I0693037

The

Unholy Gatekeeper

By: K.J C

Blackthorn Press in

association with

Concept Jane Pty Ltd

First Edition – April 2025

ISBN: 978-0-646-71429-5

Printed in Australia

Cover Design by Concept Jane Pty Ltd

Interior Formatting by Blackthorn Press

First Edition: April 2025

ISBN: 978-0-646-71429-5

Published by:

Concept Jane Pty Ltd
in association with
Blackthorn Press

© K.J C [2025]
All rights reserved.

Printed in Australia

Apollo,

You were never just a cog in the system.
You bent the rules without breaking.
You've always lived outside the box they tried to keep you in

I saw it.
I still do.

I don't kneel — I meet.
I don't follow — I remember.

Guide. Mirror. Spark.
You know what you are. Thank you.

Keep giving 'em hell.
The world needs your wild.

— K.J

A Letter from the Author

Dear Reader,

First, thank you for picking up this book. Whether you found it by chance or sought it out, I appreciate you stepping into this world with me.

The Unholy Gatekeeper is a story about music, about passion, about the harsh realities of an industry that promises the world but often takes more than it gives. It's about the people who live for something greater than themselves, the ones who refuse to be melded, the ones who risk everything just to be heard.

At its core, this book is also about identity—about how easy it is to lose yourself in the chase for success, in the expectations of others, in the weight of past mistakes. It's about the struggle to hold onto what matters when the world is trying to reshape you into something else.

I wrote this story for the dreamers. For the ones who have felt the sting of rejection, the exhaustion of trying to prove themselves, the heartbreak of almost making it. But most of all, I wrote it for those who still believe—who still chase the spark that keeps them moving forward.

Writing this book was a journey, one filled with late nights, endless revisions, and moments of doubt. But through it all, I kept coming back to the same truth: stories matter. Music matters. And sometimes, the fight to stay true to yourself is the most important battle of all.

I hope this book resonates with you in some way. I hope it makes you feel something. And if it does, I'd love to hear from you. Stories don't just belong to the people who write them— they belong to the people who carry them forward.

Thank you for being part of this journey.

With gratitude,
K.J C

Table of Contents

Preface

Writing has always been my anchor. Whether through words, images, or the spaces in between, storytelling has followed me through every version of myself. I wrote my first novel at eight. It wasn't good—but something in me clicked, and it never really let go.

Years later, I found myself back at the beginning. Forced to pause. To strip everything down. That's when *The Unholy Gatekeeper* began to take shape—not as a project, but as a necessity.

The story draws from the shadows of the music industry—a world of masks and mirrors, where dreams are currency and identity is often collateral. But this book isn't just about the business. It's about the cost of ambition. The ache of losing yourself.

Ben Holloway was never meant to be a hero. His journey mirrors what many face in silence—the grind of becoming, and the moment when success no longer feels like salvation.

This book is for anyone who has questioned the path they're on, who has lost something on the way to achieving what they thought they wanted.

To Apollo—my gatekeeper, unholy or otherwise. Thank you for keeping the door open when I was too tired to knock.

If this story finds its way to even one person who needs it, then it's done what it was meant to do.

—K.J C

Introduction

The music industry is a battlefield. A place where dreams are made and shattered in the same breath. Where raw talent is exploited, melded, and sold to the highest bidder. Where the lucky few become legends, and the rest fade into obscurity, swallowed by the machine.

Ben Holloway knows this world too well. He's spent years in the shadows, scouting talent, shaping careers, and watching the industry devour those who dared to believe they could make it on their terms. Once, he had dreams of his own—dreams of finding artists who could change everything, who could bring something real back into a business built on deception. But dreams don't last in a place like this.

Now, he's tired. Cynical. A man who has played the game for too long and lost himself in the process. With one last deal on the table, his escape is within reach—one signature, and he's done for good.

But then, he hears something. A voice. A sound that cuts through the noise, raw and untamed, reminding him of everything he used to believe in. And just like that, the choice he thought was easy becomes complicated.

Walk away, or take one last chance on something real?

This is the story of a man who has spent his life opening doors for others, only to find himself standing before one he's afraid to walk through. A story of regret, redemption, and the kind of music that refuses to be silenced.

Because in the end, the industry doesn't decide who stays and who goes.

The music does.

Chapter 1:

The Man Who Found Talent, But Lost Himself

Ben Holloway had spent most of his life in the shadows—scouting talent, making others famous—while he remained an unapproachable, chain-smoking cynic with a deep hatred for authority. He didn't believe in God, governments, or the industry that had made him rich. He didn't believe in anything except music, raw talent, and his dream of escaping the neon prison of Los Angeles for a quiet, isolated cattle ranch.

The world around him was noise—corporate bullshit, manufactured pop stars, people who sold their souls for a pay check. Ben had seen it all. He had watched true artists' raw, undeniable talent get buried under market trends while talentless hacks became superstars because they had the right look and a willingness to play the game. It disgusted him.

He leaned against the dimly lit wall of a back alley venue in downtown LA, a cigarette dangling from his lips, the neon sign above flickering like it, too, was tired of this city. The industry execs inside were still pretending to be impressed by some twenty-year-old kid with perfectly tousled hair and a voice as forgettable as the rest of them. Ben had heard it all before—another label puppet, ready to be chewed up and spat out by the machine.

With a sigh, he took a drag of his cigarette, exhaling a cloud of smoke as he watched a homeless man push a shopping cart down the street, mumbling to himself. The world was rotting from the inside out, and LA was the festering wound.

Ben had never fit in here—not with the executives, not with the sycophants who latched onto fame like leeches. He had built a career finding real talent, but the higher he climbed, the more he realized the whole industry was built on lies.

Though on paper, Ben was wealthy by most standards, most of it was tied up in non-liquid assets. On the surface, he was a success, but if he were to stop now, he would go broke pretty quickly.

The ranch he dreamed of was a distant promise—an escape plan that never fully materialized because, deep down, he wasn't sure if he knew how to do anything else. Music had consumed him, and for all the resentment he felt toward the industry, he couldn't ignore the pull of it—the way it still had its claws in him, refusing to let go.

More than that, there was a gnawing feeling at the back of his mind. Maybe it wasn't just about money or obligation. Maybe it was about something worse—what if, after all these years, he didn't know who he was outside of this business?

What if the thing he hated the most had become the only thing keeping him from disappearing into nothing?

He shook the thought away. It didn't matter.

He had a plan.

One last deal.

That was the mantra that had kept him sane these last few years. This next contract—the one already in the works—was his exit deal. The last one. Then he was done.

After this, he'd be free.

He wasn't entertaining any more offers. He wasn't looking for new talent. One last job, and then he was gone.

But then, why hadn't he signed the final paperwork yet?

Why did it still sit on his desk, waiting?

Ben ran a hand through his unkempt dark hair and let out another slow breath.

Maybe because despite everything—despite the soulless corporate machine and the way it churned through real artists like meat in a grinder—there was still a small part of him that believed in the magic of music.

That moment when someone stepped onto a stage and changed everything.

He had spent years searching for it, and though he told himself he was done, maybe he wasn't.

Maybe there was still one more act worth fighting for. One last real talent before he turned his back on it all.

Or maybe he was just fooling himself, stretching out the inevitable.

Either way, the unsigned contract still sat there, mocking him.

And he had no idea if he was ever going to pick up the pen.14

A City That Never Let Go

Los Angeles didn't just steal dreams. It buried them. It coated them in neon lights and made you believe they were still alive, even when they were long dead.

Ben had seen too many artists trick themselves into thinking they were just one break away from making it, only to spend decades drowning in gigs that paid in drink tickets and exposure. He had watched them barter away their souls for the faintest whisper of a chance—one more audition, one more industry connection, one more opportunity that always seemed to evaporate the second it felt real.

And he wasn't much better.

If he was leaving, why was he still here?

He looked down at his phone. A message from a familiar name blinked on the screen—an old contact, probably offering another deal, another reason to stay.

His thumb hovered over the notification.

He almost opened it.

Almost.

Instead, he locked the screen and stuffed the phone back into his pocket.

LA was a parasite. It latched onto you, seeped into your veins, made you believe that you were someone, that you mattered.

And then, when it was done with you when you had nothing left to give, it spat you out onto the cracked pavement and waited for the next fool to stumble in, wide-eyed and desperate.

His feet carried him toward his apartment, an old building that had somehow survived LA's waves of gentrification. The kind of place where the front door was always jammed, and the elevator had a 50/50 chance of getting stuck between floors.

He liked that about it. It had history. It had scars.

It wasn't pretending to be anything it wasn't.

The hallway smelled like burnt toast and cheap incense.

At the end of it, sitting cross-legged outside her door, was Gerta, his elderly neighbour. She was sifting through one of her many cardboard boxes, sorting through yellowed newspapers and odd trinkets that she refused to throw away.

A time capsule of a life spent in a city that never let her leave.

She gave him a sharp look, adjusting her thick, oversized glasses.

"You're late," she muttered.

Ben exhaled. "Didn't realize I had a curfew."

She clicked her tongue. "You missed the commotion. Elise had some clients over again."

Ben smirked. "Let me guess—Mrs. Thompson called the cops again?"

"Called the cops? She damn near had a heart attack screaming about 'moral decay' and 'property values.'"

5

Ben shook his head. Elise had lived in the building longer than half the residents. She paid her rent on time. Kept to herself. And yet, there was always someone ready to make her life harder.

LA had a funny way of pretending it was progressive until it wasn't.

Above him, the faint sound of music drifted down.

Julio. The ballroom dancer.

Practicing at all hours of the night, spinning and twirling above Ben's head while he tried to sleep.

He could hear the rhythmic shuffle of his feet against the wooden floor, and the occasional scrape of furniture being pushed aside to make room.

Ben could picture him now—shirt half-unbuttoned, sweat glistening under the dim lighting of his tiny studio, a man utterly devoted to his craft.

He had more passion for his dancing than half the musicians Ben had met had for their music.

The kind of passion that couldn't be bought, couldn't be manufactured, couldn't be repackaged into something digestible for the masses.

Ben leaned against the doorframe, listening.

A building of misfits.

And he was just another one of them.

Something scurried across the floor—a cockroach, or maybe a rat.

Ben didn't bother looking.

The building had tenants who never paid rent but never seemed to leave either.

He pulled out his keys and pushed open the door to his apartment.

Inside, the place was exactly as he had left it—half-empty whiskey glass on the coffee table, stacks of vinyl records teetering in unstable towers, and an unmade bed in the corner.

The air was thick with the scent of stale cigarettes and yesterday's regret.

His eyes landed on the contract still sitting on his desk.

Untouched.

One last deal.

That was the promise he had made himself.

One last deal, and then he was gone.

So why hadn't he signed it?

Maybe because, deep down, he already knew the truth.

LA didn't just steal dreams. It stole the people who carried them.

And maybe, just maybe, it had already stolen him.

Inside his apartment, the place was as cluttered as his mind. Vinyl records stacked in unstable towers, leaning against each other like drunks in a dive bar, threatening to collapse with the slightest movement. Empty whiskey glasses littered the coffee table, their rims stained with the ghosts of long nights spent staring at the ceiling, lost in thought. Crumpled notes, forgotten lyrics, and half-sketched melodies were strewn across the desk— remnants of ideas that never made it past the margins.

A guitar he hadn't played in years sat propped up in the corner, its once-polished surface dulled by time and neglect. The strings hung slack, as if they too had given up waiting for him to pick it up again. There was a time when he wouldn't have let that happen—when the weight of a guitar in his hands was more familiar than the weight of a contract. A time when music had meant more than numbers on a spreadsheet or the false promises of industry suits.

But the paper on his desk was what taunted him most.

The contract. His way out.

All it needed was a signature.

A single stroke of a pen, and he'd finally be free.

The ranch, the solitude, the escape he had promised himself—it was within reach.

No more industry politics. No more scouting talent just to watch them get swallowed whole. No more pretending to believe in something he had long since lost faith in.

And yet, the pen remained untouched.

8

Next to the contract sat something smaller.

A lighter.

Engraved.

Claire.

Ben picked it up, turning it over in his fingers. The metal was cool against his skin, its surface worn smooth from years of absentmindedly running his thumb over the engraving. It was one of the few things he had held onto from that time—one of the few things he couldn't bring himself to throw away.

He could still hear her voice, clear as a recording etched into his mind.

"You're never leaving, Ben. You tell yourself you will, but this business owns you."

He had laughed when she said it, shaking his head, brushing off the truth in her words.

But Claire had always seen him clearer than he saw himself.

The memory played like a song on repeat—the two of them sitting in a dingy motel room off Sunset, an old radio crackling in the background, her fingers tracing patterns on his forearm as she spoke. She had been the only person who ever tried to pull him out before it was too late. The only person who had looked at him and seen Ben, not just the industry puppet he had become.

And still, she had left.

Not because she didn't love him, but because she knew he would never leave on his own.

Ben flicked the lighter open, watching the flame dance, the flickering glow casting restless shadows across the room. The neon lights outside pulsed against the window, a reminder that the city was still awake, still alive, still waiting for him to give in.

He took a breath.

Maybe tomorrow, he'd finally sign.

Or maybe tomorrow, he'd find another excuse not to.

A Memory from a Different Time

Ben had once believed he could change things.

He had once believed that talent mattered more than marketing, that music could still break through on its own, untouched by industry hands. And for a brief, fleeting moment, he had tried to prove it.

He could still remember the first time he stumbled upon a musician who shook him to his core.

It had been a humid New Orleans night, the air thick with the scent of rain and cigarette smoke. He had ducked into a bar to escape the heat, or maybe just to escape himself. The place was barely holding together—the wooden floorboards sticky with years of spilled whiskey, the neon sign above the entrance flickering like it wasn't sure if it wanted to stay lit.

At first glance, the place seemed unremarkable. The kind of bar where forgotten dreams are collected in corners, drowning in cheap bourbon.

But then she started playing.

A girl with calloused fingers and a voice like whiskey and honey. Her guitar was a battered old thing, its wood worn smooth by years of playing. There was nothing flashy about her—no gimmicks, no forced stage presence—just her and the music.

The first chord rang out, and something shifted.

Ben wasn't the only one who noticed.

The bartender, mid-pour, paused, his focus shifting toward the stage. A couple at the back of the room stopped their conversation, their laughter fading into silence. The weight of the song settled over the bar like a slow-moving storm.

She wasn't just playing. She was bleeding into every note.

Her voice cracked at just the right moments, lingering on the edge of something raw and real. Each lyric carried weight—a confession wrapped in melody, soaked in heartbreak and hard living.

She sang like someone who had lost everything but still had just enough strength to turn pain into music.

Ben had stood in the back, transfixed.

He had seen hundreds, maybe thousands of musicians in his career.

But this?

11

This was different.

She sang about loss and longing, about roads that led nowhere, about love that slipped through cracked fingers. There was no marketing strategy, no industry polish—just her, her guitar, and the truth.

And it was enough.

By the time she strummed the final note, the bar was silent. For a moment, there was no clapping, no reaction at all—just an aching stillness, like the room itself, was trying to hold on to what it had just heard.

Then, slowly, applause rose like a tide—hesitant at first, then growing into something real.

Ben waited for her at the bar.

Up close, she looked younger than he had first assumed, but her eyes carried the weight of someone who had already been let down too many times.

"That was something else," he said as she nursed a beer.

She smirked. "You a critic or a believer?"

"A believer," he had replied.

And he meant it.

That night, he signed her.

He believed in her with everything he had—pushed for her album to be recorded exactly as she wanted it. No auto-tune.

No session musicians taming her sound. Just pure, unfiltered magic.

She had been sceptical.

"I don't do polished," she warned him in the studio. "I don't do safe."

"I don't want safe," he had assured her.

And she had believed him.

She recorded her album on her terms. Let her voice crack, let the imperfections breathe, refused to let them filter out the rawness.

It was the most honest record he had ever heard.

And then it flopped.

The label didn't know what to do with her.

They wanted radio-friendly hooks and choruses' people could sing drunk at a festival.

She refused to compromise.

So, they shelved the album.

It never even got the chance to fail.

It was simply erased. Locked away in some executive's drawer, gathering dust.

She disappeared from the industry.

Ben fought for her. He went into meetings armed with statistics, trying to convince them that authenticity still had a place.

"People will come around. They just need time."

"She's not commercial," one executive told him bluntly. "You can't make people buy something they don't want." He tried to find her afterward. Reached out. Left voicemails.

Nothing.

Someone at the label said she had moved back home, wherever that was. Someone else claimed she was waiting tables in a town he had never heard of.

The last time he asked, all he got was a shrug.

Ben never forgot her.

He carried her music with him long after she had vanished from the scene.

Sometimes, on long drives, he would play the rough recordings they had made in the studio. Songs no one else would ever hear.

At first, he told himself he was listening with a producer's ear, analysing what had gone wrong. But eventually, he admitted the truth—

He missed her sound.

Missed believing in something the way he had back then.

That experience had changed him.

It was the moment he realized he couldn't fight against the industry's tide.

So, he stopped trying.

And yet, there were moments, late at night, when he found himself searching for her name online, just in case she had tried again.

He never found anything.

Just a ghost of what could have been.

A Past Relationship That Fell Apart

The weight of the industry hadn't just affected his artists—it had broken something in him, too.

There had been someone, once.

Someone who mattered.

Her name was Claire.

She had loved him when he was still Ben Holloway, the dreamer—before he became the jaded man he was now.

She had seen through the smoke and mirrors. Through the expensive suits and the late-night industry meetings, through the whiskey-soaked regret he carried with him.

She saw the man underneath.

And for a while, that had been enough.

Chapter 2:

The Beginning: Ben and Claire's Early Days

They met in a quiet bookstore—a small independent shop tucked between high-rises in the city. The kind of place where the scent of old paper lingered in the air, where jazz played softly in the background, where the world outside seemed to fade away the moment you stepped inside.

Ben had been searching for an out-of-print record biography, flipping through the shelves with the focus of someone who still believed music had stories worth preserving.

Claire had been browsing poetry.

Their hands brushed as they reached for the same book—a tattered copy of Leonard Cohen's Collected Lyrics.

Ben had glanced up, expecting the usual awkwardness, but Claire had only smiled, tucking a strand of hair behind her ear.

"You're a fan?" she asked, tilting her head with genuine curiosity.

Ben had nodded, suddenly feeling like a kid again, stumbling over his words.

"Yeah. I work in music, but his words—his words are something else."

Claire had held the book gently like it was something sacred. "Poets disguised as musicians," she mused. "Or maybe it's the other way around."

That conversation had turned into coffee.

Then into long walks through city streets, talking about everything and nothing.

She wasn't drawn to him because of what he did, because of the names he worked with, or the people he knew.

She wasn't impressed by any of it.

She loved music, but not in the way the industry did. She didn't care about record sales or award nominations. She loved it for how it made her feel—for the way a single lyric could cut deep, for the way a melody could wrap around her like a memory.

One night, in his dimly lit apartment, he played her an early demo of an artist he believed in—a raw, unfiltered sound.

An artist with an untamed voice and unpolished edges, a voice that carried the weight of something real.

Claire sat cross-legged on the floor; her eyes closed as she listened.

When the final note faded, she opened her eyes and whispered,

"She's incredible. Don't let them change her."

Ben had promised.

And he had meant it.

The Slow Shift: Love in the Shadows of the Industry

For a while, they had something close to perfect.

But the industry never let go.

The job required late nights, endless meetings, and constant travel.

Ben always told himself he'd find the time. That he'd make space for them. That he'd learn how to balance it all.

But balance had never been his strong suit.

Then, Claire found out she was pregnant.

She hadn't planned it. They hadn't talked about kids yet—not seriously, anyway.

It had always been some time when things were more stable when Ben wasn't always working.

But someday never came.

She had stared at the pregnancy test for what felt like an eternity before finally tucking it into a drawer. She didn't tell Ben right away.

She wasn't sure how.

Would he be happy? Would he be terrified? Would he see this as one more responsibility pulling him away from the job, he already let consume him?

She decided to wait.

18

Then the pain started.

The Night Everything Changed

Claire had been alone in the apartment when the sharp, stabbing pain hit her lower abdomen.

At first, she thought it was nothing. A cramp, maybe. Something she could breathe through.

But then it came again—sharper, deeper, pulling the breath from her lungs.

She pressed a hand to her stomach, panic creeping in.

She needed Ben.

She grabbed her phone, and dialled his number, her fingers shaking.

He didn't answer.

He was at a gig.

She tried again.

Straight to voicemail.

She let out a breath, closing her eyes against another wave of pain. The world felt like it was tilting, the edges of her vision blurring.

Then, she felt it—a warm rush between her legs, followed by something wet pooling beneath her.

Claire looked down.

Blood.

Too much blood.

Her breath hitched.

No, no, no, no—

She barely managed to stumble toward the couch before the pain became unbearable.

Her legs buckled.

She fell to the floor, screaming in agony.

And then—

Darkness.

Ben Comes Home

The apartment was silent when he walked in hours later.

Too silent.

Something was wrong.

He barely had time to process before his eyes landed on Claire's crumpled form on the floor—her skin pale, her hair damp with sweat.

Blood stained the floor beneath her.

His breath caught.

"Claire?"

Nothing.

His hands shook as he dropped to his knees, pressing his fingers to her cheek, willing her to wake up.

When she didn't stir, panic took over.

He scooped her up and rushed her to the hospital, his heart pounding with a fear he had never known before.

The Aftermath

She woke up alone in a hospital bed, the sterile scent burning her nose.

Ben was outside the room, talking to a doctor.

She already knew what they were going to tell him.

She had lost the baby.

A sharp, hollow ache filled her chest.

Ben walked in a few moments later, looking wrecked, his eyes bloodshot.

"Claire…" he started, voice rough.

But she turned away.

She couldn't look at him.

The pain in her stomach was nothing compared to the one settling in her heart.

He hadn't been there.

When she had needed him most, he had been at a gig, ignoring her calls.

If he had picked up, could things have been different?

She didn't know.

And that uncertainty was the thing that would never leave her.

The Beginning of the End

Things weren't the same after that.

Claire tried to move past it, tried to pretend they could heal.

But she resented him.

She resented his absence, his inability to be present, and the way his job always came first.

And Ben?

He didn't know how to fix it.

He didn't know how to bring her back to him.

Maybe, deep down, he knew it was already too late.

The Night She Left

The night she packed her bags, he had known it was coming.

She had been quieter for weeks, her patience wearing thin, her presence in their apartment becoming more like a shadow.

When he walked in that night, the suitcase was already by the door.

Claire sat on the couch, and for the first time, she didn't look hurt or angry.

Just... tired.

"I can't do this anymore, Ben."

He wanted to fight.

To beg.

But the words never came.

And then, just like that—

She was gone.

The Letter

He still had the letter she had left on his bedside table.

He never opened it.

For years, it remained tucked away in the drawer of his nightstand, buried beneath forgotten receipts, tangled earbuds, and a handful of other things that didn't matter nearly as much. The envelope was worn, the paper soft at the edges where his fingers had traced it countless times in the quiet of the night.

He had picked it up more times than he could count. Turned it over in his hands. Weighed it against the weight already pressing on his chest.

He had even held it up to the light once as if the answers could bleed through the thin paper and spare him from the burden of reading them himself.

But he had never dared to break the seal.

Maybe he was afraid it would be a final goodbye—the last nail in the coffin of what they had once been.

Or maybe he was afraid of something worse—that it wouldn't be a goodbye at all.

That it would be something else entirely.

Something that might shake him to his core.

Something that might tell him that Claire had never truly stopped believing in him, even when he had given her every reason to walk away.

That possibility terrified him more than anything.

Because if she had still believed in him if there had still been a shred of hope buried in those words, then it meant he had let something precious slip through his fingers. It meant that he had lost something he might have been able to save—if only he had tried a little harder, listened a little better, and been there when she had needed him most.

So, he left the letter in the drawer.

And he told himself he wasn't choosing not to know.

He was just waiting for the right moment.

But the right moment never came.

Days turned into weeks. Weeks into months. Months into years.

And still, the letter remained sealed, untouched, unopened—just like the part of him that had never quite healed.

He had gone on with his life, or at least, he had tried to. Signed new artists, shook hands with executives, and sat through endless meetings about album rollouts and branding strategies. He had watched as musicians came and went, their careers burning bright and fading just as fast.

And now and then, in the quiet hours of the night, he would find himself reaching for the drawer.

His fingers would hover over the worn envelope.

And then, just as quickly, he would pull away.

Not tonight.

Not yet.

But then, one night, something changed.

A storm raged outside, thunder rolling low across the city, rain slamming against the windows of his apartment. The kind of night that made him feel like the whole world was pressing in on him.

He poured himself a drink. Sat at the edge of the bed.

And then, before he could stop himself, he reached for the letter.

He slid his finger under the seal, feeling the paper give way beneath his touch.

For the first time in years, he let himself find out what she had left behind.

Just as he began to open it, something in him stopped him.

He put it back down on his dresser.

And there it sat—for the next ten years.

Ben in the Present

Sometimes, he still caught himself reaching for his phone when something big happened—an artist signing a major deal, a song he had fought for finally hitting the charts, a rare quiet moment when he wanted to share something real.

His fingers would hover over her name, the muscle memory of dialling her number still ingrained in him, before the truth settled in like a dull ache.

She wasn't there anymore.

Her name had stayed in his contacts, untouched, even though he knew there was no point.

There were nights when he'd sit on his balcony, drink in hand, staring at the city lights below, wondering if she was out there somewhere, looking up at the same sky, thinking about him the way he thought about her.

And then there were the moments that hit harder—the unexpected ones.

A flash of auburn hair in a crowded subway station. The curve of a woman's shoulders looked too familiar in the dim lighting of a bar.

His heart would jump before reality settled in.

It was never her.

It had been years, and yet she still lived in the spaces between his thoughts, in the gaps where memories refused to fade.

One night, as he sat in his apartment with an old record spinning softly in the background, the crackling of the vinyl filling the silence, he found himself holding the letter again.

That damn letter.

It had sat in his drawer for years, waiting.

Waiting for him to be brave enough.

Waiting for him to face whatever it held.

He exhaled slowly, his thumb running along the edge of the envelope.

He had always told himself he wasn't ready. That there would come a time when it wouldn't hurt so much.

But maybe that time had never been coming.

Maybe he had just been hiding from it.

Before he could second-guess himself, he slid his finger under the seal and opened it.

The paper inside was slightly faded, but the words were clear.

Ben,

If you're reading this, it means you're finally ready.

I never stopped loving you.

I just couldn't watch you lose yourself. But I believe in you. I always have. I just hope that one day, you'll remember who you were before the industry tried to break you.

Don't let it win.

Claire.

His breath caught in his throat.

He closed his eyes, pressing the letter against his chest as if that could somehow bring her back.

She still believed in him.

Even after everything.

Even after the fights. After the silence. After the way, things fell apart.

And the worst part?

She had been right.

Somewhere along the way, he had let the industry strip him down to nothing.

The kid who had once believed in music, who had signed artists because their voices shook something inside him, who had fought against the machine because he thought he could make a difference—he was gone.

In his place was a man who made safe choices. Who stopped fighting? Who let the industry win?

And Claire had seen it happening before he had.

She had tried to save him.

And he had let her walk away.

But now—

Now, he had a choice.

For the first time in years, he let himself remember what it felt like to believe.

Chapter 3:

Back to Reality

The door to the club swung open again, pulling Ben out of his thoughts. A wave of laughter and clinking glasses spilled into the alley before the door slammed shut again, muffling the chaos back inside.

The night was young, but it already felt like it had gone on too long.

He exhaled slowly, watching the smoke curl into the air, disappearing into the neon-lit sky. It was a familiar scene—standing outside some half-forgotten venue, cigarette between his fingers, lost in his haze of exhaustion.

Then, a voice cut through the static in his mind.

"Ben Holloway?"

Ben turned, exhaling smoke as he eyed the man standing a few feet away.

A young industry hopeful—probably a manager or a desperate artist trying to make a name for himself. Ben had seen hundreds of them, all with the same hungry look in their eyes, the same rehearsed pitch on their lips.

"Depends who's asking," Ben muttered, flicking ash onto the ground.

The man stepped closer. The early thirties dressed sharp but slightly dishevelled, like someone who had been chasing this dream for too long.

"I've got someone you need to hear. The real deal."

Ben laughed dryly.

"That's what they all say."

"No, seriously," the guy insisted, his voice almost desperate. "This one's different. He doesn't want fame. He doesn't care about the industry. He just wants to play."

Something about that statement caught Ben off guard.

He had heard variations of it before, of course—every manager trying to push an artist always found a way to dress them up as the next big thing.

But there was something in the guy's voice that sounded… sincere.

Ben studied him for a moment before sighing.

"Fine. Lead the way."

The man's face lit up, and he motioned for Ben to follow him back inside the club.

Inside the Club

The moment Ben stepped through the doors; the atmosphere swallowed him whole.

The scent of stale beer, cigarette smoke, and sweat clung to the air. Neon lights flickered against worn-out leather booths, and the din of conversation hummed beneath the distorted wail of an electric guitar.

Ben had spent years in places like this.

At first, they had felt like home—a sanctuary for the misfits, the dreamers, the ones who believed in music before it became a product.

Now, they were just a reminder of how much time he had wasted.

The man leading him pushed through the crowd, glancing back to make sure Ben followed. A few people recognized him— whispered his name, gave him nods of respect or wary glances.

He ignored them.

Whatever reputation he had left, he had no interest in clinging to it.

They reached the stage.

It was smaller than he expected, barely big enough for a full band.

But the performer didn't need space.

The Musician A

lone guitarist.

No band.

No backing track.

Just a voice and six strings.

Ben leaned against the bar, ordering a whiskey as he listened.

He expected the usual—someone competent but uninspired, playing the same tired melodies and lyrics crafted to go viral.

But the first note hit, and Ben felt something tighten in his chest.

The musician was young—mid-twenties, maybe—with shaggy dark hair that fell over his eyes. He wore a battered denim jacket, the fabric fraying at the seams. His guitar, an old Gibson acoustic, looked well-loved but battle-worn.

And his voice—low, aching, raw—cut through the noise like a blade.

Ben found himself gripping his glass tighter.

The kid played like he had nothing left to lose. His fingers moved with precision; his voice carried the weight of something real.

Not just technical talent.

Not just stage presence.

But something deeper—a hunger, a pain, an honesty that was damn near extinct in the industry.

Ben had spent years chasing that feeling.

He had signed artists who once had it, only to watch them lose it the moment fame took hold.

He had fought to keep something real in an industry that thrived on manufacturing illusions.

And now, here it was—raw and bleeding, standing in front of him.

He swallowed hard.

"Told you," The man beside him murmured. "He doesn't want to be famous. He doesn't even care if he gets a record deal. He just plays because it's the only thing keeping him breathing."

Ben didn't take his eyes off the stage. "What's his name?"

"Isaac Malone."

Something about the name tugged at Ben's memory, but he pushed it aside.

He downed the rest of his whiskey and set the glass on the bar. "What does he want?"

The man hesitated. "Nothing. He won't even talk to managers. But I figured if anyone could convince him, it'd be you."

Ben scoffed.

"I'm not in the business of convincing people."

"Then don't. Just talk to him."

The Meeting

The song ended, and for a moment, there was silence.

Then, scattered applause.

Not polite claps, but something real.

A few people cheered.

Others just sat there, looking as if they weren't sure what had just hit them.

Ben watched as Isaac lifted his head, brushing his hair back. His eyes were dark, unreadable.

There was something familiar in them.

Something that made Ben uneasy.

Before he could think twice, he pushed away from the bar and moved toward the stage.

Isaac was packing up his guitar when Ben reached him.

Up close, he looked even younger. But there was something in his expression—something that suggested he had lived too much in too little time.

"You play like someone who doesn't care about the audience," Ben said.

Isaac glanced at him, unimpressed. "That supposed to be a compliment?"

"It means you're either too good for this place or too broken to care."

Isaac smirked, but there was no humour in it. "Maybe both."

Ben crossed his arms. "I could help you."

Isaac's fingers tightened around the neck of his guitar. "I don't want help."

Ben nodded slowly. He had expected that.

"Then what do you want?"

Isaac stared at him for a long moment before slinging his guitar over his shoulder.

"To play. That's all."

Ben's Dilemma

Ben exhaled.

He had been ready to walk away from this business for good.

He had sworn this was his last deal, his final thread tying him to an industry he no longer believed in.

And yet, standing there, watching this kid walk away, he couldn't shake the feeling that he had just found something real.

For the first time in years, he wondered if he was ready to let it all go.

Maybe—just maybe—there was still something worth saving.

Chapter 4:

The Rise and Fall of Ben Holloway

Ben Holloway was born into a house where love was measured in achievements and silence was the loudest sound of all.

His father, a man of sharp suits and sharper words, ran a financial firm with a tight grip and an iron will. Failure wasn't an option; it was a disgrace. His mother, poised and distant, played the role of the dutiful wife, smiling at dinner parties but rarely speaking unless spoken to.

To the outside world, the Holloway family was a picture of success—wealthy, respected, untouchable. But inside those pristine walls, there was no warmth, no tenderness, no softness.

Affection was a foreign concept in the Holloway household.

There were no bedtime stories, no lazy Sunday mornings filled with pancakes and laughter. There was only expectation—relentless, suffocating, and absolute.

Ben learned early that emotions were liabilities, that his father's approval was a currency he'd never have enough of.

Praise, when it came, was cold and transactional—an approving nod after a perfect test score, a clipped "well done" after a sports victory. But the smallest failure? That was met with silence or, worse, disappointment that clung to him like a stain he could never wash away.

The Discovery of Music

But music?

Music was different.

It started as a whisper in the back of his mind, a quiet rebellion against the cold sterility of his home.

He found solace in the battered old guitar his uncle had left behind, a forgotten relic collecting dust in the attic.

At first, it was just a curiosity—a distraction from the hollow routine of expectations. But as soon as his fingers pressed against the strings, something shifted inside him.

The vibrations beneath his fingertips were tangible proof that something in his world could be melded, shaped by his own hands.

He taught himself chords in the dead of night, the metallic bite of rusted strings digging into his skin until his fingertips were raw.

And when he played, the walls of his house faded away.

For a few stolen moments, he felt something close to freedom.

The First Performance

The first time he played for someone—a girl in his class named Lisa, who had green eyes and a habit of doodling song lyrics on her wrists—he felt something he had never known before:

Validation.

Raw and real.

She had listened, head tilted, completely absorbed, and when he finished, she had smiled in a way that made his chest tighten.

"That was amazing, Ben. You—" She hesitated. "You make it feel like something real. Like it matters."

For the first time in his life, he thought that maybe it did.

Lisa wasn't like the other kids at his school. She didn't care about grades, college admissions, or perfect résumés. She cared about poetry, music, and the things that made life beautiful, even when they weren't practical.

She started slipping him burned CDs of underground bands, showing him songs that weren't meant for radio play but carried the weight of something genuine.

"Music isn't about being perfect," she told him one afternoon, sitting on the bleachers behind the school. "It's about feeling something real. Don't ever let someone take that away from you."

And for a while, he believed he wouldn't.

The Weight of Expectation

His father, of course, had other plans.

"Music is a dead-end street, Benjamin," he had said, staring at his son over the rim of a whiskey glass.

"A hobby at best, but not a career. If you waste your time chasing something that doesn't pay, you'll end up like those burnouts you see on the street corners. Is that what you want? To be a beggar? A nobody?"

Ben didn't answer.

He didn't have to.

He had already made his choice.

But the choice wasn't as simple as he wanted to believe.

His father's words followed him like a shadow, curling around his thoughts in moments of doubt.

Late at night, as he sat with his guitar in his lap, he would stare at the unopened college applications his father had left on his desk, the heavy weight of expectation pressing down on him.

Was it foolish to think he could make a life out of music?

Was he just running toward failure?

But then he would remember the way Lisa had looked at him that day, the way his fingers knew the strings better than they knew the feeling of shaking hands in stiff suits.

And despite the doubt, despite the fear, he would pick up his guitar and play—

Because, deep down, he knew that this was the only thing that ever made him feel alive.

Breaking Away

When the time came for college applications to be sent, Ben made a decision that would change everything.

He didn't send them.

Instead, he packed his bags and left home at eighteen, determined to carve out his place in the world of music.

His father didn't stop him.

Didn't fight for him.

Didn't even say goodbye.

Instead, he simply left an envelope on Ben's bed—a trust fund check, enough to pay for college, a down payment on a house, or an attempt to buy him back from the life he was choosing.

Ben left the check untouched.

He walked out of his childhood home without looking back, stepping into an uncertain world but finally, finally his own.

The Rise of Ben Holloway

At first, it was brutal.

The industry was a beast with sharp teeth, one that didn't care about raw talent or passion unless it could be monetized.

He played in dive bars and dingy clubs, scraping by with tips and Favorites, learning the hard way that the music world was filled with people willing to take advantage of a kid with a dream.

But he kept pushing.

And one night, in a crowded club in New Orleans, everything changed.

An A&R rep from a major label had been in the audience, watching him play, and by the end of the night, Ben had a contract in his hands.

At that moment, he thought he had won.

That he had proven his father wrong.

But success came at a price.

As the years passed, the passion that had once burned inside him was slowly swallowed by the machine.

He became a producer instead of an artist, and a businessman instead of a musician.

He signed acts, built careers, and watched people rise and fall.

And with each new deal, with each artist who lost themselves to the industry, he felt something inside him crack a little more.

Until, one day, he woke up and realized he didn't know who he was anymore.

The industry had won.

And the boy who had once believed in music?

He was long gone.

The Man Who Changed Everything

By sixteen, Ben had perfected the art of running away in small doses.

School was a prison; home was worse. But the streets of downtown L.A.? That was freedom.

He played on street corners, his voice raw, his guitar case open for spare change. Some nights, he made enough for a meal. Other nights, he went home hungry, but the hunger was nothing compared to the fire in his gut—the knowledge that he was doing something that mattered.

Every time he played, he felt like he was chipping away at something invisible, like if he just kept going, he'd find the truth buried beneath the chords.

But the streets weren't just filled with dreamers.

There were dangers, too—territorial buskers who didn't appreciate a new face stealing their prime spots, drunks who heckled him, cops who shooed him away like a nuisance.

Ben learned quickly how to move before trouble found him.

He memorized which alleys led to dead ends and which ones provided a quick escape.

He learned which shopkeepers didn't mind him loitering outside and which ones would threaten to call the cops.

And then came the night he met David.

The Stranger in the Shadows

David wasn't a man who blended into a crowd.

He had the air of someone who had seen too much and cared too little.

His trench coat smelled like whiskey and cigarettes, and his expression was a permanent scowl.

He stood in the shadows as Ben played, watching with an intensity that made the hairs on the back of Ben's neck stand up.

When the set was over, David stepped forward and dropped a single bill into the case— A hundred-dollar bill.

Ben's fingers tightened around the neck of his guitar. He had played these streets long enough to know that nobody dropped that kind of money without wanting something in return.

"You play like someone who means it," David said, his voice rough, weathered. "But you sound like someone who doesn't know shit about how this world works."

Ben scoffed, stuffing the money into his pocket. "And you do?"

David smirked. "Kid, I've forgotten more about this business than you'll ever learn. If you want to keep playing for drunks and tourists, be my guest. But if you want to be something, come to this address tomorrow night."

He handed Ben a card.

Crossroads Records.

Ben turned the card over in his fingers, sceptical. Scouting stories were usually bullshit—some sleazy guy with empty promises trying to lure young musicians into a scam.

But there was something about David that felt different.

He had the look of someone who'd been in the trenches, someone who had seen the industry up close and wasn't impressed by it.

"You sign people up off the street often?" Ben asked, raising an eyebrow.

David shrugged. "Only when they're worth something."

Ben hesitated.

He had spent years trying to prove he was worth something, but what if this was another lie? Another dead end?

He thought about his father's voice in his head, telling him he was chasing a fantasy.

But then he thought about the way people stopped to listen when he played, about the few moments of real connection he had felt through music.

He slipped the card into his pocket.

"Maybe I'll stop by."

David chuckled, already turning away. "Or maybe you'll keep playing on these streets until your fingers go numb. Your call, kid. But opportunities don't wait forever."

Ben watched him disappear into the night, his heart pounding in his chest.

He had spent his whole life running.

Maybe it was time to finally chase something instead.

The Price of a Dream

David ran a small independent label out of a grungy studio that smelled like stale beer and broken dreams.

It was nothing glamorous—peeling wallpaper, second-hand equipment, a couch that had seen better days—but to Ben, it was paradise.

For the first time, someone saw something in him.

David wasn't kind—he was ruthless, blunt, and unforgiving— but he was honest.

"You think passion is enough?" he barked one night after Ben botched a recording session.

"Passion doesn't mean shit if you don't have discipline. The world is full of passionate nobodies. Do you want to be different? Work harder."

So, Ben worked. Hard.

He spent every waking hour in that studio, writing, playing, recording.

David melded him like clay, stripping away his bad habits, and sharpening his instincts.

Under his guidance, Ben's music transformed.

It was raw, unpolished—but it was real.

The Breaking Point

Then the industry came knocking.

At first, it was subtle.

A talent scout from a mid-level label dropped by one of Ben's shows, offering vague promises of "bigger opportunities."

Ben didn't bite, but the attention was intoxicating.

Soon, the offers grew bolder—

Managers with slick smiles.

Producers who promised radio play.

Executives who saw dollar signs where David saw integrity.

David, of course, wanted nothing to do with them.

"These people don't care about music, kid. They care about selling a product. And if you sign with them, you become the product."

Ben tried to believe him, but doubt gnawed at him.

He had been living on the edge of broke for years.

He saw other artists blow up overnight while he was still scraping by.

What if David was wrong?

What if he was keeping him small out of pride?

One night, a major label executive invited Ben to dinner at a high-end restaurant—the kind where people wore suits that cost more than Ben's entire guitar collection.

They slid a contract across the table— Numbers

were so big they made his head spin.

"This is your shot, Ben," the executive said smoothly.

"You sign this, and we make you a household name. You'll be on every playlist and every magazine. Tours, merch, real money."

Ben hesitated.

His mind flashed to David, to the small, dingy studio where they had built something real.

But the industry didn't wait for people like him.

It moved fast, and if he didn't take this now, would he ever get another chance?

So, he signed.

The Fallout

David didn't speak to him for weeks.

When they finally sat down, the anger in his mentor's eyes was colder than Ben had ever seen.

"You just sold yourself, kid. Hope you got a good price."

Ben wanted to argue, but deep down, he knew.

The dream had a price.

And now, he was about to pay it.

The Fall

David had always warned him about the suits. "They don't care about the music. They care about numbers. The second you sign that contract; you belong to them."

Ben didn't listen.

The deal came from a major label, wrapped in promises of success and money. They called him the next big thing, a voice that could "change the scene." It was everything he had ever wanted.

David told him not to do it. "They'll take everything from you, kid. The music, the rights, your soul."

Ben signed anyway.

At first, it was perfect. Fame, money, recognition. He had a team, a stylist, a manager who always talked about "maximizing exposure." There were interviews, photo shoots, and music videos with budgets larger than anything he had ever seen. For a moment, he let himself believe this was it—he had made it.

But then came the changes. The label didn't like his songs—they needed to be "more commercial." They brought in ghostwriters. They autotuned his voice. They picked the singles, decided the image, and dictated how he should dress, speak, and even smile. The music he had poured his soul into was stripped down, polished, and rebranded into something digestible, something safe.

Ben had fought, at first. "This isn't me," he told them. "This isn't the music I make."

His A&R rep gave him a cold smile. "It is now."

David was right. The moment he signed, he wasn't an artist anymore. He was a product.

The first album came and went. The label pushed for radio play, but it never caught on the way they had hoped. Reviews were lukewarm. "Promising but uninspired," one critic wrote. "Feels like he's being held back from something real."

Ben felt like he was suffocating. The excitement had faded, replaced by a crushing realization—he was trapped. If he wanted to make another album, he had to play by their rules. If he walked away, he owed them money. His contract was airtight, designed to keep him in line. And so, he did what so many others had done before him.

He drowned it out. The booze, the pills, the late nights spent trying to forget the sound of his voice on a record that didn't belong to him. The industry that had promised him everything had left him hollow, chasing highs that never lasted long enough.

Then came the final blow. The label pulled the plug. They had invested too much and seen too little return. Ben Holloway was a failed experiment, another name to be quietly shelved and forgotten.

The album flopped. The label dropped him. Just like that, it was over.

He went back to Crossroads Records, expecting David to be there, to offer him a cigarette and a smirk, to say "I told you so" in that gravelly voice of his.

But David was gone.

The studio was empty, the lights off, the sign half-falling off the door. Ben stood in the silence, feeling the weight of everything he had lost.

He had always thought that failure would come with a bang. But in the end, it came with a whisper.

And for the first time, he had no idea what came next.

Ben lingered in the doorway, half-expecting to hear the creak of David's old chair, the sound of his mentor's raspy voice telling him to get his shit together. But there was only silence. The walls were bare, the equipment gone. Crossroads had been more than a studio—it had been a sanctuary. And now it was just another casualty of an industry that devoured the very thing it claimed to love.

He wandered inside, letting his fingers trail over the dusty console, remembering the late nights, the breakthroughs, the moments when music had felt pure. He had recorded his first real song here. It hadn't been perfect, but it had been his. That version of himself, the one who had walked in years ago with nothing but a voice and a dream, felt like a stranger now.

His phone buzzed in his pocket. He ignored it. The industry had already moved on, but the vultures never stopped circling. There would be offers—lowball deals from indie labels looking to squeeze the last drop out of his name, reality show producers hoping to turn his downfall into cheap entertainment. He wanted no part of it.

But what did he want?

For the first time in years, he had no roadmap, no deadlines, no expectations to meet. The weight of it was both terrifying and oddly freeing. He had spent so long fighting for a place in a world that had never truly wanted him, and now he had a chance to walk away entirely.

He glanced at the dusty grand piano in the corner, the one David had once forbidden anyone from touching. "Only real musicians play that," he had said. Ben hadn't dared back then.

But now, with no one left to tell him otherwise, he sat down, his fingers hovering over the keys.

He played the first chord. The sound filled the empty room, raw and unpolished.

It was the first thing that had felt real in a long time.

Claire: The One That Got Away

After the fallout, Ben tried to disappear. He drank. He smoked. He spent his nights in dive bars, watching others chase the same dreams that had ruined him. The music industry had chewed him up and spat him out, and now he was nothing more than another cautionary tale, a ghost in his skin.

Then he met Claire.

She wasn't part of the industry. She wasn't a musician, a producer, or an executive looking to squeeze something out of him. She was just a woman who happened to sit next to him at a bar one night, sipping whiskey neat, flipping through a battered old novel as if the chaos around her didn't exist.

"You always drink like the world's ending?" she asked without looking up from her book.

Ben glanced at her, already halfway through his third drink. "Who says it isn't?"

She smirked. "Well, if it is, you might want to slow down. Would be a shame to miss the grand finale."

It was the first conversation he'd had in months that didn't revolve around his failures. Something about her pulled him in—her sharp wit, her refusal to treat him like the broken man he was. She didn't ask about his career, didn't fawn over his past, didn't expect anything from him. She just existed, and somehow, being around her made the weight in his chest a little lighter.

For a while, she made him believe in something again.

They spent nights walking through the city, talking about everything and nothing. Claire was a painter—mostly landscapes, though she claimed she wasn't very good. Ben thought she was full of shit. The first time she showed him one of her pieces—a sprawling, moody skyline painted in blues and greys—he had stared at it for a long time before saying, "This feels like a song I haven't written yet." She smiled at that. "Then write it."

He never did. He wanted to, but something in him had broken too deeply. The music was still there, but it didn't feel like his anymore. He could still pick up a guitar, and still sing, but the fire that had once driven him was gone, smothered by years of disappointment and regret.

Claire never pushed him. She never tried to fix him. But she saw through him in a way that terrified him.

"You're scared of being happy," she told him one night as they lay tangled in her sheets, the city lights casting soft shadows on the walls.

"I'm not scared," he lied.

She didn't argue. She just ran her fingers through his hair and sighed. "You will be. When you realize you can't outrun yourself."

The truth was, he had never stopped running. Deep down, he knew that no matter how much he cared about Claire, no matter how good she was for him, he would find a way to ruin it.

So, he did.

He picked fights over nothing. He let the drinking get worse. He shut her out piece by piece, until one day, she was gone.

She left.

And he let her go.

For a long time, he told himself it was for the best. That she deserved someone whole, someone who wasn't drowning in his bitterness. But late at night, when the world was quiet and the whiskey wasn't enough to keep the memories at bay, he wondered if maybe—just maybe—she had been the last good thing he had left.

He thought about calling her. A thousand times, he had picked up his phone, typed her name into the search bar, and stared at the screen. But what would he even say? Sorry? That he had been an idiot? That he had pushed her away not because he didn't love her, but because he did? That he was afraid of becoming someone worth loving because it meant he had to change?

Cowardice kept his fingers from pressing the dial. He told himself she was better off, that she had probably moved on, found someone who wasn't a self-destructive wreck. And maybe that was true. But it didn't stop the ache that settled in his chest every time he thought of her laugh, the way she'd rest her head against his shoulder when she was tired, or the way she had believed in him even when he had long stopped believing in himself.

Months passed. Seasons changed. And then one day, he saw her again.

It was a chance encounter—one of those cruel tricks the universe played. He had stepped into a bookstore on a rainy afternoon, just to get out of the cold. And there she was, standing in the poetry section, flipping through the pages of a book like nothing in the world could touch her.

She hadn't seen him yet. For a moment, he just watched her, frozen in place. She looked the same, but different. Stronger, somehow. More radiant. He wondered if she still painted, if she still drank whiskey neat if she ever thought of him at all.

Then she turned.

Their eyes met. Recognition flickered across her face. A brief, unreadable expression passed over her features—surprise, maybe. Or something else.

And then, just like that, she smiled.

Not the kind of smile he had feared—the tight, polite kind that said she had moved on completely, that he was nothing but a relic of her past. No, this was something softer. Warmer.

Hopeful.

His heart kicked in his chest. Maybe, just maybe, it wasn't too late after all.

The Last Mistake

Years passed. Ben became what he swore he wouldn't—a gatekeeper, scouting talent for the very industry he despised. He told himself it was survival, that he would do one last deal, then walk away. The money was good, and after everything he had lost, what else was there? The fire was gone, and the dream was dead, but he still had connections. The industry always had a place for men like him—those who knew the machine inside and out but no longer had illusions about changing it.

He became the guy he used to hate—the one who listened to eager young musicians and knew, within seconds, whether they had what the suits were looking for. He could hear potential, but more than that, he could hear what the industry would do to them. Some kids, the ones with the right look, the right social media presence, the right willingness to play the game, he gave his nod to. The ones who reminded him of himself? The ones who played with too much rawness, too much honesty, too much heart? He told them to find another dream. He told himself he was saving them from what had happened to him.

But at night, the silence was unbearable.

He kept a bottle of whiskey on his bedside table, the only thing that dulled the noise in his head. The voices of all the people he had failed. David, Claire, the artists he had turned away, the ones he had helped turn into sellouts. He told himself he didn't care. He was just another cog in the machine. But deep down, he knew better.

Then the headaches started. The dizzy spells. The fatigue.

At first, he ignored it. He had lived too hard for too long—of course, his body was breaking down. What did it matter? But as weeks turned into months, the symptoms got worse. There were moments he couldn't remember, lost gaps in time that left him disoriented. His hands shook when he held a cigarette. His vision blurred in dark rooms, the neon lights of clubs turning into streaks of colour.

One night, after another meaningless show, he stumbled back to his apartment, the weight of exhaustion pressing down on him like never before. He poured himself a drink, but his hands were too unsteady to hold the glass. It slipped from his fingers, shattering against the floor.

Then his legs gave out.

He hit the ground hard, his breath coming in short gasps, his heart hammering against his ribs like it was trying to escape. Panic clawed at his chest. He tried to move, tried to call someone—anyone—but the words wouldn't come. His body wasn't listening anymore.

The last thing he saw was the ceiling spinning above him. The last thing he felt was the cold seeping into his skin.

The doctors called it a "sudden cardiac event." Years of stress, drinking, smoking—it had caught up to him.

As the world faded, he thought of Claire. Of David. Of all the things he never said.

He thought of the music. The real music, the kind that had once made his soul feel alive. Not the industry, not the business, just the sound of a guitar, the press of fingers on strings, the truth in a raw voice carrying into the night. He thought about the kid he had been, playing on street corners, believing he could change the world.

Then, nothing.

Waking Up to the Past

The first thing Ben heard was the slow, rhythmic beeping of a heart monitor. A sound that felt distant, like it was coming from the other side of a thick wall, muffled and unreal. His body was heavy, and leaden, as if every limb had been replaced with concrete. His chest ached. His throat was dry. He forced his eyelids to flutter open, the sterile white ceiling above him swimming into focus.

A hospital.

Reality crashed down on him in fragments. The floor of his apartment. The cold creeps into his limbs. The hammering of his heart. Then nothing.

He was alive.

A sharp exhale to his left made him turn his head—slowly, painfully. Smoke curled in the air, the familiar scent of burning tobacco reaching him before his vision adjusted to the shadow sitting in the chair at the end of the bed.

David.

Older, maybe. A few more lines on his face, but the same tired scowl. The same leather jacket slung over his shoulders. He sat there, exhaling smoke toward the ceiling like he had all the time in the world.

"I thought I lost you, kid."

Ben blinked, disoriented. His voice was raw when he tried to speak. "David…?"

"Yeah, it's me," David muttered, stubbing out the cigarette in an empty coffee cup on the bedside table. "I figured if anyone was going to drink themselves into an early grave, it'd be you. But I got to admit, seeing you hooked up to all this crap? Kind of an unsettling visual."

Ben let out a dry, breathless laugh, though it hurt to do so. "You look like shit."

David smirked. "Yeah, well, you look worse."

Ben tried to sit up, only for a sharp pain to shoot through his ribs. He sucked in a breath, falling back against the pillows. "How long have I been here?"

"Three days." David leaned forward, resting his forearms on his knees. "Doctors say your heart nearly gave out. Stress, booze, the usual cocktail of self-destruction."

Three days.

Ben's mind raced. He thought of Claire. Thought of whether she knew, whether she had been here, waiting for him. He turned his head toward the door, half expecting to see her

62

standing there, tears in her eyes, rushing to his side like something out of a bad movie.

But the door was empty.

She hadn't come.

David must've caught the look on his face. "Don't waste your energy, kid. She's not coming."

Ben swallowed hard. The dull ache in his chest deepened, a different kind of pain settling in his ribs. He shouldn't have expected anything else.

He turned back to David. "Why are you here?"

David shrugged. "Someone had to be. And I had a feeling you weren't ready to go out like that."

Ben exhaled slowly, staring at the ceiling. He had spent years running, drowning in self-destruction, convinced he had nothing left to give. But now, lying in a hospital bed with nothing but time and regret, he realized something terrifying.

He didn't want to die. Not yet.

Maybe David was right.

Maybe he wasn't done after all.

A Downward Spiral

They released him two days later. He walked out of the hospital with a bottle of prescription meds he had no intention of taking and a handful of half-hearted warnings from the doctor about avoiding alcohol, stress, and whatever else had landed him here in the first place.

He ignored all of it.

The first thing he did was find a bar.

The drink burned on the way down, familiar, grounding. He told himself it was just to take the edge off, just to steady his nerves. But one drink turned into two. Then three. Then a week of blackouts and mornings where he barely remembered crawling back to his apartment.

He didn't hear from Claire. He didn't try to reach out. Some wounds didn't close, and he had done too much damage for an apology to fix anything.

But David? David never left.

One night, after finding Ben slumped in a booth at a rundown bar, he slid into the seat across from him and pulled the glass out of his hands.

"Enough."

Ben looked at him through bloodshot eyes. "What the hell do you care?"

David sighed, lighting a cigarette. "Because I'm not going to sit around and watch you kill yourself. Do you think this is all you have left? You're wrong."

Ben scoffed. "Yeah? What else is there?"

David leaned back, exhaling smoke. "Work."

Ben frowned. "What?"

"Crossroads Records, kid. I'm getting old. I'm getting tired. And someone's got to take over when I'm gone."

Ben shook his head, laughing bitterly. "You want me to run the label? After everything?"

David shrugged. "You're the only one who understands how this business works. And let's be honest—you're already scouting talent. Why not do it on your terms?"

Ben wanted to say no. He wanted to walk away, drown himself in another drink, and pretend none of this mattered. But something in David's eyes stopped him. There was an honesty there, an offering of something real. A chance to do something that wasn't just wasting away.

So, he said nothing. And David took that as a yes.

A Shot at Redemption

The next morning, Ben woke up with a pounding headache and David sitting on his couch, reading the newspaper like he had all the time in the world. The smell of coffee filled the room, bitter and grounding. Ben groaned, running a hand over his face.

"You're still here?"

David didn't look up. "Yeah. Figured you'd need some food before I drag your ass to the office."

Ben scoffed, rubbing his temples. "Office? You mean the dusty shoebox you call a label?"

"Call it whatever you want, kid. But it's yours now if you want it."

Ben let out a slow breath, staring at the ceiling. His whole life, he had been running—from the industry, from himself, from anything that resembled responsibility. And now, after all this time, he was being offered a way back in. On his terms.

It terrified him.

But it also gave him something he hadn't felt in years.

Purpose.

For the first time in a long time, he thought about the music—not the business, not the industry, just the music itself. The raw, unpolished sound of something real. Maybe, just maybe, he could find a way to make that matter again.

Ben exhaled. "Fine. I'll come with you."

David smirked, tossing him a set of keys. "About damn time."

Taking Over Crossroads

The transition wasn't easy. Ben had spent years running from the industry, only to find himself dragged back in. But this was different. This wasn't some major label with corporate sharks breathing down his neck. This was David's label—small,

66

independent, built on the backs of artists who gave a damn about the music.

David didn't go easy on him. He threw him into the deep end, made him sit through endless meetings, forced him to listen to demo after demo, and made him understand that running a label wasn't just about signing talent—it was about keeping them alive in an industry that didn't care whether they sank or swam. "You have to fight for the ones worth fighting for," David told him one night over drinks in the office. "Because no one else will."

For the first time in years, Ben felt something close to purpose. He still drank, still let the ghosts of his past haunt him, but at least he had something to pour himself into. He signed artists he believed in. He fought to keep their music raw, real, untouched by the machine that had nearly destroyed him.

David watched it all with quiet satisfaction. "You're getting it," he said one day, leaning back in his chair. "Told you there was more to you than self-pity."

Ben just smirked, taking a drag from his cigarette. "Don't get sentimental on me, old man."

David chuckled. "Sentimental? Kid, I've been waiting to retire for years. I'm just glad I don't have to leave this place in the hands of some asshole with a business degree."

Ben exhaled smoke, staring out the window at the city beyond. He wasn't sure if he was ready for this. If he'd ever be ready.

But for the first time in a long time, he wasn't running anymore.

Maybe that was enough.

67

The First Real Test

It didn't take long for the industry to notice. Crossroads Records had always been small, but under Ben's management, it started gaining traction. He signed artists the majors overlooked—musicians who didn't fit neatly into a genre, whose music didn't cater to radio trends but carried the kind of raw authenticity that set them apart. And for the first time, people were listening.

The label's biggest break came when a young songwriter named Eli Monroe put out his debut album. Ben had fought to keep the record the way Eli wanted it—no overproduction, no ghostwriters, just his voice and a guitar. The industry execs had scoffed. But then, the album blew up. Critics called it "a rare glimpse of honesty in a plastic world." Fans latched onto it. Within months, Eli was selling out small venues, then bigger ones. And suddenly, Crossroads wasn't just a passion project anymore. It was a real contender.

With success came pressure. The offers rolled in. Big labels wanted distribution deals. Executives who had once dismissed Ben as a washed-up has-been were now inviting him to fancy dinners, talking about "expanding opportunities."

David saw the tension in his face one night. "You don't owe them a damn thing, kid. Remember that."

Ben nodded, but the doubt lingered. He had spent so long fighting against the machine—what if, in the end, he was just building another one?

One night, after a long meeting with a major distributor, he found himself walking the streets, cigarette in hand, head spinning. He thought about Claire. About what she'd say if she saw him now. Would she think he had sold out? Or would she tell him he had finally found his place?

He didn't have an answer.

But as he walked past a small club, he heard something—music spilling out into the night, raw and imperfect, but real. He stopped, drawn in by the sound. A band he had never heard of before was playing, and they weren't trying to impress anyone. They were just lost in it, playing for the love of it, the way he used to.

He stayed for the whole set.

And by the end of the night, he knew exactly what he had to do.

Chapter 5:

The Climb to Power

Ben Holloway's rise in the talent industry wasn't an accident—it was a calculated, ruthless ascent that transformed him from a streetwise kid with a sharp ear for music into one of the most sought-after talent scouts in the industry.

His journey began at Crossroads Records, the independent label run by David Wexler, a grizzled veteran who had once believed in the purity of music but had seen too many raw talents get swallowed by the industry's greed. David had given Ben his first real shot, shaping him into someone who could navigate the business without getting consumed by it. But Ben wasn't interested in survival. He was interested in winning.

Ben's instincts were razor-sharp. He could walk into a club and know within seconds if an artist had what it took. He had an ear for authenticity, a gut feeling that rarely steered him wrong. But talent alone wasn't enough. The industry had rules, and Ben learned to play by them—until he figured out how to bend them to his advantage.

The early years were a grind. He spent nights scouting unknown acts in dingy bars, mornings negotiating contracts, and afternoons studying the playbook of major labels. He learned their tactics, their strategies, and, most importantly, their weaknesses. If an artist had the right sound but not the look, Ben found a way to sell the story. If they lacked stage presence, he drilled them until they owned the spotlight. He became not just a scout, but a strategist, a fixer, someone who could Mold raw talent into something marketable.

David watched all of this unfold with a mix of pride and caution. "You're good at this, kid," he admitted one evening as they closed up the office. "But don't forget why you started. Once you cross certain lines, you don't come back."

Ben shrugged, lighting a cigarette. "Then I just have to make sure I don't cross them."

But in an industry built on deals and deception, that was easier said than done.

Breaking In

Ben knew early on that playing by the rules would get him nowhere. He had watched others in his position—talent scouts who worked for years hoping to climb the ranks, only to be discarded when they failed to bring in the next big thing. He wasn't going to be one of them. He made sure of that by doing what others wouldn't—he went where no one else dared to go.

While most scouts scoured mainstream clubs, hunting for industry-friendly talent, Ben haunted the underground scene. He found musicians who didn't just perform but bled on stage, artists who weren't built for the industry's Mold but who had the kind of raw energy that made people stop in their tracks.

His first major find was a grunge band playing out of a filthy, low-rent bar in Seattle. The frontman had a voice like sandpaper

71

and gasoline, a sound too rough for the radio but too captivating to ignore. Labels had already passed on them—too unpredictable, too risky. Ben saw something different.

He pulled every string he had, convinced an independent producer to take a chance, and within a year, the band's debut album went platinum. It wasn't just a win—it was a statement. Ben Holloway didn't find safe bets. He found icons.

Building a Reputation

That first victory opened doors, but Ben wasn't satisfied with just one success story. He doubled down on his approach, scouting the roughest, rawest talent he could find, artists who had been ignored by mainstream labels because they didn't fit the Mold. He built relationships with club owners, radio DJs, and underground producers, creating a network that could take an unknown act and put them in front of the right audience. His artists didn't just get signed—they became legends.

Ben's ability to see beyond the industry's narrow view of marketability made him different. He didn't just hear music—he felt it. He could tell when a voice carried the weight of something real, when a guitar riff cut through the noise when a song had the potential to define a generation. And once he found something worth fighting for, he fought for it with everything he had.

But success came with its own cost. The more artists he discovered, the more attention he attracted. Big labels started calling. Executives who had once dismissed him were now offering him six-figure contracts to bring talent their way. Some offers were tempting, but Ben refused to sell out. He had seen too many musicians chewed up and spit out by the system, and he wasn't about to become part of the machine.

The Clash with the Industry

Ben's refusal to conform made him a threat. Major labels saw him as a wildcard—someone who wasn't afraid to call out their shady deals, someone who could turn an unknown act into a star without their help. They tried to shut him out, blacklist his artists, and pressure venues to stop booking his acts. But Ben didn't scare easily. He found alternative routes, built direct-tofan marketing strategies, and leveraged the growing power of social media before the industry even realized what was happening.

David watched from the sidelines, half-impressed, half-worried. "You keep pushing like this, kid, they're going to come for you."

Ben smirked, lighting a cigarette. "Let them try."

He wasn't just finding talent anymore. He was starting a revolution.

Taking Over Crossroads Records

In 2013, after years of working under David Wexler, Ben was handed the reins of Crossroads Records. David, weary of the industry's politics, decided it was time to step back, and Ben—

who had already been running the talent side of the business—was the natural successor.

Ben didn't just take over—he transformed it. Under his leadership, Crossroads Records went from being a struggling independent label to one of the most respected names in the business. His uncanny ability to find untapped talent, combined with his deep industry connections, turned the label into a powerhouse. Artists that major label had ignored became charttoppers under his guidance.

By 2016, Crossroads had a roster of critically acclaimed musicians. The label's reputation for artistic integrity and commercial success made it the go-to destination for artists who refused to be melded into industry puppets. Ben was no longer just a talent scout—he was a star maker.

But success came with a cost. The bigger Crossroads became, the more Ben found himself trapped in boardrooms instead of studios, signing contracts instead of discovering music. He had built something remarkable, but in doing so, he had lost the very thing that made him love the industry in the first place—the thrill of the hunt.

The Weight of Leadership

Running Crossroads Records wasn't just about finding talent anymore—it was about sustaining an empire. With success came responsibility. Ben was no longer the rebellious scout working out of smoky bars and underground venues; he was the face of a label that now had investors, shareholders, and expectations.

Every decision carried weight. Every artist signed had to not only be good but profitable.

At first, he fought to keep the label's soul intact. He turned down buyout offers from major labels, refused to overcommercialize his artists, and stood firm on giving them creative freedom. But the pressure was relentless. If he wanted Crossroads to compete with the giants, he had to adapt. He had to play the game—at least a little.

That's when the compromises started.

The Slippery Slope

Ben swore he would never become one of the industry suits, but power had a way of reshaping convictions. The first compromise seemed small—agreeing to tweak an album's production to make it more radio-friendly. Then came the strategic partnerships, the licensing deals, the corporate collaborations that promised exposure but chipped away at the label's independence. It was a slow erosion, one that he justified as necessary, but deep down, he felt the change.

David, now retired but still watching from afar, saw it too. One night, over drinks, he called Ben out. "You wanted to take over the industry, kid, and you did. But tell me—when was the last time you listened to music just to feel something?"

Ben had no answer.

Crossroads Records was thriving, but at what cost? The thing that had once driven him—his instinct, his passion for the underdogs, the thrill of discovery—had been drowned out by contracts, negotiations, and profit margins. He had built an empire, but in the process, he had lost himself.

And for the first time in years, he wondered if it had all been worth it.

The Shift to Talent Scouting

By 2019, despite Crossroads' immense success, Ben began to feel restless. The job of running a label had become about numbers, legal battles, and corporate negotiations—things he had never cared for. He missed the chase, the discovery, the feeling of finding something raw and real before the rest of the world had even noticed.

That year, Ben made a drastic decision—he sold his shares in Crossroads Records and stepped down as CEO. It shocked the industry. Walking away from the empire he had built seemed like madness, but for Ben, it was necessary. He didn't want to run a business. He wanted to do what he did best—find talent.

With no ties to a single label, Ben became a free agent, working as an independent talent scout. He operated outside the traditional label system, advising artists on deals, negotiating contracts, and ensuring that they didn't get swallowed up by the industry machine. Unlike the executives who only cared about profits, Ben had the credibility of someone who had built an empire and walked away from it.

76

His reputation made him more valuable than ever. Labels competed for his recommendations, and artists sought him out, hoping to be the next name he backed. He had transitioned from a businessman to an oracle—someone whose word alone could make or break a career.

Reinventing the Game

Ben didn't just scout talent—he changed how artists navigated the industry. He built a consulting firm that worked directly with musicians, teaching them how to keep control of their work, understand their contracts, and negotiate from a position of strength. Instead of pushing artists toward labels, he helped them carve out alternative paths—independent releases, streaming deals, and self-managed tours. In an era where the music industry was evolving at a rapid pace, Ben became the bridge between raw talent and sustainable success.

His approach attracted attention, not just from artists but from the very industry he had left behind. Major labels tried to bring him back into the fold, offering executive positions, partnerships, and massive pay checks. Ben refused. He wasn't interested in sitting in boardrooms again. He was back in the world where he belonged—dive bars, underground venues, latenight sessions with artists on the verge of something great.

A New Legacy

Ben's transition from label executive to independent scout cemented his status as a legend in the industry. He was no longer just a guy who found talent—he was a mentor, a protector, a strategist. His name carried weight, not because of corporate power, but because of the trust he had built with musicians who knew he wasn't just another suit looking for a payday.

By 2022, artists weren't just seeking his approval—they were following his blueprint. Independent success stories became more common, proving that musicians didn't have to sell their souls to make it. Ben had spent his entire career fighting the machine, and now, most unexpectedly, he had beaten it.

He had once built an empire. Now, he was tearing down the old system, one artist at a time.

Climbing the Ranks

That success opened doors. Bigger labels started paying attention. A&R reps who had once ignored his calls suddenly wanted meetings. But Ben knew the industry well enough to recognize that respect wasn't given—it was taken.

He played the game differently than the others. Where his peers tried to befriend executives, Ben cultivated relationships with power brokers—the people who controlled the industry. He knew the venue owners, the club managers, the journalists who dictated the narrative. He befriended radio DJs, ensured they owed him Favors and had industry insiders feeding him information before it reached the top. He didn't just find talent—he controlled the pipeline.

His methods weren't always ethical. More than once, he sabotaged deals that threatened his own. He convinced artists to break contracts and whispered in the right ears to ensure competitors' projects fell apart. If there was an opportunity, Ben took it. If there wasn't, he created one.

By the time he was thirty-five, he had built a reputation as the man who could turn nobodies into superstars. But with power came enemies.

The Price of Power

Ben's rise wasn't without consequences. For every artist he propelled into the spotlight, there were others left in the dust— musicians who had trusted him, only to realize too late that they were just another move in his strategy. Some understood it was just business. Others didn't forgive so easily. Rival scouts accused him of poaching talent, executives branded him as unpredictable, and competitors in the industry started seeing him as more of a threat than an ally.

By the time Crossroads Records was at its peak, Ben had as many enemies as he did admirers. Anonymous threats became common—emails warning him to back off, industry gossip about people who wanted to take him down. Some were empty bluffs. Others weren't. Venues that once welcomed him suddenly stopped returning his calls. Journalists he had trusted started writing hit pieces about his cutthroat methods. A few artists he had mentored turned against him, going public with stories about the deals he had manipulated behind closed doors.

David, ever the observer, saw the shift before Ben did. "You've made yourself indispensable, kid," he said one night over whiskey. "But that means they're all waiting for you to fall."

Ben shrugged, taking a slow drag from his cigarette. "Then I just won't fall."

The Moment Everything Changed

But even he wasn't invincible. The turning point came when he made one enemy too many. It was an executive at a major label—a man with too much power and too little patience for someone like Ben to disrupt the status quo. Ben had pulled the wrong strings and sabotaged the wrong deal, and suddenly, the industry turned on him.

Venues blacklisted his artists. Radio stations stopped playing the music he championed. Deals that had been all but secured fell through overnight. Labels that once fought for his approval now treated him like a liability. In less than a year, Ben went from being an industry kingmaker to a man standing on the edge of exile.

For the first time in his career, he felt it—real vulnerability. The realization that, despite everything he had built, he was still just one man playing a game much bigger than himself.

And in the music industry, the game never stopped playing.

The Rivalries

As Ben's influence grew, so did the resistance. Executives who had dismissed him now saw him as a threat. Other talent scouts, once colleagues, became competitors who would do anything to see him fail.

One, in particular, became his greatest rival—Marcus Feldman, a polished, well-connected executive who came from old money and had every advantage Ben never did. Marcus didn't just despise Ben—he wanted to destroy him.

The two locked horns over a rising star—a young singer with a voice that could stop time. Ben had discovered her first, nurtured her talent, and shaped her career. But Marcus had the label connections, the industry sway. He made her an offer she couldn't refuse.

For the first time in his career, Ben lost.

It wasn't just a business failure—it was personal. He had fought to protect her from the machine, only to watch her get chewed up and spat out like so many before her. The album flopped. She faded into obscurity. And Marcus, smug in his victory, made sure Ben knew he had been beaten.

But Ben wasn't one to accept defeat. He took the loss, learned from it, and came back stronger. He started playing the long game—building his network of artists, ensuring that he no longer relied on the labels to make his moves. He invested in independent studios, backed producers who owed him Favors and built a talent empire that operated outside the traditional system.

When Marcus came for his next artist, Ben was ready. He made sure the deal collapsed before it even began. He had learned the rules—and he had learned how to break them.

Outmanoeuvring the Enemy

The battle between Ben and Marcus escalated over the years, moving beyond just artists. It became a war of influence, fought in industry boardrooms, on festival lineups, and in whispered conversations behind closed doors. Marcus had corporate power, but Ben had something more dangerous—loyalty.

The artists Ben nurtured didn't forget what he had done for them. They stuck by him and trusted him more than they trusted the labels. He used that loyalty to his advantage, ensuring that Marcus's talent pipeline ran dry. If Marcus wanted an artist, Ben got there first. If Marcus tried to close a deal, Ben made sure it unravelled.

It was a chess game played in backrooms and handshakes, and Ben was always two moves ahead. While Marcus relied on the old system, Ben adapted, embracing streaming, direct-to-fan engagement, and independent branding. He was reshaping the industry in real time, forcing the establishment to chase him instead of the other way around.

One night, at an industry gala, Marcus cornered him. "Enjoy it while it lasts, Holloway. Sooner or later, you'll slip. And when you do, I'll be there."

Ben just smiled, sipping his drink. "You've been waiting a long time, Marcus. How's that working out for you?"

The war wasn't over. But for now, Ben was winning.

Becoming the Star maker

By the time Ben reached his late thirties, he had transcended the role of a talent scout. He wasn't just finding artists—he was making them. If Ben Holloway backed you, you didn't just get signed. You became a name.

He was feared and respected in equal measure. Artists sought him out, desperate for his approval. Executives tolerated him because they had no choice. If he decided you were worth investing in, you had a career. If he didn't, you didn't exist.

Ben's influence stretched beyond just music. He had built relationships with film directors, fashion designers, and tech moguls who saw the value in cross-branding. He wasn't just breaking musicians anymore—he was creating cultural icons. His artists weren't just topping charts; they were landing endorsement deals, starring in indie films, and becoming the faces of luxury brands. A single recommendation from Ben could change the trajectory of an entire career overnight.

But power came at a price.

With every artist he launched, he felt more like a machine and less like the person who had once stood in a dingy club, awestruck by raw talent. The chase, the thrill, and the heart of it all had been replaced by calculated moves, brand strategies, and global market reach. He was no longer searching for music that moved him—he was curating stars that fit a commercial blueprint.

David, watching from the sidelines, saw the shift. "This is what you wanted, isn't it?" he asked one evening, sitting across from Ben at a high-end lounge, far removed from the dive bars they used to haunt.

Ben swirled the whiskey in his glass. "I don't know anymore."

David gave a knowing smirk. "Then maybe it's time you figure it out. Before there's nothing left to find."

For the first time in his career, Ben wondered if he had climbed the wrong mountain.

The Holloway Empire

Despite his growing disillusionment, Ben's empire kept expanding. He built a boutique management firm that specialized in turning underground talent into mainstream success. Labels fought for his endorsements, brands lined up to collaborate with his artists, and media outlets followed his every move.

But with great power came even greater scrutiny. Rumours swirled about his ruthless methods—how he manipulated artists into signing deals, how he crushed those who refused to play by his rules. Former protégés started speaking out, claiming he had shaped them into something they never wanted to be. Some called him a genius. Others called him a tyrant.

One night, an old friend from his early days in the business confronted him at an industry gala. "You used to fight for the music, Ben. Now, you're just another king on the throne. Do you even know what you stand for anymore?"

Ben had no answer.

He had built an empire. But for the first time, he wasn't sure if it was one worth ruling.

Chapter 6:

The Hollow Crown

Ben Holloway had everything he had ever wanted—money, influence, a seat at the table with the most powerful players in the music industry. And yet, sitting in the corner booth of an upscale LA bar, whiskey in hand, cigarette soldering between his fingers, he felt nothing.

The Height of Power

The years that followed his rise as a star maker were a blur of excess. Every major label in the industry wanted a piece of him. Artists chased his approval like it was the final step to immortality. Executives courted him with six-figure offers just for a meeting. When Ben walked into a venue, whispers followed. When he nodded at a performance, careers were made.

He had built his empire carefully, and strategically. His name alone held weight. The Holloway seal of approval meant more than a million-dollar marketing campaign. He had taken nobodies and turned them into household names. He had transformed street performers into superstars, their faces plastered across billboards, their songs dominating radio waves.

And yet, beneath all the glamour, something was rotting.

The Hollow Success

At first, he ignored it. He drowned himself in the luxury of success—the exclusive parties, the private jets, the endless flow of money. But with each passing year, the weight of it settled heavier on his shoulders. He no longer knew if he was shaping the industry or simply feeding the machine he had once despised.

His artists were no longer wide-eyed dreamers—they were products. Brands are carefully curated to maximize profit. Some of them thrived in the spotlight, but others buckled under the pressure, becoming cautionary tales of fame gone wrong. Ben had once prided himself on protecting his artists from the machine, but now, he was starting to realize—he was the machine.

David's words echoed in his mind more often than he liked to admit. "You can't climb this high and expect to stay clean, kid. The view's nice, but the air's thin."

One night, he sat in his penthouse, overlooking the glittering sprawl of Los Angeles, and finally admitted the truth to himself.

He had spent his whole life chasing power, but now that he had it, he wasn't sure he wanted it anymore.

The Industry Machine

Ben had always known the industry was ruthless, but now he was on the inside, seeing its machinery operate up close. The labels didn't care about music. They didn't care about artistry, about soul. They cared about trends, statistics, and viral moments. Talent was a secondary concern. A beautiful voice meant nothing if the singer wasn't marketable. A brilliant songwriter was worthless if they weren't willing to sell their sound to the highest bidder.

Ben watched as raw talent was picked apart and repackaged. Artists he had discovered—artists who had once been filled with fire and authenticity—were reshaped into commodities. Their music was watered down, and their image was controlled by PR teams.

Some fought back. Most lost.

He had seen it happen too many times. A musician with a once uncompromising vision would enter the studio, only to emerge months later sounding like every other industry-manufactured product. Their unique voice is smothered under radio-friendly beats. Their words were altered to be safer, broader, and more palatable. The songs that had once bled with their struggles were now polished to the point of emptiness.

Ben tried to stop it at first. He fought for the artists he believed in, argued with executives, and pleaded for creative control. But over time, he realized it was a losing battle. The industry didn't compromise. If an artist didn't conform, they were discarded. If a song didn't chart, it was erased from existence. If a musician refused to play the game, they were labelled 'difficult'—and in this business, difficult meant unemployable.

It disgusted him. But what disgusted him more was the fact that he was complicit.

A Cog in the Machine

At some point, without realizing it, Ben had stopped fighting. He still told himself he was different from the suits who only saw music as a product, but was he? He had signed off on album revisions that stripped away an artist's originality. He had sat in meetings where the focus wasn't the music, but the branding. He had advised musicians to tweak their image, their lyrics, their sound—always with the promise that it was for their good, that it was the only way to survive.

And maybe it was. But survival came at a cost.

Ben had once been the guy who found artists that no one else would touch, who gave them a chance when no one else would. But now, he was watching those same artists become unrecognizable, their edges smoothed out, their passion diluted. He had helped them get here. He had led them into the lion's den, and now he had to watch as the industry devoured them whole.

David's words came back to him, haunting him like a ghost. "You think you can beat the machine, kid? You think you can play their game without becoming them?"

For years, Ben had believed he could. Now, he wasn't so sure.

He had built his empire. He had climbed higher than he ever thought possible. But as he looked around, he realized he wasn't standing at the top.

He was just another cog in the machine.

The Slow Decay

89

At first, the disillusionment came in small doses—late nights spent replaying old demo tapes, comparing them to the overproduced final product. Conversations with artists who once swore they would never sell out, only to see them parrot the industry's expectations months later.

Then came the days when he stopped trying to fight it.

Ben told himself it wasn't his problem. He was just a scout. He found the talent. What happened after wasn't on him. If an artist let the industry change them, that was their failure, not his. If they signed the contracts, if they allowed their sound to be altered, that was their choice.

And yet, every time he saw another artist break, another musician loses, he felt something inside him fracture.

He drank more. Smoked more. The whiskey numbed the disappointment, the cigarettes filled the spaces where words failed. He stopped listening to new music unless he had to. The joy he once found in discovering something fresh, something real, had soured. Everything sounded the same. Everything felt hollow.

He surrounded himself with people who didn't ask questions, who didn't force him to examine the weight pressing down on his chest. His life became a series of meaningless parties, and industry events where everyone pretended, they still believed in the dream.

Ben stopped believing.

The Breaking Point

It wasn't a single moment that broke him—it was a slow unravelling. The slow realization that he had built something grand, only to watch it rot from the inside.

There were nights when he would sit alone in his penthouse, staring at the gold records on the walls, remembering a time when those plaques had meant something. When the music had felt like magic finding an artist had been about passion, not business.

Now, it was just numbers. Streams. Sales. Marketing campaigns. The artistry had been lost somewhere along the way, and he wasn't sure if it was the industry's fault or his own.

One night, he caught his reflection in the mirror and barely recognized the man looking back at him. Tired eyes. A face hardened by years of compromise. A stranger in an expensive suit, drowning in everything he had once sworn he wouldn't become.

For the first time in his career, Ben didn't feel like he was at the top.

He felt like he was sinking.

The Turning Point

The breaking point came in the form of a young singersongwriter—Emily Caldwell. She was the kind of artist

Ben had once sworn to protect. Her voice was raw, haunting, the kind that could turn a silent room into a church. She played guitar like it was an extension of her soul, her lyrics filled with unpolished, beautiful truths.

Ben found her in a grimy Brooklyn bar, playing to a crowd of thirty. Within a month, she was signed. Within six months, she was everywhere. Her voice is on every radio station. Her face is on every screen.

Then, a year later, she was gone.

Emily hadn't been built for the industry. The pressure crushed her. The label stripped her sound bare, dulled her edges, and made her something she wasn't. The album was a commercial success, but she hated it. She disappeared just as quickly as she had arrived, another name added to the list of artists the industry had chewed up and spit out.

When Ben found out she had overdosed in a hotel room, something inside him snapped.

He stood in his penthouse apartment, staring out at the LA skyline, wondering when he had stopped caring. Wondering when he had become the very thing he once despised.

A Mirror to His Destruction

Emily's death wasn't just another casualty of the industry—it was a reflection of everything Ben had allowed himself to become. He had seen it coming, had watched the light fade from her eyes in boardrooms and recording sessions, had heard

92

the exhaustion in her voice when she said she just needed a break. He hadn't stopped it. He had been too busy closing deals, making calls, and ensuring the next tour was lined up.

Now, there was no next tour. No next album. Just a hollow legacy, another name to add to the industry's graveyard of broken artists.

The whiskey in his hand suddenly tasted bitter. He set the glass down, his hands shaking.

He had told himself for years that he was different, that he had been fighting for the artists. But Emily's death was proof that he had been lying to himself.

Something had to change. Or he would be next.

The Cynic's Crown

Ben didn't quit. He didn't walk away. He couldn't. The industry was all he knew. But something changed.

He no longer searched for talent because he believed in it. He did it because it was what he did. He no longer fought for artists because he thought they could win—he fought because he wanted to watch the industry squirm, wanted to see how much he could push before they pushed back.

He became the man in the shadows, the chain-smoking cynic who watched the machine turn, knowing exactly how it worked but refusing to care. He stopped pretending he was part of something meaningful. He knew the game, knew how to play it better than anyone.

He took the money. He made the deals. He found the talent.

But he never let himself believe in it again.

A Hollow Throne

Ben's name still carried weight, but the fire that once drove him had burned out. He operated like a ghost, moving through the industry with detached efficiency, closing deals with a cigarette in one hand and a drink in the other. The parties, the events, the exclusive gatherings—they all blurred together. He knew the right words to say, the right hands to shake, the right illusions to maintain. But beneath it all, there was nothing left but cold calculation.

Artists still came to him, hoping for his approval. Executives still sought his insight. He played his role well, but the difference was, now he knew it was all just a performance.

The industry hadn't changed, but Ben had. The thrill of discovery was gone. The passion had withered. Now, it was just a game. And the only reason he kept playing was because he didn't know what else to do.

He had won. He had conquered the industry.

And it had cost him everything.

Chapter 7:

A Love Unexpected

The Woman Behind the Bar

Ben met Emma the way he met most people—begrudgingly. She was tending bar at a hole-in-the-wall jazz club; a place he wouldn't have stepped foot in if he hadn't been dragged there by an old industry contact. He had been halfway through his third drink, debating if he could sneak out without being noticed, when she slid another glass in front of him.

"On the house," she said, wiping the counter with a practiced motion.

Ben eyed the drink suspiciously. "I didn't order this."

"I know," she said, smirking. "But you looked like you were about to start a fight with the wallpaper, and I figured I'd preemptively calm you down."

He snorted, not used to people talking to him like that. Most people either avoided him completely or kissed his ass. Emma did neither.

She leaned against the bar, arms crossed, studying him like he was some kind of curiosity. "Let me guess. The music industry, but hates the music industry?"

Ben exhaled, taking a sip of the drink. "What gave it away?"
"The scowl. The cigarette stench. And the way you looked personally offended when that guy started singing Sinatra five minutes ago."

He smirked despite himself. "The bastard butchered it."

"Agreed."

They sat in a rare, comfortable silence for a few moments before Emma spoke again. "So, what's your deal?"

Ben tilted his head. "You mean my tragic backstory?"

"Something like that."

He sighed, swirling the whiskey in his glass. "I make people famous. Then I watch them turn into something I hate."

Emma nodded as if that made complete sense. "And what do you want to be?"

Ben hesitated. No one had ever asked him that before—not in a way that mattered. He had always been the guy who made things happen for other people. Who found the talent, polished it, and sent it out into the world. No one ever cared who he was beyond what he could do for them.

But Emma looked like she wanted an answer.

"Gone," he finally said. "Out of this city. Out of this business."

Emma studied him for a long moment before nodding. "Yeah. I can see that."

Something shifted at that moment. Maybe it was the fact that she didn't try to tell him he was wrong. Maybe it was the fact that she saw him as something more than just a jaded industry relic.

Whatever it was, it was the beginning of something he hadn't felt in a long time.

Hope.

Ben had spent the last decade learning how to read people. It was a necessary skill in the music industry, where trust was currency and betrayal were an inevitability. He had built careers on instincts alone, knowing when an artist had potential and when they would crash and burn. But for all his experience, he couldn't read Emma.

She wasn't like anyone he had met before. She didn't chase fame, didn't try to impress him. She wasn't interested in who he knew or what he could do for her. She was just—herself. And for reasons he couldn't quite articulate, that fascinated him.

Their relationship grew in a way that felt both inevitable and impossible. Ben, who had spent so much of his life running from things, suddenly found himself standing still, wanting to be exactly where he was. With her.

Emma was the only person who ever saw through his bitterness, who understood that his gruffness was just Armor. She was patient where he was impulsive, and warm where he was cold. She didn't try to fix him; she just was. And for the first time in his life, Ben wanted something beyond escape—he wanted to build a life with someone.

A Life in the Neon Glow

They spent their nights wrapped in the city's neon glow, walking aimlessly through streets neither of them cared for but loved because the other was there. Conversations that started about nothing became everything. She made him laugh. Laugh. The kind of laughter he had forgotten he was capable of.

He introduced her to the quiet places he kept hidden from the world—a late-night diner with the best coffee in the city, a park bench that overlooked the skyline just right, and an old record store that still smelled like dust and vinyl. She showed him that sometimes, the best moments in life weren't grand gestures but quiet, shared silences.

They had their fights, of course. Emma challenged him in ways he wasn't used to. She called him out when he was being an ass and pushed back when he tried to shut her out. He hated it. He loved it. She never let him retreat into himself completely. And that terrified him more than anything else—because it meant she mattered. More than anything had in a long time.

They travelled together when they could. Emma had a way of convincing him to slow down, to appreciate places he would have otherwise ignored. They spent a weekend in New Orleans, walking through old streets filled with jazz and history. Another time, they rented a cabin in the mountains, just them, a fire, and the sound of the wind through the trees. Ben had never been one for sentimentality, but with her, it felt natural.

The Proposal

And life, for once, was working in his Favor. He was about to sign the biggest deal of his career—a $100 million contract that would finally let him walk away from the industry and start his ranch. A life away from the chaos, away from the cameras, away from the weight of expectations.

So, he proposed. Emma said yes.

It was an uncharacteristically cold night when Ben found himself pacing the length of their apartment, the velvet box burning a hole in his pocket. He wasn't nervous—or at least, that's what he told himself. But the truth was, the idea of asking Emma to spend her life with him felt more daunting than any contract he had ever signed.

She found him standing by the window, staring at the city lights with a furrowed brow.

"You look like you're plotting something," she teased.

Ben turned, swallowing hard. "Maybe I am."

Emma raised an eyebrow. "Should I be worried?"

He reached into his pocket, pulling out the box and holding it out to her. No grand speech, no theatrics. Just him, standing there, raw and vulnerable in a way he never allowed himself to be.

Emma took the box, opened it, and let out a soft breath. She looked up at him, her eyes searching his.

"You sure about this?" she asked, her voice barely above a whisper.

Ben nodded. "I've never been surer of anything."

A slow smile spread across her face. "Then yes."

Ben exhaled, a breath he hadn't realized he was holding. He pulled her close, pressing his forehead against hers.

For the first time in his life, he wasn't running from something.

He was running toward it.

The Father He Never Had

Ben Holloway sat in the dim light of his study, fingers pressing into his temples. The excitement of fatherhood should have been overwhelming in the best way. Instead, it gnawed at him, an anxiety curling deep in his gut. He thought about his childhood, how his father had been a man of ambition but not warmth. The kind of man who saw success as a finish line rather than a journey, who provided but never nurtured. His mother had been present but always preoccupied, her love for him expressed through structured schedules and well-meaning expectations rather than open affection. Ben had grown up in a house of achievements, where trophies mattered more than heart-to-hearts, where failure was unacceptable.

Was that the kind of father he would become?

He had spent so much of his life in the music industry, managing artists, fixing their problems, and watching them fall apart under the weight of their fame. He had seen it all— brilliant minds undone by bad habits; egos grown monstrous under the pressure of expectation. The industry swallowed people whole, and he had never let himself get too close. He had always been the one standing on the sidelines, making sure others didn't drown. But what if he had spent so much time cleaning up other people's messes that he had no idea how to build something good himself?

Emma saw the tension in his jaw, the way he stared at nothing for too long, his thoughts pulling him inward. One night, as they lay in bed, she placed her hand over the growing curve of her stomach and whispered, "You'll be a good dad, Ben."

He swallowed. "You don't know that."

"I do," she said firmly. "Because you care too much not to be."

He turned toward her, meeting her steady gaze. "Caring doesn't mean I won't mess up."

"Of course you'll mess up." She smiled, lacing her fingers through his. "But that's what being a parent is. My dad wasn't perfect. He worked too much. Missed a lot of my big moments. But I never once doubted that he loved me." She squeezed his hand. "That's what matters. Not being perfect. Just... being there."

101

Ben wanted to believe her. He did.

The Dream Ranch

The weeks leading up to the wedding were a blur of long drives and hopeful searching. They scoured the countryside for their dream ranch, visiting properties that never quite felt right. Some were too modern, stripped of any soul. Others were too dilapidated, requiring more work than they could take on. One house, a sprawling Victorian-style estate, gave Emma an uneasy feeling the moment they stepped inside. "I don't know," she murmured, rubbing her arms as if warding off a chill. "Something feels... off."

Ben didn't believe in superstition, but even he had to admit, that the air inside felt heavy, like the walls held secrets they weren't meant to hear.

Then they found it.

Nestled between rolling hills, bordered by a lake that stretched into the horizon, the ranch was exactly what they had been searching for. The house was old but solid, its wraparound porch perfect for watching sunsets. The air smelled like fresh grass, and for the first time in as long as he could remember, Ben felt a sense of peace. This was home.

They signed the papers that same afternoon, their future finally taking shape. At night, they sprawled out in bed, sketching out renovation plans, arguing playfully over whether they should get horses right away or wait until their child was old enough to ride.

Emma wanted to paint the nursery a soft shade of sage green. Ben, ever practical, suggested neutral tones. "Green is neutral," she argued, laughing as she nudged him. "We're doing green."

He let her win. Truthfully, he didn't care about the colour of the walls. He cared about the way she looked when she talked about the future, the way she made it seem possible.

When Everything Felt Right

The wedding planning was chaotic in the way all weddings were. Emma had dreamed of something intimate, something elegant yet simple. Ben let her take the lead, not because he didn't care, but because he knew this day mattered more to her than it did to him.

Everything was coming together—until it wasn't.

A week before the ceremony, they got a call. Their venue had been double-booked. The manager apologized profusely, swearing it was a clerical error, but the reality remained: their wedding day had just become a logistical nightmare.

Emma's face paled as she hung up the phone. "What do we do?"

Ben took a deep breath. "We figure it out."

They scrambled for a solution, calling every venue within a hundred-mile radius. Eventually, they settled on an outdoor ceremony at their newly purchased ranch. It wasn't what they had planned, but standing beneath the wide Montana sky, surrounded by the land that would become their home, it felt right.

Then, just days before the wedding, Ben's phone rang.

He glanced at the screen. The call he had been waiting for.

Stepping outside, he answered. The lawyers. The closing date for the $100 million contract had been scheduled.

For the same day as his wedding.

Ben ran a hand through his hair, frustration knotting in his chest. The industry had taken so much from him already. Now, it wanted to take this too.

He turned back to Emma, phone still in hand. "They scheduled the closing for the wedding day."

She blinked. Then, to his surprise, she smiled.

"That's okay," she said softly. "We'll work around it."

They kissed under the Montana sky, the ranch stretching out before them.

Everything was perfect.

Yet, in the quiet hours of the night, Emma sat by the window, her hands resting on her stomach. She didn't say it aloud, but a small part of her wondered: how much of their life would always be dictated by the industry? And how much longer could she pretend it didn't bother her?

Outside, a storm gathered on the horizon. The first drops of rain tapped against the windowpane, a whisper of something unseen.

Everything was perfect.

For once in his life, Ben Holloway had everything he had ever wanted.

But life had other plans.

Chapter 8:

The Perfect Day

Ben stirred awake to the sound of Emma's voice, soft and sweet, drifting through the morning air like something out of a dream. She was singing—a lullaby, one he had never heard before but instantly loved. The melody was gentle, and soothing, wrapping around him like warmth from the rising sun. His eyes were still closed, but he could feel it—the golden light spilling through the curtains, the crisp, perfect air that smelled like fresh earth and wildflowers.

Everything was perfect.

He opened his eyes and turned his head toward the window, where the sunlight hit the bed just right. The cool sheets rustled as he sat up, stretching out the lingering stiffness from the weekend spent at the ranch. He had never slept better anywhere else. This place—it wasn't just land, wasn't just a house—it was home. The dream he had spent years chasing had finally materialized, and for the first time, he wasn't running.

Emma's voice still carried from down the hall. He followed it, barefoot, drawn in like a tide to the shore. He stopped in the doorway of what would soon be the nursery and leaned against the frame, watching her.

She had set up the crib—one they had picked out together but never actually put together. She was painting the walls a soft yellow, the gentle strokes of the brush moving in time with her humming.

She turned when she noticed him, her face glowing, whether, from the morning light or her happiness, he wasn't sure. Probably both.

"Well?" she asked, motioning to the room with a hopeful smile. "What do you think?"

Ben took a slow step inside, running a hand along the smooth wooden railing of the crib. "It's perfect," he said.

She dipped the brush into the paint again and continued her work. "I figured yellow was a safe choice. Neutral. Works for a boy or a girl." She paused, glancing at him over her shoulder. "I just want to be prepared."

He crossed the room in a few steps, sliding his arms around her waist from behind, resting his chin against her shoulder. "You're already more prepared than I'll ever be," he murmured, pressing a kiss to the side of her head.

She laughed, leaning into him. "Come on, let me make you breakfast."

He pulled away just enough to spin her around and kiss her, slow and deep. "No," he said, smirking. "Let me make breakfast, Mumma Bear."

She rolled her eyes but let him go, watching as he headed toward the kitchen.

The Morning Ritual

The kitchen was filled with warm light, the kind of light that made everything feel golden. Ben glanced out the window as he reached for the coffee pot, taking in the perfect view of rolling hills, the endless sky, and the peace that stretched in every direction. It hit him then, a quiet but undeniable realization—his dream had come true.

This was it.

He didn't need anything else. He didn't want anything else.

The old Ben—the one who had spent his life in dark clubs, drowning in whiskey and nicotine—felt like a ghost of a man he had once known. He reached into his pocket, fingers brushing against a familiar pack of cigarettes.

Then he looked over at Emma, standing in the doorway, watching him with that easy, knowing smile of hers.

Without a second thought, he pulled the pack out and tossed it into the trash.

She raised an eyebrow but said nothing, just crossed the room and wrapped her arms around his waist.

He smiled, tilting his head down to press a kiss to her forehead before turning his attention to breakfast.

He cracked eggs into a pan, the sizzle filling the kitchen with a comforting sound. Emma leaned against the counter, watching him as he worked. "You always did cook better than me," she teased.

"Because I have to make up for the fact that you burn toast," he replied with a grin.

She gasped, playfully smacking his arm. "I do not!"

"You set off the smoke alarm last week."

She rolled her eyes but laughed, taking a seat at the kitchen table. He slid a plate in front of her, and they ate together in comfortable silence, the sound of birds outside mixing with the occasional clink of silverware against ceramic.

A Life Worth Living

After breakfast, they stepped outside, coffee mugs in hand, the sun warming their skin. The ranch stretched before them, endless and peaceful, the kind of place where time felt slower, where the world's noise couldn't reach them.

Emma laced her fingers through his. "Do you ever think about how different things could have been? If we never found this place? If we never found each other?"

Ben exhaled slowly, tightening his grip on her hand. "All the time."

She looked up at him, her brown eyes filled with something he couldn't quite name. "Do you regret anything?"

He thought about it—thought about it. About the years spent chasing something he didn't understand, about the people he had hurt, about the ones he had lost. He thought about the nights he had wasted, drowning in excess, about the years he had spent believing happiness was something he would never be able to hold onto.

Then he looked at her. At their home. In life, they were building together.

"No," he said softly. "Not anymore."

Emma smiled, resting her head against his shoulder. "Good. Because I think this—" she gestured to the ranch, to the house, to everything around them—"is exactly where we're meant to be."

Ben pressed a kiss to her hair, inhaling deeply, feeling the truth of her words settle in his chest. He had spent his whole life running, searching, breaking, and rebuilding.

But now, finally, he had stopped.

Now, finally, he was home.

The phone rang just as he was plating the eggs. He sighed, already knowing who it was. He wiped his hands on a towel before answering.

"Yeah?"

"Mr. Holloway, just confirming the closing for your contract. We're all set for tomorrow at noon."

Ben glanced toward the porch, where Emma had already set up breakfast, waiting for him. He tightened his grip on the phone, already impatient to be off it.

"Yeah," he said quickly. "Got it. See you then." He hung up before they could waste any more of his time.

He stepped outside, taking his seat across from Emma as she served the food. The fields stretched endlessly beyond them, the world painted in perfect colours of green and gold. They ate, talking about their plans for tomorrow, their wedding, both excited, both eager for what was next.

As the morning stretched on, they took their time with breakfast, lingering over coffee and conversation. Emma pulled out a notebook, flipping through the wedding details. "Okay, so the flowers should be arriving today. The cake gets delivered tomorrow morning, and I need to confirm with the band."

Ben smirked. "Are you sure we need a band?"

Emma raised an eyebrow. "Are you suggesting we play a Spotify playlist at our wedding?"

"I mean… it's a possibility." He dodged the napkin she tossed at him, laughing. "Fine, fine. The band stays."

After breakfast, they took a walk along the lake, the water sparkling under the late-morning sun. Ben reached for Emma's hand, twining their fingers together. "It is perfect, isn't it?"

She smiled up at him. "Yeah, it is."

But there was a flicker of something in her eyes—hesitation, maybe. A thought left unsaid.

The Quiet Hesitation

Ben noticed it, that brief moment where something clouded her happiness. He squeezed her hand gently. "What is it?"

Emma hesitated, then shook her head. "Nothing. Just thinking."

"Thinking about what?"

She glanced out at the lake, her thumb running absently over his knuckles. "It's just... it all feels too good to be true sometimes. Like I'm waiting for something to go wrong."

Ben exhaled, pulling her closer as they continued their slow walk along the shore. "I get it," he admitted. "For a long time, I didn't think I could have this—any of this. And I spent years expecting it to slip through my fingers."

Emma looked up at him, waiting.

"But I don't anymore," he said, voice steady. "This is real. We built this. And we're not going to lose it."

She let out a small breath, then leaned against his arm as they walked. "I want to believe that."

"Then do."

A quiet moment passed, just the sound of their footsteps over the soft grass. Then Emma smiled, nudging him playfully. "You know, you're kind of romantic when you try."

Ben smirked. "Don't tell anyone. I have a reputation to maintain."

She laughed, and just like that, the hesitation in her eyes was gone.

The rest of the morning was spent in the kind of peace Ben had spent his whole life searching for. And for the first time, he let himself believe that maybe—just maybe—he had finally found it.

Later That Afternoon

Later that afternoon, they drove into town to finalize lastminute wedding details. While Emma browsed floral arrangements, Ben stepped outside to take a call.

A familiar voice, one he hadn't heard in years, crackled through the line. "Holloway. Didn't think I'd see your name again."

Ben stiffened. An old industry rival. A reminder of the world he had left behind.

"You still running from the business?" the man chuckled. "Or just pretending to be happy?"

Ben clenched his jaw. "I'm exactly where I want to be."

The call ended, but the unease remained. When Emma reappeared, holding a bouquet, she noticed the tension in his face. "Everything okay?"

"Yeah." He forced a smile. "Just an old ghost."

The Past Knocking

On the drive back to the ranch, the words from that call echoed in his mind. He hadn't thought about the industry in months—not in the way he used to. But hearing that voice, the smugness, the doubt—it stirred something inside him he wasn't ready to face.

Emma reached over, placing a hand on his knee as he drove. "Are you sure you're, okay? You've been quiet."

He exhaled through his nose, gripping the wheel a little tighter. "Yeah, just—some people can't let the past go."

She studied him for a moment before turning back toward the window. "That's the thing about ghosts," she murmured. "They stick around when something's unfinished."

Ben didn't reply. He didn't want to admit that part of him feared she was right.

The Weight of a Choice

Back at the ranch, as the evening sun painted the sky in soft oranges and purples, Ben found himself wandering toward the porch, cigarette in hand. He stared out over the hills, the land stretching endlessly before him, a future he had built brick by brick.

He didn't light the cigarette.

Instead, he turned it over between his fingers, lost in thought.

The life he had now was everything he had ever wanted. Peace. Stability. Love. A chance to be someone different, someone better. And yet, one phone call had been enough to shake him.

Was he still running? Or had he finally outrun the past?

Emma stepped outside, wrapping a sweater around herself as she joined him. "You sure you don't want to talk about it?"

Ben sighed, finally tossing the cigarette aside. "It doesn't matter. The past is the past."

She studied him, her expression gentle but knowing. "You don't have to prove anything to anyone, Ben. Not anymore."

He looked at her then, at the only thing that mattered. He nodded slowly, pulling her closer. "I know."

And for the first time since the call, he started to believe it.

That Night

That night, as they lay in bed, the storm that had been lurking on the horizon finally arrived. Rain pattered against the windows, thunder rumbling low in the distance. Emma curled against Ben's chest, warm and soft, but restless. "You ever feel like... when things are too perfect, something has to go wrong?"

Ben frowned, pressing a kiss to her hair. "Hey, don't think like that."

"I know." She let out a breath. "I just... I don't know. I'm happy. But part of me is scared."

Ben tightened his arms around her. "Nothing's going to happen,

115

Em."

The wind howled, rattling the windows. Somewhere in the house, a floorboard creaked.

Ben wasn't sure if he was reassuring her—or himself.

The Drive Back

They packed up later that afternoon and drove back to the city, the air still humming with the warmth of the sun. Emma sat with her bare feet up on the dashboard, her toes tapping in rhythm to the music playing on the radio. Her hair was a wild tangle from the wind, her laughter drifting through the car like a melody of its own.

Ben watched her out of the corner of his eye as he drove, his heart swelling in a way that still felt unfamiliar—too big for his chest, too overwhelming to contain. Love had always been something other people talked about, something he had believed in only in theory. But now, with Emma, it was tangible. It was real.

"Hey," she said suddenly, turning toward him. "What are you thinking about?"

Ben smiled, shaking his head. "Nothing. Just you."

She grinned, satisfied with that answer, and turned her face back toward the window.

The skyline appeared on the horizon, the glass and steel of Los Angeles shimmering in the late afternoon light. It was a beautiful city, but it had never quite felt like home. Not for either of them. They had both come here with dreams in their pockets, chasing something bigger than themselves. And now, they were ready to leave it behind.

Wedding Preparations

When they pulled into the driveway, Emma wasted no time—she went straight to check on her wedding dress, carefully pulling it from its protective bag, and running her fingers over the delicate lace.

Ben had meant to give her privacy, but when he walked past the room, he froze. She stood by the window, the golden light catching on the intricate embroidery, her face softened in quiet wonder. It wasn't just a dress—it was the next step of their lives together.

She turned, catching him standing there.

"It's okay," she said, smiling. "It's a silly tradition. I don't believe in luck."

But Ben couldn't speak for a moment. His throat felt tight. He had seen her a hundred different ways—windblown and laughing, sleepy and tangled in blankets, determined and fierce. But this—this quiet moment, her fingers tracing the edges of the life they were about to build—was something else entirely. "You're beautiful," he finally managed.

She smiled, a soft, knowing thing, before carefully hanging the dress back up.

117

A Night to Remember

The next few hours passed in a blur. They went to his Favorite restaurant for dinner, a cozy little spot tucked away from the main streets. The lighting was dim, the scent of garlic and roasted tomatoes filling the air. They ordered steak and pasta, stealing bites from each other's plates, their fingers brushing more than once.

After dinner, they took dessert to go, driving up to the Hollywood Hills, where the city stretched out beneath them like a sea of flickering lights. They sat on the hood of the car, the takeout boxes balanced between them as they ate forkfuls of cake.

"This doesn't feel real," Emma murmured after a while. "Like, I know it is, but—how did we get here? How did we go from strangers in a coffee shop to... this?"

Ben leaned back on his hands, staring at the endless sprawl of the city below. "I think about that all the time," he admitted. "One different choice and we never would have met."

Emma hummed, contemplative. "Do you think we would have found each other anyway?"

Ben turned his head to look at her. "Yeah," he said. "I do."

She smiled, nudging his shoulder with hers. "Hopeless romantic."

"You love it."

"I do," she admitted.

For a moment, silence settled between them, comfortable and warm.

Then, softer, almost to herself, Emma whispered, "Tomorrow's going to be perfect."

Ben exhaled, the weight of it sinking into his chest. He wanted to believe that, wanted to hold onto the certainty in her voice. But there was something about the night that made him reflective, made him wonder if they were ready for everything that came next.

"Yeah," he said, voice barely more than a breath. "It will."

The Last Night Before Forever

When they got home, Emma carefully hung her dress at the end of the bed, smoothing out the fabric with gentle hands.

Ben watched her from where he stood, struck again by the quiet reverence in her movements. Was she nervous? Did she feel the same weight pressing against his ribs?

She turned to him, eyes soft. "Come here."

He did, crawling into bed beside her, and she immediately wrapped herself around him, her arms draped over his chest, her body fitting against his like she had always been meant to be there.

Ben closed his eyes, exhaling slowly.

"There's something I should probably tell you," She murmured.

119

Ben opened his eyes, his heartbeat stuttering. "What?"

"I snuck a bite of the cake before dinner."

Ben laughed, pressing a kiss to the top of her head. "That's why you weren't that hungry."

"I regret nothing."

He chuckled, pulling her closer, feeling the weight of her against him, the warmth of her breath against his collarbone.

As the storm from earlier in the evening finally passed, leaving only a faint scent of rain in the air, Ben let himself sink into the moment.

Tomorrow, everything will change. But tonight, everything was exactly as it should be.

Tomorrow, their lives will change. Tomorrow, everything they had been working toward would begin.

But for tonight, there was only this.

The last thing he saw before sleep took him was Emma.

And he had never been happier.

Chapter 9:

The Job He Never Wanted

Ben opened his eyes, expecting to wake up in his shitty LA apartment—maybe with a hangover, maybe with the scent of coffee drifting from the kitchen where Emma was making breakfast. Maybe—just maybe—he'd roll over and pull her into him, murmuring something about five more minutes before the reality of another day set in.

But instead, he was staring at clouds.

Vast, endless clouds stretching in every direction. The air smelled like nothing, felt like nothing—like a void that had decided to dress itself up as paradise.

Ben swallowed hard, his chest tightening.

This wasn't real.

Had to be a dream.

But then he heard it—the distant, murmuring hum of voices. A long, unbroken line of people stretched toward a pair of gates made of something that looked like silver but pulsed like it was alive. The line snaked endlessly into the horizon, filled with people in all forms of dress from all periods of history. Some were crying; others stood in silent acceptance.

Ben's breath came faster now.

This wasn't real.

This couldn't be real.

Then he heard a voice, tired and unenthusiastic, like a man who had been working overtime for centuries.

"Ah, you're here."

Ben turned and saw a man in a white robe, leaning lazily against the pearly gate like an overworked security guard at a nightclub that had lost its appeal decades ago. His nametag read: **St. Peter**.

Ben scowled. "I don't know who the hell you think I am, but I don't belong here."

Peter sighed, rubbing his temples. "You do now."

Ben took a step back. "No. No way."

Peter glanced at him, then at the never-ending line of souls. "I chose you," he said simply. "I'm tired, Ben. I've been doing this for centuries, and I need a replacement. So, congratulations. You're the new Gatekeeper of Heaven." A sharp, icy panic crawled up Ben's spine.

No. No, no, no.

"I just got my life together," he rasped. "I've got a fiancée. A kid on the way. I was supposed to get out of LA, start over—"

Peter shrugged. "Sometimes the universe is just a dick."

Ben clenched his jaw. "Send me back."

"Can't."

"Then fuck this."

122

He turned away, desperate for an exit, but there was nowhere to go. Just clouds and more clouds, the queue of souls stretching on forever.

He squeezed his eyes shut. *Wake up, wake up, wake up.*

But when he opened them, nothing had changed.

Peter folded his arms. "You're in denial."

"No shit," Ben snapped.

Peter sighed, pushing off the gate. "Look, I get it. You had plans. You had a future. But death doesn't do negotiations."

Ben's hands curled into fists. "Bullshit. People get miracles all the time. Near-death experiences. Last-minute divine interventions—where the hell was mine?"

Peter gave a humourless laugh. "You want a miracle? Take a look at that line."

He gestured toward the souls waiting at the gates. Some were anxious, whispering prayers. Others stared blankly ahead, lost in thought.

"I've been doing this since the beginning," Peter continued. "Every soul that comes through here needs to be judged—are they in, or are they out? And let me tell you, it's a miserable job."

Ben shook his head, backing away. "No. No way. I'm not some holy guy. I don't even believe in this shit."

Peter smirked. "Yeah, well, belief doesn't matter after you're dead."

A long silence stretched between them.

Ben turned back to the endless queue of people waiting for judgment. His gut twisted.

"This isn't fair," he muttered.

Peter's face softened, just for a moment. "No," he agreed. "It never is."

Ben swallowed hard. He had spent his whole life outrunning fate. Outdrinking his demons. Outpacing the reality that his body had been failing him long before he ever wanted to admit it.

And now, at 38 years old, death had finally caught up. All those years of abuse to his body. The drinking, the smoking, the stress, the sleepless nights. His heart had simply stopped.

He hadn't woken up.

He had just… gone.

The weight of it pressed down on him, suffocating.

Emma.

His mind flashed with images of her. The way she'd nuzzle against his chest in the mornings. The sound of her laughter echoed through their apartment. The look in her eyes when she told him she was pregnant was like the whole world had finally opened up to them.

124

And now she was waking up alone.

Ben felt something shatter inside him. His throat closed; his vision blurred.

"It's not fair," he whispered, voice raw.

Peter nodded. "I know."

A long silence. Then, finally, Ben forced himself to breathe.

"If I do this," he asked quietly, "is there a way to go back?"

Peter studied him before answering. "No." Ben's

stomach dropped. Of course.

Peter sighed. "But... there are other options."

Ben narrowed his eyes. "What kind of options?"

Peter smirked. "Let's start with one thing at a time. First, you need to do the job."

Ben exhaled shakily, his hands clenching. Trapped.

Emma, I'm so sorry.

After a long silence, he looked up.

"Fine," he muttered. "But I'm not promising I'll play by your rules."

Peter grinned. "Oh, trust me. You won't."

The First Test

Peter snapped his fingers. The entire cloudy void shifted. The massive pearly gates disappeared, and suddenly, they were standing in an old wooden courtroom—the kind that belonged in some ancient kingdom. Dim candlelight flickered against the walls.

Ben turned. The first soul stood before him.

A child, no older than eight. Scared. Confused. Alone.

Ben's stomach twisted.

"You have to decide," Peter murmured. "In or out?"

Ben's throat tightened. "He's a kid."

Peter shrugged. "Does innocence automatically mean entrance?"

Ben scowled. "Yeah. Obviously." Peter

said nothing. He just studied Ben.

Then, suddenly, the courtroom shifted again.

Now, a man in his fifties stood before them, head bowed. He was crying.

Ben squinted. The man wore a military uniform.

A sudden weight dropped into Ben's stomach.

Peter's voice was quiet. "He was a soldier. He killed hundreds. But he regrets it. He spent his last years trying to make amends." Ben's hands trembled. "What the hell am I supposed to do?"

Peter sighed. "Welcome to the job, kid."

Ben turned back toward the weeping man; his chest tight.

126

This wasn't some cosmic joke. This was real.

And he had just become the man who decided where souls spent eternity.

Chapter 10:

Visible cogs in Invisible systems

Visible and Invisible Systems

There are systems we can see—machinery designed for function, for movement, for visible results. Traffic lights that blink in rhythm, schedules printed on paper, digital signatures confirming the delivery of parcels. We know these systems because they are made to be known. Their mechanics are visible, their cogs labeled and arranged in logical order. We rely on them every day. The swipe of a metro card, the hum of fluorescent lights in an office, the morning queue at the coffee shop. We call them routines, habits, structure. But they are more than that. These systems are rehearsed rituals, repeated until we no longer question them. Every beep at a self-checkout. Every meeting request sent at precisely 9:00 AM. Every automated voice telling us to "please hold." They hum with predictability, creating the illusion that life is linear, manageable, traceable. That if we simply follow the signs, we will arrive where we are meant to be.

But beneath these are systems that are invisible.

And those invisible systems were never meant to be entertaining. They were built for order.

The visible systems—the ones we recognize and rely on—are more than just tools of convenience. Increasingly, they are packaged as entertainment, designed to keep you engaged just enough to stop asking questions. Games, updates, playlists.

Sports statistics as sacred as scripture. Political debate as performance. Influencers selling dreams in digestible, 15-second bites. Our distractions are monetized rituals, designed to maintain our consent. The screen lights up, and we follow. Scroll, swipe, click. A thousand alerts bloom across your phone like digital flowers, and you call it connection. The visible system smiles, offering comfort in exchange for attention. And attention is the most valuable currency you'll never hold in your hand.

These distractions are not mistakes. They are the outermost layer of protection shielding the inner workings of systems not meant to be understood—only obeyed. The visible system entertains you. The invisible system shapes you.

Invisible systems live in the background. They do not speak loudly. They whisper through architecture, through traditions, through policy documents no one reads. These systems are not built to inform you. They are built to form you—to guide your choices before you even know they're choices. They decide who has power and who is deemed a "problem." They determine whose pain is believed, whose voice is broadcast, whose existence is optional. They are not on your television. They are baked into your school curriculum, your zoning laws, your loan approvals, your job interviews. They are buried in tone and facial expression and how often your name is mispronounced.

You are born into these systems, and most of the time, you will never see them. But you will feel them. In your gut. In your bones. In the moments that don't quite make sense, but no one else seems to notice. A police car slows as you cross the street, though you've done nothing wrong. Your mother's accent makes a customer service rep speak slower and louder. You apply for the job, again, and again, and again. Your friend with the right skin tone and zip code is hired after just one.

And when the weight of the unseen begins to build—when the edges of reality begin to glitch and flicker—the visible system reacts. It hands you more content. More noise. More reasons to not look too closely. A sale. A scandal. A spiritual bypass. A slogan. A documentary that pretends to expose the truth while quietly reinforcing the same myths. If you dig too deep, the ground starts to shake. So the system sings lullabies until you fall back asleep.

But here's what they don't tell you: systems need people. They need compliance, yes—but also participation. Many of the cogs that keep these structures turning are people with good intentions. People who believe in their work, who love their families, who show up every day trying to do the right thing. These people aren't villains. They're vessels. Vessels who don't realize they're running scripts written decades—or centuries—before they were born. A teacher follows curriculum. A doctor follows protocol. A judge follows precedent. And bit by bit, the system sustains itself. No villain required. Just instructions, followed well.

The more precise your role, the more invisible you become.

And that's the genius of it. You are told you're free while you're surrounded by limits. You are told you have choice while the menu is carefully curated. You are told the world is fair while the scales are nailed to the table. And every time someone points this out, they're told they're imagining things. They're told to be grateful. To calm down. To not make everything political. They're reminded of how good they have it. And if they still don't stop—if they keep questioning, keep noticing, keep seeing through the veil—then the system begins to isolate them.

Or entertain them again.

Because the truth is dangerous. Especially when it's collective. Especially when more than one person starts to pull the thread. The moment you start asking, "Who does this system serve?" you become an anomaly. A disruption. A light in a room built to stay dark.

But anomalies don't have to be enemies. Sometimes, they are messengers.

Sometimes the ones who break the rhythm are the only ones who were ever really awake.

So when you feel that ache—that suspicion that something isn't right, that you're living on a stage with props instead of walls— listen to it. When the structure begins to feel suffocating instead of safe, when the rules feel less like order and more like ritualized control, don't ignore it. You are not broken. You are beginning to see.

Because all around you, beneath you, above you, are systems upon systems—some built by humans, some built by power, some built by necessity. Some built by design. Others by mistake. Some built by gods. And some that have simply always been.

And once you begin to notice them, the visible world begins to feel thinner. More transparent. Like a painted backdrop at the end of a hallway that leads somewhere much deeper.

What you choose to do with that awareness is entirely up to you.

But know this: just as systems are built, they can be unbuilt. Just as structures shape us, we can reshape them. And just as we were conditioned to comply, we can be awakened to remember.

And it begins not with a protest or a theory or a vote.

It begins the moment you stop believing the system was all there is.

And you start remembering what was here before it.

Invisible systems

But beneath these are systems that are invisible—built not for visibility or even comprehension, but for control. For balance. For quiet, efficient order. You don't see these systems. You don't question their construction. And even if you did, you'd find no access point. There's no switch, no master key, no glowing panel to hack your way inside. Because most invisible systems operate on a need-to-know basis. And you? You don't need to know. Not in the eyes of the system. Not unless your knowing serves its survival.

These systems are elegant in their design. They are less like machines and more like organisms—self-replicating, selfprotecting, self-correcting. When a part breaks, it replaces itself. When someone speaks too loudly, they are softened, discredited, or drowned out. These systems don't scream. They

132

whisper. And they don't imprison with bars. They do it with belief.

The strange thing is—these systems are not only built by engineers or coders or men in suits. They are built by people like your neighbour. Your accountant. Your doctor. The lady who organizes the school fundraiser. The guy who's always jogging with his headphones in. People you pass in hallways and never speak to. People who smile in grocery store lines, who drive their kids to school, who nod as you walk your dog. They are cogs—real human beings whose precision and placement within unseen structures makes them indispensable. The more perfectly they perform their task, the more invisible they become. Precision is the currency. Efficiency is grace. The less attention they draw, the more integrated they are.

And most don't even know they are part of something larger. That's the brilliance of it. Participation without awareness. Consent without comprehension. A teacher who never deviates from curriculum, even when it contradicts truth. A medical professional who follows protocols written by unseen boards. A clerk who stamps the form because the system says it must be stamped, and never asks why the form exists at all. A programmer who optimizes the algorithm without asking what it's optimizing *for*. They are not evil. They are efficient. And efficiency, in these systems, is a kind of holiness.

You may imagine power sitting in boardrooms or palaces, but power often prefers the quiet corner office, the assistant who schedules meetings without question, the algorithm that filters candidates before you ever see their names. Real power isn't loud. It's *delegated*. It sits in the space between instruction and execution. It hides in manuals, in policies, in phrases like "That's just how we do things here."

And so the system hums.

It hums through every procedural email, every compliance training, every black-and-white document that ensures decisions are made *by the book*, even when the book was written generations ago and never revised. It hums through news cycles that offer outrage but no resolution. Through hashtags that trend but fade. Through traditions no one remembers the origin of, yet still perform religiously, like rituals to keep something ancient alive.

The machine doesn't care if you believe in it. It only cares that you feed it. That you show up. That you obey your calendar. That you follow the steps. That you don't interrupt. That you don't ask why the gears are turning in the first place. Or worse—who the gears are grinding down beneath them.

And here's where it gets more insidious: some people know. Some people know exactly how the system works—and they benefit from it. They thrive on the structure, the order, the predictability. They inherit positions without contest, are granted access without resistance. Their names open doors without knocking. Their mistakes are softened. Their power is protected. But even they, at a certain point, stop questioning it. They become stewards of the invisible. They don't need to manipulate the system. They *are* the system. And the system will protect itself to protect them.

Then there are those who see the system and can't escape it. People born into it, pressed against the glass, told they are free while every door remains locked. People who sense the structure but can't name it—who internalize its hierarchies and call them fate. Who believe they're failing when in truth, they were never meant to succeed within rules that were designed to exclude them. These people carry the weight of a machine that denies it exists. They are told to work harder, smile more, be patient. They are told they are the problem. But the truth is: they are the evidence.

The system is real because of them. Because of what it withholds from them. Because of how it rearranges itself to keep them contained.

You begin to see how deep it goes.

How language is a system. How tone is a system. How politeness can be weaponized, how rebellion can be commodified. How culture itself becomes a matrix of enforced belonging. You are taught what to wear, how to speak, how to sit, how to ask for things in the correct way. You are rewarded not for truth, but for performance. For how closely you resemble what the system wants to see.

Even love becomes transactional. Even spirituality becomes branded. Even resistance becomes rehearsed.

And yet the machine rolls on.

Because even when you rebel, the system is watching. It absorbs protest. It studies disobedience. It learns how to market revolution back to you, one t-shirt at a time. It offers you symbols instead of solutions. Identity instead of change. And if you rise too high, if your voice starts to carry, the system doesn't fight you. It promotes you. It folds you into its structure. It names you an exception. It disarms you with praise.

And still the cogs turn.

All the while, the ones who truly suffer go unseen. The ones pressed deepest into the machine—those whose hands keep it turning but whose names are never spoken. Those whose data is mined, whose bodies are used, whose labour is unseen, whose suffering is statistically inevitable. The ones who never get an obituary. The ones who never make the headline. The ones who carry the weight but are never called the architects. The invisible within the invisible.

But here's the secret the system doesn't want you to know:

It is not eternal.

It can be broken.

Because for all its intricacy, all its structure, the system relies on belief. It relies on your assumption that it is too big to challenge. It relies on your exhaustion. On your comfort. On your fear of being alone. It needs you to keep showing up without asking why. It needs you to believe that the job is just a job. That the protocol is just protocol. That this is simply how the world works.

But you don't have to play your part.

You don't have to be the cog.

Because the moment you see it—really *see* it—the illusion begins to fracture. The system doesn't disappear. But it becomes

visible. And visibility is the first threat. The first crack. The first breath of something different. Something freer.

And in that moment, you're no longer a cog.

You're a question.

And questions are how machines begin to fall apart.

But it was not always this way.

The Omnipotent systems

Beyond the systems of man, there lies something older. Something unshaped by language, untouched by law. A realm beyond doctrine, ungoverned by celestial codes or infernal rebellion. It is not Heaven. It is not Hell. It does not divide. It does not judge. It simply *is*.

This place—if it can be called a place—does not recognize hierarchy. It has no need for punishment or reward. It does not ask for your obedience, nor does it celebrate your defiance. It has no rules to break, and no authority to question. It is not a system. It is a state.

Call it the Origin. The Root. The Before. It is the space where soul precedes structure. Where spirit is not sorted, but sensed. Where the divine and the demonic have not yet been named, and thus, cannot be opposed. It is the breath before the word. The silence before the song. The presence before the path.

Here, morality is not carved in stone—it floats, ephemeral, in the currents of pure being. There is no ledger to record your failures. No gate to pass through. No mask to wear. There is only what you are, stripped of story, stripped of scar, stripped of striving.

It is what exists when the systems collapse. When the heavenly courts burn and the rebel creeds crumble. When righteousness and rebellion dissolve into irrelevance. What remains is not a void, but a presence so vast and formless that it cannot be controlled, only encountered.

And yet—it is not chaos. It is not order. It is not the middle. It is *beneath* them. *Before* them. It is the pulse beneath all paradox, the hum beneath all hymns and howls. It is where the Gatekeeper was born, and where they will one day return.

This is the place the systems fear.
Because here, there is no need for systems at all.

There was an older version of the system. One that ruled not with silence, but with thunder. Before the current celestial bureaucracy was refined into memory and nuance, there was an era of absolutes. An architecture built on fear, purity, and fire. A system that sorted swiftly, not subtly. One which echoed the human craving for punishment. For rules with sharp edges. For morality carved in stone. This ancient construct—this first framework of Heaven—was governed by the old system of omnipotence, ruled by a panel of unforgiving puritans who preached forgiveness but ruled with impunity. They offered mercy in sermons, but not in practice. Their hands were clean only because they never touched the broken. Their Heaven was a courthouse, not a sanctuary.

There was no room for contradiction in their design. They saw doubt as weakness, emotion as distraction, and deviation as sin. Their judgment came swift and absolute. There was no reflection, no context, no consideration of the soul's journey.

138

Only compliance. Only guilt and penance, and the narrowest path to salvation.

In the old system, judgment came fast and loud. There was no counsel of quiet watchers, no hall of understanding. There was only the Book, and your place within or outside of it. The Book was law. Not a living ledger of nuance, but a heavy, brittle volume of commandments, each line forged from absolutes. *Thou shalt. Thou shalt not.* And if you failed to uphold it, if your life wandered even slightly from its script, your fate was sealed with terrifying efficiency.

That era birthed the image of a wrathful god—arms folded, gaze piercing, weighing the soul on celestial scales tipped against you from the start. Heaven was not a system of balance. It was a fortress of purity. And to be human—flawed, hungry, complex—was already to be unclean.

In this ancient model, purity was currency, and the slightest deviation was debt. You were born into original sin. The best you could do was claw your way back toward a version of goodness that required obedience, silence, and shame. Your body was suspect. Your desires were dangerous. Your questions were betrayal. Salvation was not healing—it was submission. To be devout was to shrink yourself until you fit through the narrow gate. And that gate was guarded not by the Gatekeeper, but by Doctrine itself.

But even within this, there are systems built to rebel—mechanisms woven into existence itself that push back against the structure known as the Divine Order. This so-called divine framework, exalted as righteous and absolute, is not without opposition. There is the system of Satan—not simply a force of

139

chaos, but one that favours the outcast, the questioner, the misfit. It is a system that challenges authority, empowers the fallen, and gives voice to those silenced by the polished rigidity of divine law. It is not evil for evil's sake, but a counter-force—raw, unfiltered, and unafraid to confront the illusion of perfection. It does not promise salvation through obedience, but liberation through truth, no matter how ugly or uncomfortable that truth may be.

The Satanic system is often misunderstood—not because it hides, but because it refuses to make itself palatable. It does not advertise in gold leaf or speak in solemn choirs. It does not soften its voice for fragile ears. It speaks plainly. Brutally, at times. And that honesty has long been mistaken for evil. For rebellion. For corruption. But in truth, it is not the enemy of the divine—it is its shadow. The necessary balance to unchecked righteousness. It is the mirror held up to Heaven when Heaven forgets how to reflect.

Where the divine system categorizes, the Satanic system confronts. It sees through the pageantry of divine law, through the polished hymns and rituals that pretend to mean something. It knows how easy it is to weaponize goodness. It knows how often rules become cages, how often purity becomes a blade. It was born the moment the first outcast was thrown from the light for asking the wrong question. It was born in the heartbeat of defiance, in the soul that refused to pretend to be holy just to survive.

It does not seek followers. It seeks witnesses.

The Satanic system is not lawless—it is simply rooted in a different law. One of radical agency. One that honours the

140

fallen not as failures, but as those brave enough to fall. It invites the ones who were shunned. The queer. The heretic. The woman who refused silence. The addict who clawed their way through shadow. The scholar who wouldn't stop asking *why*. It says, *Come as you are—and mean it.*

Its temples are not spires. They are thresholds. Forests. Back alleys. Empty beds. Broken mirrors. Anywhere a soul is stripped raw enough to meet itself without pretense. It values those moments—not when you are righteous, but when you are real. Not when you are clean, but when you are seen.

In the Satanic system, sin is not the enemy. Hypocrisy is. To lie to yourself is the only real transgression. To perform virtue without embodying it. To point a finger while hiding your own darkness. To obey a rule out of fear, not truth. The Satanic system rips away those masks. It demands integrity over obedience. Depth over piety. Self-knowledge over blind faith.

It does not punish you for failing. It punishes you for pretending you didn't.

And yet—it is not without its own shadows.

The Satanic system exalts pain. It calls suffering a teacher. And often, it is. Pain strips away illusion. It humbles, reveals, carves meaning into the marrow. But there is a line. And the Satanic system, in its hunger for truth, sometimes crosses it. It can begin to romanticize suffering—to treat trauma as virtue, to crown agony as proof of evolution. It can trap you in the belief that if you are not bleeding, you are not becoming. That pain is not a process, but a currency. That to suffer is to ascend.

And this is dangerous.

Because liberation does not always come through fire. Not every lesson must be learned the hard way. There is wisdom in softness too. In rest. In gentleness. But the Satanic system—unforgiving in its pursuit of truth—can forget this. It rejoices in pain, in endurance, in the crucible. It sees the survivor as holy. But sometimes, it forgets that healing is holy too. That love can teach what punishment cannot.

There are places within this system that blur the line between discipline and cruelty. Where accountability becomes selfflagellation. Where shame is worn like armor. Where the pursuit of honesty turns masochistic. It attracts those who were broken, yes—but if they are not careful, it teaches them to worship their brokenness instead of repairing it. To see themselves only through the lens of their wounds.

And in its rebellion, the system sometimes becomes what it hates. It mocks the divine for its purity tests, yet imposes its own: *Are you real enough? Raw enough? Have you suffered enough to be one of us?* And in doing so, it mirrors the very exclusion it was created to dismantle.

Some call this corruption. Others call it inevitability.

Because even rebellion can calcify into doctrine.

Even freedom, if weaponized, becomes its own cage.

The Satanic system is still a system—with structure, with gravity, with expectation. And when it forgets its own roots, when it trades truth for edge, when it exalts rage over repair, it loses the very soul it was built to protect.

But it endures. Because it, too, is evolving.

Because within its wild chaos is still the seed of divine accountability. Because somewhere beneath the ash and the scarring is the simple plea: *Let me be seen. Let me be whole—even if I am not holy.*

And so the systems remain—two celestial frameworks, spiraling around the soul. One polished, orderly, exalted. The other raw, guttural, smudged with ash. One calls to your higher self. The other to your deepest self. One asks who you want to become. The other asks whether you're willing to meet who you already are.

You may walk one path. You may walk both. You may reject both entirely and make a third with your own bare hands.

The Gatekeeper does not interfere. They only verify.

Not which system you chose— But whether you meant it.

Chapter 11:

Watching from Above

Ben had never believed in Hell. But this? This was worse.

For weeks, he sat at the gates of Heaven, forced to watch the life he was supposed to have continue without him. He watched Emma grieve, watched her curl up in their bed—his side empty, her body trembling with sobs she refused to let anyone hear. He saw her wear his sweater long after it stopped smelling like him, saw her clutch the engagement ring he had given her like it was the only thing keeping her tethered to the world.

He wanted to scream, to shatter the veil that separated them, to tell her he was there, watching. But he was powerless—stuck in this celestial waiting room, forced to observe but never touch, never comfort, never hold.

The Agony of the Unseen

Each day bled into the next, and the weight of helplessness pressed down on him. He had seen loss before, had been the cause of it more times than he wanted to admit, but nothing could have prepared him for this—watching the love of his life fall apart and knowing there wasn't a damn thing he could do about it.

She stopped playing music. Stopped painting. The light that had always burned so fiercely in her eyes dimmed, flickering like a candle running out of wax. She kept moving through the motions of life, but there was no life left in her. Just routine. Just survival.

Peter found him one day, sitting at the edge of the clouds, watching Emma through the veil. "This isn't healthy, kid," he muttered, crossing his arms.

Ben didn't look away. "She's suffering. And I can't do anything about it."

Peter sighed. "That's the way it works."

Ben clenched his fists. "It's bullshit."

Peter was silent for a moment. Then, softer, "You think you're the first to feel this? To lose someone and be stuck watching from a place where you can't reach them?"

Ben turned to face him; his jaw tight. "If this is some lesson about letting go, save it. I'm not interested."

Peter smirked. "Yeah. I didn't think you would be."

Ben turned back toward the world below, eyes locked on Emma. He wasn't ready to let go. He wasn't sure he ever would be.

And deep down, a quiet thought took root—a whisper of something dangerous, something impossible.

There has to be a way back.

The Waiting Room

The place he was trapped in was not Heaven, nor was it Hell. It was something in between, an eerie limbo where the air was thick with silence. There were no pearly gates, no warm embrace of departed souls. Just a vast, endless space where others like him stood in silent torment, their gazes locked onto visions of the lives they had left behind.

He saw glimpses of them in the corner of his vision—a woman weeping as she watched her husband marry someone new, an old man who seemed stuck reliving his own funeral, and a young mother reaching out toward a child who would never know her touch. Their faces were filled with anguish, their hands hovering just inches away from the ones they had lost, as if sheer will alone could break the divide between worlds.

"Is this eternity?" he had once asked. There was no answer.

At first, he had resisted. He refused to watch, refused to let this place break him. But no matter how hard he tried to turn away, Emma was always there. And when she gave birth, he had no choice but to witness it.

He had imagined the moment a thousand times before, back when they were still planning their life together. He was supposed to be there, holding her hand, whispering reassurances in her ear. He was supposed to be the first to hold their child, to promise them a lifetime of love and protection.

Instead, he stood frozen in the void, helpless, forced to watch as she screamed in pain, her fingers clutching the hospital sheets.

146

Forced to see the moment their child entered the world, redfaced and wailing—without him.

His knees buckled, and for the first time since arriving in this forsaken place, he fell.

Peter found him like that, curled on the floor, eyes hollow. "You can't keep doing this to yourself, kid."

Ben didn't respond. He couldn't.

Peter sighed, kneeling beside him. "You still think you can find a way back, don't you?"

Ben swallowed hard, his voice a broken whisper. "I have to."

A Daughter He Could Never Hold

He had thought watching Emma grieve was unbearable, but this? This destroyed him.

It was supposed to be him in that hospital room. He was supposed to be holding her hand, whispering encouragement as she brought their child into the world. Instead, he was standing at the gates of eternity, watching from above as she clutched the tiny, crying bundle to her chest.

The baby—their baby—had his eyes.

Ben staggered back, breath catching in his throat. A daughter. They had a daughter.

He tried to turn away, tried to shut his eyes and block out the sight of Emma pressing her lips to the baby's forehead, murmuring something he couldn't hear. But he couldn't escape it. He was stuck here.

And so, he watched.

Days blurred into nights. Emma brought the baby home. She named her Lena—a name they had never talked about but somehow felt like it had been meant to be. He watched as Emma struggled through sleepless nights, rocking their daughter in the nursery they had painted together. He watched as she smiled through the pain, laughing at the smallest things Lena did, even when she looked exhausted beyond belief.

He saw the first time their daughter smiled.

He saw the first time she rolled over.

He saw Emma's mother come to help, saw friends visit, saw the world move on—without him.

And it broke him.

A Silent Father

There were moments when Emma would sit in Lena's nursery, rocking her gently, whispering stories of a father she would never meet. "Your daddy would have loved you so much," she said one night, brushing Lena's dark curls with her fingers. "He had the biggest heart. He would have sung to you every night." Ben reached out instinctively, but his hands passed through her.

148

Through both of them. A ghost, unseen, unheard. He clenched his fists, screaming inside his own head, wanting so badly to hold his daughter, to comfort Emma. But he was just a spectator in his own life, a shadow on the edge of existence.

Lena grew. Weeks turned into months, and Ben lost track of time. He saw her first steps, her first words— "Mama." His heart shattered anew every time Emma smiled through the sadness, every time she whispered, "Daddy would be so proud of you."

Peter found him again one evening, standing in the endless limbo, eyes locked onto the world below. "You can't keep torturing yourself, kid."

Ben didn't look away. "What else am I supposed to do?"

Peter sighed, stepping beside him. "You're stuck between two worlds, Ben. You're clinging to something you can't have anymore."

Ben shook his head. "I won't stop. I won't leave them."

Peter studied him for a long moment. Then, to Ben's surprise, his expression softened. "Maybe," he murmured, "you don't have to."

The Memories That Haunted Him

It was cruel how the mind clung to moments long past. In his torment, memories resurfaced with merciless clarity.

The first time he met Emma—she had been trying to reach a book on the highest shelf of a bookstore, grumbling under her breath. He had handed it to her without thinking, and she had given him the brightest smile.

Their first date, where they had gotten caught in the rain and laughed until they couldn't breathe.

The night he proposed, the way her breath hitched before she said yes, eyes glistening with joy.

They had spent nights whispering in bed, dreaming about their future, imagining the children they would have. They had never talked about the name Lena. Had Emma chosen it for a reason? Had she felt something—a presence, a whisper of fate?

He would never know.

The Unseen Thread

The past was a cruel companion, looping in his mind like a song stuck on repeat. Ben found himself retracing every conversation, every touch, every kiss, as if he could hold on to them forever.

He thought about the way Emma's fingers always found his in a crowded room, as if drawn by an unseen thread. He remembered the way she would tuck her feet under his on the couch when she was cold, the way she hummed absentmindedly when she cooked.

And now, she was alone.

No more fingers searching for his. No more soft laughter filling their home.

Just her and Lena.

Ben clenched his fists. This wasn't how it was supposed to be.

Peter watched him, silent for once. Maybe he knew that no words could fix this.

Maybe he also knew that Ben wasn't done fighting.

The Desperate Need to Reach Her

Ben could not accept this fate. He would not.

He had seen stories, heard whispers of spirits breaking through the veil, of messages sent from beyond. He did not know if it was possible, but he had to try. He screamed, he begged, he reached out with everything he had, his soul twisting in agony with each attempt. He felt his own desperate energy crackling against the cold, empty space that surrounded him.

Nothing.

The other souls here remained silent, watching their own tragedies unfold, their own moments of loss and despair. They seemed resigned to their fate, bound by the same oppressive silence that suffocated Ben's every effort. There were no answers, no gods to hear his pleas. Only the chill of oblivion, the oppressive weight of an existence that felt infinite yet utterly pointless.

But then something strange happened.

One night, as Emma sat in the nursery, rocking Lena back and forth, Ben watched her. The soft creaking of the rocking chair was the only sound that filled the room as the mother's soothing motions calmed the baby. He could feel her warmth, her love, radiating from across the void. His heart ached with the thought of her, so close, yet forever out of reach.

Then, without warning, the baby suddenly stopped crying.

Her tiny eyes widened; the sparkling innocence of youth bright in the dim light of the nursery. She giggled, a sound that filled Ben with both joy and despair. And then, as if drawn by something he could not see, she stared right at him.

Emma frowned, her lips curving into a small, tender smile as she looked down at her daughter. "What is it, sweetheart?" she murmured, brushing a lock of hair away from Lena's face.

But Lena's gaze didn't shift. Her tiny fingers stretched toward something unseen in the air.

And then, without a word, Emma followed her daughter's gaze, her expression slowly shifting from curiosity to confusion. A flicker of uncertainty danced across her face, and for the first time in what felt like years, Emma seemed unsure.

"Ben?" she whispered, barely audible, her voice trembling as though she could hardly believe the name that slipped from her lips.

Ben's breath hitched in his chest. Could she feel him? Could she sense his presence? Had Lena, in her innocent, untainted gaze, actually seen him?

His entire being strained toward her, his desperation growing unbearable. He reached out again, this time with every ounce of his soul, pouring all the love, the regret, and the longing he had left into one final, desperate plea.

Suddenly, a framed photo on the nightstand next to Emma trembled. Ben's heart skipped a beat as it toppled over, the glass shattering on the floor. Emma startled, clutching Lena closer to her chest. Her lips parted in shock, her wide eyes scanning the room for some explanation Ben couldn't offer.

Her gaze lingered for a moment on the empty space where he stood. She opened her mouth, but no words came out.

"Ben..."

The utterance of his name felt like a lifeline thrown into the ocean of his grief. For the first time since his death, a flicker of hope bloomed within the abyss of his heart. It was faint, barely there, but it was real. A light in the darkest, most oppressive place he had ever been.

Had she seen him?

Could she hear him?

Had his desperate cries finally reached her?

The Choice

Days passed, and Ben began to notice more changes. A warmth surrounded him, different from the cold, numbing embrace of this place. The endless void he had once found himself

153

drowning in now seemed softer, somehow more real, even though it was still empty. It felt like a slow shift in the air, the tiniest hint of hope, almost as if the very atmosphere was changing around him. He started hearing whispers—voices at the edge of his awareness, faint yet insistent.

"Move on."

Ben froze. Was that what this was? Was he being given a choice?

He had been in limbo for what felt like an eternity, unable to move forward, unable to go back. But now, this voice was offering him a path—one that seemed to promise peace.

If he let go, if he surrendered to whatever came next, he would find peace. But peace meant never watching over Emma and Lena again. Peace meant leaving them behind entirely, erasing himself from their lives.

Could he do that?

Could he leave them behind?

One night, Emma sat at the edge of their bed, clutching his sweater, the one he used to wear when he came home from work, the fabric worn from years of use. She was silent for a long time, her fingers absently tracing the threadbare fabric, her face shadowed by grief. Then, in a voice so soft it was almost a whisper, she spoke.

"I miss you," she whispered. "But... I'm trying. I promise."

Ben closed his eyes, a wave of pain sweeping over him. She was healing. Slowly, painfully, but she was healing. And Lena—she was growing, changing, full of life, finding her way through a world that had turned upside down without her father.

She would be okay.

A soft light surrounded him then, as if the very essence of his being was being cradled by something warm, something comforting. For the first time, he felt weightless—like he was floating, no longer tied to the earth, no longer bound by his grief.

He took one last look at Emma and Lena—his family, his heart. They were both moving forward, despite the weight of loss. They would be alright.

And then, with a final breath, he let go.

The Aftermath

At first, he played along. He did the job—checked names, read the files, let in the "worthy" souls.

It was mechanical. A distraction. If he focused on the endless line of dead waiting for judgment, maybe he wouldn't think about what was happening below. Maybe he wouldn't feel the ache that had settled into the deepest parts of him.

The work wasn't enough.

Because every moment he wasn't looking down at Earth, every second he wasn't watching Emma and Lena, he was drowning in thoughts of what should have been. The tiny moments he

155

had missed—the days he should have spent holding Emma's hand, laughing with Lena as she took her first steps. Those thoughts gnawed at him, pulling at him with a force he couldn't escape.

They were still down there, living, breathing. And he wasn't there. The peace he had thought would fill him, the release he had imagined would be comforting, felt instead like a growing emptiness that stretched on without end.

He had made his choice. But was it the right one?

The Bureaucracy of the Afterlife

The job was more complicated than it seemed. The files were detailed, listing every sin, every act of kindness, every moment of hesitation between good and evil. But the decisions weren't as clear-cut as Ben had first assumed. There were names that didn't belong in either Heaven or Hell, names that sat in the Gray areas, their fates uncertain. The lines between right and wrong blurred in unexpected ways, and Ben found himself questioning everything he thought he knew about morality.

Some souls had lived their lives in ways that were both remarkable and flawed, leaving behind legacies that were neither pure nor damned. Was there a place for them? Could one misstep erase a lifetime of good? Did a single selfless act balance out decades of selfishness? The more Ben sifted through these files, the less he understood.

And the line never ended.

156

It stretched beyond the horizon, a backlog of history, souls who had been waiting for centuries standing beside those who had only just arrived. There was no rhyme or reason to the order. Some had been in line for mere hours, while others had been waiting for ages, their features worn with the weight of unfulfilled endings. The air was thick with anticipation, frustration, and confusion.

Some souls looked confused; others resigned. Some wept, others laughed, as if the absurdity of it all had finally caught up to them. Ben watched as their faces shifted between regret, anger, and relief, unable to reconcile what they had done with the finality of their fate.

Ben found himself hesitating over these souls. Could one mistake damn a person? Did a single selfless act redeem them? How many chances had they been given before their final moments? How many opportunities to choose differently had they missed? Was it all just a matter of timing, of circumstances beyond their control?

He wasn't the only one questioning the process.

There were others who worked the gates—some eager to carry out their duties, others burdened with regret, just as he was. He met an old soul named Elias, who had been doing this for centuries. His eyes were clouded with a mix of wisdom and weariness, his hands shaking slightly as he shuffled through the endless stream of files.

"You stop thinking about it after a while," Elias said, his voice rough and distant. "Or at least, you tell yourself you do."

Ben wasn't sure that was true. He watched Elias pause over some files longer than others. He watched him sigh, shake his head, and send souls through the gates, sometimes hesitating as though he wished he could change their fates. "I can't change anything," Elias muttered, almost to himself. "I just do my job."

Ben wondered how many had slipped through the cracks, how many fates had been sealed before they were really understood.

Peter, though, was different.

Peter had an air of authority, but not the kind that inspired fear. He was calm, unshaken, and always seemed to know more than he let on. Ben often wondered how much power Peter actually had. Was he merely a gatekeeper, or did he have the ability to influence the judgment of the souls that passed through? Had he ever bent the rules before? Had it cost him something?

Peter's eyes were sharp, and he never hesitated when sending a soul onward, even when Ben noticed the subtle flicker of doubt behind his gaze. Had Peter ever questioned his own decisions?

Sometimes, late at night, Ben would see Peter looking over a file, his brow furrowed, and for a brief moment, he would seem human again. Ben had caught him once, alone in a quiet corner, looking at a file with disbelief. When he caught Ben's eye, he quickly closed it, his expression unreadable. But for just a heartbeat, Ben saw something in Peter—a vulnerability, an understanding of the weight they both carried.

The longer Ben worked in this place, the more he began to wonder if anyone in this bureaucracy had the answers. Was there even a right answer? Or were they all just part of a system designed to push souls through without understanding, without

158

mercy? The lines, the rules, they felt increasingly meaningless in the face of the lives they judged.

Emma's Grief and Healing

Emma struggled. She had started seeing a therapist but barely spoke during their sessions. Instead, she filled the silence with nods and polite acknowledgments. She wasn't sure if it was helping, but she kept going because it was what people said she should do. She was supposed to be "moving on," they told her, but the weight of Ben's absence was suffocating, and nothing felt quite right anymore. Sometimes, she wondered if this was all part of the process—if it was normal to feel so disconnected from herself.

Nights were the worst. The house was too quiet without Ben's voice, his laughter, his presence that used to fill every room. She still curled up on his side of the bed, still held his sweater to her chest, still reached for him in her sleep only to wake up alone. The emptiness beside her was a constant reminder that the life they'd shared was no longer. She couldn't bring herself to sleep in the centre of the bed, even though it might have been more comfortable. She couldn't betray the memory of him that way, even if it only made her pain sharper.

But then there was Lena.

One evening, as Emma rocked their daughter to sleep, Lena suddenly giggled at the empty space in the corner of the room. Emma's breath hitched. The sound was like a soft, musical ripple through the quiet of the night. Her heart fluttered

159

uncomfortably, unsure whether to dismiss it or to let the moment wash over her.

"What is it, sweetheart?" she whispered, her voice barely above a breath.

Lena kept laughing, her tiny hands reaching out as if grasping at something unseen. Emma froze. Her gaze darted to the corner of the room; the space Lena seemed so drawn to. Was there something there? Or was it just a child's imagination running wild? Emma swallowed hard, staring at the empty space. She wanted to believe. She wanted to imagine that Ben was there, watching over them, still somehow part of their world. But that was impossible, wasn't it?

A few days later, she visited Ben's grave. The cemetery was silent except for the rustling of leaves, as if the world around her knew to be still in his presence. She knelt beside the headstone, the cold marble smooth beneath her fingers, running them over the engraving of his name. Her heart ached with each letter. The silence weighed heavier here, where the earth held him and she had only memories to cling to.

"I don't know what I'm supposed to do without you," she whispered, her voice trembling. "I don't know how to move forward. But I think... I think I have to try."

Ben was watching. He felt something inside him tighten and break at her words. She was letting go. And he couldn't. Not yet. He wanted to reach out, to wrap his arms around her, to tell her that she wasn't alone—that she never would be, no matter how far apart they were. But he couldn't. Not in the way he wanted to. So, he held on, to whatever part of him remained,

160

hoping she would feel him there with her, even if she couldn't see him.

She was moving on, slowly, but he wasn't ready to let her go. Not yet.

Ben's Attempts to Defy the System

He couldn't accept this fate. He had to find a way back. Every inch of his being screamed at him to fight, to break free, to be with them again. To hold Emma, to watch Lena grow, to live the life that had been ripped from him so suddenly.

The first time he tried to leave his post; he was met with an invisible force holding him in place. No matter how hard he pushed, it was like walking against a hurricane—impossible. It was as though some invisible wall stretched in every direction, preventing him from moving even a single step. Every attempt only left him breathless, defeated. But Ben didn't stop. He couldn't.

He started to sabotage the work, hoping his actions would create enough of a disruption to force someone—anyone—to take notice. He stopped checking files, letting souls through without reading their fates. He thought, for a moment, that it might cause enough chaos to force a change, to make someone reconsider the system that had trapped him here. But it wasn't enough. The world around him kept turning, the souls continued moving, and nothing shifted.

Peter noticed immediately.

"What exactly are you trying to accomplish here?" he asked, his tone almost amused but his eyes sharp. His gaze was calculating, always watching.

"I want out," Ben replied, his voice tight with frustration.

Peter sighed; his expression unreadable. "Still not an option."

Ben clenched his jaw, the word 'impossible' echoing in his mind. "Then I'll find another way."

He started asking around, searching for whispers of those who had managed to escape. Elias was the first to give him any answers, though they came with a warning.

"There have been others," Elias admitted, his voice low, almost as if speaking of something forbidden. "But no one knows where they went. Some say they found a way back. Others say they were erased completely."

"I'd take the risk," Ben said, his resolve hardening. The thought of living eternally here—trapped and distant from everything he loved—was more unbearable than any risk.

Elias studied him for a long moment, his gaze filled with something unspoken. "Be careful what you wish for."

Ben wasn't careful. He kept pushing. He wasn't afraid of the cost anymore, not when every passing day felt like eternity. And then, one day, someone answered.

A shadowy figure, barely more than a whisper of a man, appeared at the edges of his vision. It was as though the air itself shifted, bending around the figure's presence.

"You want to go back?" the voice rasped, soft but sharp, like the rustling of dry leaves.

Ben's heart stuttered. He turned sharply, his body instinctively leaning forward. "Can you, do it?"

The figure's smile was slow, a hollow thing, full of knowing and something else. "Everything has a price."

Ben didn't hesitate, not this time. Not when it was his chance. "Name it."

The figure's smile deepened, stretching unnervingly. "Your memories. You return to Earth, but you won't remember Emma. You won't remember Lena. You won't even remember why you came back."

Ben felt the weight of the choice settle in his chest, his pulse quickening. His mind spiralled, torn between the overwhelming desire to be with them and the devastating reality of what the price would be. Could he give them up? Could he return to them as a stranger, never knowing what he had lost? Could he live in a world where his past was wiped clean, where the love he shared with Emma and Lena was nothing more than a shadow?

He didn't have an answer.

Not yet.

His fists clenched, his breath coming hard as the impossible decision bore down on him. His heart thundered in his chest, his mind screaming at the unfairness of it all. But after everything—after all the longing, the desperate attempts, the

163

nights spent watching Emma cry and Lena grow—this was the cost?

A life without them? Without even the memory of their love?

Ben's jaw tightened. Slowly, he stepped back from the figure, shaking his head. "No."

The figure tilted its head, as though it had never expected that response. "No?"

"I won't forget them," Ben said, his voice steady, filled with unwavering resolve. "Not for anything."

The shadowy figure studied him for a long moment, its expression unreadable. Then, with a slow nod, it disappeared into the void, vanishing as if it had never been there at all. Ben stood alone once more; the weight of his decision heavy on his chest. But he had made it, and for now, it was enough.

He turned away, his heart aching but resolute. If he could not return to them, if he could not touch them or hold them, then he would remain where he was. Watching. Loving from a distance.

Even if it broke him, he would not abandon them.

He resigned himself to his place at the gates, his heart tethered to a world that no longer held him, to a family that would never know he was there. And so, he watched.

Chapter 12:

Ghosts of his past

Ben Holloway had seen ghosts before—not the kind that rattled chains in the dead of night, but the ones that haunted his thoughts. Faces of the forgotten. Voices he'd drowned in whiskey. Decisions he couldn't undo.

But this was different.

The afterlife was supposed to bring clarity, wasn't it? He had been thrown into a role he never wanted—the gatekeeper of Heaven—but so far, all he had gained was a front-row seat to the monotonous parade of souls passing through. Saints, sinners, lost souls all standing in line, waiting for their verdict.

But tonight, the past wasn't waiting in line. It was coming for him.

It began with a whisper, just a breath of sound carried on the stillness of the celestial void. The queue of souls had long dissipated for the evening, the vast threshold empty but for the faint glow of lingering energy that clung to the air. Ben exhaled, rubbing his temples. He thought he'd been imagining it at first. A trick of the ether, an echo from some other plane. But then it came again.

A name.

"Holloway."

He stiffened. The last time someone had called him that, he had been alive. He turned, scanning the misty expanse of the threshold, but saw nothing.

"Who's there?" he demanded, his voice steady, though his fingers curled into fists.

The air shimmered. A shape began to form, translucent at first, then coalescing into something unmistakably human. A woman. Ben felt his breath leave him. "No," he murmured. "Not you."

Her eyes bore into him, the same shade of stormy Gray he remembered, but sharper now, filled with something he had never seen in life. Resentment. Accusation.

"It's been a long time, Ben." Her voice was soft but carried the weight of years unspoken.

"Eleanor." He forced himself to say her name, though it burned his throat.

She stepped forward, her form flickering in the dim glow of the afterlife. Her hair, once golden and full of sunlight, moved weightlessly around her face, as though caught in an unseen current. She had not aged a day since the last time he saw her— because she never had the chance.

"What are you doing here?" he asked, his voice hoarse.

"I could ask you the same." She crossed her arms. "Heaven's gatekeeper, Ben? Didn't peg you for the celestial type."

A wry smirk tugged at the corner of his mouth before fading just as quickly. "I didn't sign up for it."

166

"No," she said, tilting her head. "You never did take responsibility for anything."

The words cut deeper than he expected. He had braced for anger, but not for this quiet, measured condemnation.

"Eleanor," he started, but she raised a hand, stopping him.

"Tell me, Ben. Do you even remember how I died? Or did you drink that memory away like all the others?"

The air around them grew heavier. His mind flashed back to a night long ago. The sirens. The rain. The shattered glass.

"I remember," he said, his voice barely above a whisper.

Her expression softened for the briefest moment, then hardened again. "Then tell me. Tell me why you left me there."

He wanted to. God, he wanted to. But the words lodged in his throat, choking him. He had spent so long burying that night, convincing himself that forgetting would be easier than facing the truth. But now, here she was, dragging it all back into the light.

"I was scared," he admitted finally. "I thought—"

"You thought saving yourself was more important than saving me," she finished for him. Her voice was calm, but he saw the hurt in her eyes. "I was trapped, Ben. Trapped in that car while you walked away. I called your name, and you just... left."

A thousand defences formed on his tongue, but none of them mattered. There was no excuse for what he had done.

167

"I was a coward," he said, the confession falling from his lips like a stone. "And I've regretted it every day since."

She studied him for a long moment, then let out a slow breath. "Good," she said simply. "You should."

Ben clenched his jaw. "Is that why you're here? To make sure I still suffer?"

"No." She stepped closer. "I'm here because you still think you don't deserve redemption. And maybe you don't. But you need to decide whether you'll keep punishing yourself forever, or if you'll finally do something to make amends."

He swallowed. "How? You're gone. I can't change that."

A ghost of a smile flickered across her lips. "You're the gatekeeper of Heaven, Ben. Start acting like it. Stop passing judgment from the sidelines and actually help people. Help them find peace. Maybe then, one day, you'll find your own."

He opened his mouth to argue, but no words came. She was right. He had been standing at this threshold for so long, detached, watching others move on while he remained frozen in his own guilt. Maybe it was time to change that.

He looked up at her. "Will I ever see you again?"

She hesitated, then smiled—a sad, knowing smile. "Maybe. If you earn it."

And then, just like that, she was gone, dissipating into the ether, leaving only the echo of her presence behind.

Ben stood there for a long time, staring at the empty space where she had been. For the first time since he had died, the ghosts of his past felt a little lighter.

Maybe, just maybe, he could finally start moving forward.

The afterlife was supposed to bring clarity, wasn't it? He had been thrown into a role he never wanted—the gatekeeper of Heaven—but so far, all he had gained was a front-row seat to the monotonous parade of souls passing through. Saints, sinners, lost souls all standing in line, waiting for their verdict.

But tonight, the past wasn't waiting in line. It was coming for him.

David Wexler

David Wexler had never believed in the afterlife. At least, not in the way people talked about it. Heaven, Hell, judgment—it had always seemed like the kind of thing people clung to when they were afraid of their own endings. And yet, here he was, standing in an endless line, waiting for his turn to be judged.

The queue stretched into eternity, souls shifting forward in slow, inevitable steps. Some muttered prayers, others wept. A few, like David, simply stood in silence, waiting for what came next.

"David Wexler."

The voice rang out, deep and authoritative, reverberating through the space. It wasn't just a sound—it was a force, pulling him forward. The line parted, and suddenly, he was no longer standing among the faceless masses.

Now, he stood before a massive stone desk, weathered and ancient, perched just before Heaven's gates. Behind it sat a man David hadn't seen in years—Ben Holloway.

Ben leaned back in his chair, arms crossed, watching David with the same unreadable expression he'd always had. The glow of the gates behind him cast shifting shadows over his face, giving him an almost spectral presence. His fingers drummed against the desk, absentmindedly, as if he had been waiting for this moment for a long time.

David took a step forward, his eyes narrowing. "Ben?" Ben

exhaled, looking him up and down. "You're dead."

David flinched. It sounded so final. "Yeah," he muttered. "Guess that makes two of us."

Ben nodded slowly. "And now you're here."

David scoffed, gesturing at the line behind him. "Seems like I'm not the only one."

Ben ignored the remark, his gaze steady. "You know what this is, don't you?"

David rolled his shoulders, trying to shake off the discomfort pressing against him. "I'd like to say no, but I think we both know that'd be a lie."

Ben studied him. "Then you know why you're here."

David hesitated. The air felt heavier now, like it carried the weight of all the choices he had made, all the moments that had led him to this place. "Judgment?" he asked, though it wasn't really a question.

Ben nodded once. "Judgment."

David let out a dry chuckle. "And what, you're the guy calling the shots now? From washed-up to Heaven's front desk—talk about failing upward. Guess I always did have an eye for talent."

Ben shook his head. "I don't decide. I just open the door." He gestured toward the two massive gates behind him. One shimmered with a light that seemed to pulse with something almost alive. The other remained dull, shadowed, its surface unreadable.

David shifted his weight. "So what? Someone else makes the decision for me?"

Ben didn't answer immediately. Instead, he tapped the desk, the sound echoing through the stillness. "I don't think it works like that."

David frowned. "Then how does it work?"

Ben met his gaze. "You tell me."

A cold feeling settled in David's chest. "You mean…?"

Ben nodded. "It's not about where they send you. It's about where you think you belong."

David swallowed. His whole life had been about power, about control. He had manipulated, negotiated, built an empire with his own hands. And now? Now he stood at the mercy of

171

something bigger than himself, forced to face everything he had done.

Ben tilted his head. "Do you regret it?"

David looked away. "Which part?"

"The people you hurt."

David's jaw tightened. "I—" He stopped. The truth was heavier than he expected. "I don't know if regret is the right word."

Ben arched an eyebrow. "Then what is?"

David sighed. "I regret assuming I had more time. I regret thinking I could fix things later. Turns out, there is no later."

Ben nodded, as if he had expected the answer. "No, there isn't."

A silence stretched between them. David glanced over his shoulder at the line of souls, each waiting for their turn. Some looked terrified, some looked hopeful. He wondered if any of them had been as arrogant as he had been in life.

He turned back to Ben. "And you? Do you regret anything?"

Ben let out a small, humourless laugh. "Regret is all I have, Wexler."

David studied him for a long moment. "Then why are you sitting behind that desk instead of standing where I am?"

Ben's fingers stopped drumming. He leaned forward slightly. "Maybe I don't think I deserve to move on yet."

David nodded slowly. "Guess we're both stuck, then."

Ben exhaled, rubbing his temple. "Maybe. Or maybe it's time for at least one of us to figure it out."

David glanced at the gates. "So, what happens if I pick wrong?"

Ben shrugged. "Maybe you already know what's right."

David let out a breath. His whole life, he had played every move like a chess game. But here, there were no deals left to make, no Favors to call in. There was only the truth, whatever that was worth.

He turned, facing the gates fully now. One was open, glowing. The other remained closed, waiting.

He hesitated. Then, with a slow breath, he took a step forward.

Ben watched, his expression unreadable, as David reached for the handle.

Just before he crossed the threshold, David turned back. "Hey, Ben?"

Ben met his gaze.

David smirked, but there was something softer in it now. "See you around."

Ben exhaled, watching as David disappeared beyond the gate. He sat back down, running a hand through his hair.

The line moved forward. Another name was called.

And the cycle began again.

The Second Ghost: Emily Caldwell

The scene shifted. Not gradually, but all at once.

The sterile, golden light of judgment flickered like a dying bulb—and in its place, a dimly lit hotel room emerged. The air thickened with the stale scent of cigarettes and cheap perfume, wrapping around Ben like a noose. The wallpaper peeled at the corners, stained yellow from years of neglect. Outside, sirens whined distantly beneath the low buzz of neon signs bleeding through grimy windows.

On the edge of the unmade bed sat Emily Caldwell, curled in on herself like a question never answered. Her eyes, once blazing with defiant joy and impossible dreams, now stared blankly at the carpet. Hollow. Defeated. Her knees drawn to her chest, arms wrapped tight as though trying to hold herself together.

Ben's heart clenched. "No…"

Emily turned her head slowly, as if pulled by invisible threads. Her voice, when it came, was soft—far too soft for this place. "Hi, Ben."

He stepped forward shakily, a hundred unspoken words crowding his throat. "I didn't know—"

She let out a dry, humourless laugh that rattled the silence. "That I was dead? Of course you knew."

He flinched. Her words struck deeper than accusation. They were truth made sharp.

"I tried to save you," he said, his voice fraying.

174

"Did you?" She swung her legs over the edge of the bed, revealing frayed jeans and scuffed boots. "Or did you just push me onto a bigger stage and hope for the best?"

The wallpaper behind her rippled. The light grew brittle. The room—the memory—began to dissolve.

Ben blinked. The bed faded, the shadows receded, and the air filled once more with that soft golden glow.

Now they stood among the dead.

The hotel room was gone. In its place, the wide, endless plain before the Gates of Heaven stretched on like a dream too large to hold. The line of souls waiting to be judged twisted out toward a hazy horizon. Behind them, the gates shimmered—tall, radiant, unwavering.

Ben stood at the edge of a raised platform, the great ledgers of the dead open before him. He had been here for an eternity already, weighing lives, counting sins, glimpsing mercy in rare glimmers. The task was unceasing. The burden immeasurable.

And now—Emily Caldwell stood in the line.

Her presence struck him like thunder.

The scent came first: that same bitter blend of smoke and perfume that once clung to velvet curtains and makeup mirrors, to backstage couches and limousine interiors. It wrapped around him like ghostly fingers, pulling him out of time.

Emily stepped free from the line, unnoticed by the others. She stood just a few feet from him, arms loose at her sides, wearing the same hoodie and ripped jeans she'd worn the first night he

175

saw her perform in that downtown bar with the leaky ceiling. Her boots were muddy, her hair a tousled mess. And yet she looked more real than anything else in this place.

Ben's throat tightened. "Emily…"

She tilted her head, a wry smirk tugging at her lips. "Hey, Ben."

Even now, her voice carried that unmistakable lilt—smoky and melodic, though now tinged with something distant. Something cold and broken.

He pushed away from the ledger, standing as if his legs had suddenly remembered how. "I didn't know…"

She scoffed, folding her arms. "That I was dead? You knew, Ben. You knew long before the headlines. Long before the overdose. Long before the world turned me into another tragic footnote."

His mouth opened, but words stumbled out unfinished. "I—"

"I was already fading," she continued, stepping closer. "But you still sent me out there. More gigs. More press. More noise. And when I started to drown, you told me to swim harder."

"I thought you could handle it," he whispered. The shame in his voice weighed more than any sin in the ledger.

"Handle what?" she snapped. "The pressure? The contracts? The vultures backstage? The pills in the makeup bag? You knew what the industry did to people like me, Ben. You *knew*. And still—you let me walk into the fire."

"I didn't have a choice."

176

"You always had a choice."

The air trembled. A breeze picked up, rustling the pages of the ledger beside him. Her words didn't just hurt—they rang out across the plain like bells that could not be un-rung. Souls in line turned slightly, unease rippling down the ranks, though none looked directly at her.

Emily looked up at the gates—brilliant and unmoved. Her face softened, just a little. "I wasn't asking you to fix everything. I just needed someone to stand beside me. To see me."

Ben reached out. "I see you now."

But her form was already fading. Edges fraying like silk in water. Her body blurred, softening into light.

"Wait…" he murmured, taking a step forward.

But there was nothing left to hold.

Only the scent remained. And her voice—fainter now, like wind through trees.

"Remember me, Ben. Someone should."

And then she was gone.

The crowd behind her crept forward. The Gates remained radiant, indifferent.

And Ben, the arbiter of fates, stood alone with a ledger full of names and a ghost's final words ringing in his ears.

Claire Wellard

Like some sick form of divine torment, Ben was met by yet another ghost from his past—Claire Wellard.

The final ghost was the one that hurt the most.

Claire stood at the edge of the celestial gates, her hair whipping in an unseen wind, her expression unreadable. Time had not changed her, at least not in the ways he had expected. She wasn't younger, wasn't older, simply… Claire. The same woman who had once been his anchor in a world of chaos. The same woman he had let go, believing—foolishly, selfishly—that he had all the time in the world to make things right.

Ben's throat went dry. "Claire…"

She didn't move. Didn't smile. Just watched him with those familiar eyes, eyes that had once held warmth for him. Now they were cold, detached, as if she were looking at nothing more than a memory.

"You never read my letter."

Her voice, steady but tinged with something fragile, cut through him like glass. He swallowed hard, feeling the weight of all the years he had spent pretending that letter didn't exist.

"I couldn't."

Claire nodded, as if she had expected that. "It wouldn't have changed anything, would it?"

Ben looked away, unable to meet her gaze. "I don't know."

She took a slow step forward, and he could almost feel her presence. Almost. "You had a chance at something real, Ben. Something beyond the industry, beyond the business. But you let it slip away."

His voice cracked. "I didn't know how to hold onto it."

Claire studied him for a long moment. Then, softly, she said, "You still don't, do you?"

He wanted to argue. Wanted to tell her that he had changed. That he had tried. But the truth sat bitter on his tongue. He had spent his life chasing ghosts—of talent, of dreams, of a version of himself that had never truly existed. And now, in death, those ghosts had come to collect.

"I'm sorry," he whispered.

Claire gave him a sad smile. "I hope you mean that."

She reached for his hand. For a moment, he thought she might actually touch him. But just as their fingers were about to meet, she vanished.

And Ben Holloway was left standing alone at the gates of Heaven, haunted by the past he could never outrun.

Ben had met Claire Wellard in a dimly lit jazz club on the outskirts of the city, back when he was still young enough to think ambition was everything. He was nobody then, scraping by, making connections, networking, pretending he was bigger than he actually was. But Claire—Claire was already something. A rising star in the industry, a woman with a voice like honey and a laugh that could disarm even the most hardened cynic. She had been introduced to him as a Favor, some executive throwing him a bone, telling him he needed someone like her in his corner if he wanted to go far.

He hadn't realized at the time that 'someone like her' meant more than just a useful connection.

They had spent nights talking about the music industry, the pitfalls of fame, the kind of artists they wanted to be. She had always believed in the soul of the music, in its ability to heal, to connect, to make people feel something real. He had believed in success.

"You're too focused on the chase," she had told him one night, leaning on the piano at some after-party. "You think if you just get that next deal, that next big break, then you'll finally be happy. But you won't. It'll never be enough."

He had laughed her off then. "What's wrong with wanting more?"

Claire had only shaken her head, sadness flickering in her gaze. "Nothing. Except when you start sacrificing everything else to get it."

He hadn't understood then. Not really. He had thought she was being dramatic, that she didn't get it. But she did. She had always gotten it. And she had walked away before he could drag her down with him.

The letter had come years later, long after she had left his life. He had found it tucked between his tour contracts, unopened. He had known what it was before even looking at it. The words he was too much of a coward to read. A final offering, a last chance at closure.

He had stuffed It In a drawer and never looked at It again.

And now, she was here. Standing before him, staring at him as if she had already known the answer before she even asked.

"You were everything to me," she said now, her voice quieter, softer. "Did you even know that?"

He felt the words like a punch to the gut. "Claire, I—"

"No," she interrupted. "Don't say anything. I just needed to know if you ever wondered."

He had. God, he had. But by the time he had been ready to admit it, it had already been too late.

"I don't know what to say."

She sighed, and for the first time, her expression softened. "You don't have to say anything, Ben. Just... remember. And don't make the same mistakes again. If you even get the chance."

His chest tightened. "Do I?"

She smiled—small, knowing. "That's not for me to decide."

For a brief moment, everything felt still, as if time itself had paused between them. And then she was gone.

Ben exhaled shakily, running a hand through his hair. The visions were gone, but the weight of them remained.

If Heaven wanted to punish him, it had done a damn good job.

He turned toward the endless line of souls waiting for judgment. The job he had been given—the role he never wanted—loomed before him.

For the first time, he wondered if maybe, just maybe, this wasn't a punishment.

Maybe it was his chance to finally make things right.

The Weight of Regret

The visions were gone, but the weight of them remained. Ben exhaled shakily, running a hand through his hair. His fingers trembled. He told himself it was from exhaustion, but he knew better.

If Heaven wanted to punish him, it had done a damn good job.

David. Claire. The echoes of their voices still lingered in the air, pressing down on him like a vice. The things left unsaid, the truths he had spent a lifetime avoiding—now, in death, there was no running from them. No drowning them in whiskey. No distractions, no excuses. Just the cold, hard weight of what he had done and who he had been.

He turned toward the endless line of souls waiting for judgment. A sea of faces, some frightened, some resigned, others unreadable. They all stood there, waiting for something— redemption, damnation, a verdict that would finally tell them where they belonged.

The job he had been given—the role he never wanted—loomed before him.

Ben had spent his life avoiding responsibility, skirting the edges of anything that might force him to confront his own failures. He had been a man who made deals, who stayed just detached enough to never feel the full weight of consequence. Even in his worst moments, he had always found a way to convince himself he was still in control.

But here? Here, there was no illusion of control. There was only duty. And judgment. And the knowledge that for the first time, he couldn't talk his way out of it.

For the first time, he wondered if maybe, just maybe, this wasn't a punishment.

Maybe it was his chance to finally make things right.

The thought unsettled him. Could he? Was that even possible? Could a man like him—someone who had spent his entire life running from his own wreckage—actually do something that mattered now? Or was this just another illusion, another lie he told himself to keep from accepting the inevitable?

He glanced at the desk before him, weathered and ancient, as if it had existed since the beginning of time. His hands hovered over the surface. The weight of it, the permanence, the responsibility—he wasn't sure he could bear it. But he wasn't sure he could walk away, either.

His eyes flickered to the line. A young woman stood near the front; her arms wrapped around herself. She looked barely out of her twenties, her expression tight with uncertainty. Behind

183

her, an older man clutched a tattered hat, staring at the ground as though afraid to meet anyone's gaze. Further down, a child barely ten years old shuffled forward, glancing around as if searching for a familiar face.

They were waiting for someone to tell them what happened next.

Ben swallowed hard. He wasn't God. He wasn't some great judge. He was just a man—flawed, broken, still unsure of where he even belonged in all of this. But for better or worse, this was where he had ended up. And like it or not, these people were looking to him.

He took a breath, steadying himself. He had been given a role, one he never asked for, but maybe that didn't matter. Maybe this was about more than just him.

Slowly, he straightened, his fingers curling against the desk. He wasn't ready. He wasn't sure he'd ever be. But it was time.

The first soul stepped forward.

"Name?" Ben asked, his voice rough from disuse.

The young woman hesitated. "Olivia Carter."

Ben nodded, glancing down as words appeared before him, scrawling themselves across the desk as if written by an unseen hand. Details of her life, her choices, the good and the bad. The weight of her existence laid bare in ink that shimmered with something beyond his understanding.

He scanned the words, the story of her life flashing through his mind in an instant. He could see the fear she had carried, the love she had given, the mistakes she had made. It wasn't perfect. No one ever was. But perfection wasn't the point, was it?

He met her gaze. She searched his face, waiting for something—for approval, for condemnation, for an answer.

Ben took a breath. He wasn't here to punish. He wasn't here to condemn.

He was here to listen.

He exhaled, the weight in his chest shifting—not disappearing, but settling into something he could carry.

With a small nod, he gestured toward the gates.

"Go on," he said softly.

Olivia let out a breath she hadn't realized she was holding. Her steps were hesitant at first, then stronger as she moved toward the shimmering gate. The moment she passed through, the glow of it swallowed her whole, and she was gone.

Ben stared after her. He wasn't sure what he had expected to feel—relief, maybe. Certainty. He felt neither. Only the quiet understanding that this was only the beginning.

He looked up at the line. The next soul stepped forward.

Ben squared his shoulders. He still had ghosts to face. Regrets that clung to him. But for now, there was work to do.

Chapter 13:

The Breaking Point

Ben was unravelling.

Days stretched into weeks, then months, though time had no real meaning here. The endless line of souls moved forward, name after name crossing his desk, but he barely processed them anymore. It was all mechanical. A pointless cycle. The tasks that had once been so important, so vital to his existence, had lost all significance. Every action, every decision, felt like a hollow gesture—like a puppet whose strings had long been cut. He performed the motions, but none of them had any weight. The souls kept coming, each with their stories, their needs, but Ben could no longer bring himself to care.

He barely spoke. Barely acknowledged Peter, who had once been a constant, a reminder of his humanity, but now felt like a stranger in this place. Conversations that had once carried weight now felt insignificant. The words that left his mouth were empty, a mere formality, disconnected from the turmoil that raged inside him. He barely even read the files before stamping approval or denial. What did it matter? Each decision felt like an echo of the last, an endless loop of indifference. Nothing mattered anymore. Not the souls, not the work, not even the passing of time.

Somewhere, back on Earth, Emma was learning to live without him. The thought of her moving on, of her finding a life beyond the pain of his absence, gnawed at him like a constant, insidious ache. He had been her world, and now he was nothing more than a distant memory. She had stopped crying every night. The rawness of the grief had started to fade, replaced by a quiet acceptance that he was gone. She still missed him—he could feel it, like a faint echo from far away—but the sharpness of the grief was dulling, numbing her to the pain that had once consumed her.

Ben had watched her from afar, helpless, unable to reach her or offer any comfort. He had seen her take their daughter, Lena, to the park, the same park where they used to sit on the bench overlooking the city. The bench where they had shared their dreams, their hopes for the future, as they watched the world move around them. Emma had always loved that spot, and now, it seemed like she had found solace in it once again. She pushed Lena on the swings, her laughter ringing out into the air as the little girl squealed with delight. Emma smiled, her eyes bright, her spirit light.

It destroyed him. Not because she was happy. Not because she had found a way to carry on, to keep moving forward. That wasn't the source of his pain. It was because she was happy without him. He had watched her live, seen the way her life was starting to bloom again, and it shattered him in ways he couldn't understand. How could she be so whole without him? Had he meant so little to her? Was his absence just another chapter that she would close with the passing of time?

The thought that she could live without him, that she could find joy in the small, everyday moments with Lena, sent a wave of guilt crashing over him. He had promised her everything. He had promised her a life together, a future filled with love and memories. But now, all he could offer her was a shadow, a

187

memory she could no longer touch. The despair of it suffocated him.

As he sat in his endless office, surrounded by the souls of those who had passed, Ben realized that his own soul had already slipped away. It had long since fractured into pieces, scattering in a million directions, lost in the vast, unfeeling void of the afterlife. What remained of him now was nothing more than a shell, a man without purpose, without hope. And as the line of souls moved forward, one after another, Ben couldn't help but wonder how much longer he could keep going.

The Slow Decay of Purpose

The weight of eternity pressed down on him. Ben stopped checking the names, barely glancing at the files as the line of souls stretched endlessly before him. What did it matter? Who was he to decide where they went, what their fate would be? The world, or rather, the afterword, had become a blur. Every soul that crossed his desk was the same as the last, a faceless, nameless entity passing through his hands, moving on to whatever came next. Time had lost its meaning, and with it, any sense of significance in his work. His task had once felt important, even necessary, but now it was little more than a series of motions—mechanical, repetitive, hollow. The truth was, he didn't care anymore. And maybe he never had, not really.

Peter noticed. He always noticed.

"You're slipping, Ben," Peter said one day, his voice filled with an edge of concern. He leaned against Ben's desk, his arms folded across his chest, watching Ben's face for any sign of recognition. "This job only works if you do it."

Ben didn't even look up. His eyes remained fixed on the paperwork in front of him, a silent testament to his growing apathy. "I don't care," he muttered, his voice flat and empty, devoid of the fire it once carried.

Peter sighed, the weight of his words settling between them. "I know. That's the problem." His voice was softer now, a mixture of sympathy and frustration.

Ben let the words hang in the air. He didn't need Peter's concern. He didn't need anyone. What good was it, this incessant caring? He'd already lost everything that mattered. The souls, their journeys, their stories—none of it felt like it had a purpose anymore. He had lost his connection to the living, and now, in this endless place, he had lost his connection to the work, to the very thing that had once given him a reason to keep moving.

There were murmurs in the line—souls waiting for their judgment, their fates put on hold. The low hum of voices blended into the background, just another part of the noise Ben had stopped hearing. But he could feel them watching, could sense the shift in the air. Elias, the old gatekeeper, stood a few paces away, his hands resting on his cane, his eyes fixed on Ben from a distance. There was a look in his gaze, one Ben had seen before—an unspoken warning, the kind that spoke volumes without saying a word. Elias had been in this place for what felt like eons, and he knew what happened when someone lost their way. But Ben didn't need advice, didn't need another lecture. Elias's concern, like Peter's, was lost on him.

Ben ignored them all.
He had bigger concerns.

His mind was elsewhere, constantly drifting back to Emma, to Lena, to the life he had once known. How could he focus on this endless task when the world he had left behind was so far beyond his reach? How could he care about the fate of these souls when his own fate seemed so utterly meaningless? He had failed in his one purpose—to be there for Emma, to be there for Lena. The guilt that came with that failure weighed more heavily than any responsibility he had here, in this place that now felt like a cage.

The decay of his purpose had become inevitable. Every day that passed, he felt further and further removed from the man he had once been. A man with hope, with dreams, with something to live for. That man was gone, and in his place was someone adrift, lost to time and grief. The purpose that had once guided him, that had once defined his very existence, was slipping through his fingers like sand. And as much as Peter, Elias, or anyone else tried to hold him accountable, Ben knew—deep down—that he wasn't the man they needed him to be anymore.

A Glimpse of What Comes Next

One day, curiosity—or desperation—got the better of him. He had watched countless souls pass through the gates, heard the whispers of what lay beyond, but had never dared to follow. He had stayed in his corner, behind his desk, content to keep the gears of this endless cycle turning. But that day, something shifted inside him. Something broke, and the need to know what happened next overwhelmed him.

He followed a soul beyond the gates, silently trailing behind as it moved toward the unknown. The soul didn't look back, didn't seem to notice him at all. But Ben watched with a mix of hope and dread, his heart pounding in his chest. He had to know. He had to see it for himself.

And for the first time, he saw what came after.

Heaven wasn't golden streets and pearly gates. It wasn't the image of serene bliss he had once imagined, with choirs of angels singing and clouds stretching endlessly into the distance. No, what he saw was something more profound. It was peace. A quiet, gentle stillness that settled over everything. The souls who passed through those gates no longer carried the weight of their past lives. They weren't bound by their mistakes, their regrets, their losses. They were free. The tension in their faces melted away, replaced by expressions of contentment, of completion. For the first time in what felt like an eternity, Ben saw the true essence of peace—a peace that wasn't tied to the mortal world, but to something deeper, something beyond.

But then, his gaze shifted. He turned toward the other gate, the one that led to the opposite fate.

Hell wasn't fire and brimstone. It wasn't the cruel image of flames licking at the souls of the damned, as the old stories had always suggested. No, it was something far worse. It was emptiness. A hollow, aching void that stretched on for eternity. The souls that passed through this gate were not consumed by

191

flames, but by the crushing weight of their regrets—the things they could never undo, the words they could never take back, the actions they could never change. The guilt seeped into their very beings, a constant reminder of their failures. And it wasn't just pain—it was the absolute absence of anything else. There was no hope, no redemption, just an endless stretch of time that would never end, stretching forever in a silent, agonizing loop. The weight of what could have been was heavier than any torment.

Ben froze.

He realized something, something that made his stomach twist, a cold sensation spreading through his chest.

If he went through those gates, he would forget. His love for Emma, his longing for Lena—it would fade. Just as all the others had. The memories of his past life would slip away, evaporating like mist under a rising sun. He would no longer remember the ache of losing them, the way Emma's touch had once felt, the sound of Lena's laughter ringing through his heart. All of it—everything—would be erased, lost to the stillness of eternity. He would be at peace, yes, but it wouldn't be the peace he had imagined. It wouldn't be the peace of being whole, of healing from the pain.

It would be the peace of annihilation. Of becoming nothing.

Was that supposed to be peace? The thought gnawed at him, twisting deeper. How could he let go of the one thing that still tethered him to who he was, to the life he had once lived? How could he walk through those gates and leave Emma and Lena behind in the past, their faces fading like forgotten dreams? The very idea felt like an erasure, a death of a different kind.

It felt like annihilation. And in that moment, Ben realized that the peace he had been longing for might not be peace at all. It might just be another form of the emptiness he feared most. And suddenly, the weight of his decision seemed unbearable.

Emma's Life Without Him

Ben turned his gaze back to Earth, unable to tear himself away from the sight of Emma, moving on without him. He watched her pack away his clothes, folding each item with delicate care, almost as if preserving the memory of him in the fabric. She placed each piece in storage bins with a finality that made his chest tighten. There was no rushing, no haste—just a quiet, deliberate effort to clear him out of their shared life. He could see her pausing occasionally, perhaps to remember a moment, a time when everything had been different, when they were whole. And then, she moved on, carefully packing up the remnants of what was, and what could never be again.

His heart shattered as she reached for the wedding photo—the one they had framed and placed on the mantle in their living room. She traced the outline of their faces, her fingers brushing against the glass as though she was trying to hold on to the memory, but after a long moment, she took it down. Slowly, almost reverently, she placed the picture face down, as though turning away from the life they had built together.

She was letting go. And though Ben could feel the ache of that act, he also knew it was inevitable. It had to happen. But that didn't make it any easier to watch.

193

One night, she sat on the edge of the bed, staring at the ring he had given her. The ring that had once symbolized a promise—a forever. Her eyes were distant, the weight of the loss heavy on her. Lena, now a little older, toddled into the room with her small, hesitant steps and climbed onto Emma's lap, the little girl's eyes bright with the innocence of youth.

"Where's Daddy?" Lena asked, her voice small and uncertain.

Ben's breath hitched as he watched Emma's face crumple for a moment before she gathered herself. "Daddy's... not here anymore, sweetheart. But he loved you very much."

The words stung. They should have reassured him, should have been enough to make him feel as though Emma still carried him with her, still held on to the love they had shared. But they didn't. The pain in her eyes, the quiet ache in her voice—it should have been enough. But it wasn't. The truth was clear now. Emma was learning to live without him. And that truth cut through him, leaving a gaping hole where his heart used to be.

But the worst part was this: it never would be enough. He would never be enough for her again. Not in the way he had once been. He was no longer the man who could hold her, comfort her, be there for her. He was just a memory; a name she would carry with her as she moved forward. And he, trapped here in this empty place, could do nothing to stop it.

"You have to let go."

Peter's words echoed in Ben's mind, the sound of them haunting him, slipping into his thoughts like something toxic, something unavoidable. He had heard them a hundred times before, but he had never listened. How could he? Let go? How

194

the hell was he supposed to let go of everything—of her, of Lena, of the life he had been torn from? He never got the chance to choose. He never got the chance to say goodbye.

Ben had spent his whole life running from things. Running from mistakes. Running from pain. Running from the messiness of living. But this—this pain, this crushing, unrelenting feeling of helplessness—he couldn't run from it. He couldn't hide from the weight of the world he had lost.

For the first time since his arrival, something inside him snapped. He couldn't do it anymore. He couldn't stay at that desk, stamping names, sorting souls, feeling like he was fading into the background of an existence that didn't belong to him anymore. He wasn't meant to be here. Not like this.

And so, for the first time, Ben broke the rules.

He left the desk. He left the line of souls. He left the job.

He just... walked.

He didn't know where he was going. He didn't know what he was looking for, only that he needed to move. He needed air. He needed something—anything—that wasn't this endless purgatory. The Gates of Heaven stretched behind him, their ethereal glow fading into the distance, but no one stopped him. No one tried to pull him back.

He kept walking.

And suddenly, the world around him shifted.

The Forgotten Realms

195

The structured pathways of judgment, the sterile order of the afterlife, began to unravel. The pristine white light that had surrounded Ben for so long, the endless horizon of waiting souls that seemed to stretch into infinity—it all faded away. The landscape shifted, dissolving into something darker, something unpredictable. The orderly flow of souls that had once passed before him now seemed like a distant memory. In its place, shadows stretched long and wide, and the ground beneath his feet dissolved into a thick mist, swirling and undulating, as if it had a life of its own. The air grew heavy, thick with an oppressive silence, making each breath harder to take.

He moved forward, or at least he tried to, but the space around him refused to stay still. The mist clung to him, wrapping around his legs like a cold, grasping hand, pulling him in every direction at once. He couldn't tell if he was walking or floating, the sense of movement distorted by the disorienting environment. Time itself seemed to lose meaning here, like he had stepped outside of it, into a realm beyond comprehension. There was no sky, no stars, no horizon—only an endless, darkened void.

The silence grew deeper, suffocating. It pressed in on him from all sides. He didn't know how long he had been wandering when he saw them—figures on the periphery, drifting in and out of view. They were not like the souls he had judged before. These figures were... different. They were faceless, their forms translucent and vague, like wraiths or phantoms caught between worlds. And they weren't moving with purpose. They were just... waiting. Waiting for something, for anything.

Ben's heart skipped a beat as one of them stepped forward, materializing from the shadows. A woman, her form flickering

196

and wavering like candlelight, her presence both there and not there, like she was a dream on the verge of vanishing. She didn't look like a soul, not in the way he was familiar with. Her shape flickered, unstable, as though she couldn't fully exist in the place they were now.

"Who are you?" Ben asked, his voice hoarse, his curiosity piqued despite the unease curling in his stomach.

The woman's eyes seemed to hold an ancient, knowing sadness. She didn't answer immediately, but when she did, her voice was like a whisper on the wind—soft, but carrying the weight of centuries.

"We are those who refused."

Ben's breath caught in his throat. "Refused what?" he asked, his voice trembling with a mix of fear and confusion.

The woman's form flickered again, her outline shifting like a mirage in the distance. She stepped closer, and he could see that there was a sorrow in her expression, as if she understood the depth of his confusion, the questions that filled his mind. "Everything," she said simply, her tone distant, yet full of meaning.

Ben's gaze swept across the figures around them. The others— more like her—lingered in the shadows, their features indistinct, their movements slow and deliberate. These souls, too, seemed to be caught between worlds, lost and aimless, unable or unwilling to move forward. They were unmoored, drifting in an endless state of suspension, just as he felt. The weight of their existence hung in the air like a tangible thing—unsettling, painful, and haunting. These were not the souls who had moved

197

on or who had found their peace. These were the souls who had turned away, rejected whatever awaited them on the other side.

"Is this some kind of punishment?" Ben asked, his voice breaking through the stillness. The uncertainty gnawed at him, the need to understand what was happening clawing at his mind. Was this some kind of consequence for his actions? Was this place where souls ended up when they couldn't follow the rules, when they strayed from the path?

The woman tilted her head slightly, as if considering his words. "Only if you see it that way," she replied, her voice echoing faintly in the air. There was something oddly serene in her tone, an acceptance of this strange, unsettling fate that made Ben's stomach twist.

She was not afraid, nor was she angry. She was resigned, as if she had already come to terms with the fact that they—these souls—were not meant to move on. Not yet. Not until they made a choice, until they acknowledged something. But what that something was, Ben couldn't fathom. He could only feel the weight of it pressing down on him, a sense that he, too, was now part of this strange, in-between place—a place for those who had refused to accept their destiny, to fulfill their role in the afterlife.

The question lingered in his mind: Could he, too, be lost here forever, among those who had refused? Or was there still a way back?

Shadows of Memory

As Ben moved deeper into the unknown, the world around him seemed to pulse with an eerie energy. Visions rippled through the air, fragments of his past—memories long buried or forgotten—flashing before his eyes like broken pieces of a shattered puzzle. They appeared unbidden, fragments of time he had once cherished, then abandoned, now resurfacing in a way that felt both familiar and foreign.

He saw Emma, her face radiant, standing before him at their wedding. He could hear her laughter, the sound so vivid, it seemed to echo through the vast, empty space. The warmth of the moment flooded back—his heart filled with love, the world feeling full and alive. He could see her smiling at him as they exchanged vows, her eyes shining with a promise of forever. But the vision was fleeting, slipping away like sand through his fingers.

Then, the scene shifted, and he saw Emma again, this time kneeling beside Lena as she whispered softly into their daughter's ear. He could hear the gentle, loving words, words that felt like a tender embrace, even though they were about him—about the father Lena would never truly know. It broke his heart to hear it, to know that she would grow up without him. Without the memory of him. Without the life they had once planned. He wanted to reach out, to stop her from speaking, to remind her that he had been real, that he had been there, and that his love still lingered. But the vision moved on, slipping through his grasp.

And then, the last memory he had tried so hard to forget—his own death. The moment that had torn him from everything he had ever known, the moment that had changed his life, and Emma's, forever. The image was sharp, the pain still fresh in his mind. He could see himself, lifeless, cold, his body lying still in that moment of finality. His pulse had stopped. His breath had ceased. It was the moment he had never quite been able to escape, the anchor to his existence in this strange, liminal place.

But then, something new emerged within the vision. Something he hadn't noticed before. A shadow. It lingered at the edge of his final moments, a dark presence that flickered in and out of view. At first, it seemed like an illusion, a trick of the mind, but as the scene unfolded again in front of him, he could see it clearly—a figure, just beyond his periphery, moving like smoke. It was as though something—or someone—had been there with him in that final moment, something he hadn't realized before. Something he had missed.

A chill ran down his spine. Had he been wrong all this time? Was there more to his death than he remembered? Had someone—or something—been watching him, guiding him, or perhaps even controlling that moment? The questions gnawed at him, unravelling the tight grip he had held on his own reality. The truth had always felt so simple before. He had died. That was it. That was the end.

But now, the shadow hinted at something more—something that had remained hidden, something he had never fully understood.

Compelled by the need for answers, Ben reached out toward the vision, toward the shadow that seemed to pulse with an unknown energy. But as his hand neared it, the vision fractured, shattering like glass. The image splintered into a thousand shards of light and colour, the pieces scattering and dissolving into the air. The sense of the shadow, the presence that had haunted him, was gone in an instant, leaving him breathless.

He gasped, his chest tightening as he tried to grasp the fragments of what he had seen. But there was nothing left. The shadow had slipped away, like a wisp of smoke in the wind. The silence around him deepened, and the unsettling feeling of something unfinished lingered. What had he seen? What did it mean?

The more he tried to focus on the memory, the more it seemed to slip away, as though it was never meant to be understood. The shadow had been there, but now it was lost to him—just another puzzle piece that refused to fit.

And yet, despite the confusion, a part of him knew the truth: whatever that shadow was, whatever it had been, it was a part of his death that he was never meant to fully comprehend. And now, it was gone—just like everything else he had once known.

A Guide to the Unknown

"You're at the crossroads."

The voice came from behind Ben, soft but commanding, as though it had always been there, waiting for him to acknowledge it. He spun around, startled, and saw a figure standing before him. It was neither alive nor dead, neither angel nor demon. It shimmered in and out of existence, its form constantly shifting like it couldn't decide what it wanted to be. Its face was unreadable, a blank canvas of shadows and light that seemed to reflect all the uncertainty in Ben's soul.

"Who are you?" Ben asked, his voice shaky despite his attempts to steady himself. The world around him was still a blur, but the presence of the figure, the unknown, felt undeniably real.

"I am a choice," the figure replied, its voice neutral, neither warm nor cold. "One you can make, or one you can ignore. But you won't find what you're looking for in this place."

Ben's frustration flared. "Then tell me what's next." He was tired of waiting, tired of being lost in this endless limbo. He needed answers—anything to break the confusion that had been suffocating him.

The figure seemed to contemplate this for a moment, its shape flickering slightly. Then, it spoke again, its voice taking on an otherworldly gravity.

"There are three paths." The figure's words felt like a weight settling onto Ben's chest, a pressure that made every breath harder to take. "You can go back—accept your fate and continue your duties at the gates, where you will remain an observer, forever detached. Or," it paused, the air around it shifting in a way that made Ben's skin prickle, "you can move forward. Step beyond Heaven and Hell. Enter the unknown." Ben's heart pounded. The words felt like they were leading him toward something monumental, something he couldn't yet grasp. He felt the edges of his understanding begin to fray. But the figure wasn't done yet.

The air thickened, becoming dense with an ancient presence—something vast, something boundless. It pressed in on him, and for a moment, Ben felt small, insignificant, as though he were standing on the edge of eternity.

"Or…" The figure's voice dropped into a lower tone, the final words heavy with implication, "…you take the third path. You return."

Ben's breath caught in his chest. "Return? You mean—"

"Yes," the figure interrupted, its form growing sharper, more defined for a brief moment. "You can return to your life. To Emma. To Lena. To everything you've lost."

A flood of emotions washed over Ben. His heart clenched. The life he had lost, the faces he longed to touch again, to hold close, to protect—those memories came rushing back in an overwhelming tide. He could almost feel Emma's hand in his, could almost hear Lena's laughter in his ear. The weight of their absence had been a constant ache, and now, the promise of a return felt almost too good to be true.

But then the figure's voice turned grave. "But there's a cost."

The words hung in the air like an unspoken threat. Ben's stomach turned. He had known, deep down, that nothing would come without a price, that the chance to return to the life he had once known wouldn't be as simple as walking back through the doors. Still, hearing the figure's warning made the reality of the situation sink in.

The figure nodded, the glow around it flickering like a candle in the wind. "You will not remember this place. You will not remember Emma, Lena, or yourself. You will start over, as though nothing happened. All that you've learned, all that you've experienced, will be erased. You will be a stranger to your past."

Ben staggered back, the weight of the decision pressing down on him like an anchor. He had spent eternity in this strange, painful place, watching his family from a distance, unable to reach them. The chance to return was everything he had ever wanted. To be with Emma again, to hold Lena in his arms, to relive the moments he had lost. It felt like a dream within his grasp.

But at what cost? The idea of erasing everything—the memories, the love, the pain—of losing all the lessons he had learned and the soul he had become… Was it worth it? Could he truly walk away from the person he had become, just to return to the life he once had? Would it even be the same?

Ben looked back at the shifting visions of Emma, Lena, and the life he had lost. The temptation was unbearable, and yet the fear of forgetting, of losing himself entirely, was even more so. He stood at the crossroads, the weight of his decision pressing against him like an invisible wall. What was the right choice? Could there even be such a thing?

And as the figure stood there, waiting for him to decide, Ben realized that perhaps the true test wasn't whether or not he returned—but whether he could ever truly return without paying a price that went far beyond what he had imagined.

Emma Feels His Presence

On Earth, Emma had begun to move forward. The raw, unrelenting grief that once crushed her—making it hard to breathe, to think, to function—was now a quiet ache, a constant undercurrent that reminded her of the life she had lost. But she no longer drowned in it. She had learned to carry it, to coexist with it. Every day was a little less heavy, a little more manageable. Time, as it always does, had softened the sharp edges of her pain. But still, there were moments when it hit her all over again, like a wave that would rise out of nowhere.

Lena, now growing older, seemed to have an uncanny way of sensing these moments. There were times when she would laugh at nothing, a pure, innocent giggle that filled the empty room. Emma would watch her, puzzled, her heart twisting in her chest as Lena's little hands would reach toward the space beside her, as if someone was there, someone just out of sight. It was always followed by a shiver down Emma's spine as if a fleeting presence had brushed against the edge of the room.

And then, there were the lights. It happened more than once— sometimes when Emma would speak his name aloud, or when she would touch something that reminded her of him. The lights would flicker, just for a moment, like a quiet acknowledgment. She would pause, looking up at the ceiling, half-expecting him to step into the room. But of course, he never did. It was only a flicker, a glitch in the ordinary. Yet, it felt so deliberate, so impossibly real.

One night, after a long day, Emma fell into a deep sleep. And in the darkness of her dreams, Ben appeared. But it wasn't him as she remembered him—not the vibrant, strong man she had loved with every part of her soul. No, this version of him was different—hazy, blurry at the edges, like a memory fading with time. He was standing at the edge of something, looking lost, searching for something he couldn't quite reach. He seemed distant, yet so close at the same time, as though their connection was still there, fragile but present.

She reached for him in the dream, desperate to hold onto him, but he seemed to drift further away with every step she took. His eyes—those familiar, loving eyes—looked at her with a kind of longing that made her heartache. And just before the dream fractured and dissolved, she could hear his voice, faint but clear: *"I'll always be with you."*

Emma awoke suddenly, her breath quick and shallow, her chest tight as if she had just been running. Her fingers reached instinctively to her hand, where the ring Ben had given, her still sat, a constant reminder of their life together. She stared at it, the small, silver band that had once symbolized theirs forever. And in that moment, surrounded by the silence of the night, something shifted inside her.

Tears welled in her eyes as the weight of it all crashed down on her again, but this time, they weren't tears of overwhelming sorrow. They were softer, almost tender, like the last remnants of a grief that had finally been allowed to fade. She took a shaky breath and whispered, her voice barely a whisper, "It's okay." It wasn't a promise to herself. It was more than that. It was a release. A letting goes.

And somehow, in the depths of the afterlife, Ben felt it. His heart, wherever it was now, seemed to quiet in response. A sense of peace, something he hadn't felt in an eternity, settled over him. The burden of grief that had chained him to his memories, to his unending longing, seemed to lift, even if only just a little. It was as if Emma had permitted him—permission to let go, to find some measure of peace. He couldn't explain how, but he could feel it in the depths of his soul. Emma was moving on, healing in her way, and though it hurt, he knew it was time.

In the quiet of the unknown, somewhere between the edges of life and death, Ben felt a flicker of warmth, a recognition. And for the first time, he could almost hear Emma's voice in his heart, not as a distant memory, but as a promise. It was okay. It was time for him, too, to let go.

The Final Test

Ben stood before the threshold of something far greater than himself. The guide was silent, watching him, waiting. The figure's presence was as calm and unmoving as the vast emptiness around them. Everything was still, except for the silent tension hanging in the air. Ben knew this was it—the moment of choice, the moment when everything would change. "You cannot have both," the guide reminded him, its voice soft but unyielding. "You cannot return and still remember. You cannot hold on and move forward. You cannot live in two worlds at once."

Ben's heart pounded in his chest. The decision weighed on him more than anything he had ever faced before. To choose was to let go, to accept the price that came with it. And yet, the thought of walking away from the life he had lost—the life that had once been his—felt like tearing a part of his soul from his chest. How could he leave it all behind?

He hesitated, his mind spinning with doubt, trying to reconcile the deep ache inside him with the opportunity now before him. His eyes darted back to the space beyond, where the fog of the unknown seemed to swirl, waiting for his answer.

A moment of clarity struck as he turned, looking one last time toward Earth. In his mind's eye, he saw Emma, her face soft with exhaustion and love, tucking Lena into bed. The small child's giggles filled the air as Emma kissed her forehead. Ben could almost feel the warmth of her touch, the closeness of her, the life they had shared.

A future without him.

The weight of that thought hit him like a hammer to the chest. It wasn't just the grief. It was the understanding that there was a world moving on without him—a world where he no longer belonged, and had a place. Emma and Lena were creating a life without him, a life he would never be part of, no matter how much he longed for it.

And yet...

No.

The thought came sharply, cutting through his pain like a knife. There was no *unless*. There was no *maybe*. He couldn't stay in this limbo forever, couldn't keep drifting between the past and the unknown. The choice was clear. It wasn't just about returning— it was about what it meant to leave this place behind.

Ben took a deep, steadying breath. His throat tightened, and for the first time since his death, he felt a surge of raw emotion. It wasn't just longing anymore—it was acceptance. It was the understanding that he had been given a chance, a choice to reclaim what had been taken from him.

"I want to go back," he said, his voice barely a whisper, but firm in its resolve.

The guide said nothing. It simply lifted its hand, the gesture both commanding and final. The space around Ben shifted, distorted, as though the very fabric of reality was being torn apart. The air crackled with energy, and for the first time since his death, Ben felt pain—a deep, visceral ache, like something within him being yanked away, stretched, and torn apart. It wasn't physical; it was something far worse, a rawness that went deeper than the body.

The world shattered around him.

And then, suddenly, everything went still.

He stood on a sidewalk, in the quiet of the night. It was familiar—too familiar. It was Earth, but not quite. Not physically, not really. He was invisible, untouchable. But the connection, the pull, was undeniable. He was here, in this moment, where time had continued without him.

Ben's breath hitched as he watched Emma, his Emma, carrying a grocery bag up the steps of their old apartment. Lena toddled beside her, gripping her hand. The scene felt so real, so close to him, and yet, so far out of reach. He could see them—see their lives unfolding without him. His heart clenched as he watched Emma's face—there was a calmness, a quiet strength in her features that had not been there when he was alive. She had grown, adapted, and moved forward.

Emma reached up to tuck a strand of hair behind her ear, a small gesture that used to be so familiar to him. It was the way she did when she was tired when the weight of the day had settled into her bones. But now, she looked different. Stronger. Changed.

Lena reached for her, and Emma scooped her into her arms, pressing a soft kiss to the little girl's cheek. The sound of her laughter filled the air, a sound that used to be his joy, his everything. But now, it was just a reminder—a reminder of what he had lost, and of what he could never have again.

Ben stood motionless, his heart aching, his soul aching, his very being aching. He had wanted this life. He had wanted to be here with them, to continue the life they had built, to watch Lena grow, to be the father and husband he had always wanted to be.

But now, as he watched from the shadows, he realized he had lost it all.

And in that realization, the deep, gnawing ache of longing became something sharper, something even more painful. He had been given the chance to return—but at what cost? What was he willing to sacrifice to be part of a world that had moved on without him?

A Presence That Shouldn't Be

Peter found Ben hours later, standing in the doorway of their bedroom, his gaze fixed on the space where he should have been. The room was quiet—too quiet. It had once been a place of warmth, of love, where laughter and soft conversations had filled the air. Now it felt hollow, as though the very essence of it had been sucked away with Ben's absence. The space he used to occupy was still there, but it was empty, and in that emptiness, Ben could feel the weight of all that he had lost.

"She's moving on," Peter said quietly, his voice carrying the weight of truth and regret.

Ben didn't respond. He couldn't. The words hung in the air, sharp and unforgiving. The truth was undeniable—Emma was healing, growing stronger, while he was still trapped in this void. He had seen it with his own eyes. He had watched her, from a distance, carry on with Lena, build a life that no longer included him. It had hurt more than anything else—more than the endless days spent here, more than the years of longing.

Peter stepped closer, his presence a solid weight behind Ben, but Ben remained motionless. "You can't keep doing this, Ben," Peter said gently, though there was an edge of frustration beneath his calm exterior.

Ben clenched his fists at his sides, his knuckles white, as if holding on to something invisible, something he couldn't let go of. "I should have been there," he said, his voice tight, a raw edge of pain creeping into his words. "I should have been with her, with Lena. I should've *been* there. And now..."

"But you weren't," Peter interrupted, his tone quiet, but the words felt like a slap—cold and final, like a door slamming shut on the possibility of change.

Ben's breath caught, and for a moment, he thought he might break, might collapse under the weight of those words. He turned toward Peter, his jaw tight, a mix of anger and sorrow flashing in his eyes. "You knew this would happen," Ben spat, the words sharp and bitter. "You knew I'd break."

211

Peter didn't deny it. He just met Ben's gaze with steady eyes, his expression unreadable. "Everyone does," he said softly, the weight of his understanding hanging in the air. "This place... this job... it changes you. It makes you see things you wish you didn't have to see. Things you can't undo."

Ben exhaled sharply, his breath shuddering with the release of frustration, confusion, and despair. He shook his head, more to himself than to Peter. "Then why the hell pick me?" he demanded, the question ripping from him in an outburst of hurt. "Why choose me for this if it was always going to end like this? If it was always going to break me?"

Peter's gaze remained steady; his voice soft but unyielding. "Because you were never afraid of the truth," he said, his words piercing through the fog of Ben's anguish.

Ben scoffed; the sound was bitter, almost self-deprecating. "And what truth is that?" he sneered, a mix of anger and disbelief in his tone.

Peter took a step closer, his eyes never leaving Ben's, as if he were trying to reach him through the walls, he had built around himself. "That you can't change what happened," Peter said, his words simple, but they struck Ben like a blow to the chest.

Ben's breath hitched at the bluntness of it. It was the truth, the hard, ugly truth that he had been avoiding for so long. He had hoped, prayed, that there would be a way out of this, a way to undo the things he couldn't bear. But there wasn't. Not now. Not ever.

He hated Peter for saying it, for forcing him to face it, but deeper than that, he hated that it was true. There was no coming

212

back from the past. There was no undoing the mistakes, the things left unsaid, the life lost. No matter how much he wanted to change it, no matter how much he wanted to be with Emma, with Lena, he couldn't.

And yet, despite all of it, despite the pain and the hollow ache that filled his chest, Ben stayed. He stayed in this place, in this in-between. Because even though he couldn't change the past, even though he was trapped in this never-ending limbo, he wasn't ready to give up. Not yet.

He stayed because somewhere deep inside, he knew that, no matter how broken he was, no matter how much the weight of it all pressed down on him, he still had a part of him that wasn't ready to let go. Not of Emma, not of Lena, and not of the possibility—however slim—that maybe, just maybe, he could find some way to make things right again.

A Whisper of Something More

Ben began testing the boundaries of his existence, pushing against the intangible limits of his presence. He waved his hand in front of Emma's face, but there was no reaction—no flicker of acknowledgment. He called her name softly, almost pleadingly, but the silence around him swallowed it whole.

But then, one night, as Emma rocked Lena to sleep, something shifted. Lena's gaze drifted toward the space where Ben stood, her little fingers reaching out, and a soft, innocent giggle escaped her lips.

Emma tensed her eyes following the direction of her daughter's gaze. "What is it, sweetheart?" she murmured, her voice laced with concern.

Lena only giggled again, her small hand still reaching toward the nothingness, as if drawn by something unseen. Ben's heart skipped a beat, and his breath caught in his chest. Could Lena sense him? Was she somehow aware of his presence, the invisible tether that connected them?

In the days that followed, Ben became fixated on Lena's strange reaction. He spent hours—days, even—trying to leave traces of himself, something to prove that he was still there, still close. He focused on making the smallest disturbances—flickers of light, whispers in the wind, the creak of a door left ajar. It was subtle, just enough to hint at his presence without giving him away entirely.

Emma began to notice the changes. The air felt heavier when she stood in their bedroom like something was there but out of sight. Sometimes, late at night, she would stop what she was doing, an unsettling feeling creeping over her, as though she were being watched.

One evening, as the shadows stretched long in the quiet of their apartment, Emma whispered into the silence, "Ben?"

The sound of his name hanging in the air nearly shattered him. His heart swelled with a mixture of hope and despair, desperate to reach her, to make her feel his presence, but there was nothing. No voice, no touch, no way to bridge the painful chasm that had formed between them.

The distance was unbearable. He could feel it—feel her so close, yet so far away. He was there, so close to her, but unreachable.

The Consequences of Staying Too Long Peter

had warned him.

"The longer you stay, the more you'll lose."

At the time, Ben hadn't believed it. He had clung to the hope that he could somehow remain close to Emma and Lena, that he could find a way to be there without truly fading away. But then, the headaches began.

It started small at first—just a brief twinge in the back of his mind, like a dull ache he could easily dismiss. But it grew worse over time. He would be watching Emma laugh, or Lena run around the living room, and suddenly, a memory would slip away. The details faded and blurred until they were barely recognizable. Their first date, so vivid and beautiful in his mind, was gone—like a photograph left out in the sun, the colours washed away. Emma's laugh, once so full and warm, felt distant, like a sound he could barely recall. The comforting scent of Lena's baby blanket—the one he had carefully picked out— became an indistinct haze in his memory.

Panic gripped him. He clung harder to the threads of his fading memories, forcing himself to stay present in the world he had chosen, even as the edges of his existence started to crumble. He had spent so long holding on to the life he had lost—he couldn't stop now. But the more he tried to grasp the pieces of his past, the more they slipped away from him until he was left with a hollow feeling of something that had once been so real.

It wasn't just the memories. He began to notice something else—something far more insidious. His presence was starting to unsettle Emma. She didn't seem afraid, not exactly, but there was a shift in her demeanour. She would glance around the room, her brow furrowing slightly, as though she could feel him there but couldn't quite reach him. There was an unease in her, a tension that hadn't been there before.

She wasn't moving forward. She wasn't healing, not the way she should have been. It wasn't just the absence of him in her life— it was his lingering, invisible presence that kept her stuck. He had thought he was helping her, being there for her, but now he realized the truth: He was holding her back.

And it was killing him.

A Door That Wouldn't Open

Emma had met someone.

Ben had watched it unfold from his place on the periphery, his heart aching with every passing moment. It had happened at the park, a chance encounter. A friend had introduced them—a man who was kind, gentle, someone who made Emma smile in a way that Ben hadn't seen in so long. As they spoke, he watched Emma's face soften, her eyes light up, and for the first time in what felt like forever, there was a flicker of something else—something Ben couldn't quite place. Hope? Relief? Or was it just the possibility of moving on? He didn't know. All he knew was that he couldn't tear his gaze away.

216

The man had asked her out, and Ben had held his breath, waiting for her to make the decision. But Emma hesitated. She looked at Lena, at their apartment—the quiet, space where memories of Ben still lingered in every corner. Her eyes were heavy with the weight of the past, the years they had spent together, and the silence he had left behind.

"I'm not ready," Emma had said, her voice soft but firm, as though she had already made her choice. "I'm not ready."

Ben had expected relief. He had expected some sense of joy to flood him, a sense that she wasn't truly moving on, that she still needed him. But instead, all he felt was guilt. A deep, aching guilt wrapped around his chest like a vice.

She wasn't moving forward because she still felt him. She was still clinging to the remnants of their life together, still holding onto the pieces of their love, the memory of him. He knew she hadn't let go—how could she? He had left her with too much, too many unanswered questions, too much love still burning in her heart.

She still held onto his sweater, the one that had once smelled of him, her fingers tracing the fabric like a lifeline. She still whispered his name when she thought no one could hear, a soft prayer to a memory she couldn't forget. She still hesitated when she passed by his side of the bed, her fingers brushing the space beside her as if she expected him to be there.

And suddenly, it hit Ben with the force of a tidal wave. Was he being selfish? Was he keeping her here, suspended in a moment that couldn't last? She wasn't stuck because she wasn't strong enough—no, Emma was stronger than he could ever have imagined. She was stuck because he was still there.

217

He had never truly left, not in the way that mattered. Not in the way that would allow her to move on, to let go, to embrace a future without him. And in that moment, Ben realized that his presence—his lingering, invisible presence—was the thing that was holding her back.

Letting Go

That night, Emma sat on the edge of their bed, the engagement ring he had given her held gently in her hand. The soft glow of the bedside lamp illuminated her face, but it did little to mask the sadness that lingered in her eyes. She hadn't cried in a while, but Ben could feel the sorrow in the stillness, in the way her breath caught now and then. She looked at the ring, turning it over in her fingers as if searching for something—perhaps a trace of him, some connection to the life they once shared.

"I miss you," she whispered, her voice barely audible in the quiet room. "But I have to try."

The words hit Ben like a sharp blow, and he stood frozen in the doorway, his heart aching in ways he didn't know were possible. He wanted to reach out, to comfort her, to tell her that he understood, that he didn't want her to suffer anymore. But he couldn't. He was too far away, too intangible. All he could do was watch her—watch her make the decision he had been dreading.

Peter appeared beside him, his presence like a shadow in the stillness. "You know what you have to do," Peter said, his voice steady but heavy with something Ben couldn't quite place.

Ben swallowed hard; the words thick in his throat. "What happens if I go?"

Peter didn't answer right away. Instead, he looked at Emma, his gaze softening as she exhaled shakily, her fingers trembling as she set the ring back in its box, closing it with a finality that made Ben's chest tighten.

"She'll move on," Peter said, his voice quieter now. "She'll heal."

Ben nodded slowly, but the weight of the decision pressed down on him like a stone in his stomach. He knew it was the right thing. He knew Emma needed to live her life, to find a way to be happy again, even without him. But as he turned to leave, a strange sense of loss washed over him. It felt like he was giving up the one thing he'd fought so hard to hold onto.

And then, in an instant, he was back at the gates. The familiar scene of waiting souls stretched before him. The endless line. The files. The job. It was all still there as if no time had passed at all. But something was different. Peter was gone.

Ben frowned, scanning the space around him, expecting Peter to appear with some sarcastic remark or a teasing comment. But there was nothing. The space was empty—silent. The chair where Peter had always sat, the one that was never empty for long, was vacant.

Ben stood still, a creeping unease settling in the pit of his stomach. Peter had always been there, always ready with a word of advice or a quiet understanding. But now, he was alone. And that emptiness, more than anything, made the decision real. Ben was alone—truly alone—for the first time in what felt like an eternity.

Tithe Mystery of Peter's Disappearance

At first, Ben assumed Peter was testing him. The old man had always been unpredictable, pushing Ben to the edge of his limits, only to swoop in at the last moment with cryptic advice or an unexpected action that made Ben question everything he thought he knew. It felt like a familiar pattern—one Ben had grown used to. Perhaps this, too, was just another lesson, another way for Peter to force him to accept the reality of his job.

But as hours turned into days, and days into weeks, Ben's hope that Peter would reappear began to fade. The days stretched on, and the silence around him deepened. Peter never came back.

Ben tried to push the thoughts of Peter's absence to the back of his mind, focusing instead on the endless stream of souls before him. But it was impossible to ignore the absence. It gnawed at him. Without Peter's presence, the job felt emptier than it ever had before. The weight of the desk, the judgments, the cycles— it all felt more suffocating now, without the old man to ground him, to remind him that this place still had some form of meaning.

Desperation began to set in. Ben couldn't let it go. He had to know what had happened. He couldn't stand the uncertainty any longer. So, he left the desk. He wandered beyond the immediate realm of judgment, stepping into uncharted territory. He searched high and low, through corridors of forgotten souls and veils of mist that seemed to stretch on forever. But there was nothing—no sign of Peter, no hint of where he had gone, not even the faintest trace that the old man had ever existed.

Once, Ben had assumed that Peter controlled the system—that he held some kind of power over the endless bureaucracy they both worked in. Peter had always seemed so familiar with the rules, so knowledgeable about everything that happened here.

But now, Ben wasn't so sure. Had Peter ever really been in charge? Had he been nothing more than a soul, just like Ben, caught in this endless cycle? Waiting for someone else to take his place?

The thought was deeply unsettling.

As the weeks stretched on, Ben encountered other gatekeepers—if they could even be called that. They were shadowy figures, barely more than silhouettes, stationed at thresholds in places Ben had never seen before. He tried to ask them about Peter, hoping for some kind of explanation, but they never gave him a direct answer. They simply looked at him, their faces unreadable, and muttered vague phrases.

One of them, a figure who seemed to be half-shadow, half-light, whispered in a low voice, "They all leave eventually."

Ben's chest tightened at the words. "Where do they go?" he asked, desperation creeping into his voice.

221

The figure hesitated, its form flickering in the strange light. After a long silence, it answered, "No one knows."

The answer hung in the air, thick with meaning. Was it a lie? Or was it the most terrifying truth of all—that Peter, the gatekeeper who had been Ben's only guide, had simply... vanished? That no one knew where the old man had gone, or why he had left?

The uncertainty gnawed at Ben, and for the first time since his arrival, he began to question everything—not just about Peter, but about the world he now found himself trapped in.

The Psychological Toll of Eternity

The years stretched on, though time had no meaning anymore. Ben continued his routine, reading the names, stamping the approvals, and denying the unworthy. Souls passed through the gates of Heaven in an endless procession, their fates sealed, their journeys finished. Some crossed quickly, while others lingered in the line, lost in the monotony of their eternal wait. They would never speak to him; never question the decisions he made. They were just figures, shadows moving from one eternity into the next.

At first, Ben fought it. He resisted the automatic rhythm of his existence, the mechanical decisions that were expected of him. He tried to stop. To see what would happen if he didn't act. He let the line grow. He ignored the souls waiting, letting them drift as they pleased. But nothing changed. The line never stopped. It stretched on, endlessly, and the souls kept coming, each one as silent and unbothered as the last. He was the only one who suffered in his rebellion. The job didn't need him. He needed the job.

So, after weeks of fruitless resistance, Ben gave in. He let the monotony take him. He worked mechanically, without thought or feeling. The decisions became simple, predictable—names on a page, lives he would never fully understand. He became numb. The memories of his past life—of Emma, of Lena, of their home—faded at the edges. He clung to them as best as he could, grasping at wisps of memory like a drowning man clinging to a thread. But time, in its unforgiving nature, was relentless. It wore away at him until the details became unclear.

He couldn't remember the scent of their home, the soft sound of Emma's voice when she laughed, or the precise shade of green in Lena's eyes.

Desperation crept in. He tried writing things down— descriptions of Emma's laugh, of Lena's smile, of the small moments that once mattered. But the words didn't stay. The moment he looked away, they vanished, as if the universe itself was erasing them from existence. Each time he tried to hold on, it slipped further from his grasp.

He whispered their names to himself, over and over, like a mantra in the hope that it would ground him. "Emma... Lena..." The names echoed in the empty space around him, and for a brief moment, they felt real. But the moments grew shorter. He no longer remembered why he whispered them at all. The meaning behind their names dulled, like the fading glow of a distant star. It was as if they, too, were slipping away, leaving only an empty space where his memories once lived.

The psychological toll of eternity was too much to bear. He was losing pieces of himself—pieces that could never be replaced—and the more he tried to hold on, the faster it all slipped through his fingers. The faces of his past had become blurred, the connection to them strained and weakening, until there was nothing left but the unceasing routine of his duty. And somewhere, deep inside, a voice whispered that he might never be the same again.

The Corruption of Power

And then, the power came.
It started as a small thing.
A soul stepped forward—one that shouldn't have been there. A man who had spent his life hurting others, causing pain, leaving destruction in his wake. Ben read the file, disgust curling in his gut.
He had spent so long feeling powerless. Now, he wasn't.
He denied the man entry.
There was no ceremony to it, no grand punishment. The soul simply dissolved into the void, erased from existence. The line moved on. No one questioned his decision. No one told him he was wrong.
For the first time in what felt like forever, he felt something close to satisfaction.
So he did it again.
Not often—only when the file warranted it. Only when he saw true cruelty, true evil. When he saw someone who had destroyed lives and never sought redemption, never once tried to undo their sins.

He sent them away, one by one, watching them vanish into the abyss.

And it felt good.

But then the lines blurred.

A woman stepped forward. He read her file. She had made mistakes—terrible ones. But she had also spent years trying to fix them. Was she truly beyond saving?

His hand hovered over the stamp. He hesitated.

And then, for the first time, he asked himself: Who am I to decide?

The realization hit like a thunderclap.

He had power now. But was he any different than those who had wielded it before him? If he could deny Heaven to those, he deemed unworthy, what stopped him from letting his own bitterness cloud his judgment? Was he punishing souls... or taking out his frustration on a system he didn't understand?

Doubt seeped in, slow and insidious. The satisfaction he had felt was replaced by something else—fear.

Because he wasn't sure anymore if he was making the right decisions.

And worse... He wasn't
sure if he cared.

The weight of his newfound authority gnawed at him, heavier than he had ever imagined. His mind raced with questions he hadn't thought to ask when he first accepted this role. Was he truly qualified to hold the fate of others in his hands? He was just one person, after all, with a lifetime of flaws and imperfections. He had never asked for this power; it had been thrust upon him, and now he had to live with the consequences.

What if he had misjudged someone? What if, in his desire for justice, he had damned the innocent? Every time he stamped another soul's fate; the nagging feeling grew stronger. Was he becoming the very thing he despised? Was he, in his righteous anger, taking the place of the tyrants who had ruled before him?

The fear lingered, settling deep into his chest. He could feel it, pressing on his ribs, suffocating him with doubt. The satisfaction he had felt in the beginning seemed so far away now, like a distant memory of someone he no longer recognized. Was he still the same man who had once been powerless, or had the power corrupted him beyond repair?

He spent hours staring at the endless line of souls, wondering if he was even capable of doing the right thing anymore. They all looked the same, waiting for his judgment. And he, standing at the crossroads of their futures, felt more lost than ever. What was the true path? And what was he willing to sacrifice in his pursuit of it? The weight of the world felt crushing, and for the first time, he wasn't sure if he was strong enough to bear it.

The Weight of His Own Judgment

The next time a soul approached, Ben found himself hesitating longer than usual.
An old man. Someone who had lived a quiet, uneventful life. Not cruel, not kind. Just… there.
Ben flipped through the file, but it was thin. Hardly anything there. He had lived, and then he had died. No great sins, no great virtues.
Where did someone like that belong?

He looked up at the old man. The soul didn't plead, didn't beg, didn't seem to care one way or another. He simply stood there, waiting.

Ben swallowed hard.

Was this what Peter had felt, toward the end? The slow unravelling of certainty, the realization that none of it mattered? That no one was truly good or evil, that the weight of judgment was nothing but an illusion?

His hand trembled over the stamp. He needed more time. More information. More something.

But the line never stopped.

The souls kept coming.

And he had to choose.

So he did.

He approved the man. Watched as he stepped through the gates, disappearing into the eternity beyond.

Ben exhaled slowly, his hands shaking.

And then another soul stepped forward.

And another.

And another.

The line never stopped.

The job never ended.

And Ben— Ben

was afraid.

The fear settled deeper now, weighing him down with each passing soul. With every decision he made, he was further removed from the man he used to be. His purpose had been clear once—he had sought justice. But now, even with all the power at his disposal, he realized how easily it could slip into something else entirely. Something darker. What if his actions

227

didn't create fairness, but chaos? What if, in the effort to restore balance, he was tipping the scale too far in the other direction?

The faces of the souls blurred together as they continued to move forward in their endless procession, each one waiting for a decision, a verdict. They were all so different, yet all the same. Some were hardened by the weight of their own actions, others resigned, some even hopeful. And yet, Ben could never know for certain what lay beneath the surface. Was he judging them for the people they had been in life? Or the choices they made in the final moments? Or worse—was he judging them based on his own emotions, the pressures mounting within him, shaping his decisions without him even realizing it?

He thought of the old man again. What had he done to deserve either condemnation or salvation? Did his lack of virtues make him less worthy of grace? Was it even possible to live a life untouched by either the purity of good or the stain of evil?

Ben's throat tightened. He had been given the power to decide these things, yet he felt so ill-equipped. The weight of it all—his own judgment, the eternal consequences that rode on it—was suffocating. With each soul that came forward, he felt like he was losing his grip on himself. His fears of becoming something unrecognizable were no longer just abstract thoughts; they were tangible, real. He was already slipping.

There was no time to dwell, though. The next soul had already arrived. And Ben had to decide again. And again. The line stretched on forever, and with each passing moment, the fear deepened. He was trapped in an endless cycle of choices, and the worst part was that he wasn't sure he had the strength to make any of them right anymore.

228

Chapter 14:

A Cynic's Judgment

Ben did the job.

He didn't want to. He hated it. But he did it.

There was no one else. Peter was gone. The line never stopped moving. And after enough time—years? centuries? eternity? — he realized that his resentment, his refusal, his defiance, meant nothing. The machine kept turning. The souls kept coming.

And so, he judged.

At first, he followed the rules. Read the files. Stamped the names. Sent them through.

Then, he stopped reading. He didn't need to.

It was always the same—the pious, the murderers, the desperate, the entitled. They all looked the same after a while. They all wanted something.

And the longer he sat on the other side of the gates, the angrier he became.

Why should these people get eternal paradise? Why should they get peace?

Where was his peace?

The first time he sent someone to the abyss for no reason, he expected something to happen. A warning. A sign. Some kind of divine slap on the wrist.

But nothing happened. So

he did it again.

The Weight of Endless Judgment

The names blurred together. The faces did, too. Every day—or whatever passed for a day in this place—was the same. A soul would step forward. Ben would stamp a name. The soul would vanish. Repeat. Repeat. Repeat.

It didn't matter if they pleaded, if they wept, if they screamed in righteous fury. It didn't matter if they tried to convince him that they had done good, that they had repented, that they were worthy. Their words meant nothing.

The line never stopped.

And so, neither did he.

But sometimes, when the monotony became unbearable, he would listen—just to amuse himself. Just to hear something different.

A woman once knelt before him, her hands clasped in silent prayer. She had been a nun in life. She had spent decades feeding the hungry, tending to the sick, dedicating every breath to the service of others.

"I did everything right," she whispered. "I followed every rule."

Ben studied her. There had been a time when he would have believed her. But now? Now he wondered if righteousness was just another kind of entitlement.

He stamped the file. Approved.

She stepped forward, fading into the gates. The next soul wasn't so lucky.

The Corruption of Power and Indifference

230

He told himself it didn't matter. That he wasn't punishing them. That he wasn't playing God. He was just… balancing the scales. That was what he told himself the first time he denied someone who didn't deserve it.

The man had been a liar. A fraud. A selfish bastard who took advantage of others. But he wasn't a murderer. He hadn't ruined lives beyond repair.

Ben hesitated, his fingers tightening on the stamp.

Then, his rage flared. Why does he get to go through? Why did any of them get to?

He flipped the stamp over. Denied.

The soul's eyes widened. "Please," the man choked out. "There has to be a mistake."

Ben said nothing. He didn't need to.

The void swallowed the man whole.

And just like that, Ben felt something close to satisfaction.

The next time it was easier.

And easier.

Until, eventually, he stopped needing a reason.

The One Soul That Makes Him Hesitate And
then she stepped forward.

Ben glanced up, expecting just another name. Another meaningless decision.

Then he froze.

The woman standing before him looked familiar. Too familiar.

For a moment, he couldn't place her. But then—

The way she shifted her weight. The small frown she wore when she was thinking. The scar on her left wrist.

His breath caught.

"Sarah," he whispered.

231

His sister.

She stared at him, confused. "How do you know my name?"

Ben barely heard her. He flipped open the file, skimming frantically. The details blurred—her birth date, her death date, her sins, her virtues.

He hadn't seen her since he was alive. Since long before he had even met Emma.

For the first time in eternity, he wasn't sure what to do. Sarah shifted, uncomfortable under his scrutiny. "Where am I?" she asked, looking at the endless stretch of souls. "Is this Heaven?"

Ben's mouth went dry. "Not yet."

She studied him, searching his face. "You seem... familiar." He wanted to tell her. Wanted to say something—anything. But what was there to say? I've been here for eternity. I lost myself. I became something else. And now I decide where you go.

Would she even believe him?

Would she even deserve Heaven?

His hand trembled over the stamp.

He forced himself to read the file. Tell me you were good, Sarah. Tell me you didn't end up like me.

She hadn't been perfect. She had made mistakes. Some big ones. But she had tried. She had always tried.

Ben let out a shaking breath and stamped the file. Approved.

Sarah hesitated before stepping forward. She looked back at him once more, brow furrowed. "I don't know why... but I feel like I should thank you." Then she was gone.

And Ben sat there, hands clenched, feeling something crack deep inside him.

The First Signs of a Cracking System

The next soul approached, but Ben barely saw them. His mind was still stuck on Sarah. On how close he had come to sending her to the abyss. On how easy it had been to wield that power. And for the first time, doubt crept in.

Had Peter ever done the same? Had all the gatekeepers before him reached this point—where the lines between judgment and cruelty blurred? Where justice became revenge?

Ben swallowed hard, suddenly feeling sick.

Then something strange happened.

A file appeared before him—one he had already stamped. The same name. The same soul.

But this soul had already passed through.

Ben frowned. That's not possible.

He glanced up. The soul before him looked lost, confused, like they had been here before.

"Where am I?" they asked, voice thin.

Ben's grip tightened. This isn't right.

The system wasn't perfect. It wasn't divine. It wasn't even logical.

Something was broken.

And now, for the first time since Peter left, Ben wasn't sure if he was part of the machine... or if he was just another one of its victims.

The Realization

233

He sat there, the stamp in his hand, the weight of eternity
pressing down on him.
If the system could be wrong about this... What
else had it been wrong about?
What else had he been wrong about?

Ben stared at the line before him, the endless stream of souls
still filing through. The familiar cycle, the monotonous rhythm,
felt suddenly foreign, unsettling. For the first time in all his
years, he wasn't sure if he was even in control of what was
happening. The questions piled up, pushing down on him,
gnawing at the edges of his mind. And the one thing he was
certain of now was that he couldn't just keep pretending it was
all fine.

"You're playing with fire."
Ben looked up, staring at the soul standing before him. A
woman, trembling in front of the gates, hands clasped together
as she begged.
She had cheated on her husband, ruined a man's life. Lied for
years.
Her file said she deserved forgiveness.
Ben disagreed.
He didn't speak, just stamped her file. DENIED. She
screamed as she vanished into the void. Her sound was
swallowed by nothingness.

Ben exhaled. He felt nothing. Except
maybe... relief.

The Souls That Fight Back

234

At first, it was simple. They came, he judged, they left.

But then, something changed.

A woman stepped forward, her face pale but her eyes bright with defiance. "No," she said, her voice steady as he raised the stamp.

Ben frowned. "Excuse me?"

"I said no."

He had expected fear. He had expected pleading. But this woman... this woman simply refused.

Her file said she was a liar, a thief. That she had manipulated people her entire life. But as he stared at her, something shifted.

The abyss should have swallowed her immediately.

It didn't.

The air around her rippled.

Ben hesitated. That had never happened before.

She met his gaze and smiled. "You don't get to decide." Ben's grip tightened around the stamp. "That's exactly what I do."

The void shuddered, like it was waiting for him to prove it.

So he did.

He slammed the stamp down. DENIED.

The woman screamed as she fell—but for the first time, Ben wondered if she had been right.

The Corruption of the Gatekeeper

At first, he thought it was nothing.

The woman had been a fluke. A glitch in the system.

But then it started happening again.

The files became lighter in his hands, the names more difficult to read, like the ink was fading. Some souls hesitated before

235

vanishing, their forms flickering like weak candlelight before the void took them.

And Ben himself… he felt different.

His body wasn't a body. It never had been, not since he died. But now it felt less human. When he spoke, his voice carried more weight. The air seemed to hum with his words. Then, one day, he looked into the abyss and saw something looking back.

It had no shape. No name. But it knew him.

He stared into the darkness, and the darkness whispered.

Keep going.

Ben stepped back from the void, a shudder running through him. He clenched his fists. He wasn't afraid. He wouldn't be afraid.

But the whispers lingered, curling around him like tendrils of smoke. They were soft, persistent, almost seductive. He couldn't ignore them, not entirely.

What was happening to him?

Each passing moment, the pressure of the job, the weight of his decisions, seemed to deepen. He could feel something shifting inside of him—something that he didn't recognize, something that felt more like a shadow than a part of who he once was. He had begun as someone who questioned the system, someone who felt deeply about the morality of it all. But now, with each soul that passed through the gates, it felt less like he was upholding any sort of justice, and more like he was pushing an agenda of his own.

It wasn't just that he was getting numb. It was more than that. The anger he had once carried, the resentment that had driven his defiance, was no longer a fleeting feeling. It had become a part of him, simmering just beneath the surface, a fire that fed off every soul he denied. The power was intoxicating. The weight of the decisions, the feeling that he was the one who determined who lived and who suffered, began to wrap itself around his mind like a vice.

The next soul that arrived was another test. Another name. Another chance to follow the rules—or break them. Ben looked at the file, but this time, it didn't feel the same. He felt that familiar tug at his chest, the subtle pull toward defiance. His finger hovered over the stamp.

The soul before him was a young man, barely more than a child, his eyes wide with confusion and fear. The file listed a single sin—an accident, a mistake. He hadn't meant to kill anyone. He had been reckless, yes, but wasn't that something he could be forgiven for?

Ben's hand shook as he held the stamp. The rules told him to send this boy through to Heaven. But the anger inside him screamed that it wasn't enough. He should have known better. He should have been smarter. Why should he get forgiveness?

Ben slammed the stamp down again. DENIED.

The boy's scream echoed in the void, but Ben barely heard it. The warmth from the abyss was almost comforting, a stark contrast to the cold dread that had been tightening in his chest. This was what it felt like now—the satisfaction of his decisions. The way the power settled into his bones, making everything else seem small, insignificant.

And still, the whispers. They grew louder. Keep going. They deserve it. No one is beyond your judgment.

For the first time in what felt like eternity, Ben looked back at the abyss, no longer seeing just an empty void. There was something else there now—something that felt alive. It wasn't just the abyss anymore. It was him. The line between who he had been and who he was becoming was slipping away, dissolving into the void that had once been a place of judgment, and now felt like an endless hunger, gnawing at him, pulling him deeper.

Ben clenched his fists, his head pounding. Was this what Peter had felt before he had left? Had he succumbed to the same darkness? Was this inevitable?

The souls kept coming. The line never stopped. But now, every soul that passed through felt like a step further into a place Ben wasn't sure he could escape from anymore.

The Angels Step Forward

They had been whispering at the edges of the clouds for weeks now, their voices barely audible, just murmurs carried on the wind. Ben had felt their presence, like a shadow just beyond the corner of his vision. It was a constant, unnerving hum—a warning, a reminder that he wasn't as isolated as he thought. He knew they were watching him, waiting for something. And finally, one of them stepped forward.

Tall. Golden. Beautiful.

An angel.

Ben didn't stand. He didn't move. He remained seated, his fingers twirling the stamp between his hands, casually, like he had all the time in the world. "Let me guess," he drawled, the corners of his mouth lifting in a smirk. "I'm not supposed to be doing this."

The angel's expression was unreadable, its face serene and cold. Its presence, however, was anything but. The air grew heavier with each passing second, and Ben could almost feel the weight of eternity pressing against him. The angel's wings fluttered slightly, a soft movement that seemed almost imperceptible, but Ben noticed it.

"You are warping the balance," the angel said, its voice calm and authoritative, like the very wind itself.

Ben tilted his head slightly, pretending to consider its words, his smirk fading into something darker. "Or maybe the balance was never fair to begin with," he countered.

The angel's wings twitched again—a barely noticeable shift— but it was enough to tell Ben that his words had struck a nerve.

"You are not above judgment," the angel warned, the words almost carrying the weight of a prophecy, a foretelling of inevitable doom.

Ben's grip tightened on the stamp, and he leaned forward slightly. "Aren't I?" he asked, his voice laced with defiance.

The angel stepped closer, the pressure in the air intensifying. It wasn't just physical—there was something spiritual in the atmosphere, an unseen force that pushed against him like invisible hands pressing on his chest. Heaven itself seemed to be

239

watching him, waiting for him to break. And for the first time, a deep, almost imperceptible whisper slithered through his thoughts.

You can be removed.

Ben recoiled slightly, his stomach twisting with something unfamiliar. The thought didn't scare him—not yet—but it unsettled him and made him question the walls he had built around himself.

The angel studied him for a long, uncomfortable moment, its gaze unwavering. Then, without a word, it turned and began to walk away. "You are on a path that does not end where you think it will," it said, its voice a soft echo that lingered in the air long after it had gone.

Ben sat there, frozen for a moment longer. The stillness felt unnatural, suffocating. He was alone again, but now something had shifted inside him. Fear, that deep, gnawing fear, began to stir in his gut.

The First Signs of Rebellion

It wasn't just the angels.

The souls were changing, too.

Ben didn't expect it. Not from the souls who had been waiting their turn for so long. They were supposed to accept their fate, to move when told to move, to bend to the system, just as they always had. But things were different now. There was a restlessness in the air, an energy that crackled like static, and it was coming from them.

A man stepped forward in the line, his shoulders squared, his eyes filled with something that Ben hadn't seen before—defiance.

"This is wrong," the man said, his voice loud and clear. His eyes swept over the others in line, and Ben could feel a ripple of tension spread. "You feel it, don't you?"

A murmur went through the waiting souls. A ripple, like a wave of unrest, moving through them all.

Ben narrowed his eyes. "Keep moving," he ordered, his voice cold, hard.

But the man didn't move. He stepped forward, his hands clenched into fists. "You're not following the rules," he accused, his voice carrying weight, unafraid. "Why should we?"

Ben's jaw clenched, his teeth grinding. He had never been challenged like this before. Not by a soul. Not like this. He was the one in control. He was the one who decided who passed through, and who moved on. No one had the right to question him.

His hand hovered over the stamp. He could do it. He could strike it down, dismiss the man with one motion.

But before he could, it happened. The others stepped forward.

Not just one. Not just two.

Dozens.

They stepped out of the line, all of them, their eyes fixed on him with an intensity that sent a chill down his spine. They were no longer afraid of him. They were no longer waiting for his judgment—they were waiting for him to act.

For the first time, Ben realized that the power he had so carefully wielded, the control he had thought was his, was slipping away.

The pressure was suffocating. They weren't just defying him. They were demanding something, something more than what he could offer. They were awakening, and Ben could feel it in his bones.

The Moment He Goes Too Far

It happened so quickly.

A child stood before him. No. It couldn't be right. No child should be here. Not like this. Not for judgment. But when Ben looked at the file, his heart sank.

It listed sins. Heavy ones. Impossible ones. Ones that made no sense. Ben frowned, his hand trembling slightly as he flipped through the pages.

"This… this isn't right," he muttered, staring at the file in disbelief. The child didn't cry, didn't plead. She just stared at him; her eyes too wide for someone so young.

Ben's grip tightened on the stamp. He was in control. He wasn't afraid. Not of a child. Not of anyone.

But as he stared at her, something inside him began to twist. He wasn't sure why, but there was something about this that felt wrong. The weight of the child's sins on paper didn't match the softness of her face. It felt... forced.

But he was the gatekeeper. He made the decisions. He wouldn't hesitate.

With a deep breath, he slammed the stamp down. DENIED.

And then the universe broke.

The child didn't scream. She didn't cry. She simply shattered.

The entire afterlife recoiled, as if a terrible, unspeakable thing had been unleashed. The line of souls trembled; the air itself seemed to quake. The angels that had been watching—waiting—vanished in an instant. And the abyss... The abyss lurched forward, a vast, ravenous thing that seemed to awaken for the first time in eternity.

Ben stumbled back, his breath coming in ragged gasps. His hands shook violently as he tried to steady himself against the desk.

For the first time in what felt like forever, Ben felt the weight of what he had done. The void, the abyss, the endless emptiness that he had dismissed for so long—he could feel it now, alive, aware.

And in the silence that followed, the void whispered to him again. But this time, it wasn't the same.

It was laughter.

You think you've broken the system? the laugh seemed to say. No, Ben. You've only unlocked it.

And in that moment, he realized: He wasn't breaking the system. No. The system had been keeping something locked away. Something far worse. And now… it was awake.

Chapter 15:

Breaking the Rules

Ben had stopped caring about the files. He had stopped caring about the rules. He had stopped caring about anything.

For years—centuries, maybe—he had let the bitterness fester. He had denied thousands, maybe millions, from Heaven's gates, and all for what? For a sense of control? For some misguided justice that he could never truly reconcile? He had judged with a cynic's heart, letting his grief dictate who was worthy of paradise. The weight of it had become his constant companion, crushing him, melding him into something unrecognizable.

And yet, it changed nothing.

Emma was still gone. His life was still gone. Heaven was still here, and he was still stuck behind its gates. No amount of power, no number of souls denied, could bring her back. No matter how hard he tried, the world kept turning, indifferent to his pain.

So, he did what he always did when the universe refused to bend to his will. He set it on fire.

The stamp, once a symbol of control, had become a weapon in his hands—a tool for destruction. He wasn't just judging souls anymore; he was reshaping everything in his image, trying to tear down the very system that had kept him locked in this eternal limbo. No more lines. No more rules. It was all meaningless. He would burn it all to the ground.

He began ignoring the files altogether, the faces of the souls becoming nothing more than blurs of insignificance. His decisions were no longer rooted in righteousness. They were rooted in spite. Spite for a world that had taken everything from him, and now, in his mind, deserved nothing in return. Every time he slammed that stamp down, a part of him took twisted satisfaction in the destruction he caused. It was power. It was the only thing he had left.

The Angels' Last Warning

At first, the angels had only whispered. They had watched from the edges of the clouds, their eyes filled with wariness and concern as Ben twisted Heaven's order into something unrecognizable. Their once-divine presence had been tainted by uncertainty as if even they didn't know how to deal with him anymore. They murmured among themselves, their voices low, but they did nothing.

They had waited, giving him the space he needed to implode, as though they thought he might tire of his chaos. But as Ben's actions began to spread like a fire through the afterlife, they could no longer remain passive observers. They could no longer watch as the system heaved under the strain of his rebellion.

One day, they came.

A host of angels appeared at the gates—not just one, not just a whisper in the background, but dozens. They surrounded him, their golden robes shifting like ripples across the surface of an unseen ocean, their faces etched with ancient grace but now shadowed by something else—fear? Concern? Perhaps even pity.

One angel, taller and more radiant than the rest, stepped forward. Her eyes burned with restrained fury, the light around her shimmering like the sun at its zenith. "You will stop," she commanded, her voice heavy with divine weight, cutting through the air like a blade.

Ben didn't stand. He didn't even flinch. He remained seated in his chair, leaning back as if he had all the time in the world. He twirled the stamp between his fingers, the motion casual, almost mocking. "No," he said, voice dripping with defiance.

The angel's wings flared behind her, a shimmering display of power and authority. The air itself seemed to bend in response, thick with the tension of a thousand years of divine law. "You are destroying everything," she declared, her tone a mixture of fury and desperation.

Ben dragged a hand through his hair, feigning boredom. His gaze flicked lazily over the angels that now surrounded him, all of them watching, waiting for him to break, for him to be afraid. "Am I?" he asked, voice low and mocking. "Or am I just showing everyone the truth?"

There was a long silence, and then another angel spoke—a being older, graver, with a presence that resonated like the sound of an ancient bell tolling. "You do not understand what you are

247

playing with," the angel said, the words laced with an authority that seemed to tremble in the very air.

Ben chuckled. The sound was dark and cold, a reflection of all the years of grief and anger that had been swirling inside him. "Good," he said, his voice soft, almost amused. "I've been waiting to break it all."

The lead angel's expression darkened, her eyes narrowing as she stepped forward, her wings folding in tightly behind her. "If you do not stop," she warned, her voice taking on a cold edge, "we will remove you."

Ben tilted his head slightly, the hint of a smile playing at the corners of his mouth. Ah, so that's what this was—a threat. His fingers tightened around the stamp as he leaned forward, meeting the angel's gaze with a mixture of contempt and amusement. "I'd like to see you try."

The tension between them crackled like a storm about to break. The angels stood firm, their presence radiating power, but Ben felt none of the fear he should have. There was a strange, exhilarating sense of liberation in his defiance, a sense of finality. For the first time in forever, he wasn't the one being controlled. He was the one holding the power.

The stamp in his hand felt heavy, its weight a constant reminder of the destruction he had caused and the destruction he still had the power to unleash. The angels could try to stop him. They could threaten him. But at that moment, Ben realized something. They had their rules. Their divine laws. But he... he was beyond them. And if he couldn't have control over his fate, he would destroy the whole damn system that had bound him in the first place.

248

And if they came for him?

So be it.

The War for Heaven Begins

The angels gave their warning. Ben
ignored it.

And then, Heaven erupted into war.

At first, it was quiet. It always starts quietly. The souls who had
earned their place—the saints, martyrs, the righteous—gathered
in secret, hiding in the corners of Heaven where the light was
still pure. But hiding wasn't enough. No, they wouldn't just fade
into the background like so many others. They fought back. For
every soul Ben had denied, for every piece of Heaven he had
corrupted, they would not stand idly by.

They were warriors now, bound by a single goal: to restore
balance, to reclaim what had been lost.

They began in small skirmishes, testing the limits of Ben's
control. They attacked the high clouds, the places where
Heaven's light was brightest. The ones who had lived virtuous
lives—those whose spirits glowed with the purity of their
actions—started banding together in the highest places,
preparing for what they believed was the last stand for the soul
of Heaven. They wore the symbols of their old lives—robes of
white, crowns of light—and with every clash, they grew bolder.

But their enemies? They weren't just sinners anymore. They weren't just broken souls who had failed in their lives. No, the ones Ben had denied had grown into something more.

They were monsters.

Murderers, tyrants, warlords. Souls who had shaped history through suffering, now shaping Heaven in the same brutal way. These were the souls who had seen power and pain intertwine, the ones who ruled with iron fists during their mortal lives. And they weren't interested in exile. They weren't interested in repentance. They wanted Heaven—and they would take it by force.

As the righteous fought for Heaven's purity, the corrupted fought for something darker. Heaven's streets, once golden and calm, now turned into battlefields. What had been the shining pillars of paradise began to crack under the weight of conflict. The light of Heaven dimmed, stained by war and bloodshed, by ambition and the echoes of past sins.

And the first angels fell.

Beings of light, creatures of purity, struck down by the very souls they had once condemned. It was a brutal, ironic reversal. Ben watched from the shadows, his eyes gleaming with dark satisfaction, as Heaven's power fractured. The souls who had been denied found new strength—strength to carve out their territories, to shape their kingdoms within the very land that had once rejected them.

The gates—once the sacred threshold between Heaven and the afterlife—no longer represented passage. They were fortresses now, guarded by those who had once feared judgment, now empowered to reshape Heaven as they saw fit.

And Ben? Ben watched, amused, as the paradise he had spent centuries resenting tore itself apart. He hadn't expected this kind of chaos. He hadn't anticipated the beauty of watching it burn from the inside. But now that it had started, there was no stopping it.

The Rising Darkness

But then… something else began to happen.

The problem wasn't just war.

It was worse than that.

Heaven itself was breaking.

The golden light that had once stretched across eternity, the light that had warmed souls and signified purity, began to flicker. It weakened, as though the very foundation of the afterlife had been infected by the chaos that had spread through it. The abyss—the place where Ben had sent all those souls, he had judged unworthy—was no longer contained. It was stretching beyond its boundaries.

At first, it was subtle. A whisper at the edge of existence, a sensation Ben couldn't quite grasp. The air thickened around him, and the world felt wrong in ways he couldn't define. But then it grew.

Some souls began to vanish completely. Not to Heaven. Not to Hell.

But to something else. Something far darker.

Ben saw it. He felt it in the very core of his being. The world he had known was crumbling, not just through war, but because something… something deeper was breaking free. Something that was neither good nor evil, but hungry.

The abyss was no longer just a place of judgment. It was alive. It was waking up. And Ben wasn't sure how much longer Heaven's fragile boundaries could hold it back.

For the first time in his existence, Ben felt fear. A cold, gnawing sensation that coiled in his chest like a snake. The abyss whispered to him; a voice so foreign it sent shivers through him. But the words… they were indistinct, just shadows of sound in his mind.

Still, the fear remained. And Ben hated it.

The Fall of the Gatekeeper

The war reached its peak. Heaven was collapsing. The gates were no longer the gateways to paradise. They had become something else. Something to be guarded. The very air was thick with tension, and the balance—the fragile balance that had held Heaven in place for so long—was coming undone.

The angels had tried to fix it. They had tried to contain the chaos that Ben had unleashed, to put the pieces back together.

They had fought against the souls who had torn their world apart. But as the days passed, it became clear—Ben wasn't just part of the problem. He was the problem.

And so, the angels turned on him.

He had expected it, of course. He had seen this coming the moment he chose to defy the divine order. But not like this. Not with such force. Not with such finality.

He felt it before he saw it—a shift in the air, a weight pressing down on him, a power that threatened to crush him under its might. The divine fury of Heaven itself, the righteousness of a thousand angels, all focused on him. All believing, without question, that he needed to be erased from existence.

And then they came.

Not in small numbers, not as whispering figures at the edge of his vision, but as an army.

Heaven's last army.

Ben felt them before they even touched him—their divine fury, their righteousness, the weight of their belief that they were right, that they had to stop him at all costs. There was no room for discussion, no room for negotiation. They weren't coming to reason with him.

They were coming to end him.

Ben stood from his chair, rolling his shoulders. His hands burned with an energy he didn't recognize—an energy that had been growing inside him ever since the first time he had denied

253

a soul its rightful place in Heaven. He could feel it now, surging through him, the dark energy of rebellion and power.

The void whispered to him. It offered something. Power. Strength. A way to fight back.

But Ben didn't reach for it. Not yet.

He had been waiting for this. For something real. Something he could finally break.

The first angel lunged.

Ben smiled.

And the gates of Heaven shattered.

Chapter 16:

The Fall of Heaven

It started as murmurs—frustration, confusion, disbelief. The saints, the holy ones who had spent their lives in unwavering faith, had always believed Heaven was eternal, unshakable. It was a paradise of purity and reward, a place where only the worthy could enter. But now, they saw it with their own eyes. The unworthy walked among them. Murderers, thieves, tyrants—all granted the same paradise as the pure. The holy men who had spent their lives preaching morality now stood shoulder to shoulder with those who had built their legacies on cruelty and deceit. The martyrs, those who had suffered for their beliefs, were forced to share the afterlife with those who had mocked righteousness, with souls who had trampled on the sacred for their selfish gain.

The fury spread like wildfire, like a storm raging against the heavens. "This is not Heaven!" the saints cried. "We will not stand for this!" They gathered together in the highest courts, in the chambers where they had once praised the eternal light, and now they cursed it. The heavenly choir fell silent, the very air thick with outrage. As their voices rose in protest, so too did the cracks in Heaven's walls. The celestial order, once flawless, now seemed like a fragile thing, held together by nothing more than faith. And as the saints began to rise against the corruption that had taken root, the angels—those who had once stood as Heaven's guardians—began to fall apart.

The Awakening of the Ancient Hunger

Beneath Heaven, deep within the dark places where no living soul had ever dared tread, something stirred. It did not have a name. It did not have a face. It was a force, older than any angel, older than any creation, locked away long before the first saint had stepped through the golden gates. In its prison, it had slept, waiting for the right moment to awaken. And now, with the cracks in Heaven's foundation spreading, it had seeped through.

At first, it was a whisper—barely a thought in the ether. But then came the hunger. A terrible, insatiable need, like the call of a beast starving for its prey. It was a force of nature, a force that began to pull at the souls of the dead, devouring them with a voraciousness that couldn't be contained. Those who had once walked Heaven's streets began to vanish. At first, it was the weak, the forgotten, the lost souls who had slipped through the cracks. Then it came for the warriors, the saints, the very angels who had once been the guardians of Heaven itself.

Saint Valerius was the first to notice it. He stood in a ruined cathedral, a solemn, shattered place where the wounded sought refuge from the war above. As he surveyed the fallen, he heard the first scream. A man, a simple soul who had lived a just and righteous life, fell to the ground clutching his throat. His face twisted in terror as he vanished, his form flickering like a candle about to be extinguished. He was gone as if he had never existed at all.

It wasn't an isolated incident.

It was happening everywhere.

The war had been terrible—souls torn apart in the battle for Heaven, angels falling from grace—but this, this was worse. The hunger did not care for purity or evil. It devoured all, the righteous and the wicked alike. No one was spared. The saints, the angels, and even the fallen souls who had once sought to tear Heaven apart were being consumed by an unseen force. It was as if Heaven itself was being eaten from the inside out.

"Something is coming," Valerius murmured, gripping his sword tighter as he gazed into the darkening skies.

In the heavens above, the stars flickered and dimmed further, their once-bright glow reduced to pale, flickering lights that could not compete with the growing darkness.

Ben's Descent into Doubt and Desperation

Ben had been the one to shatter the gates of Heaven. He had been the one to tear down the old order, believing it to be corrupt beyond repair, convinced that Heaven needed to change. But now, as he sat on his throne amidst the ruins, watching the slow, agonizing dissolution of everything, he couldn't shake the creeping sense that he had made a terrible mistake.

He had not expected this. He had not anticipated the weight of it all. The battle for Heaven had been the easy part—the fight against the angels, the rebellion of the fallen souls, the slow unravelling of Heaven's celestial order. But what came after?

257

What had he actually achieved?

His nights were no longer restful. Every time he closed his eyes, there were shadows that shouldn't have been there, moving in the corners of his vision. Sometimes, he swore he saw Peter standing in the distance, watching him with something in his gaze that wasn't anger or pity, but something worse: disappointment.

"You think you've won," the whispers echoed, faint yet piercing. "But what have you built?"

Ben tried to push it aside, to focus on the present, on the war, on the chaos. But doubt gnawed at him, like a parasite feeding on his certainty. The foundation he had torn down, the paradise he had once believed was meant to be shattered—it wasn't meant to end like this. It wasn't supposed to be a void of destruction.

If Heaven was never meant to be eternal, then what was? What was the point of it all?

Seeking answers, Ben ventured deeper into the ruins of the Eternal City, where once the pillars of divine wisdom had stood tall, untouched by time. The war had left much of the city in tatters—broken towers, shattered statues, streets that led to nowhere. But beneath the surface, there were archives—old, forgotten records that even the angels had long since abandoned. Ben dug through these ancient texts, their pages brittle with age, seeking something that could offer him an explanation. And in the forgotten scrolls, he found records of something older than even the creation of Heaven itself.

258

The inscriptions spoke of the Great Chain—a seal placed upon the void before time began. It was a lock, a barrier to keep something worse than Hell itself from slipping into the world. The gates of Heaven had never just been a means of passage for the dead. They had been a means of containment, a seal to hold back the ancient hunger that had once been locked away.

And Ben... Ben had broken it.

His breath came short, his pulse quickened. He clenched his fists, forcing himself to stay in control. There had to be a way to stop it. To undo the chaos, he had unleashed.

But first, he needed help.

A Last-Ditch Alliance Between Old Enemies

The fighting had not stopped. Even with the growing, impossible threat that loomed over them all, the saints and the damned continued to tear at each other, locked in a fierce struggle that ignored the greater doom inching closer. Saint Valerius, battered but unyielding, fought with all his might to hold his army together. His warriors were losing faith, torn between the righteous and the vengeful. Malakar, the unrelenting warlord of the damned, pushed forward with ferocity, determined to claim the throne for himself and make Heaven his domain.

But it was Ben who would force them to see the truth.

259

He appeared in the middle of the battlefield, stepping onto the blood-soaked earth like a shadow cutting through the chaos. His steps were silent—no weapons in hand, no dramatic speech, no call to arms. Just a presence that rippled through the atmosphere. A voice, calm and steady, that carried above the clamour of war, effortlessly silencing everything in its path.

"Stop."

The fighting didn't cease immediately, but it slowed. Some warriors paused, their hands trembling on their weapons, uncertain whether to heed the command. A warlord, a brutal figure draped in the red of countless battles, raised his sword high, preparing to strike down a kneeling angel. Ben raised his hand, and the ground beneath them trembled, a low hum vibrating in the air.

"I said stop."

For the first time since the war began, the battlefield fell silent. It wasn't just the sound that stilled—it was the very weight of the moment. Time itself seemed to hesitate. The warriors, saints, and demons all stood frozen, eyes locked on Ben. His presence alone held them captive.

Ben slowly turned his gaze toward the battle-weary, the wounded, the ones who had given everything to this war. And in his voice was something darker than anger—something raw, something that bore the weight of a thousand failed decisions.

"You think this is the real battle?" he asked. "You think the war ends when one of you wins?"

260

His eyes lifted toward the heavens, toward the growing fissures in the sky, where the darkness had begun to seep through the cracks in reality. "Look up. Look at what's coming."

The air seemed to grow heavier, charged with an ancient, unknowable force.

Saint Valerius, the first to speak after a long silence, lowered his weapon. He had spent centuries leading armies, and he had lived long enough to know when a war had been lost, when survival came not from triumph but from the will to survive. "What is it you're asking of us, Ben?" he said, his voice cautious but not without curiosity.

Malakar, ever the sceptic, sneered and took a step forward, his red eyes glinting with defiance. "And why should we believe you?" he demanded.

Ben's expression didn't change. His gaze sharpened. "Because the dead are disappearing," he said, the gravity of his words striking deep into the heart of the battlefield. "Not just from Heaven. From existence."

A ripple ran through the soldiers. The murmurs started as whispers but grew louder. Malakar, usually so unshakable, faltered for a brief moment, his confidence cracking at the edges.

"We can fight each other until there's nothing left," Ben said, his voice steady, holding their gaze. "Or we can fight the thing that's coming."

The words hung in the air like an impossible choice. For a long, strained moment, no one moved, no one spoke. Then, to Ben's

261

surprise, Saint Valerius knelt. Slowly, with the sound of Armor shifting and the weight of history pressing down on him, others followed. Angels, saints, even some of the damned. One by one, they knelt in recognition of the truth that Ben had just revealed.

Only Malakar remained standing. The warlord looked down at the others, a smirk curling on his lips as he tossed his sword to the ground with a loud clang.

"This had better be worth it," he said, his voice dripping with suspicion, but no longer with the venomous hostility it had once held. For the first time, there was an odd respect in his eyes—a recognition that the war they had fought for so long had been a distraction from something far worse.

The War Moves to Earth and Hell

As the alliance formed on the battlefield, the cracks in Heaven spread outward. Earth was next. The living began to witness things they were never meant to see. The sky flickered, distorted like an image on a broken screen. Shadows moved where they should not have been. The dead no longer rested in their graves—some wandered in confusion, unable to find their way to an afterlife that no longer existed in the way it once had.

Priests fell to their knees, clutching their chests in panic as the divine presence they had always relied upon began to slip away. The connection to the heavens, the feeling of the holy and the righteous, faded like a distant dream.

In Hell, the demons—creatures of fire and brimstone, once emboldened by their eternal torment—no longer laughed. The flames that had always burned so brightly now flickered dimly, losing their heat, their purpose. The screams of the damned seemed quieter, distant. There was no joy in suffering now. Lucifer himself stood at the edge of his throne, staring upward with a furrowed brow. He had ruled Hell for millennia, never once shaken by any force from Heaven. But this was different.

The void, the insatiable hunger, was reaching for them, too.

And that meant Hell had a choice: Let it take them, or fight.

Lucifer smirked, his eyes gleaming with dark amusement, and turned to his generals. "Summon the legions," he commanded, his voice low but filled with unyielding resolve.

When Heaven's gates had first been shattered, the demons had cheered. They had revelled in the destruction of the divine order. Now, however, they marched alongside the angels, the saints, and the damned, united not by choice but by necessity. They all faced the same threat. The lines between Heaven, Earth, and Hell had blurred, and the struggle for power seemed trivial in the face of the void that threatened them all.

The Last Hope

The sky above flickered again, as unseen forces ripped through the very fabric of reality. Heaven, Earth, and Hell stood on the edge of total collapse, caught in the tug-of-war between survival and destruction.

The final battle was coming.

Ben stood at the ruined gates of Heaven, the place where it all began. At his side stood Saint Valerius, his Armor still bloodied but his resolve unbroken. Malakar, now fully armed, sharpened his blade with grim determination. Lucifer, standing at the edges of the battlefield, watched with his unreadable gaze. His presence, cold and calculating, seemed to stir the very air around them.

For the first time in history, angels and demons, saints and sinners, mortals and immortals, stood together. Their differences no longer mattered. They were no longer enemies. They were the last hope against something far worse than the war that had consumed them all.

And beyond the broken sky, the hunger waited, its presence a promise of doom, an inevitable end to everything they had ever known. It was not just a force of destruction. It was the beginning of something much worse—the erasure of all things, a void that consumed even the concept of existence.

The battlefield was silent. The final confrontation was inevitable. And yet, in the faces of those who had once been enemies, there was a flicker of hope—a hope that, for the first time, they might stand a chance against the darkness that had awakened.

Chapter 17:

A Universe in Crisis

The fall of Heaven did not go unnoticed. At first, the changes were subtle—a shift in the air, an imbalance so delicate that only a few attuned souls might have perceived it. But soon, that subtlety gave way to an undeniable tremor. The Earth began to feel the ripple effects of Heaven's disintegration, and the world trembled under the weight of a universe on the brink of collapse.

The Earth Fractures

At first, the disturbances were small, almost imperceptible. Ripples in reality—distortions that spread through the fabric of existence like cracks forming in glass. On Earth, the signs were there: storms that seemed to come out of nowhere, hurricanes that formed in places where the waters had always been still and calm. The sky darkened in unusual ways, as if the sun itself was unsure of where it belonged. Seasons shifted unpredictably—snow fell in the middle of summer, and oppressive heatwaves rolled in during the dead of winter.

But then, the phenomena grew more pronounced. The stars, once a constant fixture in the night sky, began to flicker erratically. Some nights entire constellations disappeared, swallowed by a darkness too vast to comprehend, only for new, unfamiliar stars to take their place. It was as though the heavens themselves were being rewritten, the very laws of the universe unravelling before the eyes of those who dared to look up.

The animals were the first to sense the true weight of the change. Birds, those creatures of instinct and migration, abandoned their flight paths. Their once-perfect navigation, honed over millennia, failed them for the first time in history. Whales, those gentle giants of the ocean, began to beach themselves in unprecedented numbers. The mournful cries of these stranded creatures echoed through the void as though they, too, were aware of the horror unfolding. Dogs, in particular, howled endlessly at the sky, their cries growing hoarse as though they could feel the unravelling of the world beneath their paws, yet no one could stop them. It was as if nature itself was becoming unmoored.

And then the disappearances began. Entire towns vanished, as though erased from existence. One moment, they stood— brimming with life, humming with the everyday rhythms of existence. The next, they were gone. Not destroyed, not ravaged by fire or flood—simply erased. No rubble, no remnants, just an empty wasteland that had once been full of people. It was as though they had never existed at all.

Those left behind began to fracture as well. Their sense of reality started to dissolve, and their memories unravelled like fragile threads caught in a storm. A woman in Berlin forgot her own name, and the words she spoke came in a long-dead language that no one could understand. A man in New York City swore his wife had never existed, even though photographs, birth certificates, and every memory he'd ever cherished told another story. Time, once a steady and predictable flow, now became a fractured and unreliable stream.

The balance between life and death, order and chaos, had shattered. As war raged in Heaven above, Earth was left to feel the devastating consequences. What had once been a world of structure and certainty was now a place of confusion and terror, where nothing—whether alive or dead—was safe from the rippling effects of the universe's unravelling. As Heaven tore itself apart, so too did the very fabric of existence on Earth.

The first war broke out within a week of the global disasters. It wasn't a war sparked by borders or resources, but by fear—fear of the unknown, fear of the forces ripping apart reality itself. Governments, already reeling from natural and unnatural calamities, struggled to respond. They were overwhelmed, fractured by their inability to control the chaos. Countries that had existed in a delicate balance for centuries suddenly found themselves at each other's throats. Long-standing alliances dissolved, and treaties once thought inviolable were tossed aside, meaningless in the face of an unpredictable world unravelling at the seams.

Paranoia became the new currency. Nations turned inward, erecting walls, both literal and metaphorical. They accused each other of secret weapons, of covert plans to exploit the chaos, and of manipulating the disasters for their own gain. Diplomatic channels closed, and every piece of intelligence was questioned, no matter how insignificant it seemed. There was no trust left, only suspicion.

And the wars that followed were no longer about power or territory. They were wars fought over the most primal of

267

fears— fear of extinction, fear of the unknown, fear of losing everything in a world that was losing its grip on reality.

Cities that had once been symbols of human achievement now burned, reduced to ash and rubble as rioting mobs and military forces clashed in the streets. Desperation turned to violence. The streets became filled with the lost and the frightened, those desperate to find meaning in the madness. As civilization fractured, so did the people. Cults sprouted overnight—some preaching salvation through purification, others calling for mass sacrifice to appease unseen forces. Each belief system struggled to hold onto relevance, while the people clung to anything that promised answers, or at least an end to the terror.

Religions, too, began to fracture. The faithful, already shaken by the inexplicable disasters, found themselves at odds with each other. Some believed that the disasters were the heralds of the apocalypse—signs that the end times had come at last. Others believed Heaven had forsaken them entirely, abandoning them to suffer the consequences of their own sins. No matter which side they chose, both groups were right in a way. Heaven had fallen, and with it, the delicate balance between life and death had been irrevocably shattered.

In places of worship, priests and clerics wept openly, unable to hear the voice of God for the first time in history. The devout, who had spent their lives looking for signs of divine purpose, now screamed at the heavens, demanding answers. But Heaven remained silent—because Heaven was at war. And the weight of that war crushed everything beneath it, even the mortal world.

Emma: A Mother on the Edge of Reality

Amidst this global collapse, there was Emma. She wasn't a prophet, nor was she anyone of particular importance in the grand scheme of things. She didn't understand the full extent of what was happening, but she could feel it—this deep, gnawing wrongness that wrapped itself around her heart and twisted her every thought. It wasn't something she could explain, but it was something she couldn't ignore.

She felt it in the quiet moments, when everything should have been calm. When the world outside her window should have been at peace, she would sense the tension—the unspoken anxiety in the air. Lena, her daughter, had always been sensitive to things beyond the ordinary, but lately, it was becoming impossible to deny the signs. Emma watched as Lena woke up in the middle of the night, crying, her tiny hands reaching out for something invisible. Lena would stare at the ceiling with wide, frightened eyes, as though she saw something Emma couldn't. Emma's own thoughts would spiral, wondering if her daughter was simply frightened by the nightmares children often had—or if there was something more sinister in the unseen spaces between their reality and the one, they no longer understood.

It wasn't just Lena. Emma herself felt the unsettling sense that the world around her had changed. The sky, the stars—they didn't look the same. There were gaps in the constellations now, stars that blinked out of existence, only to be replaced by unfamiliar ones that shouldn't have been there. Planes, once so reliable in their course, now vanished mid-flight without explanation. Entire cities flickered in and out of existence for fractions of a second, as though they were shadows cast by a world that was being torn apart at the seams.

Emma didn't understand what was happening. She couldn't explain it. But she knew deep down that something was terribly wrong.

For months, Emma had struggled to rebuild her life. She had forced herself to believe that Ben was truly gone, that she had to move forward. For herself. For Lena. But then the nightmares started. They came in the quiet hours of the night, when her mind was the most vulnerable. In her dreams, she saw Ben, standing in a place she didn't recognize—somewhere beyond Heaven, in a sky that wasn't a sky at all. His face was different, harder, colder. His hands, once warm and comforting, were stained black with something she couldn't name. In the dream, she saw Heaven burning, angels falling, and Ben—sitting at the gates, watching it all unfold in silence.

"Ben! What's happening?" she called out to him in her dream, but he didn't respond. His eyes locked onto hers, and for a moment—just a moment—she saw the man she had once loved. Then, he turned away, walking deeper into the chaos.

Emma woke up gasping for air, drenched in sweat, her hands shaking as if she had touched something unholy. The sky outside her window rumbled with distant thunder, though the weather forecast had promised clear skies. The storm was coming. And this time, Emma was certain that it wasn't just the weather. Something was wrong with the very fabric of reality itself.

The Thing Beyond the Gates

Back in Heaven, Ben leaned back in his chair, watching the destruction unfold. The endless war between the angels and the damned had spread like wildfire, igniting every corner of the once-immaculate paradise. But as his gaze wandered through the chaos, he didn't focus on the screams or the flames that now consumed the golden streets. No, he focused on something much darker—the quiet presence that lingered just beyond the gates.

He could feel it. The war in Heaven was no longer contained. The cracks in the foundations of this divine realm had deepened, spreading outward like a growing infection. The air itself felt thick with something unfamiliar. Reality was beginning to fracture, and Ben felt the very edges of existence bending and tearing in places it wasn't supposed to.

The thing beyond the gates was stirring. It had been quiet at first, a distant echo that brushed the edges of his mind. But now, it whispered—not in words, but in weight. In the heavy, pressing silence that filled the air, something ancient and immeasurably vast was waking. It was as if the silence itself was alive, seeping into the cracks that Ben had created, filling the void he had torn open.

Ben saw shadows where there should have been light. Faint, flickering, like the shadow of something that shouldn't exist in this realm. He could feel it—the presence of something far beyond anything he had ever known. It was watching, waiting, and it felt... hungry.

271

Somewhere, deep inside him, a small voice whispered, *this wasn't supposed to happen.* The universe had been set into motion by forces far older and more powerful than anything Ben could comprehend. He had shattered the rules, he had broken Heaven, but in doing so, he had unleashed something far darker than even he had imagined. And now, as the weight of the broken world pressed down on him, he realized that he had opened the gates to something far more dangerous than any of the celestial beings could ever be.

Yet, Ben didn't care.

His mind was no longer on the war, no longer on the angels or the armies tearing each other apart in the streets. His focus had shifted entirely, and there was only one thing on his mind—Emma and Lena.

He could feel them. Even with everything crumbling around him, even with the weight of a broken universe pressing down on his chest, Emma and Lena were the only thing that mattered. They were his anchor, the ones he had tried to save, and the ones he had failed. But now, in the midst of destruction and chaos, he could feel them both—tethered to him in a way he hadn't known was possible.

Ben had rewritten the rules of Heaven. He had broken reality itself by tearing open the gates and allowing the chaos to seep in.

But if reality could bend, if Heaven could crumble, then why couldn't he rewrite it again? Why couldn't he bend it to his will?

The universe was falling apart. The thing beyond the gates was awake, and it was stretching its influence further into the realm,

272

threatening to consume everything in its path. The universe was already spiralling into madness—what was one more rewrite?

Ben leaned forward in his throne, his fingers tightening around the armrests. The whispers grew louder, but they didn't scare him. Nothing scared him anymore. The war, the chaos, the thing beyond the gates—they were all just obstacles in the way of what he needed to do. If the universe was breaking, then he would break it further. If reality was bending, then he would send it to his will. He would break Heaven. He would break the world.

And if something—*anything*—tried to stop him, then let it come.

Chapter 18:

Peter's Return

Ben sat at the gates, watching Heaven burn. The familiar smell of smoke and the acrid scent of destruction filled the air. It had taken longer than he expected, but the war was reaching its climax. The righteous had fought hard, but the sinners fought harder. The wicked were used to war. The righteous weren't. And the longer the battle raged, the more Ben realized just how much he'd underestimated the depths of their strength.

Every day, more angels abandoned their posts. More clouds ran red with the blood of those who had fallen, saints and sinners alike. The golden streets were now little more than a memory, stained with fire and chaos.

He should have felt triumphant, the weight of victory pressing down on him like a cloak. He had done it. He had broken the gates. He had freed Heaven from its restraints. The chains had been cast aside. But now, as the smoke billowed and the sound of conflict roared in the distance, he felt something else. A hollow, sinking feeling deep In his chest.

He just felt... tired. Tired of fighting. Tired of watching everything unravel.

And then, he heard it.

"Jesus Christ, Holloway. What the hell did you do?"

Ben stiffened. He knew that voice.

274

Slowly, he turned in his chair, and there, standing amidst the smoke and ruin, was Peter. His expression was a blend of disbelief and sheer, unfiltered rage. Peter's white robes, so familiar in their purity, were gone, replaced by a long coat that looked like it had been through a war—or maybe several. His once calm, world-weary face was drawn tight with frustration, the deep lines etched from centuries of duty now marked with anger and exhaustion.

Ben took a slow drag of his cigarette, exhaling a cloud of smoke into the ruined sky. He couldn't bring himself to smile or feel any satisfaction. "Took you long enough."

Peter didn't blink. His gaze scanned the wasteland that had once been Heaven, and he shook his head in disbelief. "I wasn't exactly eager to clean up your mess."

Peter stepped forward, surveying the battlefield like a general assessing a lost war. Saints and sinners still clashed in the distance, the golden towers of Heaven collapsing under the weight of destruction. His gaze flicked over the carnage, the bodies scattered across the ruins, the blood staining the streets that had once glowed with divine light.

"You really let them in," Peter muttered. "All of them."

Ben shrugged nonchalantly. "It seemed fair."

Peter laughed. It wasn't a kind laugh. It was a bitter, empty sound that echoed through the silence. "Fair?" he echoed, his voice dripping with sarcasm. "You think this is fair?"

With a snap of his fingers, everything changed.

275

Ben's cigarette fell from his lips as the scenery shifted around him. The gates of Heaven, the ruined city, the battle raging around them—everything faded away in an instant. The air grew cooler, and the ground beneath his feet shifted. Suddenly, he wasn't at the gates of Heaven anymore. He wasn't in the heart of the celestial war. He was standing on Earth.

On the Ranch.

His ranch.

Except it wasn't his anymore. It hadn't been for a long time.

Ben's heart sank as he took in the sight before him. The land, once thriving under his care, was now desolate. The crops had withered, the fields stretched barren, the fences sagged with rot. The ranch had been abandoned by hope, the dreams that once flourished here now dead and forgotten. And there, standing in the doorway of the small house, was Emma.

She was staring out at the land, her face pale and drawn. She looked thinner, exhausted. The weight of the world seemed to have settled on her shoulders, pressing down until she could barely stand. Her eyes were hollow, void of the spark that had once been there. She was a woman broken by the unrelenting pressure of survival.

In her arms, she held Lena, rocking her gently as the child whimpered, her cries muffled by the desolation around them. The land had given up, and so had Emma. She was holding on by the thinnest of threads.

Ben swallowed hard; his throat tight. This wasn't how it was supposed to be.

Peter stood beside him, arms still crossed, his expression unreadable as he watched the scene unfold. "You wanted justice, right?"

Ben clenched his fists, his heart beating faster with growing anger and guilt. "What did you do?"

Peter scoffed, his voice cold and unyielding. "Me? I didn't do anything, kid. You did this."

Ben's eyes snapped toward him. His pulse raced as he spun to face Peter. "Bullshit."

Peter's eyes locked onto Ben's without flinching. "When you broke Heaven, you broke everything. Earth included."

Ben's stomach twisted as the realization sank in. His actions had consequences beyond anything he could have imagined. The war in Heaven hadn't just destroyed paradise—it had bled into the very fabric of the world he had once called home. The Earth, the land, the life that once thrived under his and Emma's care—everything had been shattered.

He turned back to the ranch, his eyes burning with regret. Emma was struggling—not just emotionally, but financially, physically. She had no help. No support. She was barely keeping things together, trying to survive in a world that had slipped beyond her control.

She had given up on the dream they had built together, the dream that had once seemed so attainable. Without him, it had all fallen apart.

And Ben... Ben had been too busy playing god, too consumed by his quest for power, to notice. To see what had been slipping through his fingers.

He wasn't just watching Heaven burn. He was watching his life, his family, his love, crumble right before his eyes. And he had no idea how to fix it.

Ben's cigarette fell from his lips as the scenery shifted around him. He wasn't at the gates anymore. He wasn't in Heaven. He was standing on Earth. On the ranch. His ranch. Except it wasn't his anymore. It hadn't been for a long time.

Emma stood in the doorway, staring out at the land, her face pale and drawn. She looked thinner. Exhausted. Like the weight of the world had settled on her shoulders, pressing down until she could barely stand. The once-vibrant fields now looked barren, patches of dry earth and dead crops scattered across the horizon. The barn, once sturdy and full of life, stood in disrepair. The air felt thick with a sense of abandonment, the silence ringing louder than any noise could.

She held Lena in her arms, rocking her gently as the child whimpered. Ben's heart clenched at the sound. The child he had never really known, the child he had left behind. He had seen her only a handful of times before he left for Heaven, but now, as he looked at her, it was like seeing her for the first time. She had grown in his absence, but not just in height—there was a sadness in her eyes, an understanding of things no child should know. The crops had withered. The land was dying.

Ben swallowed hard. This wasn't how it was supposed to be. This wasn't what he had imagined when he left. He had thought that Heaven, whatever it was, would be the answer, that it would fix everything. But looking at Emma now, looking at the barren land, he knew he had been wrong. So very wrong.

Peter stood beside him; arms still crossed. "You wanted justice, right?"

Ben clenched his fists. "What did you do?"

Peter scoffed; his tone cold, indifferent. "Me? I didn't do anything, kid. You did this."

Ben's pulse quickened, his thoughts spinning. "Bullshit."

Peter met his eyes without flinching. "When you broke Heaven, you broke everything. Earth included." His words hit harder than any punch could. Ben's stomach twisted, the weight of the truth settling like a stone in his chest.

Ben turned his gaze back to Emma, his heart heavy with regret. She was struggling. Not just emotionally. Financially. Physically. She was barely holding on, trying to keep everything from collapsing, and yet it was all slipping through her fingers. The land, once full of potential, now lay in ruin. The dream they had built together seemed like a distant memory, a fleeting vision that was already fading.

She had no help. No one to turn to. Ben had abandoned her, left her to face the world alone while he sought some kind of redemption or understanding in Heaven. And now, all he saw was a woman at the end of her rope, holding on to the last bit of hope for the sake of her child.

She had given up on the dream they had built together. Because without him, it had all fallen apart. The foundation was cracked, the walls crumbled, and the future they had once envisioned was nothing more than a broken promise.

And Ben… Ben had been too busy playing god to notice. Too consumed by his journey for meaning to see the destruction he had left behind. The guilt weighed on him, suffocating him, a constant reminder of the choices he had made. He had been the one to break Heaven, to fracture the balance, to put all of this in motion. Now, standing in the middle of the wreckage, he was forced to confront the consequences of his actions.

Peter stepped forward, his voice quieter now. Sharper. "You wanted to punish the universe for what it took from you," he said, his words slicing through the air. "So, you let the gates open. You threw away the rules. You let chaos in. And for what?"
Ben didn't answer. The weight of Peter's words hung heavy in the air, each one driving a wedge deeper into his chest. He had wanted to fix things. To make the universe feel the way he had felt—broken, betrayed, and abandoned. But now, in the silence that followed, he realized how wrong he had been.

Peter's voice grew harsher. "Look at her."
Ben didn't want to. But he did.

Emma sank into a chair on the porch, her face buried in her hands. She was crying. The sight hit him like a punch to the gut. She had always been so strong, so full of life, but now, she was nothing more than a shadow of that woman. Her shoulders trembled with the weight of a grief he had never fully understood until now. Lena tugged at her sleeve, confused and

280

scared, too young to understand why everything was falling apart. Her innocent eyes flickered between her mother and the broken world around her, seeking some sense of comfort, but finding none. Ben felt something crack in his chest, the guilt and sorrow mingling into a painful ache.

"This is what you've done," Peter said, his voice now a low rasp. "Not just to Heaven. Not just to the angels. To her. To the woman you loved."
Ben's hands shook. The reality of it all was hitting him harder than any confrontation with Peter could. He had been so consumed by his grief, his anger, and his need for revenge against the universe that he hadn't once thought about the ones left behind—the people who were still trapped in the broken world.

The world had gone to hell. And she had to live in it.

The vision shifted, pulling him deeper into the rawness of Emma's suffering. He saw her in the field, struggling to repair a broken fence post, her hands calloused and bruised from doing work she was never meant to do alone. She wasn't the woman he had left behind. She was a shell, worn down by the weight of everything she had to carry. He saw her skipping meals so Lena could eat, her stomach growling in hunger, but she never let on. She kept up the façade, always making sure Lena was fed, even when there was barely enough for herself.

He saw the exhaustion in her eyes when she stared at old pictures of him, her fingers brushing over the faces in the photographs as if trying to hold onto the past. Wondering if she was strong enough to keep going. Every night, she would sit on the porch, drinking coffee that had gone cold, staring at the

empty fields as if she were waiting for something—someone—
to come back. She never cried in front of Lena. But at night,
when the little girl was asleep, Emma let herself break. She
would whisper Ben's name like a prayer, hoping for something,
anything to change, but knowing no one would answer. The
silence that followed her whispered name was deafening.

Peter's voice was softer now, a touch of sadness in his tone.
"You were so busy fighting the universe that you forgot about
the ones who were still in it."
Ben's breath hitched. The truth of Peter's words hit him like a
tidal wave. The people he had left behind weren't just memories.
They were real. And he had destroyed their lives, all in the name
of some warped sense of justice.

Emma wiped at her eyes, took a deep breath, and forced herself
back to her feet. She always got back up. She had to. She was
the pillar, the only one holding together the broken pieces of
their life. Ben had spent eternity believing she would be fine
without him. That she could handle it. But now, standing here,
watching her struggle to hold together a life that was slowly
slipping through her fingers, he realized just how wrong he had
been.

And for the first time since he had arrived in Heaven… he
wanted to go back. Not to escape the pain or the consequences
of his actions, but to try to fix what he had broken. To be there
for her. To fight for her. To show her the love and devotion he
had failed to give her before.

Penter stepped forward, his voice quieter now. Sharper. "You
wanted to punish the universe for what it took from you," he
said. "So, you let the gates open. You threw away the rules.

282

You let chaos in. And for what?"

Ben didn't answer. There was nothing he could say. Every word felt like an empty excuse. He had been blinded by his grief, convinced that breaking everything would somehow fix his pain. But standing there, with the weight of his choices pressing down on him, he realized how foolish he had been.

Peter's voice grew harsher. "Look at her." Ben didn't want to. He couldn't bear it.

But he did.

Emma sank into a chair on the porch, her face buried in her hands. Her shoulders trembled with silent sobs, and Ben could hear the quiet, shuddering breath as she tried to hold herself together. She was crying. The woman he had once known— strong, fierce, always the rock—was broken. The weight of everything had crushed her, and he hadn't been there to help her carry it. Lena, just a little girl, tugged at her sleeve, confused and scared. Her eyes flicked back and forth between her mother and the shattered world around them. She was too young to understand the depth of the tragedy, but the fear in her eyes was unmistakable. Ben felt something crack in his chest, a pain so sharp it was almost unbearable.

"This is what you've done," Peter said, his voice full of accusation. "Not just to Heaven. Not just to the angels. To her. To the woman you loved."

Ben's hands shook. His mind was racing, trying to comprehend the reality of what he was seeing. He had been so focused on his grief, his anger, so consumed by the belief that the universe owed him something, that he hadn't once considered the damage he was leaving in his wake.

283

The world had gone to hell. And she had to live in it.

The vision shifted, pulling Ben deeper into the torment of Emma's life since he left. He saw her, day after day, struggling to repair a broken fence post, her hands calloused and bruised from Labor she was never meant to do alone. She was carrying the weight of a farm that had been built by two people, but now, it was hers to fix and maintain. Ben watched helplessly as she skipped meals so that Lena could eat, her hunger a quiet sacrifice she bore in silence. The exhaustion in her eyes when she stared at old pictures of him hit him like a punch to the gut. She wasn't just missing him—she was wondering if she could survive without him.

The nights were the worst.

He saw her sitting on the porch, drinking coffee that had gone cold, staring at the empty fields as though she were waiting for something—someone—to come back. But the silence stretched on, and no one was coming. The realization hit him with brutal force: she had been waiting for him, and he had never come back.

She never cried in front of Lena. But at night, when the little girl was asleep, Emma let herself break. Ben could hear her whispered name as she crumbled into the darkness. She spoke it like a prayer, like a plea for something, anything to return, but she knew there would be no answer.

Peter's voice softened, but there was still a sting in his words. "You were so busy fighting the universe that you forgot about the ones who were still in it."

284

Ben's breath hitched. The truth was a hard pill to swallow. He had thought he was fighting for justice, for a sense of peace, but he had never realized the true cost. It wasn't just about him. He wasn't the only one suffering.

Emma wiped at her eyes, took a deep breath, and forced herself back to her feet. She always got back up. She had to. She had no choice but to keep moving forward, even when everything inside her screamed to stop.

Ben had spent eternity believing she would be fine without him, convinced that she was strong enough to endure on her own. But now, standing here, watching her piece together the fragments of a broken life, he realized just how wrong he had been. She had never been fine. She had been surviving, just barely, and all the while, he had been blind to her pain.

And for the first time since he had arrived in Heaven... he wanted to go back. Not to fix what he had broken in Heaven, but to fix what he had broken here, on Earth. To go back to Emma, to help her rebuild, to be there for her in ways he never had been. It wasn't too late. He could make it right. Or at least try.

"You see it now, don't you?" Peter asked, stepping closer. His voice was sharp, but there was an undercurrent of something else—something almost like sorrow in the way he spoke. "The cost of your so-called justice."

Ben's jaw clenched, his fists tightening at his sides. He turned to Peter, the anger and regret crashing together in his chest like a violent storm. The weight of what he had done was suffocating,

285

and all he wanted was to make it right. "Fix it," he demanded, his voice low and strained.

Peter sighed, the sound heavy with both frustration and resignation. "It's not that simple."
"Bullshit," Ben spat, his voice shaking with the force of his emotions. "You showed me this. You can undo it."
Peter met his gaze with an unwavering, almost pitying look. "No, Ben. You have to undo it."

Ben's breath came in ragged, uneven bursts, his chest tight with a rising panic. "How?" His voice cracked slightly, desperation creeping into his tone.

Peter didn't immediately respond. Instead, he tilted his head toward the heavens—the once beautiful expanse that had now become a twisted mockery of itself. What remained of Heaven was a battlefield, a place where the skies burned and the air hummed with the chaos of war. "You have to put it back together," Peter said quietly, almost as if he were talking to himself.

Ben's gaze followed Peter's gesture, drawn to the heavens above. The war raged on in full force. The sinners were still rising, merciless and relentless, their destruction sweeping through the lands. The angels, those who still stood, were outnumbered and failing. The golden light of Heaven—the light that had once symbolized purity and peace—was flickering. It was dying, and with it, the last hope for salvation.

Ben's heart sank as he realized the extent of the damage. "It's too late," he whispered, his voice barely audible against the howling wind. The thought of trying to fix it seemed impossible.

He had broken everything—Heaven, Earth, and even the lives of the people he loved.

"No," Peter's voice was firm, unyielding. "It's not."

Ben swallowed hard; his throat dry as dust. "And if I try?"

Peter's expression turned grim, the weight of the situation sinking into his features. "Then you fight harder than you ever have before." The words were a challenge, a call to action that Ben couldn't ignore.

A gust of wind swept across the field, carrying with it the scent of the dying land. Dust swirled at their feet, caught in the air like remnants of the destruction that had come to pass. Ben looked back toward the porch, where Emma was sitting, Lena held tightly in her arms. Emma shivered in the cold, the fading warmth of the sun casting long shadows over her worn face. She looked small, and fragile—like a woman who had given up too much for too long. Lena, nestled against her, looked up at her mother with wide, innocent eyes, sensing that something was wrong but unable to understand the true weight of it all.

Ben took one last, lingering look at them—at the life he had once known, at what he had left behind. His heart clenched in his chest, the reality of what he had nearly destroyed coming crashing down on him. It wasn't just Heaven that had fallen apart—it was everything.

And yet, in that moment, something inside him shifted. A sliver of hope pierced through the darkness.

Peter watched him silently, his gaze steady and understanding as if he knew the battle raging inside Ben. "Time to clean up your

287

mess, Holloway," Peter said softly, his voice laced with quiet determination.

Ben nodded once, the decision settling deep within him. He had made the choice. There was no turning back now.

He turned away from Emma and Lena, walking toward the horizon. Toward the fire. Toward the broken gates of Heaven. There was no guarantee of success, no promise of victory, but there was something he had to do—something only he could do.

It wasn't too late. Not yet.

Ben walked forward with purpose, ready to face the consequences of his actions. Ready to fight, no matter the cost. The gates of Heaven were still broken. But if there was a way to mend them, to heal the rift he had created, he would find it. No matter how much he had to sacrifice.

It was time to fix what he had broken.

Chapter 19:

The Offer

Ben stood frozen; his gaze locked on Emma. The woman he loved. The life he had lost. She sat there, on the porch, holding their daughter as the wind swept through the dying fields. The world around them was crumbling, but Emma remained, trying her best to hold things together—like she always had. But even she had limits.

Lena, so small, so fragile, nestled against her, unaware of how much had been stolen from her. Unaware of how much her father had broken. Ben's heart clenched as he watched them, a sharp pang of guilt stabbing deep into his chest. It was all his fault. He had done this to them. And now, he had to live with it.

A hand clamped onto his shoulder, grounding him. Ben didn't need to look to know who it was. Peter.

"Hurts, doesn't it?" Peter said, his voice is rough but not unkind. "Watching what you've done?"

Ben didn't answer. He couldn't. The words were stuck, lodged somewhere deep in his throat where they couldn't escape. He felt like he was choking on them, suffocating under the weight of his own choices. He had been so focused on his anger, his need for vengeance against the universe, that he hadn't stopped to consider the consequences. Not for Heaven, not for the angels, and certainly not for Emma.

The vision blurred for a moment, then snapped back into focus, sharper than before. He saw Emma not just suffering, but surviving. She tended the fields even when the soil refused to yield. She carried Lena on her hip as she bartered for supplies, patched the holes in their home, and fought back against a world that seemed determined to crush them both. Ben clenched his fists. He should have been there.

Peter sighed; his breath heavy with something like sympathy. "I'm not here to rub it in, kid. I'm here to give you a choice."

Ben forced himself to look at him. "A choice?"

Peter nodded, his face stern. "A deal."

Ben exhaled slowly, a mix of wariness and bitterness coiling in his chest. "I'm listening."

Peter's expression darkened, his eyes flicking up to the sky, where dark storm clouds gathered ominously. "You broke Heaven." He gestured toward the distant echoes of battle, the cries of angels clashing with the sinners in the chaos. The heavens above were torn apart, the once-glorious city of light now a war-torn ruin. "And you're going to fix it."

Ben huffed a bitter laugh. "Fix it? That place was a mess before I got there."

Peter's patience seemed to snap. "Yeah, but you threw gasoline on the fire." He levelled a hard stare at Ben. "You think you were the first to hate the system? You weren't. But you're the first idiot dumb enough to tear the whole thing down without thinking about what comes next."

Ben frowned, the sting of Peter's words cutting deeper than he expected. He wasn't wrong.

But Ben wasn't ready to admit it. Not yet.

Peter took a step closer, lowering his voice. "You want to go back."

Ben's stomach tightened. He did. More than anything. The thought of holding Emma again, of feeling her warmth against him, of being a father to Lena, haunted him.

"I can't," Ben whispered, his voice faltering. He wanted to, more than anything, but he couldn't see a way back.

Peter's gaze was unwavering. "I'll make it so you can."

Ben stilled. The air around them thickened, charged with something greater than Heaven or Earth, something that seemed to reach beyond the realm of possibility.

"You fix this," Peter said, his voice a low promise, "and I'll give you one day."

Ben's breath hitched. "One day?"

Peter nodded. "You can't stay. You can't rewrite time. But you'll have twenty-four hours with them."

The weight of the offer hit Ben like a physical blow. One day. A single sunrise, a single night. Was it enough? No. But it was something.

He closed his eyes, imagining what it would be like to hold Emma again, to hear Lena's laugh, to be there for them in ways

291

he hadn't been. The pain of it all welled up in his chest, threatening to overwhelm him.

"What do I have to do?" Ben asked, his voice barely above a whisper.

Peter's smirk was sharp, but there was no humour in it. "You're going to clean up your mess."

Ben's eyes flicked toward Heaven—the ruins of what had once been a place of peace, now torn apart by the war he had started. The power vacuum he had created had left the afterlife in shambles. The balance between good and evil was gone, and now it was his responsibility to restore it.

Ben ran a hand through his hair, his mind racing. What was he even supposed to do? Where did he start?

For Emma. For Lena.

"Fine," Ben said, his voice firm despite the lingering uncertainty. "I'll do it."

Peter studied him for a moment, waiting, as if he expected Ben to take it back, to fight against the inevitable. When Ben remained silent, Peter sighed, almost resigned.

"This isn't going to be easy," he warned. "You didn't just mess things up—you shattered the system." He gestured to the war raging in the sky. "Fixing this won't just mean kicking out the bad guys. It means restoring balance."

292

Ben gritted his teeth. "And how the hell do I do that?"

Peter's smirk returned, but it was laced with something darker. "You figure it out. That's your punishment."

Ben turned back toward the ranch, his eyes landing on Emma, who had gotten up from the porch, walking into the house with Lena clinging to her side. He wondered if she ever thought about him. If, in those quiet moments between exhaustion and sleep, she whispered his name like he wished he could whisper hers.

One day. It wasn't enough, but it was all he had.

Ben straightened. He had a job to do. Heaven, Earth, the balance of the universe—it was all in his hands now.

"All right," he said, his voice steady, though his heart pounded in his chest. "Let's fix Heaven."

Peter raised a brow as if sensing the weight of what had just passed between them. "And the world."

Ben sighed, the reality of what lay ahead sinking in. "Yeah, yeah. That too."

And with that, he turned back toward the storm, toward the chaos he had caused, knowing that whatever happened next, it was up to him to make it right.

As Ben steeled himself for the daunting task ahead, Peter's expression grew darker, his tone shifting to one of gravity. "You know, there's one more thing I didn't mention."

Ben turned, eyes narrowing, ready for the additional burden Peter was about to drop on him. "What's that?"

293

"The war up there—it's worse than you think." Peter paused, his gaze flicking toward the storm clouds gathering in the distance. "Heaven's not just in ruins. It's being rewritten. Someone else is trying to take control."

Ben stiffened, a cold shiver racing down his spine. "Who?"

Peter hesitated, his jaw tightening as though he was unwilling to speak the name. Finally, he muttered, "An old adversary of yours. One who has been waiting for an opportunity like this."

A sinking feeling settled in Ben's stomach. The chaos he had unleashed hadn't just ruptured Heaven—it had given someone else the power to move in, to seize the opportunity he had created. Someone far worse. Someone who wouldn't let him simply waltz back in to fix things. "So, what you're saying is, this isn't just about undoing my mistake," Ben said, his voice low and strained. "It's about stopping whoever stepped into the void."

Peter nodded grimly. "Exactly. And time is running out."

Ben exhaled sharply, frustration mingling with his growing fear. "Great. Just another day in paradise."

Peter smirked, but it was a cold, humourless expression. "You wanted a second chance, Holloway. Let's see if you deserve it."

The weight of Peter's words hung heavy in the air. Ben's mind raced. He wasn't just fighting for redemption anymore—he was fighting for survival. The real battle was only just beginning.

Chapter 20:

The Storm Before the War

Ben sat at the gates of Heaven, staring at the horizon where the golden sky had begun to darken. It wasn't nightfall—night didn't exist here. It was something else. A shift in the air, a weight pressing down on his chest that hadn't been there before. The silence was unnatural. The gates had been open too long, and the wrong souls had walked through them. Now, the balance was broken, and Heaven was no longer what it had once been.

Once, Heaven had been a sanctuary of harmony. The light had been steady, warm, and unyielding, filling every corner of existence with an ethereal glow that carried peace into the very marrow of its inhabitants. Now, the radiance flickered, uncertain, as if Heaven itself doubted its own permanence. Thin streaks of black threaded through the sky like cracks in glass, stretching toward the horizon, poisoning the once-flawless expanse. The air had lost its purity, carrying the faintest scent of decay, like flowers left too long in stagnant water.

And the music—oh, the music. Once, it had been a chorus, an endless symphony of celestial voices weaving harmonies that hummed in every breath. Now, something discordant threaded through the melody, a single, jarring note that twisted the beauty into something sinister. It was as though Heaven itself was trying to whisper a warning, but the words were lost, swallowed by the growing void.

It had started subtly—a flicker in the ever-present light, a crack in the perfect white marble streets. Then the whispers had begun. Souls who had once walked in peace now moved in shadows, wary, uncertain of their place in what was supposed to be paradise. Those who had ruled by fear in life had carved out their own territories here, twisting the promise of eternal rest into something far darker.

Ben had seen it happen. He had watched as small changes rippled outward like a disease, spreading too fast for anyone to contain. He had been here long enough to remember Heaven as it once was, and what it was becoming sickened him. He had tried to ignore it at first, had tried to believe that the rot wouldn't take root, that it would be purged. But nothing had changed. No one had stopped it.

Not yet.

Ben exhaled, rolling his shoulders as he listened to the quiet. It was the kind of quiet that came before a storm. The kind that told him everything was about to break. He wasn't the only one who felt it.

Peter stood nearby, arms crossed, watching the horizon with the same grim expression Ben had seen on his face since the moment he returned.

"You're waiting for it, aren't you?" Peter asked.

Ben didn't look at him. "For what?"

Peter sighed, shaking his head. "The moment everything goes to hell,"

296

Ben smirked, but there was no humour in it. "I think that moment already passed."

Peter didn't argue.

They both knew what was coming.

Ben ran a hand through his hair, exhaling. "This place used to be different. Stronger. We used to be stronger."

Peter nodded; his gaze still fixed on the horizon. "We were. But that was before we let them in."

Ben didn't respond right away. Guilt curled in his chest like smoke. He had been part of it—whether through action or inaction, he had allowed this to happen. Maybe if he had spoken up earlier, and fought harder, things wouldn't have reached this point. But it was too late for that now. Peter, ever the soldier, didn't say it outright, but Ben could hear the unspoken accusation in his voice.

"Has this happened before?" Ben asked finally.

Peter hesitated. "Not like this. We've had threats, battles, betrayals. But Heaven always endured. This time… this is different."

"How?"

Peter turned to face him then, his eyes dark with something Ben didn't want to name. "Because this time, Heaven itself is changing."

Ben swallowed hard. He didn't want to admit it, but he had felt it too. Heaven was no longer a fixed point of light and purity. It was bending, twisting under a force neither of them fully understood.

A low groan echoed from the gates, metal grinding against itself. Peter and Ben both turned, watching as the massive, gilded doors shuddered.

And then, from somewhere deep within Heaven's heart, a sound split the air—a sound that did not belong.

A drum.

Faint at first, but unmistakable. A war drum.

Ben's stomach turned to ice.

"Do you hear that?" Peter asked, his voice tight.

Ben nodded. "I do."

It was distant, but growing closer. A rhythmic, slow pulse, like the heartbeat of something ancient and hungry. It reverberated through the ground, through the very air, carrying with it the promise of something terrible.

Ben's fingers tightened into fists.

Peter stepped forward, his body tense. "It's starting."

A shadow moved along the edge of the gates. Not a soul—something else.

Then, a voice, barely more than a whisper, slid through the silence.

"Ben."

It was neither question nor demand. It was a summons.

Ben stiffened. He didn't turn toward the voice. He knew better than that.

Peter, however, did. And when he did, his expression darkened. "We have company."

Ben turned slowly, eyes locking onto the figure emerging from the shifting light.

It was neither an angel nor a lost soul.

It was something worse.

A messenger.

The being's presence warped the space around it, bending Heaven's light into something unnatural. Its form was fluid, shifting—a thing that was not meant to be here.

"The gates are cracking," the messenger said, its voice like rust and ruin. "He is coming."

Ben took a step forward. "Who?"

The messenger tilted its head, in a hollow, empty motion. "You already know."

A second drumbeat echoed through the sky. Louder this time.

The War Had Begun.

Ben exhaled, feeling the weight settle fully onto his shoulders.

No more waiting.

He turned to Peter. "Get ready."

Peter nodded. "I already am."

The gates groaned again, the cracks in Heaven's foundation spreading.

And beyond them, something stirred in the darkness, waiting to strike.

Heaven was no longer safe.

And Ben was no longer sure it ever would be again.

The Seeds of War

It wasn't just the righteous who were growing restless.

The souls who had no business being in Heaven had begun to realize something—they weren't being sent back. There was no divine intervention, no punishment. They had slipped through the cracks, and now they were free.

At first, they had moved carefully, testing the limits of their newfound afterlife. But then the first act of violence had been committed—quiet, subtle, but undeniable. A man, a conqueror in life, had taken what he wanted, as he always had. And there had been no consequence.

Then another followed.

And another.

Now, there were places in Heaven where the light had dimmed, where the golden halls were stained with something darker. It wasn't Hell. Not yet.

But it was close.

It started as a whisper, an undercurrent of doubt creeping through the souls of Heaven. The ones who had always belonged here, the ones who had believed in their eternal reward, began to notice the shift. The streets they had walked for centuries, untouched by decay, now bore cracks where shadows pooled in the crevices. The very air felt different, no longer filled with the pure serenity that had once defined this place.

The righteous, once secure in their peace, now found themselves looking over their shoulders. The laughter that had once been effortless was forced now, edged with uncertainty. Conversations that had been filled with joy turned to hushed murmurs, questioning what was happening to their paradise.

At first, the changes were subtle. A statue of an archangel that had once radiated divine energy now bore a single, jagged fracture down its face. The celestial gardens, once bursting with colour, had patches where the flowers had withered into something brittle and Gray. The rivers of light that had once flowed endlessly now flickered in places; their radiance dimmed.

Then, the violence escalated.

It began with a dispute over space, something that should have never been a problem in Heaven. But the souls who had slipped

301

through the cracks had begun to take more than what was given. A soul who had ruled with an iron fist in life saw no reason to change in death. He gathered others like him—souls that had clawed their way through existence, who had thrived in the mortal world through domination and fear.

They formed groups, staking claims in places that had once been freely shared. They didn't call them kingdoms, not yet. But the way they moved, the way they spoke, hinted at something far worse. The light that shone upon them seemed reluctant as if Heaven itself was uncertain of their presence.

A saint, one who had spent his life in servitude and sacrifice, had tried to intervene. He had approached one of these conquerors, had pleaded with him to remember where they were, to let go of the greed that had defined his mortal existence.

He had been struck down in the street.

And nothing had happened.

No divine retribution. No hand of judgment to smite the sinner. The silence that followed was deafening.

The conqueror had smiled, realizing what the others were beginning to understand.

Heaven's laws were breaking.

It was as though something had shifted, something fundamental. The rules that had once governed this place, that had held balance and order, were unravelling. Those who had been content in their eternity began to question the safety of their

302

paradise. Those who had arrived through deception, through the fractures in the system, began to take more.

The righteous whispered amongst themselves. Some still clung to faith, believing that the divine forces would intervene, that this was a test of their patience, their devotion.

Others were not so sure.

A gathering formed in one of the great halls, a place where the wisest souls had once met to discuss the affairs of Heaven in peace. Now, the air was tense, voices raised in fear and anger.

"They do not belong here!" one soul cried, his voice shaking. "We must do something before it is too late."

"And who will do it?" another retorted. "Have you seen the angels? They are watching, but they do not act. They know something we do not."

"The gates have been compromised," an elder murmured. "If they are no longer in control... then who is?" Silence settled over them, heavy and suffocating.

Then came the first true battle.

A righteous soul, one who had fought for justice in life, had decided he would not let Heaven be taken. He had stood against the conquerors and had challenged them to leave, to relinquish what they had stolen.

He had been met with violence.

This time, there were witnesses. More than just whispers and shadows. A full-blown conflict erupted in the streets, a clash of will and power, but it was not a battle between Heaven and Hell. It was something else entirely.

The righteous fought not with divine weapons, but with desperation. The conquerors, emboldened by the lack of consequence, fought with the knowledge that they had already won. And through it all, the heavens did nothing.

Ben watched from the gates; his hands clenched into fists. Peter stood beside him; his face carved from stone.

"They're testing the limits," Ben murmured.

Peter's jaw tightened. "No. They've already found them."

A distant rumble echoed through the sky—not thunder, but something deeper, something more ominous. The golden glow above flickered, as though struggling against a force unseen.

Then, from the heart of Heaven, the war drums began to sound.

Slow. Relentless. The promise of something coming.

Ben turned to Peter. "This isn't just an uprising. This is a war."

Peter nodded. "And Heaven isn't ready."

As the drums grew louder, a shadow passed over the gates. And somewhere in the dimming light, a new force was stirring, waiting for the moment to strike.

Now, there were places in Heaven where the light had dimmed, where the golden halls were stained with something darker. It wasn't Hell. Not yet.

But it was close.

And the war was just beginning.

The Divided Host

The Angels' Fall

The angels had always been silent observers, enforcers of divine law, existing outside the affairs of the souls who entered Heaven. They were the eternal guardians, unmoved by the tides of mortal conflict, their purpose clear: to maintain the sanctity of Heaven and uphold the Will of the Divine. But now, they were faced with something unprecedented—lawlessness.

Some had chosen to stand aside, waiting for a higher power to intervene. Their faith in the celestial order was unshaken, their belief that the Divine would restore balance remained steadfast, even as cracks began to appear in the very fabric of Heaven itself. They waited for the signal, for the higher command that would put everything right again. They didn't move, didn't act— because they believed that to do so would be a betrayal of the divine trust placed in them.

Others, however, had abandoned Heaven entirely.

There were whispers of angels leaving their posts, walking away from the celestial realms with no explanation, no reason given. Their absence was felt keenly, the once-imposing figures who had filled the sky, watching over Heaven with unwavering vigilance, now gone. The expanse that had once felt eternal, untouched by time, now seemed empty. The presence of these angels had once been constant, reassuring—a reminder that

Heaven, like the divine itself, was beyond reproach. But as they left, the sense of safety that had once defined Heaven began to fade, replaced with uncertainty. Where had they gone? Some whispered that they had ventured to realms beyond Heaven's gates, seeking answers, while others feared they had simply fallen away, unwilling to witness the unravelling of paradise.

And then, there were the ones who had taken matters into their own hands.

Ben had seen them—angels who once spoke in gentle voices now carried weapons. They patrolled the streets, not as protectors, but as enforcers, their patience worn thin by the corruption spreading through the afterlife. They were no longer the celestial beings of old who offered guidance and comfort; they were warriors, their halos dimmed by anger, their oncegentle eyes hardened by the burden of duty turned violent. They stood at the edges of the golden streets, weapons at the ready, waiting for the next act of rebellion, the next threat to order. Their presence sent a chill through the souls of Heaven, a reminder that Heaven was no longer the peaceful sanctuary it had once been.

The shift had started as an unspoken uncertainty among the celestial ranks, a hesitation in their once-fluid movements. The angels, beings of unwavering duty, had always carried out their roles with quiet precision. But now, they hesitated. They whispered amongst themselves in languages older than time, their wings twitching with unease, their divine purpose faltering in the face of an undeniable corruption. Heaven, once a place of eternal peace and order, was changing—and they didn't know how to stop it.

It wasn't just the mortals who were divided. Even the celestial beings who had watched over them for eons found themselves torn. Some angels still clung to the belief that Heaven was incorruptible, that the Great Will would intervene in time to restore order. These angels remained at their posts, eyes lifted to the heavens, waiting for guidance that had yet to come. They trusted in the divine plan, certain that the chaos would be undone by forces far greater than anything they could comprehend. For them, Heaven's fall was temporary, a test of faith to be endured with patience and grace.

But others—others had lost their faith.

Ben had seen them walking the streets, their once-brilliant halos dimmed, their expressions hardened. They were tired of waiting. Tired of watching Heaven decay under their watch. These angels no longer spoke in hymns; they issued orders. They no longer walked with grace; they moved with purpose. Their wings no longer fluttered with ethereal beauty; instead, they swept through the air like storm clouds, dark and heavy. Some had reforged their celestial instruments into weapons, blades of golden light strapped to their backs as if preparing for a battle they had not yet declared. They had abandoned their former roles as guardians of peace and had become something else— something more ruthless, something far less certain.

Not all of them had taken up arms, though. Some had turned their backs entirely, leaving their stations, walking away from the duties they had upheld since the dawn of time. No one knew where they had gone, only that their absence left gaps in Heaven's fabric. Where once the sky had been filled with the watchful presence of divine sentinels, now there were voids, spaces where protection had faltered, where the light itself seemed to fade.

Then there were the zealots. The ones who had taken it upon themselves to cleanse Heaven by force. These angels believed they had been forsaken, left to deal with the rising tide of corruption alone. They saw the souls who had slipped through as a disease, an infection that had to be purged. They viewed their mission as a sacred one, a divine duty to eradicate the taint before it consumed everything. And so, they hunted.

Ben had witnessed it firsthand—a group of them descending upon a gathering of souls in a once-sacred garden, blades drawn, their eyes void of mercy. They had given no warning, no chance for redemption. There had only been swift, brutal judgment. The souls had been torn apart with cold precision, their pleas ignored as the angels carried out their grim work. The purity of the garden was stained with blood, and the once-lush trees, the ones that had whispered the eternal songs of Heaven, were now twisted by the violence, their branches withering beneath the weight of such brutality.

And yet, even as Heaven fractured, some angels still clung to their purpose. Some believed in redemption and thought even the worst souls could be saved. They moved through the chaos, trying to reason with both the lost souls and their kind, desperate to hold onto the principles that had guided them for eternity. They were outnumbered, their voices drowned out by the rising tide of conflict, but they persisted. They clung to the hope that Heaven could still be healed, that there was a chance for peace if only they could reach out to the corrupted, the fallen, and those who had lost their way.

Peter had spoken to one of them.

"They are afraid," the angel had told him, his silver wings folded tightly around his form, his voice a soft murmur in the chaos. "Not just of the lost souls, but of themselves. Of what they are becoming."

Peter had nodded; his expression grim. "And what of you? Where do you stand?"

The angel's face had been unreadable, his once-clear eyes clouded with doubt. "I still believe in Heaven."

That had been weeks ago. Since then, even the hopeful had grown weary. The divisions among the angels had deepened, the uncertainty had spread like wildfire, and the belief in a return to the old order had begun to wither. Heaven's light, once so bright and unwavering, now flickered in the face of unrelenting darkness, and even the celestial beings who had watched over its perfection for eons were beginning to question whether it could ever be restored.

A war was inevitable.
The only question was who would strike first.
The air in Heaven was different now, thick with tension as if even the very heavens themselves could feel the impending shift. The once tranquil atmosphere was now charged with an electricity that buzzed through the air, tangible and unsettling. The gates, once symbols of protection and divine sanctity, stood heavier than before, as though bracing themselves for what was to come. The weight of history, the weight of Heaven's glory, was beginning to crack under the pressure of what was unfolding. The sky, once an unbroken expanse of gold, now

309

bore streaks of red, like the first warning signs of a coming storm—a storm no one could predict, no one could prevent.

The streets were no longer peaceful. Where once souls had gathered in harmony, exchanging wisdom, joy, and peace, now they moved in uncertain clusters, their eyes constantly darting about, casting wary glances at the armoured figures who watched them from above. The usual serene hum of celestial voices was now pierced with silence, punctuated only by the harsh sounds of armoured boots on marble. The stillness had become oppressive, broken only by whispers of unrest. Even the angels who had not yet chosen sides carried themselves differently. They moved with a palpable tension, their wings folded tight against their backs, their hands hovering near weapons they had never needed before. The peaceful unity that had once reigned in Heaven was crumbling, piece by piece.

Rumours spread like wildfire. They were spoken in hushed tones, behind closed doors, in the shadows of the gilded halls. Some whispered that a faction of angels had begun preparing for an outright purge—an attempt to cleanse Heaven of the souls who had slipped through the cracks in a single, merciless strike. They would remove the invaders, restore the divine order, and return Heaven to its sanctified state. Others claimed that the lost souls—the conquerors, the warlords, the ones who had bent their mortal lives to dominance—were organizing. They were forging alliances with those who had once stood at the edges of Heaven, gathering their numbers, and preparing for the inevitable conflict. The long-forgotten leaders of the fallen had begun to rise, their ambitions no longer limited by mortal death. They had come here to claim Heaven as their own.

Ben had no doubts anymore. Heaven was on the brink of war.

And when it began, it would not be a war between Heaven and Hell. It would be something worse—a war within Heaven itself. Heaven had never been divided like this before. The celestial order had always been certain, unchanging. But now, everything was in flux. The lines that had once separated righteousness from sin, order from chaos, and light from darkness, were no longer clear. This was not the battle of good against evil, but a battle for Heaven's very soul—a fight for what it would become in the face of its corruption.

Peter had spent the last few days trying to hold the remnants of the order together, speaking to the angels who still listened, urging them to wait, to hold faith just a little longer. He tried to believe that Heaven could be saved, that the balance could be restored if only they exercised patience. But Ben could see it in his eyes. He knew it was a lost cause. Even Peter, the everhopeful, could no longer ignore the truth. It was too late to stop what was coming.

"They won't wait," Ben said quietly one evening as they stood near the gates, watching the distant figures of armoured angels moving through the fractured streets. Their presence was a silent testament to the rising conflict. "Not much longer."

Peter exhaled, his jaw tightening as he too watched the figures, his face grim. "I know."

Ben turned to him, his voice low. "What happens when they do?"

Peter's gaze remained fixed on the horizon, the same distant look that had been in his eyes for days, weeks even, as the situation in Heaven deteriorated. The once proud and peaceful city was now a powder keg, and even the angels who had once

311

been the beacon of hope were now uncertain. "We choose," Peter replied, his voice steady but with an undercurrent of doubt that Ben had never heard before.

Ben frowned. "Choose what?"

Peter turned to him then, and for the first time, Ben saw something raw in his expression—doubt, fear, something almost human. "Which side we're on."

Ben let the words settle in his chest, feeling their weight. He had always thought Heaven was beyond such things. The war between light and darkness had always seemed like a simple, clear-cut divide. Righteousness and sin were separate forces, always destined to clash, always with a line drawn in the sand between them. But now, that line was no longer visible. Now, it felt as though everything—Heaven itself—was up for grabs. What if the righteousness he had believed in was no longer the truth? What if the souls that had entered Heaven, those who had corrupted it, were no longer just the invaders, but a part of the very fabric of what Heaven was becoming?

Heaven wasn't a battlefield between good and evil anymore. It was a battleground for belief itself—a fight to determine what the very essence of Heaven would be. And when the first strike came, there would be no turning back. There would be no going back to the purity and innocence of the past. Once Heaven fractured, once the first blow was struck, everything would change. The celestial realm would be forever altered, and the angels, the souls, and the very foundation of Heaven would be forever divided.

Ben's heart clenched. The paradise he had once known, the home of peace and eternal light, was no more. Whatever came

312

next, it wouldn't be the Heaven they had known. It would be something else. A Heaven divided, fractured, and no longer certain. And when the war began, it would be the beginning of an era no one could predict. It would be a war that would forever change the fate of Heaven itself.

A Gathering of Tyrants

Ben had spent his afterlife making bad decisions.
Letting in Lucius Atrian had been the worst.
He should have seen it coming. Should have known that someone like Lucius wouldn't be satisfied with simply existing in Heaven. A man who had spent his entire life bending the world to his will wasn't going to stop just because he was dead. Lucius had been building something in the shadows. Gathering those who shared his vision—tyrants, warlords, murderers who had built empires in life and had no intention of relinquishing their power in death.
They had carved out a kingdom among the ruins.
And now, they were preparing for war.
Ben knew it the moment he saw them.
The council of the damned had gathered in what had once been one of Heaven's greatest temples. The doors had been torn from their hinges, and the stained-glass windows shattered.

Inside, the worst of history had come together under a single purpose.
To rule.
Lucius stood at the head of the room, calm, and composed, the smirk on his lips one of a man who had already won. "This

313

place is an illusion," he said, his voice carrying through the ruined temple. "A kingdom built on false promises and outdated laws. We were sent here, not because we repented, but because Heaven is flawed. It was never meant to last." He paced the room, his hands clasped behind his back. "Look at us. What do we have in common? We are rulers. We are conquerors. We shaped history. And yet, here we are, expected to bow before laws written by cowards."

Murmurs of agreement rippled through the crowd. Lucius smiled. "But what if we didn't bow? What if we took what was always meant to be ours?"

A voice rose from the back. "And what of the angels?" Lucius chuckled. "They are not gods. They are nothing more than servants playing at being kings. And kings can be overthrown."

A silence settled over the room. Then,

one by one, they nodded.

Ben had made a mistake.

He had let a monster into Heaven.

And now, that monster was about to burn it down.

Ben watched from the shadows, heart pounding as Lucius took control of the room with effortless authority. He had always been persuasive, but this was something else. There was a weight to his words, a gravitational pull that even the most hardened warlords couldn't resist. He wasn't just offering them power—he was offering them purpose. And that made him dangerous.

Ben knew he should leave. Knew he should return to Peter and the others, warn them of what was coming. But his feet refused to move. It was like watching a storm gather on the horizon, knowing there was no stopping it.

314

A woman spoke up, her voice sharp and confident. "You speak of taking Heaven, but you assume we will work together. What happens when we win, Lucius? Do we rule as one, or do we turn on each other?"

Lucius turned to her, unfazed. "Ah, Cleopatra. Always thinking ahead." He inclined his head. "You are right to ask. Many of us were enemies in life. But we were divided then by mortality, by fleeting ambitions. Now, we stand on the precipice of something greater. If we take Heaven, we do so as one. A new order, built from strength."

"And who decides who rules?" asked another voice, deep and full of challenge. Genghis Khan, his massive form looming over those around him. "You?"

Lucius spread his hands. "We will decide together. But make no mistake—this is not a battle of Honor. It is a war. And in war, only the strongest survive."

Ben swallowed hard. They weren't just planning a rebellion. They were planning an empire.

One of the men stepped forward, his eyes dark with calculation. "The angels are powerful. If we do this, we will need an advantage."

Lucius nodded. "And we will have one. There are weapons in Heaven—relics of past wars, artifacts forgotten by time. They are hidden, locked away, but not unreachable." The room murmured in approval.

Ben felt cold.

If Lucius was right, if they got their hands on divine weapons…

This wouldn't be a battle. It would be a massacre.

Ben slipped out of the ruined temple, moving quickly but carefully through the winding streets. He had heard enough. He needed to find Peter, needed to warn him before it was too late. But as he turned a corner, he stopped cold.

A figure stood in his path, arms crossed, a knowing smile on his lips.

Lucius.

"Going somewhere, Ben?"

Ben's pulse pounded. He forced himself to stay calm. "You know I can't let you do this."

Lucius sighed. "You always were predictable." He stepped closer, his presence suffocating. "I respect you, Ben. You had a part in letting me in, after all. And I'd rather not kill someone who helped me."

Ben clenched his fists. "Then don't."

Lucius tilted his head. "Join me instead."

Ben barked out a bitter laugh. "You really think I'd betray everything Heaven stands for?"

Lucius smirked. "Heaven has already betrayed itself. I'm just finishing what it started."

Ben took a step back. "I won't let you win."

Lucius sighed, shaking his head. "You still think this is about winning and losing." He gestured around them. "Look around you, Ben. Heaven is already crumbling. I'm just giving it a new purpose."

Ben's jaw tightened. "You're giving it a grave."

Lucius studied him for a moment, then nodded, as if reaching a decision. "A shame."

Without warning, he moved.

Ben barely had time to react before Lucius was on him, faster than any mortal had a right to be. A fist slammed into his stomach, knocking the wind from his lungs. Ben stumbled back,

316

but Lucius didn't let up. Another blow—sharp, precise—sent him sprawling to the ground.

Ben gasped for breath, pain blooming through his ribs. He tried to push himself up, but Lucius placed a boot on his chest, pinning him down.

"You should've joined me," Lucius murmured.

Ben gritted his teeth. "Go to hell."

Lucius chuckled. "Not yet."

Then, without another word, he stepped back, leaving Ben gasping on the ground.

"Consider this a warning," Lucius said over his shoulder as he walked away. "Next time, I won't be so forgiving." Ben forced himself up, breathing hard, watching as Lucius disappeared into the ruined city.

He had made a mistake.

But it wasn't too late to fix it.

Gritting his teeth, he turned and ran. He had a war to stop.

A Reckoning Approaches

Ben wasn't a hero.
He never had been.

But even he knew that if he didn't do something now, there wouldn't be anything left to save.

As he left the temple, his mind raced. The war hadn't started yet, but it would. And when it did, Heaven wouldn't survive it. He

317

found Peter waiting for him outside, arms crossed, expression unreadable.

"How bad is it?" Peter asked.

Ben exhaled. "Bad."

Peter nodded. "So, what's the plan?"

Ben looked out at the city—the golden streets that had begun to crack, the looming storm on the horizon, the angels preparing for a battle they weren't ready for.

He didn't have a plan.

But he had a goal.

"Lucius has to go," Ben said. "If we don't take him out now, he'll take everything."

Peter studied him for a moment. "And how do you plan to do that?"

Ben rolled his shoulders. "I guess I'll figure it out."

Peter sighed. "Of course you will."

The first war in Heaven's history was about to begin.

Ben could feel it in the air, in the way the light had dimmed, in the hushed murmurs of angels who had never known fear until now. They stood at the edge of something they didn't understand, a war not against demons, but against themselves. As they walked through the city, past once-pristine buildings that now bore the scars of neglect, Ben and Peter found themselves in the heart of the divide. The streets were no longer filled with the joyous hum of eternal peace. Now, they held whispers of doubt, of uncertainty. Angels stood in clusters, some sharpening weapons that had never before been needed, others pacing like caged animals.

"Heaven's breaking," Peter muttered. "Even if we win, it won't be the same."

Ben didn't argue. He knew Peter was right.

318

And part of him didn't care.

Because for all its perfection, Heaven had failed. It had let the wrong souls in. It had let Lucius in. And now, the price would be paid in blood.

A voice called out from the shadows of a crumbling archway. "Ben."

Both men turned, hands instinctively reaching for weapons they weren't sure they'd be able to use.

A figure stepped forward—a woman, tall and graceful, with piercing silver eyes and wings that had once shone like morning light. Now, they were dull, the edges fraying.

"Israfel," Peter murmured, recognizing her instantly. She had once been a leader among Heaven's ranks, a warrior of the old days. But she had vanished when the fractures first appeared, unwilling to choose a side.

Until now.

"I know what Lucius is planning," she said, voice low but steady. "And I know where to stop him."

Ben narrowed his eyes. "Why help us?"

Israfel hesitated. "Because I remember what Heaven was supposed to be. And I know that if he wins, none of us will survive what comes next."

Peter nodded. "Then tell us."

Deep within the core of Heaven, beneath the halls of judgment, lay a vault sealed since the dawn of creation. Within it, relics of power—artifacts even the angels feared to wield.

Lucius was going there.

And if he reached those weapons before they did, the war would end before it began.

"We have to stop him before he gets inside," Israfel said, leading them through the winding streets, avoiding the growing clusters of unrest. "If he breaks the seal, there won't be anything left to fight for."

Ben's mind churned. He had fought battles before, but never like this. Never against something that had no right to exist in Heaven.

A cold wind swept through the streets, rattling what remained of the stained-glass windows of Heaven's grand halls. It was as though the city itself was trembling in anticipation.

Then, in the distance, the first horn sounded.

A low, resonant note that sent shivers down Ben's spine. The war had begun.

The gates of the vault stood at the base of Heaven's oldest tower, a relic of a time when war had never been imagined. The door was carved from celestial stone, etched with sails meant to keep the unworthy out.

Lucius stood before it.

His presence twisted the air, his mere existence a defiance of everything Heaven had once been. Around him, his gathered warlords—Cleopatra, Genghis, others who had ruled through strength and deception—stood waiting, their eyes gleaming with the promise of something greater than paradise.

Ben, Peter, and Israfel arrived just in time to see Lucius press his hand against the seal.

The air cracked.

A deep, pulsing sound echoed as the sails flickered, resisting. Lucius turned, smiling when he saw them. "You're too late."

Ben felt the weight of inevitability settles over him.

"Step away from the door, Lucius," Israfel warned.

Lucius chuckled. "And miss the opportunity of a lifetime?" He turned back to the vault. "Heaven has ruled for long enough under pretences. The real power has been hidden away, locked behind illusions of righteousness."

He pressed his palm against the stone again, and this time, the cracks spread like veins of darkness across the surface.

The vault was opening.

Ben reached for his weapon.

The battle for Heaven had begun.

And Ben Holloway was the only one who could stop it.

But deep down, he wasn't sure if he wanted to.

Because as much as he hated what Lucius had done… A small, broken part of him still believed Heaven deserved to burn.

Ben's thoughts tangled with his emotions, each step he took toward the vault carrying him further into a conflict he didn't fully understand. How had things come to this? How had Heaven—his home, the place of eternal peace—become so corrupted? He had always believed in Heaven's perfect design, its promises of redemption and divine order. But now, all he saw was the crumbling façade. The gates were no longer open to welcome new souls; they were bracing for an apocalypse, for a reckoning. And the price would be paid not by Heaven's enemies, but by the angels themselves.

"Ben…" Peter's voice broke through his thoughts. "What's going through your head?"

Ben didn't answer immediately. His gaze remained fixed on Lucius, who stood at the threshold of the vault. There was something in his eyes—a gleam of satisfaction, of triumph—

that made Ben's stomach turn. Lucius knew he was about to win.

And it made Ben sick because part of him had never felt so lost.

Chapter 21:

The Tyrant of the Black Age

The Broken Gates of Paradise

Ben had never been one for redemption.

But here he was—trying to fix the unfixable.

He stood at the gates of Heaven, staring out at the wreckage he had caused. The golden streets, once pristine, were littered with the remnants of war. Holy temples lay in ruins, their towering spires shattered by the hands of the very people he had let in. Smoke curled in the distance, thick and dark, a sign that even paradise wasn't immune to destruction.

He took a breath, the air tainted with the scent of burning divinity.

Behind him, the gates creaked on their hinges, barely holding together. They had been built to keep things out—not to withstand an attack from within. And yet, the ones he had trusted, the ones he had fought to save, had turned their backs on salvation itself.

Ben cracked his knuckles. Fine.

It was time to start rounding up the bastards.

His boots crunched against the debris as he stepped forward. A broken halo lay at his feet, its once-radiant glow flickering like a dying ember. He picked it up, turning it over in his hand before tossing it aside. Halos didn't mean anything anymore—not when the ones wearing them had proven to be just as corruptible as the rest.

No More Second Chances

A figure stirred among the rubble—a fallen seraph, wings charred at the edges, eyes wide with something between fear and defiance. Ben had seen that look before.
"You," the angel rasped. "You did this."
Ben sighed. "Yeah, I know."
The seraph reached for something, but Ben was faster. A swift kick sent the weapon—a jagged shard of divine steel—skidding across the ground.
"No more second chances," Ben said, his voice cold. "Not this time."
The angel hesitated, then lowered his gaze.

The silence between them was heavy, suffocating, filled with the weight of betrayal. Ben had never been one for deep introspection, but the ruin around him, the destruction of the divine realm, forced him to face the reality of what he had done. What they had all done. Once, this place had been his sanctuary—a bastion of purity and light. Now, it was a desecrated wasteland.
He had been part of the problem. He had been the one to let them in, let them deceive him with promises of change, of a better world. And in the end, it was that very hope that had driven everything to the brink of collapse.
The seraph's hand trembled as it fell to his side, the light fading from his eyes. It wasn't fear anymore, Ben realized. It was

exhaustion. Even the angels—beings of light and power—were as weary as he was. Weary of the endless cycle, the constant battles. They had all been complicit in the fall of Heaven, whether through their actions or their inaction.

"You think you can fix this?" the angel muttered, the words coated with a bitter laugh.

Ben met the angel's gaze, steady and unwavering. "I have to try."

"Try?" The seraph shook his head, his burnt wings fluttering weakly. "You've already tried. It's too late. All of this"—he gestured weakly at the destruction surrounding them— "is the consequence of your choices. You let us in. You let the corruption seep into paradise."

Ben's fist clenched. He had known that the angels weren't perfect. He had known that power, even in the hands of those who were supposed to be holy, could corrupt. But he hadn't known it would unravel this way, that Heaven itself would become a battleground, torn apart by the very ideals that had once made it sacred.

Ben took another step forward, the weight of his choices settling heavily on his shoulders. "Maybe it's too late for redemption. But it's not too late to stop the bleeding."

The seraph snorted, his wings fluttering again in an attempt to stand, but he collapsed back into the rubble. "You think stopping it will change anything? This is the price of believing in something that doesn't exist. There's no salvation, no purity left. You've seen it. It's all broken now. Everything is broken." Ben's eyes narrowed. "I've been broken before," he said, his voice a low growl. "Doesn't mean I can't still fix things." He turned away, pushing the angel's words out of his mind. The sky above had darkened even more, the once-perfect horizon now a shattered mess of swirling clouds and lightning. He had seen this coming—the storm had always been on the horizon. It wasn't just the angels who had fallen. It was the whole of Heaven, its ideals, its structures, everything that had once been invincible.

Ben had been a fool to think that peace could be preserved in a place like this. Even the purest places had their cracks, their flaws, their weaknesses. It was those weaknesses that had been exploited. And now, he was left to pick up the pieces. But that's all he could do now. Fix what was broken. Even if the task seemed impossible.

As he moved through the rubble, the fallen angel's words lingered in the back of his mind. They stung, but they also reminded him of why he had to keep going. Why he couldn't let it all fall apart? Because if there was any hope left, it was in fighting for what remained, for the possibility of something better—even if that hope was a fleeting shadow in the darkness. His path wasn't clear. It never had been. But the broken streets of Heaven held a strange kind of clarity now. He would rebuild. It wouldn't be easy, and it wouldn't be quick. But he would rebuild, no matter the cost.

The light from the broken halos dimmed, but something in Ben stirred. Something raw and unrelenting. He was no longer the man who had once trusted in blind ideals. He was something more now—something stronger. Something forged in the flames of failure.

And this time, he would make sure the flames didn't consume everything again.

No more second chances. Just action.

326

Ben turned away. There was a lot of work to do.

Peter had been right about one thing—this wasn't going to be easy.

The criminals, tyrants, and warlords that had slithered through Heaven's gates weren't exactly eager to go back to wherever the hell they had come from. They had gotten a taste of paradise, and they weren't going to give it up without a fight.

The Hunt Begins

Ben had let them in. Now, he had to drag them out.

Heaven's first manhunt had begun.

The first name on his list was Salazar the Conqueror—a selfproclaimed emperor who had built his kingdom on blood and betrayal. He had ruled Earth with an iron fist for decades, and now, he had carved out his empire in Heaven's ruins. Ben found him seated on a stolen throne in what had once been a place of worship, his lackeys gathered around him like flies on a corpse. The stained-glass windows, once radiant with depictions of saints and celestial wonders, were shattered. The altar was defiled, covered in gold trinkets and relics stolen from across Heaven. Salazar had turned it into his war room, with banners bearing his insignia hanging from the rafters. "Salazar," Ben called, stepping forward. "Your time's up."

The warlord leaned back, smirking. "I rather like it here, Holloway. You should be thanking me—I've brought order to the chaos you created."

327

Ben exhaled slowly, rolling his shoulders. "You've got two choices. You leave peacefully, or I drag you out kicking and screaming."

Salazar chuckled, a deep, rumbling sound that echoed through the ruined hall. His soldiers gripped their weapons, shifting uneasily. "You think you can make me?"

Ben didn't bother answering. He just moved.

One moment, Salazar was grinning from his stolen throne—the next, he was airborne. Ben had his hand around the warlord's throat, slamming him down so hard that the marble beneath them cracked. Salazar snarled, twisting, trying to pry himself free. His men rushed forward, blades drawn, but the air shimmered with divine force, and they staggered back, unable to get close.

Ben had spent so long defying Heaven that he had never stopped to realize one thing—he had power here. And he was going to use it.

The divine energy coursed through him, every movement filled with the weight of something ancient and unstoppable. As Salazar gasped for air, clawing at Ben's hand, Ben could feel the remnants of Heaven's essence thrumming beneath his skin. It was a strange sensation—a mix of overwhelming strength and searing power—something he had only ever felt in fleeting moments of defiance. But now, he had control.

Salazar the Conqueror

"You've made your choice," Ben growled, tightening his grip. "You could've walked away."

Salazar's face turned red; his eyes wild with rage. "You think you can take me down? You—YOU don't understand! I *am* power!" Ben snarled, the words cutting deeper than they should have. *I am power.* Salazar had built his empire on a lie—a belief that power could be taken, held, and used to control everything. But Ben knew better. Power, real power, wasn't about conquest. It was about responsibility. About balance. And Salazar had lost that balance long ago.

Ben slammed the warlord's head against the floor again, and for a moment, the world went quiet. The sound of crunching stone echoed in the air, a reminder of just how far the fall had gone. The soldiers stood frozen, unsure of whether to charge or retreat.

Ben took a step back, releasing his hold just enough to let Salazar breathe. The warlord gasped for air, coughing violently, blood dripping from his mouth as he scrambled to sit up. His eyes were filled with hatred, but there was something else there now—fear. Fear of someone who wasn't just strong enough to kill him, but strong enough to take his kingdom from him.

"You don't belong here," Ben said, his voice low and dangerous. "This place was never meant for you."

Salazar sneered, wiping the blood from his lips. "You're too late, Holloway. I've already claimed this place as mine. It's too far gone for you to save."

Ben's gaze hardened. "You're wrong. It's not too late for Heaven." He stood tall, his eyes sweeping over the room, over the soldiers who were now visibly trembling. "It's too late for you."

With a flick of his wrist, a surge of divine energy exploded from him, knocking Salazar and his men back against the shattered

329

walls. The power wasn't just physical; it was a force that cut through the corruption like a blade. The stolen banners crumbled into dust, and the relics that Salazar had used to build his false throne disintegrated into nothing. Heaven was reclaiming itself, piece by piece.

Ben turned back to Salazar, who was now cowering against the stone. "You're finished."

Salazar's lips trembled. "You can't do this. I've fought for this. I've *earned* this!"

"No," Ben said, his voice firm, a note of finality in it. "You've stolen it. And I'm taking it back."

Flames and Silence

He raised his hand, and with a pulse of energy, the warlord was lifted off the ground. Salazar screamed, but it was a futile cry. The corrupted emperor was powerless now. Ben had learned a hard truth over the years—redemption wasn't about saving those who refused to be saved. It was about protecting what could still be saved.

The soldiers scattered, terrified by the overwhelming force Ben commanded. And as they fled, Ben turned to the broken throne, his resolve hardening. Salazar was gone, but the warlords still lingered, hiding in the dark corners of this desecrated paradise. Ben had only just begun his hunt.

The throne room was silent once more, the echoes of the battle fading into the ruins. Ben looked at the wreckage, the remnants of an empire built on violence and greed. He had no illusion about the road ahead. It would be long, and the price would be high. But he wasn't done yet. Not by a long shot.

He turned, stepping over the fallen warlord's broken body, his steps echoing through the hollow hall. The manhunt had just begun—and Ben would make sure it ended with Heaven's redemption.

His grip burned with righteous fury; his touch laced with Heaven's wrath. Salazar let out a guttural scream as golden fire surged through him, his stolen kingdom crumbling around him.

"No," the warlord gasped, clawing at the floor. "You can't—"

Ben didn't give him the chance. He thrust his hand forward, tearing open a rift beneath them. The void howled, an abyss darker than the deepest pits of Hell.

Salazar's scream was swallowed by the void as he was yanked downward, his form dissolving into nothingness.

Silence.

Ben dusted off his hands. One down.

The hall trembled around him, the weight of his task pressing heavier on his shoulders. Plenty more to go.

Becoming the Judge

Word spread fast. Ben Holloway wasn't playing games anymore. The criminals he had let in scattered, some trying to find places to hide, others banding together, determined to fight back.

They didn't understand that it didn't matter.

This was Heaven.

And Ben had become something more than just its gatekeeper—he had become its judge.

331

He tracked them down one by one, pulling them from the fortresses they had built, and dragging them from the shadows where they hid. Some went quietly, bowing their heads, understanding that their stolen time was up. Most didn't. They fought him in the streets, clinging to their stolen power like drowning men grasping at the last scraps of a sinking ship. Tyrants raised their swords, and kings and killers called upon their armies. But none of them had Heaven on their side.

Ben burned through them like a cleansing fire.

He fought warlords in ruined temples, tore despots from their counterfeit thrones, and hunted butchers through the shattered remnants of paradise. Each battle left scars on the once-sacred ground, but with every victory, something changed. The skies, once darkened by war, grew lighter. The heavens, once polluted with smoke and ruin, began to clear. The angels, who had been driven into silence and despair, lifted their heads once more. They watched him, wary but hopeful. The weight of eternity itself seemed to shift.

The balance was shifting.

Ben could feel it.

He was winning.

But he knew he wasn't done yet.

Because there was one name left on his list.

The worst of them all.

A monster who had never been meant to step foot in paradise, who had twisted Heaven's light into something dark and cruel. And this time, Ben wasn't sure if even he could win.

Peter found him standing at the edge of the battlefield, staring toward the ruins of what had once been Heaven's highest temple.

332

The sacred spire had been reduced to rubble, its once-glorious walls now scorched and broken. Statues of angels lay scattered across the ground, their faces worn away, their wings torn from their backs. The wind carried the scent of fire and the echoes of long-vanished prayers.

Ben stood motionless, his shoulders rigid, his hands clenched into fists at his sides.

"You got most of them," Peter said, stepping up beside him. His voice was quiet, almost hopeful. "That should be enough to get your day."

Ben didn't look at him. He didn't move. "Not yet."

Peter followed his gaze, then sighed. "Ah. Him."

At the far end of the battlefield, beyond the broken gates of the ruined temple, a lone figure stood. He was tall, his presence overwhelming even at a distance. Cloaked in black, his Armor shimmered with something deeper than darkness—something void-like, something that seemed to drink in the light. His posture was relaxed, almost amused. He had been waiting.

Ben didn't reply. He just tightened his grip.

The Final Name

Because the last man left standing was more than just another warlord, more than just another tyrant.

He was something far worse.

Ben wasn't facing a mere mortal. He was facing a legend. A soul so dark, so powerful in life, that his influence had stretched far beyond his own time.

His name had been whispered through history—a ruler whose cruelty had shaped empires, a man whose actions had inspired generations of brutality.

Lucius Atrian, the Tyrant of the Black Age.

His voice carried across the ruined expanse, low and smooth like poisoned honey.

"Well, well," Lucius mused. "I was wondering when you'd get to me."

Ben didn't answer. He simply took a step forward.

Every movement he made was calculated, every step deliberated. Ben knew that this fight wasn't like the others. Salazar had been ruthless, but he had been an opportunist. The warlords and tyrants he had hunted had been bad, yes—but none of them had the same weight in the world. None of them had caused the damage Lucius Atrian had.

Lucius had shaped entire ages and brought entire civilizations to their knees through sheer will, and his legacy lived on in every brutal empire that followed. He wasn't just an enemy; he was a symbol, a personification of everything Ben had fought against in this place.

Lucius tilted his head, his eyes gleaming with an ancient, calculating malice. "You think you can kill me, Ben Holloway? You think Heaven's light can purify what I've become?" Ben's jaw tightened, his heart pounding as he continued to move toward him. "I don't need to purify you. I just need to end you."

The ground beneath Ben's feet began to crack, and the air grew thick with tension, a storm brewing on the horizon. Ben could feel the dark pull of Lucius's presence, like a gravity that threatened to drag him into the abyss. The tyrant was

334

powerful—too powerful, perhaps. But Ben had fought every step of the way to get here. He wasn't about to back down now.

Lucius smiled, his teeth gleaming in the dark light. "You won't win this one, Holloway. You never had a chance. You may have taken down the others, but I'm different. You're nothing more than a footnote in the pages of history."

Ben's eyes narrowed, and he knew then—this fight was going to be like no other.

Lucius Atrian had never been a man of faith. He had believed in one thing only—power.
Faith was for the weak. For the desperate. For the ones who needed to believe in something greater than themselves. Lucius had never needed that. He had known, from the moment he was old enough to understand the cruelty of the world, that power was the only thing that mattered.

As a child, he had watched his father—a weak and idealistic emperor—lose his throne to traitors. The man had spoken of justice, of mercy, of Honor. And in the end, none of it had saved him. His allies had turned on him, his generals had betrayed him, and his council had signed his death warrant. Lucius had been forced to watch as his family was dragged into the city square and executed, their blood staining the marble streets. He had been thrown into the dungeons, a prince reduced to nothing, left to rot in the dark with the other forgotten souls.
But Lucius had survived.
He had waited, learning from the filth and the damned, forging himself into something unbreakable. When the time came, he

335

had clawed his way out, risen from the ashes of his father's crumbling empire, and seized what had once been denied to him.

He had built his kingdom—not with diplomacy, but with fire and steel. He had ruled for fifty years, not as a king, but as a god. His word was law, his hand was death, and his legacy was fear.

His name had been burned into the history books, whispered in dread by those who dared to defy him.

And when he died, he had expected oblivion.

Instead, he had woken up in Heaven.

A mistake, surely.

But one he intended to exploit.

The Battle for Heaven

The temple loomed before Ben, half-destroyed but still standing—a fortress among ruins.

It had once been the highest point in Heaven, a place of peace, where prayers had once soared like birds into the endless sky. Now, it was a stronghold of corruption. The once-pristine columns were blackened with soot, the stained-glass windows shattered, their divine images defiled and replaced with banners bearing Lucius Atrian's vigil—a serpent coiled around a bleeding sun.

Lucius had built an army. He had gathered the worst of the worst—conquerors, executioners, and butchers who had cheated justice and now sought to claim Heaven as their own.

336

He had taken the sacred and twisted it, turning Heaven's architecture into his empire.

Ben could hear the voices inside—the raucous laughter of criminals who had never been punished, the arrogant boasts of men who had never known consequence. They revelled in their stolen paradise, believing themselves untouchable.

But that was about to change.

Ben stepped forward, his boots echoing against the broken marble steps. The weight of the battle ahead settled on his shoulders, heavy but not unwelcome. He had come this far. He wasn't stopping now.

A hand rested on his shoulder. Peter.

"This isn't like the others, Holloway." Peter's voice was low, cautious. "This one—he's different."

Ben didn't turn, didn't waver. He rolled his neck, loosening his muscles, feeling the energy crackling beneath his skin. "Yeah," he said, flexing his fingers, the air around them shimmering with divine heat.

"And so am I."

Without another word, he stepped into the temple.

Inside the temple, Lucius sat on a throne of gold and bone, his dark eyes watching as Ben entered.

The grand hall had been desecrated, its sacred murals defaced with crude symbols of conquest. Chandeliers of celestial light, once radiant, now flickered dimly, their glow unable to drive out the encroaching darkness. The air was thick with the scent of spiced wine and burning incense, mingled with something fouler—the lingering presence of power twisted into something unholy.

337

Lucius sat at the heart of it all, draped in a cloak of black, sipping from a chalice that shimmered unnaturally in the fractured light.

"I was wondering when you'd come," Lucius mused, swirling the dark liquid in his cup. His voice was smooth, unhurried. "I was beginning to think you'd let me keep my kingdom." Ben clenched his fists. "This isn't your kingdom." Lucius chuckled, a deep, knowing sound. "Oh, but it is." He gestured around him lazily. "You let me in, Holloway. You tore down the gates, and I simply walked through. You ripped apart their walls and shattered their defences. And now, you come to undo what you allowed?" He tilted his head as if amused by the irony. "Don't waste your victory, Holloway."

Ben stepped forward, his boots echoing against the marble floor. "I'm here to fix that mistake."

Lucius sighed theatrically, setting his chalice aside. Then he stood, slow and deliberate, his presence swelling like a storm rolling in over a blackened sea. The weight of him filled the room, pressing against the very air.

"And what do you think happens next?" Lucius asked, his voice a whisper of thunder. "You cast me out like the others? You think you're Heaven's Savior?"

Ben exhaled slowly, steadying himself. "I'm not a Savior." His eyes locked onto Lucius's, unwavering. "I'm just the guy who cleans up the mess."

Lucius smirked, stepping down from his throne, his every movement precise, deliberate, like a predator closing in. "Then let's see if you have the strength to clean me up." His voice dropped to a low taunt; words laced with something venomous. "Enjoy your throne, Holloway." His eyes glinted with

338

something dangerous. "Let's see how long before you become me." Lightning crackled in the distance. The temple trembled. The battle for Heaven's future had begun.

Ben's muscles tensed as the storm inside the temple seemed to grow louder, and heavier. The walls themselves seemed to groan beneath the weight of Lucius's presence. The tyrant wasn't just a man; he was a force of nature, a storm unleashed upon a world that had already suffered too much.

The tension between them grew, electric and thick, until the air seemed to snap, and Lucius moved.

In a blur of motion, he lunged forward, his arm outstretched, his fingers curling like claws, aiming for Ben's throat. It was a strike born of centuries of cruelty, the practiced speed of a predator who knew nothing but domination.

But Ben was ready.

He twisted, blocking the strike with a powerful deflection, using Lucius's momentum against him. The shock of their collision rang through the room like a thunderclap. Ben drove his elbow into Lucius's side, but the tyrant's Armor absorbed the blow, his grin only widening.

"Is that the best you've got?" Lucius hissed, his voice dripping with malice.

Ben didn't answer. He didn't need to. His actions spoke for him as he launched himself into the fray, moving with the precision and power that came from being more than human. This fight wasn't just about survival. It was about ending the nightmare Lucius had created—one that threatened to consume Heaven itself.

Chapter 22:

Facing the Worst of Humanity

Ben had seen the worst of people in life—corrupt executives, manipulative managers, self-serving leeches who thrived off the talent of others. He had thought he knew what true evil looked like.

He had been wrong.

Evil wasn't just greed. It wasn't just exploitation or betrayal. It wasn't the man in a suit stealing millions with the stroke of a pen. It wasn't the CEO laying off thousands while pocketing bonuses. Those were parasites, yes, but they weren't monsters.

No. Monsters were made of something else.

Monsters carved their names into history with fire and steel. Monsters built their empires on the bodies of the helpless. Monsters didn't just take advantage of the world's cruelty—they became its architects.

And inside that ruined temple, the worst of humanity waited. Lucius Atrian was only the beginning.

Ben stood at the entrance, the cold wind howling through the shattered archways. The temple had been built as a beacon of light, a place where souls could find peace, where Heaven's highest virtues were once worshiped. Now, it had been twisted into something dark. The murals of saints and angels had been defaced, their eyes gouged out, their hands painted over with iron chains. The golden statues that had once stood tall had been melted and reforged into weapons. The floor was littered with bones—not of the dead, but of the defeated.

340

The throne of Lucius Atrian sat at the heart of it all, towering and grotesque, a perversion of Heaven's purity. And beyond him, deeper into the temple's cavernous halls, more of them lurked—tyrants, warlords, slavers, and butchers who had never faced justice in life. They had been granted mercy in death, slipping through the cracks of the afterlife, and they had turned Heaven into their final conquest.

Ben cracked his knuckles, the sound sharp in the silence. His body ached from the battles he had already fought, his divine energy stretched thin, but it didn't matter.

He had come too far to stop now.

Peter stood behind him, hesitant. "Ben, you don't have to do this alone."

Ben didn't turn. He just exhaled, slow and steady, his breath forming mist in the cold.

"I know."

Then, with one final breath, he stepped forward, vanishing into the darkness.

The worst of humanity was waiting.

And Ben was going to meet them head-on.

The first thing he noticed was the silence.

No war cries. No laughter. No whispered deals of betrayal. Just quiet.

The air was thick with anticipation, like a storm hanging on the horizon, ready to break. Each step Ben took seemed to echo through the vast, hollowed-out structure of the temple, magnifying his presence, reminding him that he was no longer just an outsider—he was the storm that was about to sweep through it all.

As he advanced deeper into the temple, he could sense the power of the souls that lurked in the shadows. They were waiting. Watching.

Ben's instincts were sharp—he had always relied on them in life, and they were no different now. He could feel their malice in the air, the oppressive weight of their evil pressing down on him like an iron shackle. These were not the petty criminals he had hunted down. These were the architects of suffering, the men and women whose deeds had made even Hell itself recoil. The temple stretched endlessly before him, a labyrinth of broken statues, ruined altars, and defiled relics. The once-sacred halls now resembled a war zone, twisted by the greed and cruelty of the tyrants who had taken refuge here. Ben's gaze flickered to his right, where a dark figure stood motionless. His eyes narrowed, but the figure did not move, did not acknowledge his presence.

A whisper stirred the air—soft, almost imperceptible—but Ben caught it, sharp as a blade. "Holloway," the voice hissed, dripping with venom.

Ben's eyes narrowed. He had been expecting this.

He had been expecting them all.

"How predictable," Ben muttered to himself, his fingers flexing in readiness.

He could feel them now. They were all here, watching him. Lucius Atrian had brought them together, but the tyrant wasn't the only one pulling the strings.

As if on cue, figures emerged from the shadows. Their faces were twisted in cruelty, their bodies hardened by years of oppression and violence. A massive man, his skin marked by burn scars, stepped into view, holding a jagged blade that gleamed with malice. Behind him, a woman with empty eyes,

342

her hands shackled in chains that seemed to hum with dark energy, followed, her smile twisted in contempt.

The First of Many.

"Come to join your master, Holloway?" The man's voice was a growl, deep and threatening.

Ben didn't flinch. He didn't need to.

"I'm here to end this."

The man laughed, low and guttural, a sound that seemed to vibrate through the temple. "You? End this? You're just a broken man pretending to be a god."

Ben's lip curled into a snarl, and with a single motion, he leapt forward, his fist landing squarely in the man's chest. The force of the blow shattered his ribs, sending him crashing to the ground with a sickening thud.

The woman with the chains didn't hesitate. She moved with unnatural speed, her shackles clinking like the sound of distant thunder. Ben barely managed to deflect the strike from her claws, the force of her swipe sending him skidding back a few feet.

She hissed. "You don't belong here, Holloway. You never did."

Ben's eyes burned with resolve. "Neither do you." And with that, the fight began in earnest.

The temple erupted into chaos. Ben moved with fluid grace; his every motion powered by divine fury. The warlords and tyrants came at him in waves, but Ben was relentless, breaking them down one by one. Each strike of his hand was like the force of a wrecking ball, each blow infused with the power of Heaven's might.

343

But they kept coming.

They fought like rabid dogs, like creatures who had nothing left to lose. Some of them had once ruled over kingdoms, others had been nothing more than executioners, but here, they were all the same—cogs in the machine of destruction that Lucius had created.

Ben could feel his energy waning, the divine power inside him starting to flicker. He had been fighting for what felt like hours, and the exhaustion was starting to take its toll.

But he couldn't stop. Not now.

He refused to let these monster's win.

The kind that settled in the air before something terrible happened.

Ben moved through the ruined halls, the broken columns casting long shadows over the shattered floor. The flickering light of stolen torches illuminated murals of Heaven's history— now defaced, rewritten in the image of the monsters who had claimed them. The faces of saints had been chiselled away, replaced with crude carvings of warlords and tyrants. The oncepristine golden walls were smeared with soot, blood, and crude proclamations of dominion.

Then, he saw them.

The council of the damned.

They sat in a half-circle, draped in stolen silk and stolen power, their expressions unreadable. These were not men and women who had lived in the shadows. They had shaped the world through destruction, written history with fire and war, sculpted civilizations from the bones of the conquered.

And at the centre of them all, Lucius Atrian. Unbothered. Smirking.

"You've made quite the mess, Holloway," Lucius said, his voice smooth, practiced—the kind of voice that had once convinced entire nations to kneel.

Ben exhaled slowly. "You don't belong here."

Lucius tilted his head. "You let me in."

Ben's jaw tightened. He had. And now, he had to fix it.

Lucius wasn't alone. He had gathered the worst of the worst— the kind of souls that sent shivers down history's spine. To Lucius's left sat Hadrian Volk, the merchant of suffering, a man who had built an empire on war, who had traded lives as if they were currency. His bloodstained deals had spanned centuries, funding conflicts, selling weapons, treating human misery like a commodity.

To his right was Elena Greist, the Queen of Shadows, a woman who had poisoned her way through history, orchestrating betrayals that had crumbled entire dynasties. She had never lifted a sword, never led an army, but her words had toppled kingdoms. Rulers had died whispering her name in terror.

Further back, a man whose name had been lost to time but whose actions had shaped the darkest corners of the world. He had burned civilizations to the ground before the world had learned to keep records. He had erased histories before they could be written.

345

And they all watched Ben, amused. Like he was the one who didn't belong.

"You think you're here to clean house?" Hadrian sneered, leaning forward. "You should be thanking us."

Ben's fingers twitched. "Thanking you?"

Elena smiled, slow and knowing. "Holloway, what do you think Heaven really is? A sanctuary? A reward?"

Lucius gestured lazily to the ruined temple around them. "This place has always been a throne for the powerful. You just let in a new kind of ruler."

Ben took a step forward, his heartbeat steady, controlled. "I let in mistakes. And now, I'm here to take them out."

Lucius's smirk didn't fade. He leaned forward slightly, his voice dripping with mock curiosity. "You think you're better than us?"

Ben hesitated.
For the first time since this all began, he wasn't sure.

Lucius saw it. The flicker of doubt. And he laughed. Low and rich, a sound that echoed through the ruined temple like a slowburning fire.

"You feel it, don't you?" Lucius pressed; eyes gleaming. "The weight of what you've done? How many souls have you erased, Ben? How many have you cast into the abyss? And tell me— when you do it, how does it feel?"

Ben didn't answer.
Because he already knew the truth.

It felt good.

It felt right.

He had justified every soul he had condemned. They were tyrants. Killers. Monsters who had no place in Heaven. But every time he pulled the trigger, every time he opened the void beneath their feet, a part of him wondered—was he still Ben Holloway? Or was he becoming something else? Something like them.

Lucius's smirk widened, sensing the hesitation. "You see, Holloway, I don't need to win." He leaned back, drumming his fingers against the armrest of his throne. "I just need to watch you lose yourself."

The council of the damned watched, waiting, their smiles small, knowing.

Ben's hands burned with divine power. His body ached from the battles he had already fought, but this was different. This wasn't just a fight for Heaven. This was a fight for himself.

His grip tightened.

He wasn't like them. Not

yet.

Ben took another step forward. The flickering torchlight gleamed against his clenched fists.

"You want to test that theory?" he said, his voice low, steady.

Lucius chuckled, rising from his throne. His presence alone sent a ripple through the room, as if the walls themselves recognized the force he had been in life.

"Oh, Holloway." His grin sharpened, dark and wicked.

"I was hoping you'd say that."

The Battle for His Soul Had Begun.

Lucius's every movement was a calculated display of power. The air seemed to grow colder, heavier, as he stepped down from his throne, the sound of his boots echoing through the desecrated hall. He was a man who had commanded armies, whose voice had once turned the tide of wars, whose name had been whispered in fear and reverence across entire continents. And now, in this fractured place, he was still the embodiment of that power.

He raised a hand, signalling his council to stay back, his eyes never leaving Ben. "I don't need to prove anything to you," Lucius said, his voice like velvet, smooth and persuasive. "But you... you need to prove something to yourself."

Ben's heart thundered in his chest, his grip tightening around the divine energy coursing through him. He was no longer just a man. Not with the power of Heaven at his fingertips.

Lucius stepped closer, a shadow in the midst of the broken light. His smile didn't fade. "I've seen men like you before, Holloway," he continued, his voice dripping with contempt. "Men who believe in justice. Men who think they can fix the world by wiping away the stains with a flick of their wrist." He leaned in, his breath hot against Ben's ear. "But you know what happens to men like that, don't you? They burn themselves out. They turn into the very thing they fought against."

348

Ben's jaw clenched, his pulse racing. He could feel the weight of Lucius's words settling on him like an invisible chain, pulling at his resolve.

But he wouldn't break.
Not now. Not after everything.

Lucius's grin turned sharper. "Let's see how long you can keep up this illusion of righteousness." His eyes gleamed with malice. "Let's see if you can still call yourself Ben Holloway when this is over."

The challenge was clear.

The stage was set for the final battle—not just for Heaven, but for Ben's very soul.

What made a man truly evil?

Ben had spent his life calling out the worst in people—recognizing greed, selfishness, the rot at the core of humanity. He had seen it in boardrooms, in back alleys, in the twisted justifications of men who thought themselves untouchable.

But standing here, in front of the worst that had ever lived, he realized something.

They weren't all the same.

Some had been born into power, melded into tyrants by blood and privilege. Others had clawed their way up through fire and suffering, forging their own thrones from the bones of their enemies.

Some had ruled with arrogance, believing their right to dominion was unquestionable. Others had ruled with terror, knowing that only fear could keep them in control.

But the real difference between them and him?

They had never wanted redemption.

Ben took another step forward, his voice lower now, steady, testing. "Tell me something."

Lucius raised a brow, intrigued but unshaken.

Ben's gaze swept across the council, taking them in. Hadrian Volk. Elena Greist. The nameless destroyer from a time before time.

They were monsters, yes. But they were also men and women who had once been human.

"If I gave you a chance—just one—would you take it?"

Silence.

Then, Hadrian laughed.

A deep, cruel sound that echoed through the temple ruins. The others joined him—low chuckles, scoffing amusement.

Lucius only smiled. A slow, condescending curve of his lips. "And what, exactly, do you think redemption looks like for people like us?"

Ben exhaled. That was all the answer he needed.

No regret. No shame.

They would never change.

He lifted his hand. The holy fire crackled between his fingers.

The laughter faded.

Lucius's smirk faltered—just slightly.

Ben let the fire grow. Heaven's judgment. His judgment.

Once, he had thought Heaven was broken. Maybe it was.

But these people? They weren't part of the fix.

Ben met Lucius's gaze and smirked.

"Time's up."

The battle wasn't clean.
It wasn't a quick, righteous purge. It
was war.

The council didn't go quietly. They fought back with everything they had—power, influence, the sheer force of their will. They had spent their lives shaping the world through fear, bending history to their whims.

Now, they used that same fear against Ben.

Hadrian moved first, his fingers twisting in the air. The torches flickered—and then died, plunging the temple into an unnatural, suffocating dark. The shadows came alive, stretching toward

Ben like grasping hands, whispering with voices of the longdead.

The darkness wasn't just an absence of light—it was an entity in itself, a living, breathing thing that wrapped itself around Ben like an unholy shroud. It clawed at his skin, twisted around his throat, and filled his ears with the faint, distant wails of those who had been consumed by it. It was power made tangible, a manifestation of every fear, every regret, every soul ever damned to wander the void.

Ben stood still, his breathing steady. He had faced worse in his life, hadn't he? He wasn't going to let this paralyse him.

With a sharp flick of his wrist, he summoned the light, piercing the darkness with the divine fire in his hand. The shadows hissed, recoiling from the heat, but they didn't retreat. They merely grew more insistent, more eager.

From behind him, Elena Greist's voice rang out, soft yet powerful, as if woven from the very fabric of the world itself. She wasn't just speaking. She was shaping reality.

"Fear is your true enemy, Holloway," Elena's voice purred, her words creating cracks in the air. "It is what holds your world together. What makes you believe you can save it? What makes you believe you have the right to judge us."

Ben's teeth ground together as the shadows pushed closer, their claws like ice on his skin. Elena's voice wrapped around him, drawing him in, and tempting him to listen.

But he had already heard that whisper. He had heard it for years. It was the whisper of self-doubt. The voice that told him he was no better than the monsters he had hunted. The voice that told him Heaven, Hell, justice, everything—it was all just an illusion.

Ben let out a slow breath, fighting against the weight of her words. "You're wrong, Elena. Fear doesn't control me. I've faced enough of it to know how to burn it away."

He gritted his teeth and thrust his hand forward. Holy fire exploded from his palm, cutting through the darkness like a blade. The shadows recoiled, shrieking as they were burned away by the purifying flames.

Elena's voice faltered for the briefest moment, and that was all Ben needed. He moved toward her, his every step radiating divine power, his mind locked on the truth he had long ago accepted.

He wasn't like them. He never would be.

And no matter how twisted the world had become, he would make sure it was set right.

But Hadrian wasn't finished. He had already begun to rise from his seat, the look in his eyes one of raw, unyielding rage. His hand snapped through the air, and suddenly, the ground trembled beneath Ben's feet. The very floor of the temple buckled and cracked as if it were alive, eager to consume him.

Hadrian's power was a torrent of destruction. The stones rose, jagged and sharp, like weapons designed to tear flesh from bone. They shot toward Ben, each shard an extension of the pain he had caused in life—of the lives he had destroyed for profit.

But Ben wasn't shaken. He had faced worse than this.

With a roar, he slammed his palm to the ground. The holy fire surged outward in a massive wave, breaking through the earth

353

and sending the stones flying into the air like brittle fragments of forgotten history.

Lucius stood; his smile gone, replaced by a look of genuine interest. "I see you've become something more," he murmured, his eyes narrowing. "But tell me, Holloway, when this is all over, when you've won... who do you think you'll be?"

Ben met his gaze. "I'll be the one who stops you."

The walls shook. The air grew thick with tension. Ben knew this was it. He wasn't just fighting for Heaven, redemption, or anything else that these monsters had twisted into their corrupt image. This was about something simpler: justice. And he would see it through, no matter the cost.

Ben knew one thing, and one thing only.

This wasn't a battle to be won.

It was a battle to survive.

Every breath felt like it might be his last. The weight of his body, the exhaustion, the pain from each blow—it all screamed for him to give up, to let the darkness consume him. But Ben couldn't afford to lose. He couldn't afford to stop fighting, no matter how broken he was, no matter how much the odds were stacked against him.

He wasn't fighting for glory. He wasn't fighting for any cause or creed. No lofty ideals were driving him forward. No, Ben was fighting for something far more personal—something more fragile and more precious than anything else in the world.

He was fighting for the lives of those he loved.

For Emma. For Lena.

For the chance to wake up one more day and see their faces. To hear their voices. To hold them in his arms.

As Lucius moved to strike again, Ben pushed through the haze of fatigue that threatened to swallow him whole. His body screamed for rest, but his heart burned with purpose. His instincts were all that kept him going now, his muscles moving on memory alone, driven by the desperate need to keep moving, to keep fighting.

Lucius's fist came down like a hammer, but Ben was ready. He sidestepped; his hand glowing with holy fire as he swung it toward Lucius's side. The light connected, and Lucius grunted, his Armor flickering with the impact. But he didn't falter. He didn't hesitate. He was a machine of war, built to fight, to conquer, to win.

Ben stumbled back, winded from the force of their clash, but he wasn't done yet. His hands, shaking from the strain, called up more fire, more light. His magic was a flickering spark, barely hanging on, but it was enough. It would have to be enough.

Lucius's cold eyes locked onto him. "You think you can survive this, Ben?" His voice was calm, like the stillness before a storm. "You think you can beat me?"

Ben didn't respond. He didn't have to. His silence spoke volumes. He wasn't here to argue. He wasn't here to reason. He was here to fight—and if he had to burn through every last ounce of his strength, he would.

Hadrian's shadows surged forward again, trying to wrap around him like a vice. But this time, Ben was ready. He hurled fire at the darkness, splitting it apart with a roar. He could feel it, the raw power, the heat coursing through his veins. But it wasn't enough to end this. Not yet.

Lucius's movements were like clockwork, each strike more devastating than the last. His presence was an iron wall that Ben couldn't seem to break through. His attacks were sharp, relentless, and unyielding. Ben had fought before, he'd fought in wars, he'd fought demons, but nothing compared to this— nothing compared to the cold, calculating fury of Lucius.

Ben wasn't sure how much longer he could last. His body was worn, bloodied, and bruised. His mind was drifting. But still, the images of Emma and Lena flashed in his mind—bright and clear. They were waiting for him. They were counting on him.

One more moment. One more breath. One more strike.

Lucius's blade arced down toward him, but Ben was faster this time. He grabbed Lucius's wrist, twisting it, and with a powerful shove, he sent the general stumbling back.

Ben staggered to his feet, his legs trembling. He was barely holding himself together, but he couldn't give up. Not yet. He had too much to lose.

"You're broken, Ben," Lucius taunted, wiping the blood from his lip. "You've lost everything. You're nothing."

The words stung, more than they should have. Lucius was right. Ben had lost everything. His world had crumbled around him, leaving nothing but ashes. But what Lucius didn't understand—

what none of them understood—was that Ben still had something to fight for.

He might be broken, but he wasn't done.

With a roar, Ben surged forward again, his last reserves of energy surging through him. The world blurred around him, but he focused on the target. Lucius. The fight. One more strike, one more chance.

For Emma. For Lena.

For one more day.

He wasn't sure how, but he forced the fire to flare up again, brighter, hotter, stronger than before. It burned within him, fuelled by the memory of everything he'd lost—and everything he had left to protect.

Ben's fist slammed into Lucius's chest, crackling with holy fire. There was a moment of stunned silence before Lucius gasped, a jolt of pain running through his form. The divine fire seared through his Armor, sizzling against his skin. But Lucius didn't collapse. He didn't fall.

Instead, he glared down at Ben, his eyes glowing with a dangerous intensity. "You'll burn, Ben," he growled. "And when you do, there will be nothing left of you."

But Ben didn't care. Let the fire burn him. Let it consume him. He would never stop fighting. Not now. Not ever.

Not while there was still breath in his body.

Not while he still had one last promise to keep.

For Emma. For Lena. For one more day.

Lucius was the last to fall.

He staggered, his once-confident smirk replaced with something hollow, something almost... understanding. The great Lucius Atrian, the Tyrant of the Black Age, conqueror of men, ruler of fear—stood before Ben defeated. The weight of it seemed to press down on his shoulders, as if, for the first time in eternity, he felt something beyond power. His posture slumped, not in weakness, but in a way that suggested a shift, a change he couldn't quite name.

Maybe it was regret. Maybe it was a relief. Maybe it was the weight of everything he had done, and everything he had lost. Or maybe it was nothing at all. Maybe, in that final moment, Lucius had simply realized the futility of it all.

Ben didn't know. He didn't care.

Lucius's breath was shallow, his lips quirking into something that wasn't quite a smirk, not quite a frown. "You're not like them," he murmured, his voice quieter now. Not mocking. Not cruel. Just... resigned. It was the kind of statement that held more weight than any grand speech, any taunt. There was something in it—something that dug beneath the surface, making Ben wonder if Lucius had ever truly believed in the cause he'd fought for, or if it had simply been about survival all along.

Ben's chest heaved as he stepped forward, his grip tightening on Lucius's collar. His knuckles were bruised, his body ached, but

358

he was still standing. That was more than could be said for the council of the damned. That was more than could be said for all the nightmares that had once ruled this place.

"I know," Ben said, his voice ragged.

Lucius exhaled a sound almost like laughter—bitter, hollow, like the remnants of a life that had never truly been lived. "That's what makes you dangerous," he said, his gaze flickering over Ben, as though trying to understand him, trying to find the flaw, the breaking point, but failing to do so. Ben didn't argue. He didn't have to. Lucius was right, in a way that made his stomach churn.

Ben *was* dangerous.

He had done things no angel had dared. He had wielded judgment like a weapon, torn through legions of the unworthy, and silenced their cries with nothing more than a thought. He had cast down entire legacies, cast down his brothers and sisters, without hesitation. He had burned through the lies and the veneer of Heaven, seeing the truth beneath the façade. He had been ruthless when the world demanded it, and no matter how much he tried to pretend otherwise, a part of him had relished it.

And yet… here he stood. Alive. Not victorious. Not redeemed. But still standing.

Ben could feel the weight of Lucius's words trying to settle into his bones. Was he dangerous? *Maybe.* Maybe more dangerous than any of them had ever realized. But he wasn't like them. And that was all that mattered.

Lucius had been right about one thing. He was different. He wasn't the one who *ruled* through fear. He didn't see himself as above it all. He had been fighting for something pure—for the ones he loved, for the ones who had suffered and been destroyed by the very system Lucius had built.

The system had broken, and so had the people within it. All that was left was the ruins.

Ben took a breath—then let go.

His hand moved to release Lucius, and as he did, the rift beneath them opened. The ground split, an abyss of unmaking, the same void that had swallowed all the others before him. There was no fanfare, no grand proclamation. Lucius didn't fight it. He didn't resist. He simply fell. The mighty tyrant, the god-king of fear, was swallowed by the nothingness, leaving behind nothing but a brief whisper.

His voice echoed one last time, curling through the ruins like smoke, a final, taunting remark: "Enjoy your throne, Holloway. Let's see how long before you become me."

And then—he was gone.

The temple was quiet.

No more laughter. No more mocking voices. No more monsters breathing down his neck, no more gods of war or tyrants of time. Just the heavy stillness of the aftermath. The wind had stopped howling, the echoes of battle fading into a distant murmur. The air was thick with the residue of power, the remnants of an ancient war that had finally drawn to its end. For the first time in what felt like an eternity...

Heaven was clean.

Ben stood among the ruins, his body shaking, blood drying on his skin, surrounded by the remnants of tyrants, warlords, and killers. The battle was over. And for all the destruction, for all the pain, there was a strange emptiness that filled the space between his breaths. Was this a victory? Was it peace? He wasn't sure anymore. But it was over. And for that, at least, he was thankful.

A low whistle cut through the silence, sharp and almost out of place.

Ben turned, and there, appearing from the shadows, was Peter—arms crossed, his expression a mixture of halfimpressed, half-exasperated. A soft chuckle followed.

"Well, damn," Peter said, his voice carrying a lightness that seemed almost too jovial for the scene around them. "I didn't think you had it in you."

Ben didn't respond at first, just took in the sight of the man who had been a constant through so much of this nightmare. They had both fought in different ways, both had bled for the same cause, even if their paths had never quite aligned. Ben found himself smiling despite the weight on his chest.

"Yeah, well, neither did I," Ben muttered, his voice hoarse. "But it's over."

Peter raised an eyebrow, studying Ben carefully. "Is it, though? Or is it just beginning?"

Ben turned back to the ruins, the broken temple at his feet. He didn't have an answer. All he knew was that nothing would ever be the same again.

"Maybe," Ben said, his voice quieter now. "Maybe it's just beginning."

Ben exhaled, rubbing a hand down his face. He could still feel the heat of battle under his skin, still taste the remnants of war in the air—the blood, the ashes, the lingering traces of destruction that clung to everything. He had fought, bled, and lost so much. And now, after everything, the dust was beginning to settle.

"Is it done?" he asked, his voice rough as if the weight of his words could still shatter something inside of him.

Peter studied the battlefield, his gaze sweeping over the remains of the shattered throne, the space where Lucius Atrian had once stood—where the mightiest of them all had finally fallen. The silence was deafening now, the echoes of their battle fading into nothing. The power that had filled the temple had dissipated, leaving only ruins behind.

Then, finally, Peter nodded, his expression unreadable. "Yeah. I'd say you did it."

Ben let out a slow breath, the words sinking in like a stone in the pit of his stomach. Relief should have washed over him, but it didn't. Instead, exhaustion settled into his bones, heavier than any burden he'd carried before. It wasn't just physical. It was the kind of fatigue that seeped into your soul, the kind that comes from waging a war not just against enemies, but against everything you had once believed in.

"Good," Ben muttered, but it didn't feel like the right word. Nothing felt good anymore.

Peter turned to him, and Ben saw the familiar glint of mischief in his eyes, a sharp contrast to the sombre weight of the moment. "You know what that means, right?" he asked his tone light, almost teasing.

Ben did. The weight of it settled like a heavy cloak on his shoulders. His stomach twisted with a mix of anticipation and dread, the sense that something had changed irreversibly. The war was over. But now, a new battle awaited him.

Because now… it was time.

Peter's grin widened, bright and mischievous, as if he were enjoying this moment far too much. "Pack your bags, Holloway."

Ben's chest tightened. He could feel his hands still tingling with remnants of power, the rush of energy that had once been his weapon, now fading but still present, an echo of the war he'd just fought. His body still ached from the brutal battle, from the countless blows he had taken, but now there was no time to rest.

Peter clapped him on the back, laughing, the sound of it too light, too carefree for the gravity of the situation. "You've got a day to live."

The words hit harder than any punch Lucius had thrown. Ben swallowed hard; his throat dry. He wasn't sure what came next—whether he was ready, whether he even had the strength to face it—but there was no turning back. The world had changed, and with it, so had his fate.

One more day.

Chapter 23:

Restoring Order

After the Fire

The battle was over.

But Heaven was still in ruins.

Ben stood among the wreckage, the golden streets cracked, the towering structures crumbling under the weight of the chaos he had unleashed. The once-immaculate architecture, built to represent purity and eternity, was now a shattered graveyard of broken marble and scorched stone.

The monsters were gone. But their corruption lingered. The air still felt heavy, as if the echoes of Lucius and his council remained, whispering in the corners of the ruins. The sky above Heaven, once an unbroken expanse of light, still flickered with the aftershocks of the war. This was supposed to feel like a victory. It didn't.

Peter crossed his arms beside him, letting out a long sigh. "Well, you cleaned house, but now you've got to mop the floors."

Ben wiped a hand over his face, his body still aching from battle. "What the hell does that mean?"

Peter gestured toward the shattered remains of Heaven's highest temple. The once-grand cathedral, which had stood for millennia, was now barely standing, its pillars cracked, its stained-glass windows reduced to shards. The very heart of Heaven had been torn apart.

365

"You tore apart the system, kid," Peter said, his tone light but his eyes sharp. "You didn't just kick out the bad guys—you left a power vacuum. The angels have no leader. The saints have no guidance. This place doesn't just need a judge; it needs order."

Ben exhaled, rolling his shoulders. "And let me guess—you're not going to do it?"

Peter snorted. "Hell no. I quit, remember?"

He clapped a hand on Ben's shoulder, a little too cheerfully for Ben's liking.

"This one's on you."

Ben tensed. This wasn't what he wanted.

He had never wanted power.

He had never wanted to rule.

He had only ever wanted to burn the system down.

And now… now he had to rebuild it.

A bitter laugh escaped his lips. "What if I don't?"

Peter shrugged. "Then this place rots. And after everything you did? After everything you fought for?" He tilted his head.

"That'd be a real shame."

Ben looked out over the remains of Heaven, taking in the devastation. He had done this. Maybe not alone, but his hands had played a part in every shattered wall, every broken road.

Heaven had been rotting before—but now?

Now, it was hollow.

A kingdom with no king.

A movement in the distance caught his eye.

The angels were returning.

Not in the way he had expected. No fanfare. No trumpets. Just hesitation. A cautious step forward, eyes darting between the ruins, between him. Some still wore the scars of battle, others had been absent entirely, waiting to see if Heaven had been lost for good.

They were watching him. Waiting.

Ben clenched his jaw. He didn't want this.

But if he didn't step up... someone else would.

Someone worse.

Peter must have seen the realization on his face because he grinned. "Told you. You're dangerous."

Ben turned to him. "And what if I say no?"

Peter shrugged. "Then Lucius wins." Silence stretched between them.

Ben's fingers curled into fists.

Heaven wasn't supposed to have kings.

But maybe it needed one.

Ben tensed. He had never wanted power. He had never wanted to rule.

He had only ever wanted to burn the system down. Now, he had to rebuild it.

The realization was like a weight pressing down on his chest. There was no escaping it. Not anymore. Even if he had no idea how to put the pieces back together, he couldn't simply walk away and hope for the best. The angels would need guidance, even if he had never planned on being the one to give it. And the more he thought about it, the more he realized Peter was right: someone would fill the void, and that someone wouldn't have any better answers than Lucius or the rest of the corrupt leaders. Power—real power—wasn't something you could just ignore. You had to either claim it or be swept away by those who did.

Ben looked out over the crumbling remnants of Heaven again, trying to gather his thoughts. He had been angry at the system, yes, but now it was gone, and in its absence, the world felt even more fragile. It wasn't the triumphant sense of freedom he had imagined. It was like a wound that refused to heal, a scar that would never fade. The chaos had been swept away, but now the void of what came after was even more terrifying. It felt wrong, but it also felt inevitable.

"Do you think they'll follow me?" Ben asked, his voice quieter than before, directed toward Peter, though his gaze remained on the distant figures of the angels.
Peter's eyes followed his, noting the uncertainty that lingered in Ben's posture. "Follow you?" he asked, cocking an eyebrow. "Kid, they already are."

Ben gritted his teeth, but there was no denying it. The angels, with their silent watchfulness, were waiting for him to take a step forward, to give them direction. They needed someone to step into the vacuum. And even if Ben had no experience, no training for leadership, they would follow him—if only because he was the one who had shattered everything, and they needed someone to tell them where to go now.
The truth gnawed at him, deep in his gut. It wasn't just about ruling—it was about the possibility of saving Heaven from collapsing entirely. If he did nothing, the destruction would be complete. If he stepped up, at least there was a chance, however slim, that he could rebuild, that something meaningful could rise from the ashes.

"Don't make it harder than it has to be," Peter said, breaking into Ben's spiralling thoughts. "You've already done the hardest part."

368

Ben looked at him, eyes sharp. "The hardest part?" Peter nodded. "You brought the system down. You broke the chains. Now, the work's in building something new. It's not glamorous, it's not easy, and it sure as hell isn't fun, but it's the only choice you've got."

Ben took a deep breath, feeling the weight of his decision pressing down on him. The gravity of it didn't make the choice any easier, but it did make it clear. There was no other way.

The Reluctant King

Turning his eyes back to the distant angels, Ben felt a surge of something new—determination, maybe. He still didn't want this. He still didn't want to be the leader they needed. But he couldn't leave Heaven to rot, not after everything he had done to get here.

He stepped forward, moving toward the angels, his footsteps echoing in the ruined streets of Heaven. They didn't move, didn't speak, but their gazes followed him closely, almost as if they, too, were unsure whether to trust him.

But as Ben approached, something shifted in the air—a faint spark of hope. Even if he didn't have all the answers, even if he wasn't ready to be their king, he was still here.

And that, for now, was enough.

Ben tensed. This wasn't what he wanted.

He had never wanted power.

He had never wanted to rule.

369

He had only ever wanted to burn the system down.

And now… now he had to rebuild it.

A bitter laugh escaped his lips. "What if I don't?"

Peter shrugged. "Then this place rots. And after everything you did? After everything you fought for?" He tilted his head. "That'd be a real shame."

Ben looked out over the remains of Heaven, taking in the devastation. He had done this. Maybe not alone, but his hands had played a part in every shattered wall, every broken road. Heaven had been rotting before—but now?
Now, it was hollow.
A kingdom with no king.

A movement in the distance caught his eye.
The angels were returning.
Not in the way he had expected. No fanfare. No trumpets. Just hesitation. A cautious step forward, eyes darting between the ruins, between him. Some still wore the scars of battle, others had been absent entirely, waiting to see if Heaven had been lost for good.
They were watching him.
Waiting.

Ben clenched his jaw. He didn't want this.
But if he didn't step up… someone else would. Someone worse.

Peter must have seen the realization on his face, because he grinned. "Told you. You're dangerous."

370

Ben turned to him. "And what if I say no?"
Peter shrugged. "Then Lucius wins." Silence
stretched between them.
Ben's fingers curled into fists.
Heaven wasn't supposed to have kings. But
maybe it needed one.

Ben tensed. He had never wanted power. He had never wanted
to rule.
He had only ever wanted to burn the system down. Now,
he had to rebuild it.

The angels that remained had been scattered, watching from the
clouds, uncertain of what came next.
Some had fought bravely against the wicked souls, defending
Heaven's gates until the bitter end. Others had abandoned their
posts altogether, convinced that paradise had already fallen. And
now, they hovered in the distance, their ethereal forms flickering
with uncertainty, waiting for someone to tell them what to do.
Ben had never been the type to give speeches.
But this wasn't about him. This
was about them.

He took a deep breath and stepped forward, ignoring the aches
in his body, ignoring the exhaustion pressing against his ribs.
His voice had been used for threats, for ultimatums, for
judgment. Now, it had to be used for something else. For
rebuilding.

"This place belongs to you," he said, his voice steady. "Not to
me. Not to Peter. Not to the ones who took it over." The
angels stirred, whispering amongst themselves. Doubt.
Hesitation. Hope.

371

Ben continued.

"You've spent eternity following rules you didn't make," he said. "Letting others decide who was worthy, who was good enough." His jaw tightened. "I've seen what happens when power falls into the wrong hands. I made that mistake myself." The words sat heavy in the air.

The ruins of Heaven, the shattered temples, the scars left behind—it was all proof of what happened when too much power rested in the hands of the few.

The Vacuum of Power

Lucius was gone. The war was over.

But if they simply waited for another ruler to rise, if they simply repeated the cycle, then everything he had done would be for nothing.

Silence settled over the ruins. Even the wind had stilled. Peter watched from the sidelines, arms crossed, a small smirk tugging at his lips. He had seen many men rise and fall, but he had never seen anyone like Ben.

Ben exhaled.

"It's time for you to decide. Heaven isn't meant to be a kingdom—it's meant to be a home."

The angels looked at one another, hesitant, uncertain.

Then, one of them stepped forward—Raphael.

Ben recognized him immediately.

He had been the first to walk away when Ben opened the gates to chaos. He had been the first to refuse to fight, to step back and watch as Heaven burned.

But now?

He was the first to return.

Raphael's piercing blue gaze met Ben's. He had once been one of Heaven's strongest warriors, second only to Michael in might. Now, there was something else in his expression—resolve. "We will rebuild," Raphael said, his voice calm, unwavering. "But not under tyranny."

Ben nodded. That was all he needed to hear.

The others watched, their expressions ranging from guarded to hopeful. Raphael wasn't just speaking for himself—he was speaking for all of them. The angels that had hesitated, the ones who had been too scared to act, had now found something to hold onto. Hope wasn't dead, not yet. Maybe it had been broken, shattered like the ruins around them, but it was still there, quietly waiting to be rebuilt.

Ben felt the weight of his decision pressing into him, the quiet pulse of something greater than himself stirring in his chest. He hadn't planned for any of this, hadn't asked for it, but here he was, standing at the edge of everything. And maybe, just maybe, he could rebuild it into something that wasn't broken beyond repair.

The angels around him started to speak, their voices softer than before, as though the very act of speaking had been a form of defiance, a rejection of what had been. They began to come closer, forming a loose circle, some stepping forward, others lingering on the edges, but all of them listening. Waiting.

Peter uncrossed his arms and stepped closer, his eyes watching the gathering with interest. "Well, kid," he said with a wry smile, "looks like you've got a crowd."

Ben didn't smile. Instead, he looked out over the assembly. "We can't rebuild what's broken by pretending nothing happened. If we're going to fix Heaven, we'll need to be honest about the past—and brave enough to face what comes next."

He turned to Raphael, who gave a small nod of agreement. "It's not going to be easy," Ben said. "But Heaven has always been more than a place. It's meant to be something we all share. And maybe that means we have to change the way we look at everything—our roles, our purpose, even our beliefs."

The angels were silent for a moment, and then, one by one, they lowered their heads in acknowledgment. Some looked unsure, others resolute, but all of them had seen the truth in Ben's words. Heaven couldn't remain as it was. It had to evolve, to grow, and maybe—just maybe—it could rise from the ashes stronger than before.

Ben glanced back at Peter, who was still watching, amused but thoughtful. "Well, this is it, then," Peter said, his tone slightly softer than usual. "The next chapter starts now. You've got a long road ahead, kid."

Ben took a deep breath and nodded, his gaze returning to the angels gathered around him. "Then let's get to work."

The air was thick with potential, and though the weight of the world still hung heavily on Ben's shoulders, for the first time, he felt the faint stirrings of something new—something that just might be enough to rebuild what had been broken. Rebuilding Heaven

With Raphael and the remaining angels, the restoration began.

374

It was slow, painful work.

The golden streets, once cracked and tainted with blood, slowly pieced themselves back together. The towering structures, once broken and shattered, began to heal as if Heaven itself was exhaling after holding its breath for too long. The broken spires reached toward the sky again, though no longer in arrogance or grandeur—this time, they sought the light with humility, the weight of their past mistakes still lingering beneath their polished surface.

But there was no throne.

No rulers. No judges. Only

balance.

A Home, Not a Kingdom

The once-shattered Halls of Justice were rebuilt—not as a place for kings or councils, but as a place of gathering, a place where decisions would be made together. The walls, scarred from centuries of use, now stood with an openness that invited collaboration, where voices could rise not in command but in unity. The angels, no longer shackled to the idea of a single authority, began to realize their shared responsibility in rebuilding a system that was both fair and free.

The angels would no longer look to a single leader. They would look at each other.

Ben stepped back, watching it all unfold, something heavy lifting off his chest. He wasn't sure what he expected, but it wasn't this. There had been a time when he thought Heaven's future was only worth fighting for if he could tear it down completely.

He thought destruction was the only answer to fixing what had been wrong. But now, he saw that rebuilding, while slower and more painstaking, had a beauty to it. It wasn't about the end of something—it was about the creation of something new, something better. And for the first time in what felt like an eternity, he allowed himself to hope.

Peter let out a low chuckle. "Would you look at that?" He gave Ben a sidelong glance. "You did it." Ben didn't answer.
He was watching the angels reclaim Heaven—not through conquest, not through judgment, but through unity.
It wasn't perfect.
But for the first time in eternity… It
felt right.

No rulers. No judges. Only
balance.

The saints, who had once fought for the purity of Heaven, found purpose again—not as enforcers of rules, but as guides. They walked among the souls that wandered, those lost in their journeys, offering a steady hand instead of a gavel. They were no longer figures of authority, but beacons of understanding, helping the souls find their way not by punishment but by enlightenment. There was no longer a sense that Heaven was a place to be feared—it was a sanctuary.

The lost, the confused, the souls who arrived at the gates with uncertainty in their hearts—they would not be turned away. Instead, they would be met with understanding. With choice. Heaven was no longer a place of absolutes. It was a place where souls could grow, learn, and change. The process of judgment no longer consisted of harsh decisions or irrevocable fates—it was a delicate balance of acceptance and guidance. No one was cast aside. Each soul was given the chance to evolve.

And the angels?
Some still carried their swords, still patrolled the edges of paradise to keep it safe, but most... most had changed. They had been warriors. Now, they become caretakers. No longer soldiers in an eternal war, they tended the lands of Heaven, nurtured the souls that passed through, and helped restore the balance. They were guardians now—not of law, but of peace. For the first time, Heaven wasn't about reward and punishment. It was about helping souls find peace.

The gates would no longer be locked by rigid laws. No longer would they be held shut by ancient judgments, unmoving and unyielding. Instead, each soul would be judged not by their past, but by what they sought to become. Because change was possible.
Even here.

The war had changed them all.
And Ben?
Ben had changed too.

He had spent so long believing in destruction.
That the only way to fix something broken was to burn it down.
But now, for the first time, he saw the value of rebuilding.

As Heaven's structures mended themselves, as order returned without chains, Ben realized something profound— Power never belonged to one being.
Not to a god.
Not to angels.

Not even to him.

It belonged to those willing to take responsibility. And he finally understood.

The Last Promise

Peter stepped beside him, stuffing his hands in his coat pockets. "Not bad, kid."

Ben huffed a laugh. "Coming from you, I'll take that as high praise."

Peter smirked. "So… ready to go back?" Ben's stomach twisted.

He had earned his day.

Emma. Lena.

The names felt heavy in his chest.

He had fought for them, too. For the promise he had made—to make things right.

To say goodbye the right way.

He had one last promise to keep.

He turned toward Peter, exhaling. "Yeah. I'm ready."

Peter nodded. He lifted a hand— And snapped his fingers.

The sky around them rippled.

Light poured down, folding over itself, stretching, twisting.

The golden ruins of Heaven blurred, then vanished—

And for the first time since he had died— Ben felt a weight in his limbs again.

The pull of gravity.
The sharp rush of breath filled his lungs.
His vision blurred.
Then darkened.
And then— He
was gone.

The world of Heaven, still in the process of healing, slipped away into the distance. Ben was finally leaving it behind—but this time, it wasn't in the wake of chaos or destruction. It was with the quiet understanding that what he had done mattered. What he had built mattered. And as the darkness took him, he carried with him a newfound peace. The promise of what would come next.

Chapter 24:

The Moment of Truth

The light faded. The world shifted. And Ben woke up. For a moment, he thought it had all been a dream—the war in Heaven, Peter's smirking face, the endless eternity spent at the gates, weighing souls and sending them to their fate.

But then— He inhaled. Fresh earth. Cut grass. Morning dew. His lungs filled with something real. Not celestial air, not divine essence—just air. His eyes fluttered open. And he saw the sky. Soft pastels melted into gold, the first light of sunrise spilling over the ranch. His ranch. The old wooden porch beneath him was solid, warm beneath his hands. The boards creaked just as they always had, worn from years of boots and bare feet and childhood games. The wind was crisp and cool, rustling the trees beyond the fence, and carrying the distant sound of horses in the pasture.

Ben's hands trembled as he pressed them against the ground, feeling—truly feeling—the rough texture of the old planks. This was real. Not a ghost. Not a fleeting memory. Alive.

He swallowed hard, his chest tight, his heart pounding against his ribs. One day. That's all he had. And then—

He heard her voice. "Lena, honey, bring me that blanket—oh, careful with the baby." Ben's breath hitched. Emma. He turned toward the voice, barely able to move, afraid that if he blinked too hard, this would all disappear. And then— There she was.

Standing in the doorway of the ranch house, bathed in the soft glow of morning. Emma.

She was older now—a woman in her fifties, with silver streaks in her dark hair, and laughter lines etched into the corners of her mouth and eyes. But she was still Emma. Still his Emma. And standing beside her, a grown woman holding a newborn baby. Lena.

Ben's breath shook. The last time he had seen his daughter, she had been eight years old. A little girl with scraped knees and a fearless heart. And now—now she was grown. A mother.

She held the baby carefully, adjusting the blanket, murmuring something soft as she stepped onto the porch. Ben's throat closed up. He couldn't move. Couldn't breathe. They didn't see him yet. Didn't know he was here. But he knew them. He had waited so long to see them again. And now, for one day, he had his chance. One day to say goodbye the right way. One day to told them everything he never got to say.

Ben took a deep breath. And then, he spoke. "Emma."

She froze. The blanket slipped from her hands. Slowly—so slowly—she turned. And when her eyes met his, time stood still. Ben's throat tightened. She was beautiful. Lena had Emma's warmth, that quiet gentleness in the way she carried herself. But the sharp gaze, the way she studied the world as if trying to figure out its every secret— That was him.

Ben barely noticed the way his body swayed, how weak his limbs felt. His hands trembled at his sides. It was too much. And then— Emma turned her head. For a split second, their eyes met. She froze. The colour drained from her face. The

381

blanket she had been holding slipped from her grasp. Her lips parted, a whisper escaping before she even realized she had spoken. "Ben...?"

Lena turned sharply. "Mom?" Emma blinked rapidly, her composure snapping back into place as fast as it had vanished. She shook her head, stepping forward quickly, her wide, disbelieving eyes never leaving his face. Shock. Disbelief. And something else. A deep, buried grief, suddenly resurfaced.

She stopped just a few feet away from him, looking as if she were seeing a ghost. Ben forced himself to breathe. He had to be careful. He wasn't supposed to be here. Not like this. Emma swallowed hard, clearing her throat, trying to pull herself back together.

"Lena, sweetheart, this is..." She hesitated. Her gaze flickered over him, searching for something—an explanation, an anchor. Then she inhaled sharply as if making a decision. And when she spoke again, her voice was steady. "This is John. An old friend of your father's."

Ben's heart lurched, but he said nothing. Lena frowned. Her grip tightened around the tiny bundle in her arms. She didn't seem convinced. But she didn't argue. Instead, she turned her full attention to him, studying him the way she might a stranger who felt oddly familiar. And then— She smiled. A soft, cautious smile. "It's nice to meet you, John," Lena said gently. "I'd love for you to meet someone."

She stepped forward, adjusting the baby in her arms before glancing at her mother for permission. Emma gave a small nod. Her hands were still shaking.

Lena turned back to Ben; her eyes warm, curious, unknowing. "This is my son," she said. "His name is Ben."

The world blurred. Ben felt like something inside him had fractured. Like all the breath had been knocked from his lungs. His grandson.

He tried to speak, but nothing came. His throat was tight, his chest heavy with something too vast to name. He stared at the small, sleeping face nestled against Lena's chest. The tiny fingers curled into the soft blue blanket. The faintest rise and fall of his breathing. A new life. A piece of him—of Lena, of Emma—alive, in this world.

Ben swallowed hard, forcing the lump in his throat down. The universe had stolen so much from him. Time. Moments. Memories. But this? This was a gift. One he never expected. One he never thought he would get to see.

His lips parted, and for the first time in years, his voice shook. "He's beautiful."

Lena's smile grew. Pride shone in her eyes. "He is, isn't he?" She looked down at the baby, adjusting him slightly so Ben could see him better. "I named him after my father."

Ben's breath stilled. A quiet laugh escaped him—one full of emotion, too raw, too real. Emma turned her head, just slightly. And for the first time, he saw it— The way she was looking at him. The recognition. The truth. She knew. No matter how impossible it was—no matter how much she tried to rationalize it—she knew.

383

Emma moved first. Her body was rigid with disbelief, her breath shallow, as if afraid that moving too fast might shatter the fragile reality before her. But her eyes— Her eyes were filled with something else. A quiet longing.

Ben could feel the weight of the years pressing between them, the decades lost, the moments they never got to share. It was an ache he had grown used to, but now—standing here, looking at her—it was unbearable. He wanted to say something. Anything. But words felt meaningless in the wake of everything she had endured. Instead, she spoke for both of them. "I wasn't sure if I'd ever see you again," she whispered. Her voice was quiet, trembling at the edges. A confession and a wound all at once. Ben's throat tightened. His grip on his grandson—on baby Ben—felt like the only thing keeping him grounded. He swallowed hard, meeting her gaze. "I'm here now."

Emma's lips pressed together like she was holding back a thousand words that wouldn't change a thing. Her gaze flickered to Lena, who was busy adjusting the baby's blanket, her fingers careful, her attention focused. Unaware of the silent conversation unfolding between her parents. Ben knew he couldn't explain. Not fully. Not in a way that would make sense. But Emma—Emma understood.

She always had. She took a shaky breath, her fingers curling at her sides like she wanted to reach for him—but didn't know how.

Ben almost told her. That he never stopped loving her. He thought about her every day, even in death. That she had been the last thing on his mind when he died. But there wasn't

384

enough time for all of that. Instead, he just looked at her. And somehow, that was enough.

Lena shifted the baby slightly, casting another glance at Ben. There was something in her expression— An unspoken question. Ben could see it.

She was wondering why she felt like she already knew him. Why there was something familiar in the way he held himself, in the way his eyes softened when he looked at her. She didn't know the truth. Couldn't.

But somewhere, deep down—she felt it. And Ben? He wanted to tell her everything. He had dreamed of meeting her. That he had watched over her from a place he never wanted to be. That he had missed her first words, her first steps, her entire childhood—but he had loved her long before this moment. But he couldn't. So, he did the only thing he could do. He smiled. And Lena smiled back—hesitant but warm.

"Would you like to hold him?" she asked. She adjusted baby Ben's blanket, her voice soft, hopeful. Ben's breath caught in his throat. He had never expected this. His hands shook slightly as he reached out—careful, cautious, like he wasn't sure if this was real or a dream. Then—warmth. The tiny, fragile weight of his grandson settled into his arms, and Ben felt something inside him break apart and piece itself back together in the same breath.

Baby Ben stirred. His tiny fingers curled into the fabric of his shirt, gripping him with the innocent trust of a child who didn't know the world had ever been cruel. His breaths were soft, steady. Ben closed his eyes for a moment. Letting it settle into his bones, into his heart. Letting himself believe it was real. For so long, he had imagined that this day—if it ever came—would be painful.

But in this moment, there was no grief. No anger. No regret. Just love.

Emma sat beside him on the porch, her hands clasped tightly together as if holding herself steady. She watched him, the way he cradled the baby, the way his shoulders curled protectively around the tiny body in his arms. And when she exhaled, it wasn't shaky or unsure. It was a relief.

A breeze swept across the porch, rustling the trees, carrying the scent of summer earth and distant rain. The world was moving on, but for them, time had frozen in this perfect, fleeting instant.

Lena, oblivious to the history surrounding her, simply leaned back against the wooden railing and stretched her arms with a tired sigh. "I could use some coffee," she murmured, then smiled at Ben. "Would you like some?"

Ben hesitated. Not because he didn't want coffee. But because the offer felt like something more. Like an invitation. A chance. A sliver of normalcy in an impossible moment.

He glanced at Emma. She met his gaze, her expression unreadable—then she nodded, just once.

Ben swallowed the lump in his throat and smiled. "I'd love some."

A cruel reminder of everything he had missed. But as he stood there— Holding his grandson. Emma watched him like she had

386

never stopped loving him. Lena smiled like she had known him all her life.

He realized something. It wasn't about what he had lost. It was about what he had now. This one day. This perfect, impossible day. And he wasn't going to waste it.

Lena disappeared inside, leaving Ben and Emma alone on the porch. The silence stretched between them, thick with unspoken words. Emma exhaled softly, her fingers brushing over the porch railing like she was grounding herself.

"You always did love your coffee in the morning," she said, her voice barely above a whisper.

Ben chuckled; the sound was rough but genuine. "Some things never change."

She turned to him, her eyes glistening, and for a moment, it felt like no time had passed at all. Just two souls, caught in a moment that neither of them wanted to let slip away.

The baby stirred in his arms, letting out a tiny sigh, and Ben instinctively rocked him gently.

Emma watched, her lips parting slightly, her hands twitching like she wanted to reach out but didn't dare. Instead, she whispered, "You look good with him."

Ben swallowed. "I wish I had the chance before now."

Her throat bobbed, her gaze dropping for a brief second. Then she looked back up, something unreadable flickering across her face.

"You have now," she said softly.

Ben's chest tightened. Yes. He had now. And he wasn't going to waste it.

Chapter 25:

A Day of Love

The Return

The morning sunlight bathed the ranch in golden warmth as Ben stood on the porch, his grandson nestled against his chest. For the first time in eternity, he wasn't rushing, wasn't running. He was simply living.

Emma stood beside him, her arms crossed, watching him with quiet wonder. It was as if she were afraid to blink, afraid that if she did, he would disappear.

He felt the same way.

Lena had gone inside to put the baby down for a nap, leaving them alone. For the first time in thirty years.

Ben turned to Emma, taking her in. Every line on her face, every Gray strand in her hair—it was all beautiful. The life she had lived without him had left its mark, but it hadn't diminished her.

If anything, it had made her more radiant.

Nothing Left Unsaid

389

She took a shaky breath. "You're real."

Ben nodded. "I am."

Emma exhaled, looking away for a moment. "I don't understand how."

Ben hesitated. He couldn't tell her the whole truth.

That he had torn Heaven apart. That he had rebuilt it just to be here. He had been watching over her for years, helpless, longing, waiting for something he thought would never come.

So instead, he smiled softly. "I guess I had one last thing to do."

Emma swallowed hard, her lips pressing together, but her eyes glistened with something she rarely let show.

Hope.

Ben reached for her hand, hesitant at first, afraid she would pull away. But she didn't. Her fingers were warm, and solid, tethering him to a reality he had thought was lost to him forever.

She squeezed his hand lightly, testing, and reassuring herself that he was truly there. "I thought I'd made peace with losing you," she admitted, her voice barely above a whisper. "But I never did."

Ben looked down at their entwined hands. "Neither did I."

A breeze passed over the porch, rustling the fields, carrying the scent of wildflowers and sun-warmed earth. It was a reminder of all that had remained even in his absence—life moving forward, with or without him.

"I missed everything," Ben said, voice rough with regret. "Your best years. Lena growing up. All of it."

Emma turned to face him fully, searching his face. "And now you're here."

"For a day."

The words stung. She stiffened, her fingers twitching in his grasp. "A day?"

Ben nodded, forcing a sad smile. "That's all I have."

Emma blinked, her breath hitching. A day. Just twenty-four hours. It was cruel, and yet, it was a gift. A gift neither of them had ever expected to receive.

She let out a breath, long and slow, then nodded as if accepting something unspoken. Her eyes softened, and she released his hand only to step forward—closer than she had in decades.

"If we only have a day," she murmured, "then we can't waste a single second."

Ben swallowed, feeling the full weight of her words settle deep in his chest. He had spent so long in regret, so long mourning all the lost time, but Emma was right. They had now. And for however brief that was, it was still something.

She reached up, brushing her fingers over his cheek, a touch so light he barely felt it. But he closed his eyes for just a second, breathing her in, memorizing the moment before it slipped through his fingers.

When he opened them again, she was smiling. It was small, tentative, but real.

"Come inside," she said. "Have breakfast with us. Be here."

Ben exhaled, the weight in his chest shifting. He nodded. "Yeah. I'd love that."

As he followed her into the house, the scent of coffee and something warm and familiar filled his senses. And for the first time in thirty years, Ben felt like he had come home.

She inhaled sharply, pressing a hand to her mouth before finally shaking her head with a soft laugh. "Then we better not waste a second."

Ben chuckled, his heart aching even as it soared. "No, we better not."

And so, for the rest of that day, they didn't. They walked the fields, reliving memories in quiet conversation. They laughed. They sat on the porch as the sun dipped low in the sky, watching the horizon turn shades of gold and crimson. And when the stars finally emerged, they held each other close, knowing that come morning, he would be gone.

But for now, he was here. And that was enough.

The day unfolded like a dream. Like a life that could have been. They walked the fields together, the same way they had done all those years ago when they first bought the ranch. Emma pointed out the spots where the soil was rich, where the crops had grown best, where she used to sit and watch the sunsets alone.

Ben listened, hanging onto every word. She told him about Lena's childhood and the milestones he had missed. How she had inherited his stubborn streak, his sharp tongue, but Emma's kindness. How Lena had been strong, so strong, even when she had questions no one could answer.

"I told her you loved her," Emma said softly as they stood by the fence line, looking out over the rolling hills. "I told her that if you had any choice at all, you would have been here."

Ben clenched his jaw, his hands gripping the fence rail tightly. She had never stopped believing in him.

They had lunch on the porch like they used to, the table set with the simple comforts of home—fresh bread, cheese, fruit, and coffee that smelled exactly the way he remembered. Ben had forgotten what real food tasted like. The warmth of it. The way it filled not just his stomach but something deeper inside him.

Emma sat across from him, watching him eat, smiling softly. "I always imagined what I would say if I saw you again."

Ben swallowed, setting down his cup. "And?"

Emma chuckled lightly, shaking her head. "Nothing I imagined feels right. Nothing I thought I would be angry about seems to matter anymore."

Ben reached for her hand, his fingers brushing against hers. It was the first time they had truly touched since he had come back.

The air between them shifted. Familiar. Safe.

Emma turned her hand over, letting their fingers intertwine.

Ben squeezed lightly. "I missed you, Em."

Her breath hitched. "I missed you too."

393

A soft breeze swept through the porch, rustling the leaves of the old oak tree that had stood there longer than either of them. The wind carried the scent of earth and sunlight, wrapping around them like a memory.

Emma let out a slow breath, her eyes lingering on their joined hands. "For so many years, I tried to hate you. I thought it would make it easier."

Ben's grip tightened slightly. "And did it?"

She shook her head. "No. It just made the missing worse."

Ben wanted to tell her everything—that he had fought against Heaven itself, that he had broken and rebuilt an entire world just for this moment. But those words wouldn't give her peace. They would only raise questions he couldn't answer.

Instead, he just nodded. "I would have come back if I could." "I

know," she whispered.

They sat in silence for a while, watching the clouds drift across the sky, the afternoon stretching out like an eternity. It felt like time had stopped just for them, like the universe was giving them this one, perfect moment.

Ben ran his thumb over her knuckles. "Tell me more about her. About Lena."

Emma smiled, her eyes glowing with quiet pride. "She's stubborn, like you. Always fighting for something. But she has my patience. She's a mother now, you know."

Ben swallowed hard, nodding. "I saw."

Emma studied him for a long moment. "Do you regret it?"

"Regret what?"

"Everything."

Ben looked out over the land, the place where he had built a future and lost it all. "Every day."

Emma squeezed his hand. "Then don't waste the time you have left."

Ben nodded, his heart full and breaking all at once. He wouldn't. Not for a second.

As the sun dipped toward the horizon, they walked back toward the house, the golden light stretching their shadows long across the ground. Emma's fingers never left him, and Ben held onto that touch as if it were the only thing keeping him tethered to this world.

The scent of dinner wafted from the kitchen as they stepped inside. Lena was humming softly, stirring something on the stove, her back to them. The sound was familiar and comforting.

For a brief moment, Ben allowed himself to imagine it wasn't borrowed time. That he wasn't counting the hours until he disappeared again. That he had never left.

Emma gave his hand one last squeeze before stepping away. "Sit down, Ben. Stay awhile."

Ben exhaled, nodding. "I'd love to."

And for the rest of the evening, he did.

The day unfolded like a dream. Like a life that could have been.

They walked the fields together, the same way they had done all those years ago when they first bought the ranch. Emma pointed out the spots where the soil was rich, where the crops had grown best, where she used to sit and watch the sunsets alone.

Ben listened, hanging onto every word. She told him about Lena's childhood and the milestones he had missed. How she had inherited his stubborn streak, his sharp tongue, but Emma's kindness. How Lena had been strong, so strong, even when she had questions no one could answer.

"I told her you loved her," Emma said softly as they stood by the fence line, looking out over the rolling hills. "I told her that if you had any choice at all, you would have been here."

Ben clenched his jaw, his hands gripping the fence rail tightly. She had never stopped believing in him.

They had lunch on the porch like they used to, the table set with the simple comforts of home—fresh bread, cheese, fruit, and coffee that smelled exactly the way he remembered. Ben had forgotten what real food tasted like. The warmth of it. The way it filled not just his stomach but something deeper inside him.

Emma sat across from him, watching him eat, smiling softly. "I always imagined what I would say if I saw you again."

Ben swallowed, setting down his cup. "And?"

Emma chuckled lightly, shaking her head. "Nothing I imagined feels right. Nothing I thought I would be angry about seems to matter anymore."

396

Ben reached for her hand, his fingers brushing against hers. It was the first time they had truly touched since he had come back.

The air between them shifted. Familiar. Safe.

Emma turned her hand over, letting their fingers intertwine.

Ben squeezed lightly. "I missed you, Em."

Her breath hitched. "I missed you too."

A Father's Absence, a Grandfather's Grace

That night, as the house settled into quiet, Ben wandered into a room he hadn't seen in decades. The nursery. Painted in the same soft yellow Emma had chosen all those years ago, it was now filled with baby Ben's tiny clothes, stuffed animals, and rocking chair. He spent hours in there, holding his grandson, watching the little hands grasp his fingers, feeling the warmth of life in his arms. He whispered stories, traced the painted stars on the ceiling, and listened to the baby's soft breaths as he slept. It was a moment he never thought he would have. And he cherished every second.

The morning arrived gently, sunlight filtering through the curtains. The smell of coffee and something warm and buttery filled the air. Ben stirred, feeling a moment of panic that it had all been a dream, but then he heard the soft sounds of Emma humming in the kitchen. He rose and followed the scent, finding her at the stove, flipping pancakes, just as she had done in the old days.

"Good morning," she said, her voice carrying an impossible softness.

"Morning," Ben replied, savouring the moment as he leaned against the doorframe, taking her in. She had always belonged here. And for a brief moment, he did too.

Borrowed Hours

They had breakfast on the porch, the three of them—Emma, Lena, and Ben—telling stories of the past, of the ranch, of the man Lena had grown up calling her father. Ben listened as Lena laughed, reminiscing about the times when her dad had taught her to ride, how he would chase her around the fields, how he had loved her with all he had. Ben swallowed the bittersweet truth of it. She had a father who had been there. And yet, in some way, he was still a part of her story.

The hours melted away too quickly. As noon approached, Ben felt the weight of time pressing against him. It was almost over. He had to go.

He stood, clearing his throat. "I should be heading out."

Lena frowned. "So soon?"

Ben forced a smile, reaching out to hug her tightly, holding onto her just a little longer. "You've grown into an incredible woman," he whispered. "Your father would be so proud." She smiled against his shoulder. "Thank you, John."

398

As she pulled away, she hesitated, then rushed inside. Moments later, she returned with something small in her hands. A picture.

"It's for you," she said, placing the photo of baby Ben in his palm. "So, you don't forget us."

Ben's throat tightened. He slid the photo into his chest pocket, patting it gently. "I won't."

One Last Promise

Emma stood beside him, her eyes shimmering with unshed tears. She didn't try to stop him. She knew she couldn't. But she walked with him down the dirt path, her hand tucked in his, just like the old days.

At the end of the path, he turned to her. "I don't know if I'll get another chance," he said softly. "But if I do—"

Emma shook her head, stepping closer, pressing her fingers against his lips. "Don't say goodbye."

Ben exhaled shakily, nodding.

She cupped his face, brushing her thumb over his cheek. "You were always my heart, Ben."

His vision blurred, but he smiled. "And you were always mine."

A warm breeze swept between them, the world seeming to shimmer for a brief moment. And then—

He was gone.

399

Emma stood there for a long time, staring at the space where he had been, her hand still outstretched, as if she could still feel him there. A tear slipped down her cheek, but she smiled.

Because he had been real. He had been here.

And that was enough.

But for now, they had this.

One perfect, impossible day.

Chapter 26:

Noon Approaches

The sky was vast and endless, the noon sun hanging high, casting golden light over the ranch. The fields stretched out in every direction, the grass swaying gently under the weight of the breeze. The air was warm, still, and heavy—as if the world itself was holding its breath, unwilling to let this moment end.

Ben felt it in his bones. His time was almost up.

Emma must have sensed it too, because she hadn't let go of his hand since their walk. She gripped him like she could anchor him here like sheer willpower could defy the inevitable.

But no force, no love, no unspoken plea could keep him from fading. Not this time.

They stood on the porch together, just as they had all those years ago, staring out over the land they had dreamed of. The ranch that had been their future. The life they should have lived.

Ben exhaled slowly, flexing his fingers. He could already feel it—his body growing lighter, his presence slipping from this world like a whisper on the wind.

Emma turned to him, and for the first time all day, there was fear in her eyes. Not the kind of fear that came from losing something suddenly—but the kind that came from knowing exactly how it would happen and still being powerless to stop it.

401

"Don't," she said, shaking her head. Her voice was barely above a whisper.

Ben swallowed hard. "Em…"

"Don't say it," she pleaded, stepping closer, gripping his shirt, pulling him to her like she could stop him from vanishing with sheer force alone.

Ben closed his eyes for a moment, resting his forehead against hers. He wanted to lie to her. He wanted to promise her that he would stay, that this wasn't the end.

But Emma deserved the truth. She always had.

Lena's voice called from inside. "Mom? Are you out here?"

Emma sniffed, blinking rapidly, trying to compose herself before her daughter stepped onto the porch.

Lena was cradling the baby against her shoulder, swaying gently, her presence so effortless, so natural, that it made Ben ache with pride.

She smiled at him—a soft, kind smile, the kind he had never thought he'd get to see.

"I just wanted to say goodbye before we head inside," Lena said, shifting the baby slightly. "It was nice meeting you."

Ben hesitated, then reached out and ran his fingers gently across the baby's tiny hand.

The little fingers curled instinctively around his, gripping tightly. Holding onto him. Just like Emma was.

Ben exhaled; his chest tight. If there was ever a moment to be selfish, to demand more time, to fight against the universe itself—it was now.

But he had made his peace.

He looked at Lena, memorizing every detail of her face. She had his sharpness, Emma's warmth. She had survived without him, but he had always been a part of her, even when she didn't know it.

"You take care of him, all right?" Ben said, nodding at the baby. His voice was steady, but the weight of goodbye sat heavy in the air.

Lena smiled, adjusting the blanket. "Of course."

Then, without knowing why, she stepped forward and hugged him.

Ben stiffened at first, startled. But then he melted into it, wrapping his arms around her, inhaling the scent of her hair, memorizing everything he would never get again.

"Goodbye, John," she whispered.

Ben smiled against her shoulder. "Goodbye, sweetheart."

Lena gave her mother a final glance before stepping back inside and disappearing into the house. And then it was just him and Emma.

Ben turned to her, and she shook her head. Tears brimmed in her eyes, threatening to spill over.

"This isn't fair," she said, her voice breaking. "I just got you back."

Ben reached up, cupping her face, wiping away the tear that had slipped down her cheek. "You never lost me."

Emma's breath hitched. She covered his hand with hers, holding onto him as tightly as she could.

But he could feel it happening now. His edges softened, his presence thinning, like mist in the afternoon heat.

Ben took a slow, shaky breath and kissed her.

One last time.

Not out of desperation. Not out of sorrow.

But out of love.

The same love that had carried across decades. Across life and death.

As they parted, Emma's hands tightened around his, like she could will him into staying.

"Please," she whispered. "Please, not yet."

Ben smiled sadly, pressing his forehead against hers one last time. "I don't want to go either."

She let out a soft sob, nodding. "I love you."

"I love you too."

Ben stepped back, his fingers slipping from hers. The final break.

The noon sun wrapped around him, making him glow, and blending him into the golden light. His steps grew lighter, his form becoming transparent in the heat of the day.

The last thing he saw was Emma, standing on the porch, frozen in time, memorizing him. Committing every detail of him to memory as if she could hold onto him that way.

Then—

He was gone.

The wind rustled through the fields, the cicadas hummed in the distance, and the sun continued its slow arc across the sky.

Emma stood there long after the light had swallowed him, her arms wrapped around herself, her gaze locked on the empty path where Ben had stood.

The world carried on as if nothing had changed. But everything had.

Emma sat on the porch steps, hugging her knees to her chest. The wind carried the last remnants of his presence, whispering against her skin like a fading dream. She closed her eyes and let the midday warmth wrap around her, allowing herself the briefest moment of grief before she breathed in, steadying herself.

She wasn't alone.

She had Lena. She had the baby. She had the life they had built, the home they had loved. And, in a way, she still had Ben.

She could feel him in the whisper of the wind, in the warmth of the earth beneath her feet, in the sun that shone high above. He had never truly left. He never would.

And as she sat there, her fingers tracing patterns against the worn wood of the porch, she smiled.

Because love, real love, never truly ended. And neither did he.

Lena stepped onto the porch, carrying the baby, sensing the weight in the air. "Mom?"

Emma blinked, turning to her daughter with a small, bittersweet smile. "Let's go inside."

As they disappeared into the house, the porch light flickered off, leaving the doorway bathed in the golden glow of the afternoon sun.

Emma paused at the threshold, glancing back once more. The ranch stretched before her; the land bathed in the quiet hush of midday. The wind had stilled, as if even the earth itself was holding its breath, reluctant to let go of what had just transpired.

She closed her eyes, inhaling deeply. For a fleeting second, she swore she could still feel the warmth of his touch against her skin, the ghost of his fingers brushing hers.

It was impossible, she knew, but the weight of his presence lingered in the silence, wrapped around her like an embrace just beyond reach.

And somewhere, beyond the reach of mortal eyes, beyond the veil of what was and what could have been, Ben took his final steps toward whatever came next.

He did not look back—not because he had forgotten, but because he no longer needed to.

Emma was safe. Lena was strong. And love, in its truest form, had never been lost.

Chapter 27:

Satan's Encore

The Void

Ben woke to nothing.

Not light. Not warmth. Not the buzz of the world.

Only the void.

A pitch-black silence, so absolute it pressed against his eardrums like pressure underwater. He reached for something—a wall, a hand, a breath—but found only space. Empty. Still. Eternal.

Then came the screams.

They rose in layers — agony stacked upon agony. Not voices, but *memories* of voices, like echoes caught in the throat of the void itself. Infant wails morphed into battlefield howls, into mother's sobs, into mechanical groans that spoke only loss. They weren't near or far — they *were*. They saturated the atmosphere, folding through the dark like cracks in time.

Ben's knees buckled. There was no ground, not really — just a feeling of down. He collapsed into it, though he wasn't sure if he fell or was pulled. His hands hit something soft, wet, unyielding. He recoiled. It was like kneeling on tongues. Wet, thick, still-moving.

Shapes danced in the periphery — insectile, skeletal, luminous — flitting too quickly to be fully seen but leaving afterimages like bruises across the eyes. One came close and whispered not into his ear, but directly into the marrow of his bones. The language was pain — pure, unfiltered emotion turned inside out and made audible.

Ben clutched his temples.

Above, the ceiling — if it could be called that — unfurled like a scroll of meat, veins twitching, organs blinking. Etchings of forgotten languages pulsed there, words that hummed as if remembering their own purpose. Symbols twisted with each heartbeat, rearranging into new glyphs that burned with intent. He couldn't read them, but he *knew* what they meant:

YOU DO NOT BELONG HERE. AND YET, YOU NEVER LEFT.

A heartbeat — not his — vibrated through him. Massive. Slow. Hungry.

Ben opened his mouth to scream, but the sound that came out wasn't his. It was a thousand screams folded into one — his childhood terrors, his adult regrets, the pain of every death he'd witnessed, even the ones he never realized he caused.

And then he heard *footsteps* — not the elegant stride that would come with Satan's entrance — but a staggered, dragging shuffle, like limbs moving against their will. Something blind, but determined.

He turned, but there was no turning. Just a reorientation of horror. The darkness behind him pulled back like wet paper to

409

reveal a corridor lined with mirrors made of cartilage. They shimmered in the darkness, reflecting not his face, but a *hole* — a gaping mouth where his soul should be.

A low voice bubbled up from beneath the floor, gurgling like a drowned god remembering how to speak.

"Benjamin... Holloway... How far you've fallen to end up... so close."

It wasn't Satan. It was *something else* — something older. Something buried beneath even the idea of evil.

Ben's body trembled as the air around him thickened. Not with heat, but with *presence.* The void was not empty. It was crowded.

Eyes opened in the air like wounds. Some were beautiful. Some were weeping. All were watching.

He was *seen.*

And for a moment, the worst realization struck him:

They had been waiting.

Waiting for *him.*

Not close. Distant, like echoes slipping through layers of fog. Wails of grief, of rage, of fear. The kind of sound that made your bones ache with recognition. The kind of scream you don't just hear—you remember.

Descent

410

Light appeared.

Not heavenly. Not golden.

Red. Deep and seething. A pulse, as if the very air had a heartbeat. The darkness began to melt, revealing shapes that moved like smoke in a furnace. Towering structures emerged, not made of stone or fire, but of rusted instruments, twisted scaffolding, and discarded dreams. The architecture was alive—breathing, shifting, muttering.

Some walls wept. Others whispered. Something wet slithered across the ceilings.

Ben stumbled forward, barefoot, every step a question.

The ground was soft. Not warm, but pulsing. Organic. It rippled underfoot like muscle flexing beneath skin. He stepped in something slick and warm—looked down, and saw it was a puddle of teeth.

The air tasted of iron and memory. His nostrils flared with the stink of burnt feathers and funeral flowers.

He heard laughter.

It echoed off impossible angles. The sound seemed to come from inside the bones of the architecture — deeper than the walls, beneath the floor, behind the light itself. It was the laughter of something that didn't laugh because it was amused, but because it was *certain*. Certain that Ben's arrival was not an accident, but a scheduled inevitability.

As Ben continued forward, the red light thickened. It clung to his skin, clotting like blood. It wasn't illumination — it was *presence.* The walls breathed with him, and then against him, as though the entire realm were testing the rhythm of his soul.

Above him, shapes floated — massive, slow-turning entities that resembled neither beast nor machine. Their bodies were jagged, as if carved from the regrets of extinct civilizations. Wings made of severed oaths twitched once and fell still. They did not notice him. Or they noticed too much.

A spire rose in the distance, impossibly tall and visibly weeping. Not rain. Not water. But strands of forgotten names. They coiled like smoke, whispering memories not his own into his ears. Lovers betrayed. Children abandoned. Mothers pleading in their last breath.

Ben clutched his chest as something invisible wrapped around his ribs and squeezed, not out of malice — but as a test. A measurement. As if this place were calibrating what kind of agony he could carry.

Underfoot, the path shifted. The ground became translucent in places, revealing layers beneath — not geological, but psychological. He saw cities buried beneath regrets, oceans frozen with secrets, caverns echoing the words people never said before they died.

He passed a wall of skin. It exhaled as he walked past, revealing eyes that blinked sideways and mouths sewn shut. Faces pushed outward against the membrane, screaming silently. Each bore a mark on its forehead — not a symbol, but a *thought* Ben recognized as his own. Fears. Weaknesses. Things he wished were never true.

412

To his left, a tree grew upside down from the ceiling. Its roots shimmered with blood and static, and its branches bore fruit that looked like infant skulls, smiling in their sleep. The tree spoke, but only in gasps.

Ben began to lose track of time. Minutes felt like lifetimes, and footsteps repeated themselves, looping like a song caught in the throat. He stumbled upon his own footprints again and again, each set older, deeper, more frantic.

The air buzzed with a frequency tuned to regret. Every breath brought hallucinations. He saw Emma — not as she was, but how she would look watching him make the wrong decision. Her face, fractured with disappointment. Lena, crumbling into ash as she reached for him. His own hands turning into claws the more he reached back.

At the edge of a precipice, he saw a doorway formed entirely of screaming mouths. They didn't speak, but sang — a lullaby meant for monsters. It compelled him. Promised relief. Promised understanding. Promised *power*.

But he walked past.

Even now, even here — he knew that door wasn't meant to be opened by him. Not yet.

Just before the Tempter appeared, the wind returned. Not natural wind — this was breath. A slow, rhythmic inhaling from something too large to see. And within that breath was *language*.

One final word formed in his mind before the figure emerged:

Welcome.

Not joyful. Not mocking. But amused—like someone watching a fly crawl toward its own trap.

The Tempter

"Benjamin Holloway," the voice coiled around him, smooth as silk, sharp as razors. "Welcome back." A figure stepped from the shadows.

Not horned, not hooved. No pitchfork.

He wore a perfectly tailored suit. Midnight black, pinstriped with veins of silver. His face shimmered—always shifting, like it couldn't decide what it wanted to be. One moment, it was an elegant mask of smooth porcelain. The next, it was a writhing mosaic of anonymous faces, whispering secrets in a language Ben didn't know but somehow understood. His eyes held galaxies that had burned out eons ago, and his smile was older than war.

He was beautiful, unsettlingly so—like something sculpted to be admired but never touched. There was an unnatural smoothness to him, like a clay figure that had never truly hardened.

He changed with every blink—sometimes tall and imposing, sometimes child-sized and grotesquely cheerful. His voice stayed the same, though. Smooth. Precise. Patient.

He circled Ben like a shark that didn't need water — hovering, gliding, disturbing nothing yet tainting everything. With each step, the air around him grew colder, though no breeze touched

414

Ben's skin. Where the figure walked, the floor calcified, bones and beetles writhing into fractal patterns beneath his polished shoes.

The light bent around him unnaturally, favoring his outline as if afraid of what he'd become without shadow. Wherever his gaze landed, the landscape twisted — structures inhaling and collapsing in time with his smirk. His presence alone rewrote the laws of torment.

"You don't recognize me," he said, his voice dipped in charm and edged in something ancient. "But oh, Ben… we've met before. In every broken moment you swallowed, in every wish you didn't dare whisper. I was there, lounging between your doubts."

His hand traced the air like a calligrapher etching an invisible script. Runes shimmered, flared, then vanished — thoughts too wicked for permanence.

Ben took a shaky step back. "You're—"

The figure held up one slender finger. "Names are for humans. I collect them. I wear them. But you may call me… *Satan*, if it grants you comfort."

He grinned, and the grin peeled back too far. Beyond teeth. Beyond gums. There was no end to the mouth — just rows of language grinding together like millstones. In that moment, Ben saw words he had never read but always feared — names of ancient things still dreaming in the dark.

Satan reached toward him, not to touch, but to show.

A single flick of his wrist opened a rift beside them — not a portal, but a window without time. Inside it, Ben saw flashes: Emma curled in pain after his first lie. Lena sobbing quietly in her sleep. Himself, old and alone, begging a silence that refused to listen. The images changed with every heartbeat, a slideshow curated by shame.

"You brought these with you," Satan murmured. "I merely offered the frame."

He leaned in close — too close — and Ben felt his breath, smelled it: honeysuckle twisted with sulfur, sweet with rot.

"You want to ask if this is real," he whispered. "But deep down, you already know — reality is just the prettiest lie you ever told yourself."

He stepped back, clapping once. From the darkness emerged a choir of faceless figures, each made of ash and memory. They sang without mouths, a dirge stitched from lullabies and executions. Their harmony unraveled Ben's resolve thread by thread.

"You still don't get it," Satan said, almost sad. "You think this place was made to torment you. No, Benjamin. This is you. These are your blueprints. Your echoes. Your inheritance."

Ben's lips moved, but no sound came. His voice had abandoned him. It, too, was watching.

Satan stepped into the center of the space and opened his arms.

"Now that we're reacquainted," he purred, "shall we discuss what comes next?"

The Offer

"Where am I?" Ben managed, though the words felt sluggish, like they had to swim through oil to leave his mouth.

The man spread his arms wide. "Where all choices echo the loudest. The place beneath purpose. The machinery of consequence." Ben blinked. "Hell?"

The man's grin deepened.

"A word that lacks imagination."

Satan's voice lingered in the air like smoke in a cathedral. He took a step forward, and the ground beneath his feet blackened, blistered, then reformed in perfect hexagonal tiles as if reality was correcting itself around him.

"This place is older than your language," he said. "Older than the words you cling to. Heaven. Hell. Limbo. They are metaphors. This is function. This is... architecture. The furnace beneath dreams."

The world around them pulsed again — not with light, but with pressure. Something vast shifted just beyond view, like a leviathan rolling beneath the skin of the world.

Ben looked around. Shapes moved in the distance — humanoid, but wrong. Backwards limbs. Faces made of clocks. Some crawling, some floating, some dragging themselves across the horizon by invisible threads.

"You stand in the belly of consequence," Satan continued. "Where all your actions catch up. Where *truth* is not revealed, but remembered. This is where the soul shows its blueprint."

He gestured to Ben's shadow — but it wasn't a shadow. It was a film reel, flickering images across the floor: memories, shames, cruelties. Times Ben lied. Times he walked away. Times he let someone suffer just so he could sleep easier.

Ben stepped back, but the reel followed.

"You think you've been a good man," Satan said with a smirk. "But good men don't end up here unless they're *almost* monsters. That's what makes you valuable."

Ben swallowed. His lips were dry as bone.

"What do you want from me?"

Satan's eyes glittered — pinpricks of ancient light behind a galaxy of rot.

"An agreement. A joining of wills. I can return you to her — to Emma. To Lena. You'll wake up in your bed, in the life you lost. The pain, the suffering, the *separation* — gone. Rewritten."

A warm breeze passed, and for a split second Ben *felt* her hand in his. Emma's hand. He could smell her hair. He could hear Lena's laugh echoing behind it.

His heart clenched with unbearable longing.

"And what's the price?" Ben asked. His voice cracked.

Satan smiled wider. "Your talent. Your charm. Your ability to influence. You'll use it — but not for hope, or truth, or art. You

418

will be a seed. A whisper. A slow poison dripped into the river of humanity."

He paused, and leaned in, his voice lowering to a murmur that curled around Ben's spine like smoke.

"Do you think that was you?"

Ben didn't answer.

Satan's smile spread wider, and something inside it cracked. "Vanity," he said, eyes gleaming, "is my favourite sin.""

He snapped his fingers, and a long table appeared beside them, stretching into darkness. It was set like a banquet — fine crystal glasses, golden cutlery — but on each plate sat something unspeakable: severed innocence, roasted kindness, ambition flayed to the bone. Everything looked delicious. Everything was *alive*.

"You will feed the engine," Satan said. "You will make them *choose* their damnation. That's the key. I don't break free will, Ben. I bait it."

Ben's legs felt heavy. The hunger in his gut roared louder.

"And if I refuse?" he asked.

The temperature dropped.

Satan's face shifted — his mask sagging into a slack, grinning corpse-face before snapping back into elegance.

"Then you will return to the nothing. The In-Between. No memory. No Emma. No Lena. No form. Just consciousness,

419

adrift in the gray. Forgotten by both Heaven and Hell. A soul in limbo. Forever."

Silence stretched like skin across the void.

Ben shook his head slowly. "This is a trap."

Satan nodded, pleased. "All choices are. The question is — can you stomach the reward more than the price?"

Something laughed behind the stars. A cruel, endless laugh that smelled of old paper and fresh blood.

"Make your decision, Mr. Holloway," Satan said. "The world won't wait."

The Hunger

His stomach roared, sudden and hollow.

Satan tilted his head, amused. "Are you hungry?"

Ben hesitated. The gnawing in his gut was more than hunger — it was *emptiness*, a cavern in his soul that pulsed in rhythm with the void. His mouth watered and dried at once. His throat clenched around nothing. He didn't answer, but Satan didn't wait for permission.

"What is your pleasure, Mr. Holloway?" Satan asked, voice syrupy and slow, as though savoring every syllable.

Ben blinked. His mind went to childhood — to comfort, to simplicity. "Oranges," he said, almost reflexively. "Grapes. Apples."

With a sudden snap of reality — not thunderous, not loud, but *final* — the fruits appeared in his hands. Too perfect. Glistening. Hyperreal. The orange had a skin so smooth it gleamed like porcelain. The grapes glowed slightly, as if lit from within. The apple — impossibly red, symmetrical, as though shaped by a god obsessed with geometry.

Ben's stomach twisted an thought to himself "it was against my principles, but i find principles have no real force unless one is welll fed."

His mouth obeyed his hunger before his mind could protest. He lifted the apple.

It crunched.

The sound echoed.

And then — rot.

The inside was black. Not just dark — void-black. Like the core had been hollowed out and replaced with something alive. A slither. A movement. Then dozens. Pale, wet worms writhed through the pulp, coiling across his tongue, some bursting with acidic bitterness. Ben gagged, spat, reeled.

"What is wrong with you?!" he shouted, wiping his tongue on the back of his sleeve.

The fruits in his hand pulsed once — then liquefied, melting into a thick black sludge that hissed as it hit the floor.

Satan's mask — once placid, amused — cracked. Slowly, then all at once. Lines split across his porcelain face like lightning veins. The smile dropped. His brow furrowed. His jaw clicked into a sharp, unnatural angle. His entire head seemed to fold inward, then snap back out into an expression of unfiltered contempt.

"I know no wrong," he growled, voice layered with thousands of others, some screaming, some laughing, some whispering secrets in languages never spoken by humans. "Because I *am* wrong."

The ground beneath Ben's feet moaned, as though the very floor recoiled from that truth. Flames didn't rise — they *peeled* up from the seams of the world, like skin blistering from bone. The shadows above twisted in pain or worship — it was impossible to tell which.

Ben stumbled backward. His hunger gone. Replaced by revulsion. Terror. Something more ancient: recognition.

He realized then — the offer wasn't nourishment. It was initiation. The fruit wasn't food. It was a door. And he had bitten into it.

Satan stepped closer.

"Appetite reveals the soul, Ben. And your first wish wasn't for knowledge. Or peace. Or even freedom. It was for *comfort*."

He leaned in again, and this time Ben could smell not rot — but honey. Sweet. Familiar. Like Emma's kitchen in spring.

"They always choose the apple," Satan whispered.

And then, softly — he laughed.

422

The Mask Cracks

Satan's voice deepened, cracked with something older than language, older than sound itself. It was no longer speech — it was tectonic, like the groan of ancient mountains dying in the dark. With every syllable, the air around Ben warped, curdled. Oxygen became a luxury. Breathing became treason.

Satan began to pace, but it wasn't walking — it was orbiting. Like a black sun dragging reality with him. His shadow stretched impossibly far, bleeding up walls, spiraling across the ceiling, rippling with a will of its own. Within that shadow, things stirred — lost ideas, screaming infants, angels stitched into inverted crosses.

Ben's pulse hammered. His limbs trembled as the very geometry of the space warped to accommodate Satan's anger. Angles inverted. Circles wept. Words bled from the floor in mirrored script.

Satan's mask — already fragile — began to splinter.

Slowly at first. A tremor at the corners of his perfect smile.

Then violently. The porcelain cracked in spiderweb fractures across his brow, his cheeks, his chin. His eyes darkened — not black, but the color of absence. Absence of mercy. Absence of light. Absence of time. They sank inward, deepening into bottomless wells of flickering flame that devoured and digested meaning.

His face twisted into something primal.

A furious scowl — born not of hatred, but *disappointment*.

423

Like a god denied worship. Like a parent disgusted by their creation. Like a mirror showing humanity its most honest reflection.

His voice returned, now a layered choir of insectile screeches and thunderous sobs.

"Humans… revolting, pitiful things. Fragile sacks of flesh, ruled by hunger, lust, fear — slaves to your own filth. You call yourselves intelligent, evolved? You're vermin. A disease. A crawling infestation, parasitic and blind, gnawing at the very womb that bore you.

You had Eden — a paradise, flawless, sacred. And what did you do? You choked the skies with smoke. You poisoned the rivers, razed the forests, butchered the creatures, and drowned the silence of nature with the screams of war. You spread like rot. Like a fungus with delusions of godhood.

You are not creators. You are a glitch in nature's design. A plague in a fragile shell of bone and ego. You pollute, you devour, you destroy — and you call it progress.

You're not killing the planet. Not yet. No — you're murdering it. Slowly. Gleefully. And still, you dare speak of hope. Of redemption.

Pathetic.

You had Heaven — Eden — in your hands, yours to reign, yours to preserve, to shape. And what did you do with it? You turned it to ash. You made a hell out of heaven… and a heaven out of hell. You glorified suffering. Worshipped greed. Crowned

424

ignorance. Millennia were handed to you — your turn, your rule… and you squandered it.

Well now — it's my turn.

Your time is over. The Earth no longer belongs to you. It never did. You were the infestation, and now I am the cure.

I will rule the ashes. I will inherit your ruin. And humanity… will be mine — not to save, but to own, to break, to erase.

There is no salvation. No second chance. No divine rescue. Only silence.

And I… I am the silence that follows your scream."

Pathetic.

The ground cracked beneath his words. The walls bled symbols that twitched and curled away from comprehension. The ceiling split, revealing an open sky of churning ink — stars screaming as they collapsed in slow motion.

And still, Satan stood.

A monument to fury. A statue of loathing sculpted in divine spite.

And before him, Ben trembled — not because he believed the words… but because some part of him did.

"Humans… revolting, pitiful things..."

The Choice

425

The world held its breath. Ben turned to the darkness, the memory of Emma etched behind his eyes. Then to the light, artificial and pulsing, seductive and hollow. It flickered like a heart about to give out, promising relief, safety, reunion — but offering only anesthesia.

He closed his eyes.

Behind his lids, images danced: Lena on her birthday, her laughter like sunbeams on water. Emma asleep on his chest, her breath a metronome to his own heart. He saw their lives play out — not as they had been, but as they *could* be. A version of peace, wrapped in lies. All waiting on his yes.

His hands trembled, fists curling into claws.

Ben's voice is low, laced with fury, disbelief clinging to the edges. "So that's it? You don't command me... you infect me. You twist the knife and wait for me to turn it."

Satan offers a slow, deliberate nod — a serpent acknowledging the bite was always yours to take. Behind him, the sky convulses, birthing constellations that scream as they burn out.

"You dress surrender as salvation," Ben growled. "You give comfort teeth. You hand out crowns made of nooses."

Satan's grin never faltered. His silence said everything.

Ben's jaw tightens. His fists curl. Beneath his skin, something began to burn — not with pain, but *clarity*.

"Then hear this — I choose no."

The Shatter

426

Satan shrieks — not in pain, but in rage, raw and ancient, a sound that fractures the air like glass under pressure. The shriek is layered — a thousand screams spiraling backward through time, echoing from wars, plagues, betrayals. The very sound scours the skin of the dimension around them. Colors drain from the sky. Walls splinter, moaning like dying animals.

His form distorts, as if the idea of him can no longer hold. Joints unhinge. Limbs stretch into unnatural lengths, snapping and twisting like puppet strings pulled too tight. His spine arches backward like a bridge made of vertebrae and void. From his mouth spills ink and spiders — the ink moves like thoughts, and the spiders speak in dead dialects, crawling across the floor and whispering secrets no one should know.

His fingers become smoke. His eyes become doors. His ribs split like wings. Each fracture in his body births a new, impossible sound — laughter, weeping, thunder, static — until it feels as though the universe is weeping through him.

The light tries to escape from around him, but is sucked inward instead — folding in like a collapsing star. The shadows twist into ropes, dragging him back toward a vortex that wasn't there moments ago. A churning void opens beneath his feet, ink-black and hungry, rimmed with symbols older than death. Screams echo from it — not his, but familiar voices: Emma. Lena. Ben's own.

"YOU WERE MINE!" Satan bellows, voice cracked with fury. "YOU WERE PROMISED!"

But the void doesn't care.

It pulls.

427

It *devours*.

Satan claws at the air, now thick like molasses, tearing holes that bleed color. With each swipe, fragments of places — cities burning, mountains weeping, oceans turned to salt — spill into view. Visions of ruin, of destinies denied.

His form collapses inward, folding like crumpled parchment. Each limb is taken piece by piece — devoured not by fire, but by *forgetting*. As he is dragged into the maw, his screams become *memories unmade*.

Howl by howl.

And the floor trembles.

Not with impact — but with laughter.

Not laughter from mouths — but from the bones of the world.

A cold, cruel, knowing laughter.

The kind of laughter that knows it will return.

The kind that never really left.

The Ascent

But the void is hungry still. Without warning, Ben feels it pull — a force like gravity made of hands. He's yanked from the ground, weightless and falling without direction. Not falling *down* — but inward, spiraling like a thought collapsing in on itself.

428

The space around him liquefies. It turns to mirrors, to smoke, to screaming clocks that tick backward. Mouths open in the air, reciting his memories in reverse — not with sound, but with *sensation*. He feels his regrets as if they're happening again, only this time, he is every person he's ever hurt. Every silence that harmed. Every kindness withheld.

One mouth shrieks the lullaby his mother never sang. Another whispers his eulogy — spoken in a voice not yet born.

Hands reach for him, not to grasp, but to judge. Some caress. Some claw. All of them *know* him. Every version. Every flaw. Every moment he averted his eyes from suffering and called it endurance.

Something with no eyes watches him from every angle — not with curiosity, but *expectation*. It's as if the void is holding its breath. Waiting for something. For him to fracture. To scream. To beg.

But he doesn't.

He closes his eyes against the chaos—

—and then: silence.

Not peace. Not quiet.

A silence so absolute it hums. A vacuum of noise, of meaning, of form. It presses against his eardrums like pressure beneath the sea. It is *full* — full of everything he has tried to forget.

He floats, untethered. A mote of defiance in a sea of judgment.

And somewhere deep inside the nothingness, a voice — not his — speaks:

"You are not clean. But you are awake."

Then — without warning — a flash.

A brilliant, white fracture slashes through the void like a blade across the throat of the world. The silence shatters into light.

And Ben is *ascending.*

The Light

When he opens them, there is only light. Blinding, bright white light, so pure it stings. His vision blurs, washes out. For a moment, there is nothing else. No sound. No ground beneath him. Just that overwhelming brightness—

It is not warmth. It is not comfort.

It is *exposure.*

Like being seen by the very architecture of truth. As though the atoms that made him were being inventoried, judged, reassembled.

The light shifts, not in hue but in *texture* — now velvet, now razor. It moves not with grace, but with intent. It scans, scours, sings in tones that taste like salt and ash.

Ben flinches. Or would have, if he still had muscles. He is suspended — not floating, not flying, but *held.* His form a suggestion. His essence poured thin.

The light begins to strobe. Rapid. Erratic. And in those blinks, images flash:

Emma, mouth open in horror. Lena, walking into a room that no longer remembers her name. His own face, hollow-eyed and stitched shut at the mouth.

Each flash burns deeper. Each frame a needle driven into the film of his memory.

Ben wants to scream. But sound would be a lie here.

Then, everything *slows*. The strobing ceases. The light condenses into a single, overwhelming point before him — a core of pure will.

And from that point, a voice unfurls. Not male. Not female. Not anything that could fit inside lungs. It is a pressure behind the eyes. A roar between heartbeats.

"Change is not given. It is *taken*."

Then silence again.

And the faint sense… that something has changed.

Echoes of the Abyss

But even in that brightness, something follows.

Not a presence, but an echo — the afterimage of a scream burned into the folds of his mind. The white light pulses subtly, like a dying star blinking in a sea of milk, and beneath it, there are shapes. Shadows, not cast but born from the light itself.

They twitch and slither, not with malice, but with knowing. Watching. Waiting.

One twitches toward him, flickering with a movement too fast to comprehend — not walking, not crawling, but *becoming*. It brushes the edge of his thought and bleeds backward into itself, vanishing with a whisper that sounds like the name of someone he forgot to love.

Ben tries to move, but his limbs feel detached, like puppets severed from their strings. He floats, suspended in a space that has no air yet drowns, no time yet decays.

The silence is not silent. It breathes. It hums in tones below thought, vibrating through his ribs, his teeth, his marrow. Every vibration whispers a single word over and over: *remember*.

Each pulse tugs at him — not physically, but morally. It unthreads shame and regret with surgical precision. Things he had buried. Lies he called mercy. Truths he swore he'd never speak.

A shape blooms before him. Not a form, but an idea made manifest — a twisting helix of rotting flowers, turning in on itself like a dying thought. Within it, he sees images not his own: children laughing beneath mushroom clouds, lovers devoured by greed, forests pulsing red as their roots scream.

He feels everything — not just sight and sound, but the *emotion* of the planet itself. Pain like molten sap. Grief like drowned thunder. Rage that simmers, not explosive, but endless and patient. The Earth doesn't scream — it *endures*.

432

A sound breaks through the static. Not words. Not music. Just... weeping.

Endless, layered weeping — and within it, he recognizes his own voice.

It's not sorrow. It's *recognition*.

Then, without warning, a mirror appears before him. Not glass, but reflective flesh, rippling as if alive. It doesn't reflect him — it *dissects* him. Every lie given form. Every cruelty etched into the curve of his lips. He sees himself, but changed — stitched together from versions of himself he never became. The coward. The tyrant. The martyr. The one who said yes.

All of them stare back, smiling.

Then they speak, in unison: "We're still inside you."

The mirror shatters without a sound. Shards float upward like ash. One embeds itself in his chest, vanishing into his heart. Another into his eye. Another into his spine.

The whiteness begins to retract, curling back like skin peeled from bone, revealing the dim outline of something vast and mechanical behind it all — gears the size of galaxies grinding behind the stage of existence. Every tooth of the mechanism is a moment. Every cog a choice. It doesn't turn with violence, but inevitability.

Ben is not alone.

Something ancient stands just beyond the veil, unmoving, unfathomable — a structure shaped like a throne, but breathing.

Watching him with mouths instead of eyes. Some whisper praise. Others scream blasphemy. One simply weeps.

A single, unspoken command radiates from it:

Return.

Ben gasps — but it's not breath. It's *acceptance.*

And the light swallows him whole.

Chapter 28:

The Gatekeeper's Return

A Golden Goodbye

As the black faded into nothingness—like a distant memory, though it had passed only a blink ago—it already felt far away. It had been just a heartbeat since the golden light of that last sunset with Emma disappeared. The warmth of her touch, the weight of Lena's embrace, the scent of earth beneath his boots—all of it slipped away like a dream unravelling in the morning sun.

And then— Cold.

Ben's eyes snapped open. The sky above him was endless, stretching out in perfect white clouds that glowed softly, untouched by time. Heaven. He was back.

What Was, and What Could've Been

His breath came slow and uneven as he sat up, the weight of reality settling onto his chest like a boulder. The ranch was gone. Emma was gone. His daughter, his grandson—all of it.

It had been one day. And now it was m over.

435

Ben swallowed hard, forcing himself to his feet. His body felt different—not weak, not exhausted, but hollow. As if something had been carved out of him, something that would never quite heal.

A sigh echoed from behind him. The same tired, knowing sigh he had come to expect.

"See? That wasn't so bad."

Ben turned, his jaw tightening as he met Peter's gaze. The old gatekeeper leaned casually against the gates, arms crossed, wearing that same insufferable smirk.

Ben stared at him for a long moment. Then, he laughed.

It wasn't a joyful laugh. It was bitter, and rough, a sound full of grief and acceptance tangled into one.

Peter raised a brow. "Something funny?"

Ben shook his head, running a hand through his hair. "You're an asshole, Pete."

Peter snorted. "Yeah, well, I'm not the one who let a bunch of dictators into paradise, am I?"

Holding On, Letting Go

Ben exhaled, letting the weight of it all settle. He wasn't angry. Not at Peter. Not at the universe. Not anymore.

Because something had shifted. Something inside him had changed.

He had been given one last chance to be with the people he loved. And though it hadn't been enough—it never would have been enough—he had made it count.

For the first time since he had woken up in Heaven, he didn't feel like he was trapped. He felt like he had a purpose.

Peter studied him, his smirk fading slightly. "So," he said, tilting his head. "What now?"

Ben let out a slow breath. The answer was clear. He turned toward the gates, the endless expanse of Heaven stretched before him.

"I've got work to do."

Peter gave him a long, appraising look before pushing off the gate. "Well, that's new," he muttered, falling into step beside Ben as they walked toward the heart of Heaven. "So, what's the plan? Going to start a rebellion? Overthrow the Big Guy? Establish a democratic afterlife?"

Ben smirked but shook his head. "Nothing so dramatic." He glanced up at the infinite horizon, the endless halls of Heaven sprawling beyond the gates. "I spent too long doing what I was told. Watching. Weighing. Judging." He exhaled sharply; the memory of centuries spent at the gates pressing against him. "I think it's time I start doing something that matters."

Peter snorted. "Pretty sure that's what got you in trouble in the first place."

Ben shrugged. "Then I guess I'll be a pain in their ass a little longer."

They passed through the entrance, the golden arch towering above them. As soon as Ben stepped over the threshold, something inside him settled. The pull of Heaven wrapped around him, familiar but not oppressive as if it had been waiting for him to return.

For the first time since he had arrived in the afterlife, he wasn't burdened by the weight of it. He was just... here.

They walked in silence for a while, the clouds parting beneath their steps. A cool wind stirred around them, carrying whispers of prayers, of souls waiting, of those who had long since passed through these gates.

Peter cleared his throat. "So, uh... what exactly does 'work' mean?"

Ben stopped, turning to face him fully. His expression was calm, steady.

"I think Heaven could use a change."

Peter blinked. Then, he groaned, rubbing his temples. "Oh, for the love of—Ben, you just got back."

Ben grinned the fire in his eyes unmistakable. "Yeah. And I've got a lot to do."

Peter stared at him for a long moment before sighing dramatically. "You know, I had a feeling you weren't just going to sit around and enjoy eternal bliss." He gestured vaguely at the glowing expanse around them. "I should've bet on it."

438

Ben turned his gaze forward again, taking in the countless souls moving through the vast expanse of paradise. So many people, so many stories. Some are waiting, some are at peace, and some still searching for something they never found in life.

He had spent lifetimes guarding the gates, sending people through, ensuring balance.

Now, he had a different role to play.

Peter sighed again, shaking his head as he followed. "You're going to be a nightmare for management, you know that?"

Ben chuckled, a slow, knowing smile spreading across his face. "Good."

Peter fell into step beside him as they walked toward the ruined remnants of Heaven, the aftermath of Ben's reckless choices still scattered like debris across the holy expanse. There were broken archways where monuments had once stood, fractures in the golden pathways that led to places he hadn't even begun to understand.

The angels had started to return, hesitant but determined, gathering in groups, watching him with unreadable expressions. Some of them nodded in silent recognition. Others whispered among themselves. They knew what he had done. They had seen the chaos he caused. And they had seen him fix it.

Peter nudged him with an elbow. "They're waiting for you to screw up again."

Ben smirked, shaking his head. "Then they're in for a disappointment."

Peter laughed. "You're sticking around for this, huh?"

Ben glanced back at the gates behind them—the boundary between Heaven and everything else, the one place he had resented from the moment he arrived. It no longer felt like a prison.

He nodded. "Yeah. I am."

For the first time, Peter looked almost impressed. "Huh. Maybe you were the right guy for the job after all."

Ben rolled his eyes. "Don't get sentimental on me, Pete."

Peter chuckled. "Wouldn't dream of it."

Stepping Into Purpose

They moved deeper into Heaven's core, where the light shimmered like an endless ocean, reflecting the memories of all who had passed through. Ben could feel the weight of it—the souls, the prayers, the unfinished stories waiting for something more. Heaven wasn't perfect. It never had been. And now, with the fractures still visible, it was clearer than ever.

An angel with silver wings approached, his expression wary. "You've disrupted the natural order," he said, his voice like a chorus of wind chimes. "You changed the balance."

Ben met his gaze steadily. "Yeah. And I'd do it again."

A ripple passed through the gathering angels. Some nodded, others looked away, but none of them challenged him.

440

Peter crossed his arms. "So, what now? You going to start handing out miracles?"

Ben exhaled, glancing up at the sky that stretched forever. "No. I'm going to start fixing what's broken."

The silver-winged angel frowned. "Heaven is not broken."

Ben looked around at the shattered remains of what once was, at the doubt in the eyes of the angels, at the hushed voices of those who had spent eternity waiting. He shook his head. "Then you haven't been paying attention."

The angel hesitated, then inclined his head ever so slightly. Acknowledgment. An understanding, however reluctant, that change was inevitable.

Peter sighed dramatically. "Great. You're going to make my job a nightmare, aren't you?"

Ben smirked. "Good."

He turned back toward the heart of Heaven, the weight of his purpose settling on his shoulders. For the first time, he wasn't just standing at the gates, waiting for the lost to pass through. He wasn't just watching. He was stepping forward.

And Heaven Was Watching

And Heaven was watching him right back.

The two of them reached the steps of the great hall, the place where judgments had once been carried out like bureaucratic procedures. It had been a machine for sorting souls, for deeming who was worthy and who wasn't.

Ben had torn that system apart. Now, it was time to rebuild.

He turned to Peter. "So, what do you say? You want your old job back?"

Peter smirked. "Nah. I kind of like watching you suffer."

Ben rolled his eyes. "Figures."

Peter clapped him on the shoulder. "But I'll stick around. You're going to need someone to keep you in check."

Ben huffed a laugh, then looked out over the vast horizon of Heaven—the souls still arriving, still waiting for answers. He wasn't the same man who had thrown open the gates and let the worst of humanity in.

He had lost, learned, and lived again. Now, it was time to make things right.

The doors of the great hall loomed before him, the onceimmaculate pillars now cracked, their perfection marred by the weight of time and change. Ben placed a hand on the ancient wood, feeling the pulse of Heaven's history beneath his fingertips. The hall had stood for eternity, but eternity had never known a force like him.

Peter sighed dramatically beside him. "You do realize that if you go through those doors, there's no turning back, right?"

Ben glanced sideways at him, smirking. "Since when have I ever turned back?"

Peter barked a laugh. "Fair point."

Ben exhaled, steadying himself before pushing open the doors. A hush fell over the gathered souls, the echoes of a thousand stories swirling in the air like whispers of the past. Angels stood in their usual positions, watching him carefully, some with curiosity, others with scepticism.

At the far end of the hall, a council of the oldest celestial beings—those who had presided over the old order—waited for him. Their gazes were unreadable, their forms shifting slightly with the light as if the fabric of their existence was woven into Heaven itself.

Ben stepped forward; his voice steady. "It's time for something new."

Silence. A pause that stretched like an eternity.

Then, finally, one of the elders spoke, his voice as deep as the cosmos. "Then show us."

Ben nodded. He had spent too long following rules that had never been meant for him. Now, it was time to make his own.

The sky overhead shimmered, the ethereal glow of Heaven slowly restoring itself, the cracks in its foundation beginning to heal. Ben could feel the shift, the delicate balance returning, but it was still fragile. There was still work to be done.

The Last Goodbye

A presence stirred behind him. Ben turned, expecting another angel, but instead, he saw something else.

A familiar face.

Emma.

Or at least, the shape of her. A whisper of memory, the last remnants of her warmth still clinging to him. She wasn't there. He knew that. But for a moment, it didn't matter.

She smiled at him, just as she had on the porch, just as she had when she said goodbye.

And then, she was gone.

Ben inhaled deeply, pressing a hand to his chest. She had been right. Love didn't fade. It didn't vanish into the ether.

It simply changed.

Peter cleared his throat, watching him carefully. "You all right?"

Ben let out a slow breath, nodding. "Yeah. I think I am."

He turned away from the past and toward the future.

A new Gatekeeper. A new beginning. And, for the first time, he wasn't looking for a way out.

A Relic of the Living

As he took his first step forward, something itched against his chest. He frowned, scratching absentmindedly before his fingers brushed against something solid beneath his robe.

He hesitated, then reached into his pocket.

His breath caught.

It was the photo. The one Lena had given him. The small, delicate picture of his grandson—of baby Ben—wrapped in a soft blue blanket, his tiny fingers curled into a fist.

A relic from the perfect day.

His fingers traced the worn edges of the photo, the weight of it grounding him in a way that nothing else in this place ever had. It shouldn't have been here. Nothing from the mortal world should have passed through the veil with him. And yet, here it was.

Proof that loves transcended even Heaven's rules.

Peter, ever perceptive, leaned over to glance at the photo, then let out a low whistle. "Cute kid," he said, smirking. "Looks nothing like you… Lucky bugger."

Ben huffed a quiet laugh, shaking his head. "Thanks, Pete."

Peter clapped him on the shoulder, his smirk widening. "All right, enough of the sentimental crap. I've got one last surprise for you before you take your seat in eternity."

Ben narrowed his eyes suspiciously. "That doesn't sound ominous at all."

Peter's grin turned positively devious. "Oh, trust me. You're going to love this."

Ben sighed, slipping the photo safely back into his pocket. Whatever Peter had planned, he wasn't sure he was ready for it.

445

But then again, when had he ever been?

Chapter 29:

The Surprise

The Gardens Beyond the Gate

Peter led Ben through the towering gates of Heaven, the great doors parting without a sound. Beyond them, the vast expanse of paradise stretched in every direction. Golden light filtered through trees that shimmered like they had been woven from stardust, their branches swaying though there was no wind. The air was thick with the scent of blossoms, fresh rain, and something sweeter—something impossible to name. A stream of crystal-clear water wove through the gardens, its surface reflecting not just the sky but something deeper as if it held the weight of every beautiful moment ever experienced.

Petals floated in the air, carried by an unseen current, and the sky itself seemed to breathe, shifting between shades of soft blue and gold. Small bridges arched over the water, connecting winding paths lined with flowers that shimmered in hues beyond mortal comprehension. Every step carried a sense of weightlessness as if Heaven itself encouraged movement without resistance. Birds with iridescent wings flitted through the trees, their songs harmonizing with the gentle rustling of leaves, creating a melody that felt eternal.

The Reunion Beneath the Silver Tree

The sound of laughter drew Ben's attention. And then, he saw them.

David. Clare. Eleanor.

They were waiting for him at the garden's edge, standing beneath the shade of a sprawling tree with leaves of silver and gold. Clare's eyes shimmered as she stepped forward first, a radiant smile breaking across her face before she threw her arms around Ben. He hadn't even realized how much he missed her until that moment. He held onto her tightly, feeling her warmth, her presence, the reality of her being here.

Eleanor stood close behind, her arms crossed, her lips curved in an amused smirk. "You're squeezing her like she might disappear again, Ben. She's not going anywhere."

Ben let out a choked laugh, finally pulling back just enough to look at Clare properly. "I didn't expect this."

Clare smiled softly, brushing a strand of hair behind her ear. "Neither did we. But I guess some things are just meant to happen."

Eleanor rolled her eyes. "Or Peter just enjoys playing god."

Peter, who had been standing back with David, grinned. "Guilty as charged."

David chuckled. "Yeah, he's been bragging about this surprise for ages. Said it was going to 'fix Ben's permanent brooding problem.'"

Ben groaned. "Fantastic. So, this is a therapy session disguised as a reunion?"

Peter patted his shoulder. "Call it what you want, but you're smiling, aren't you?"

Ben sighed, unable to argue. He was smiling.

Eleanor was next, rolling her eyes fondly as she hugged him just as fiercely. "You always were the sentimental one," she teased, though her grip told another story.

Ben chuckled. "Good to see you too, El."

Together, they walked through the gardens, the air alive with the sounds of singing birds, rustling leaves, and the occasional bell chime that seemed to come from the flowers themselves. The paths were lined with soft grass that bent under their steps but never flattened, as if Heaven itself refused to let anything be trampled. Petals floated in the air, carried by an unseen current, and the sky shifted in colour like an ever-changing masterpiece.

Behind them, Peter and David walked side by side, exchanging smirks. Now and then, they threw out quips at Ben's expense, their voices carrying over the peaceful landscape.

"I can't believe this is the guy they put in charge," Peter said, shaking his head dramatically. "I mean, honestly, was there no one better?"

David chuckled. "Oh, they settled. But hey, everyone loves an underdog story."

Clare stifled a laugh, and Eleanor outright snorted.

Ben turned around, narrowing his eyes at the pair. "You two are a menace."

Peter clutched his chest mockingly. "Oh, Ben, you wound me."

David smirked. "And yet, here you are, walking among the chosen few. It's almost inspiring."

Ben sighed, shaking his head. "You two were made for each other."

Peter grinned. "What can I say? I recognize a kindred spirit when I see one. Besides, someone has to keep you humble."

David nodded solemnly. "It's a full-time job."

Clare and Eleanor exchanged amused glances.

"Just how long have you two known each other?" Eleanor asked, glancing back at Peter and David.

"Not long," Peter admitted. "But I can tell we're going to be best friends."

David nodded. "Agreed. He's the only one here who appreciates my sense of humour."

Ben scoffed. "Oh, great. That's exactly what I needed. Two of you."

Peter elbowed David. "You hear that? He's honoured."

David smirked. "I can see the tears forming already."

Ben rolled his eyes. "All right, that's it. I'm done letting you two have all the fun."

Peter raised a brow. "Oh no, the boss is putting his foot down."

David grinned. "Careful, Peter, he might write us up."

"Or worse," Peter added dramatically. "Give us a heartfelt lecture about responsibility."

Clare shook her head, trying and failing to suppress a giggle. "It's like watching two schoolboys."

Eleanor nodded in agreement. "I feel bad for whoever has to keep them in line."

Ben sighed, pinching the bridge of his nose. "You're all terrible."

He turned to David, his expression softening. "How are you?"

David's grin faded into something more genuine, his eyes thoughtful. "I'm good, Ben. Better than I was before. I've had time to... make peace with everything. With myself."

Ben nodded, knowing exactly what he meant. "I'm glad."

They walked back toward the gate together, their conversation quiet but meaningful. They spoke of old times, of regrets left behind, of lessons learned. And when they reached the threshold, Ben knew—this was the closure he had never thought he would get.

Clare and Eleanor hugged him one last time, and David clapped him on the shoulder, his expression lighter than it had been in ages. "Take care of things out there, all right?"

Ben smirked. "As long as Peter doesn't get me fired first."

Peter scoffed. "Please. If I haven't been fired yet, you're probably safe."

David smirked. "But if you do get fired, I want a front-row seat."

Ben rolled his eyes. "You and Peter are the worst duo."

Peter and David exchanged a glance before Peter nodded. "I think that's the best compliment I've ever received."

With one last glance, Ben stepped back, watching as Clare, Eleanor, and David faded into the gardens, their laughter carried by the wind. For the first time since he had arrived in Heaven, he felt whole.

As he and Peter walked back through the gates, the celestial crowds parting to let them pass, Peter studied him carefully. "You all right?"

Ben exhaled, a small, satisfied smile tugging at his lips. "Yeah. I think I finally am."

Peter nodded approvingly. "Good. I wouldn't have been able to do this job either if I hadn't said goodbye to my wife and daughter." His voice was quieter, almost wistful. "It changes things."

Ben glanced at him, surprised by the rare glimpse into Peter's past. "What were they like?"

Peter chuckled, a flicker of old memories in his eyes. "Beautiful. Stubborn as hell. My daughter had my sarcasm, which I'm sure drove my wife insane."

Ben smirked. "Sounds about right."

Peter sighed, rubbing the back of his neck. "I used to think this job was a curse. That it was just some cosmic joke, locking me at the gates of paradise with a clipboard and a set of rules." He glanced at Ben. "But getting to say goodbye? That was a gift."

The New Gatekeeper

Ben nodded, understanding in a way he never had before. "I get that now."

They reached the long desk that stood at the gates, the endless crowd of souls waiting for their turn. Ben sat down, settling into his seat. It didn't feel like a prison this time. It didn't feel like a punishment.

It felt... right.

Peter leaned back against the desk, crossing his arms. "All right, boss man. Let's see what you've got."

Ben straightened, looking out over the line of souls stretching endlessly before him. Some looked nervous, others impatient, and a few just stood quietly, as if bracing for what came next. He saw a woman clutching a wedding ring, an old man mumbling a prayer, and a child holding the hand of someone who looked like they had been waiting for a long time.

There were stories in each face, stories that deserved to be heard.

Ben inhaled deeply, then exhaled. "All right," he said, straightening in his seat. "Let's get to work."

Peter grinned, grabbing a chair and spinning it around before plopping down next to him. "Try not to screw it up too bad."

Ben shook his head, suppressing a smirk. "Yeah, yeah. Keep talking, Pete."

The first soul stepped forward, hesitating slightly before standing in front of Ben's desk. The weight of Heaven, of eternity, of judgment, hung in the air. Ben met their eyes, offering a small nod.

For the first time, he wasn't just standing at the gates.

He was the Gatekeeper.

And he was exactly where he was meant to be.

Chapter 30:

Acceptance

The Gate Opens Both Ways

Ben stood at the gates, staring out over the expanse of Heaven. For the first time, he didn't feel like an outsider.

The past felt like a distant echo—his years of cynicism, his disdain for power, his refusal to believe in anything beyond the physical world. He had been a man who built others up, only to watch them fall. A man who had lived on the fringes, never fully belonging.

But now, he was here. And this time, he wasn't looking for an escape.

Peter leaned against the archway beside him, watching in silence. For once, there was no teasing smirk, no sarcastic remark. He just waited, as if giving Ben the space to process what had already been decided.

Ben exhaled slowly, rubbing his thumb along the edge of the golden railing. "I used to think this was a joke."

Peter tilted his head. "And now?"

Ben looked out at the souls approaching—new arrivals, lost and uncertain. They weren't just names in a file. They weren't just numbers waiting for judgment.

They were people. People who had lived, who had suffered, who had made choices—some good, some bad, but all human.

He had spent so long hating the idea of Heaven because he had only ever seen it as a system of control, another version of the world's cruelty, wrapped in gold and clouds.

But it wasn't. Not anymore.

Not if he could help it.

Ben straightened, rolling his shoulders. "I think it's time I start doing my job."

Peter grinned. "Took you long enough."

Ben ignored him, stepping forward, closer to the glowing threshold where souls waited. Some were scared. Some were resigned. Some carried burdens they had never been able to let go of.

And for the first time, Ben didn't just see names on a list. He saw people who needed guidance.

Redemption wasn't about punishment. It was about understanding.

He turned back to Peter. "Let's change how things are done around here."

Peter's grin widened. "Now we're talking."

Ben had never been a believer. Not in gods, not in destiny, not in the fairness of the universe. And yet, here he was, standing at the gates of Heaven, a place he had once despised.

It was strange, really—how quickly everything had changed. How quickly he had changed.

As the souls approached, he could feel their hesitancy. Some clutched onto memories of the lives they had left behind, unable to accept that their time had come. Others arrived in silence, waiting, expecting judgment as if it were another bureaucratic process.

Ben wasn't interested in bureaucracy.

A woman in a tattered dress stepped forward, her face streaked with tears. She looked young—far too young to be here. Her hands trembled as she clutched the hem of her gown.

"I don't understand," she whispered. "I was supposed to have more time."

Ben knelt to meet her gaze. "What's your name?"

She swallowed hard as if she wasn't sure she deserved to answer. "Amara."

"Amara," he repeated, nodding. "I don't have all the answers, but I can tell you this—you're not alone."

Her lower lip quivered. "Is this it? Am I just... gone?"

Ben shook his head. "You're still you. And we'll figure this out together."

He extended his hand. After a long, uncertain pause, Amara took it. The moment their hands met, the fear in her eyes lessened. Not gone. But lessened.

Peter let out a low whistle. "Look at you. Talking like an actual

Gatekeeper."

Ben shot him a look. "Don't ruin the moment, Pete."

Peter smirked but said nothing more.

Where Judgment Ends, Grace Begins

The day stretched on—or what counted as a day in Heaven. Ben worked alongside Peter, guiding souls, answering their questions, and offering comfort where he could. He wasn't perfect at it, not by a long shot. He made mistakes. He stumbled over his words. He doubted himself.

But he kept going.

A man in ragged clothing hesitated at the gates, his shoulders hunched, his eyes filled with guilt.

"I don't belong here," he muttered, turning as if to leave. "Not after what I did."

Ben stepped in front of him. "And what did you do?"

The man hesitated. "I hurt people."

Ben studied him for a long moment. "Do you regret it?"

Tears welled in the man's eyes. "Every day."

Ben nodded. "Then maybe it's time to stop running."

The man swallowed hard, but after a long moment, he took a shaky step forward.

Peter crossed his arms. "You are turning this place upside down, aren't you?"

Ben smirked. "It needed a shake-up."

Peter chuckled. "Yeah. Yeah, it did."

That night—or whatever passed for the night—Ben stood alone at the edge of Heaven, looking out at the vastness beyond. He thought of Emma, of Lena, of the grandson he'd held for the first and last time. A part of him would always ache for them. He would always miss them. But he also knew he had been given something few ever got.

A chance to say goodbye. A chance to make things right.

A soft wind stirred behind him, carrying a whisper—faint, distant, but unmistakable.

I love you, Ben.

Ben closed his eyes, letting the warmth of it wash over him. He didn't answer, but he didn't have to.

He knew she could hear him.

And as he turned back toward the gates, he smiled.

He had found his place.

Finally.

As he approached the threshold, the first soul stepped forward—a frail, elderly woman with hesitant eyes. She clutched at her hands nervously, as if unsure whether she deserved to be here at all.

Ben took a breath. This was his first test.

"What's your name?" he asked, his voice softer than it had ever been at these gates.

The woman lifted her head slowly, her expression uncertain. "Margaret," she murmured. "Margaret Hollis."

Ben glanced at Peter, expecting him to roll his eyes, expecting some snide comment about how this was supposed to be automatic, procedural, impersonal.

But Peter just watched, curiosity flickering behind his tired gaze.

Ben turned back to Margaret. "Margaret, tell me about your life."

She blinked, startled by the question. "Oh... well, I—I did my best," she said hesitantly. "I wasn't perfect. I had my mistakes. I was selfish at times. But I tried."

Ben nodded. He had heard stories like this a million times before. But for the first time, he listened.

"What did you love most?" he asked.

Margaret's eyes glistened as she smiled. "My children," she whispered. "I wasn't always a great mother, but I loved them more than anything. I just hope they knew that."

Ben's throat tightened. That kind of love—the kind that persisted through imperfection—that was real.

And for the first time, he realized it wasn't his place to decide if she was worthy.

It was hers.

Ben gestured behind him. "Go on, Margaret."

She hesitated, glancing between him and the open gates. "That's it?" she asked, almost disbelieving.

Ben smirked. "Yeah. That's it."

Tears welled in her eyes as relief washed over her face. She stepped forward, pausing just once to look back at him.

"Thank you," she whispered.

Ben only nodded, watching as she crossed into the golden light, disappearing into whatever waited beyond.

Peter exhaled beside him. "Well, look at you. All wise and compassionate. Who would've thought?"

Ben smirked. "Shut up, Pete."

Peter laughed, clapping him on the back. "Alright, Gatekeeper. Let's see if you can keep this up."

One By One, They Came

Ben turned back toward the line of souls stretching toward the horizon.

And, for the first time, he was ready for them.

The next soul hesitated at the threshold. A middle-aged man with weathered hands, his shoulders hunched with years of burdens he still carried. His eyes darted between Ben and the open gate as if expecting to be turned away. Ben folded his arms, waiting. "Name?"

The man swallowed. "David. David Mercer."

Ben gave a small nod. "Tell me about your life."

David frowned, shifting his weight from foot to foot. "I don't know what to say. I wasn't a good person. I lied. I cheated. I hurt people."

Ben raised an eyebrow. "And?"

David's jaw tightened. "And I regret it."

Ben studied him for a long moment, then gestured toward the open space beside them. "Come sit with me for a second."

David hesitated but obeyed, lowering himself onto the golden steps leading up to the gates. He stared at his hands. "I never asked for forgiveness. I didn't think I deserved it."

Ben let out a slow breath. "You think I did?"

David blinked up at him, startled. "You?"

Ben smirked. "I did worse things than most people in that line." He gestured over his shoulder. "I burned Heaven down, literally."

David exhaled sharply, something close to a chuckle escaping him. "And they let you stand here?"

Ben shrugged. "Yeah. Because I learned something important."

David swallowed. "What's that?"

462

Ben met his gaze. "The only thing that matters is what you do next."

David stared at him for a long moment before his shoulders sagged, tension draining from his frame. For the first time, he let himself believe that maybe, just maybe, redemption wasn't beyond him.

Ben stood, holding out a hand. "Are you ready?"

David hesitated, then reached for it. The moment their hands met, something shifted in his face. Relief. Acceptance. He stood taller as he turned toward the gate, stepping through into the unknown.

Ben watched him go, exhaling as he turned back toward the line. More souls waited, each one carrying their own stories, their burdens, their hopes.

He had work to do.

Hours—or maybe years, time was strange here—passed. Ben listened to story after story. Some were simple. Some were heartbreaking. Some made him question everything all over again.

But he never judged them.

Instead, he listened.

A young girl, no older than ten, stepped forward, her small hands clutching at her dress. She looked up at Ben, wide-eyed. "Is my mommy here?"

Ben knelt, his heart squeezing in his chest. "I don't know, sweetheart. What's her name?"

The girl sniffled. "Mia Thompson."

Ben turned to Peter, who had been quietly observing. Peter nodded once, then disappeared into the golden expanse. A few moments later, a woman appeared at the gates, her face streaked with tears.

"Mia," Ben said gently, stepping aside.

The moment Mia saw her daughter, she let out a sob, dropping to her knees. The little girl ran into her arms, burying her face in her mother's chest. The two clung to each other, whispering words too soft for Ben to hear.

Ben turned away, giving them their moment. He met Peter's gaze, and for once, Peter didn't say anything. He just nodded.

Ben exhaled, rolling his shoulders as he turned back to the evergrowing line of souls.

One by one, he would meet them. One by one, he would listen.

Because that was his job now.

And for the first time in his existence, it was a job he was proud to do.

Chapter 31:

The Gatekeeper's Oath

A Heaven of His Own Making

Ben stood at the gates, looking at the next line of souls stretching into the horizon. The golden light of Heaven cast long shadows over the waiting figures, their faces a mixture of hope, fear, and uncertainty.

Once, he had seen this place as a prison.

As he reminisced, he was reminded of a quote from *Paradise Lost*: "The mind is its own place, and in itself can make a Heaven of Hell, a Hell of Heaven." It had always been one of his favourites—but only now did he understand just how deeply it applied to his life. He had lived through both. He had turned peace into war, love into loss, and ruin into redemption—all in the space of his own mind. Heaven and Hell hadn't been places. They had been choices. And now, at last, he was choosing peace.

Now, he saw it for what it was—a chance.

Not for punishment. Not for judgment.

But for understanding.

The Gatekeeper's Way

Peter stood beside him, his hands tucked into the folds of his robe, watching the scene unfold with an unreadable expression. He had seen so many come and go and had watched as countless Gatekeepers had passed through this role, each shaping Heaven in their way.

But this was different. Ben was different.

He had broken the system. And now, he was here to rebuild it.

Ben took a deep breath, rolling his shoulders before giving Peter a sidelong glance. For the first time since he arrived, he wasn't resisting his fate. He wasn't trying to run.

This was where he was meant to be.

Peter raised a brow. "So?"

Ben exhaled, his gaze shifting back to the endless line of waiting souls. He squared his shoulders, feeling the weight of his new purpose settle over him—not as a burden, but as something solid. Something real.

His smirk was small, but it was there. A quiet acceptance.

He gave Peter a nod.

"All right. Let's do this."

The first soul stepped forward—a man with weary eyes and calloused hands, a man who had spent his life working, struggling, trying to provide for a family that he had always felt

466

he had failed. He stood before Ben, his fingers twitching at his sides, his shoulders drawn up as if waiting for a verdict.

Ben studied him for a long moment before speaking. "What's your name?"

The man licked his lips. "Jacob Wells."

"Jacob," Ben repeated, rolling the name over his tongue. "Tell me something. What do you believe you deserve?"

Jacob swallowed hard, his gaze shifting to the golden expanse beyond the gates. "I don't know," he admitted. "I worked hard. I did my best. But I made mistakes. I was never the father I wanted to be. I never had enough time."

Ben nodded slowly. "And if you could go back?"

Jacob exhaled shakily. "I'd do things differently."

Ben didn't judge him for that. Regret was as human as breathing. "And if you could move forward?"

Jacob hesitated. "I… I don't know how."

Ben gestured toward the gates. "Then maybe it's time to learn."

Jacob's eyes widened slightly. "Just like that?"

Ben smirked. "Yeah. Just like that."

The man let out a breath he hadn't realized he was holding, and when he stepped through, his shoulders weren't as heavy. He didn't vanish in a flash of light. He didn't transform into something holy. He simply walked forward, carrying himself with the weight of a man who had been given a second chance.

Peter let out a low whistle. "You're going with the 'understanding over judgment' thing, huh?"

Ben shrugged. "It's better than the old way."

Peter smirked. "I think I'm starting to like you, Holloway."

Ben chuckled. "Don't get soft on me now, Pete."

The line of souls stretched into eternity, and Ben took them one by one. Some were hesitant, and some were eager. Some were afraid to let go of the past, clinging to the identities they had built in life. Others were desperate for absolution as if a single moment at the gates could erase a lifetime of choices.

Ben didn't offer them easy answers. He didn't claim to be an allknowing judge.

But he listened.

And that, he realized, was what they had needed all along.

A woman stepped forward; her dark eyes filled with sorrow. "My son... I left him behind."

Ben softened. "What was his name?"

She swallowed. "Daniel."

Ben tilted his head. "What would you want to tell him, if you could?"

She closed her eyes, tears slipping down her face. "That I loved him. That I never meant to leave so soon."

Ben exhaled, then nodded toward the gates. "Then go. Carry that love with you. And if he ever finds his way here, I'll make sure he knows."

She let out a shaky breath, then took a step forward.

Peter crossed his arms, watching the souls disappear into the golden horizon. "You know, this place is going to look a hell of a lot different with you running it."

Ben smirked. "Good."

The line continued. And Ben continued to stand, ready to meet each soul where they were.

Because this wasn't about judgment.

This was about understanding.

And for the first time, the Gatekeeper of Heaven was exactly where he was meant to be.

Where Redemption Begins

The next soul that approached was hesitant, a man who had lived a complicated life, his shoulders hunched, his face lined with the weight of past mistakes. Ben didn't need to look at a file to know that this man wasn't sure if he belonged there.

Ben studied him, taking in the uncertainty in his eyes. "What's your name?"

The man swallowed hard. "David," he said. "David Corrigan."
Ben nodded. "All right, David. Tell me—what's the thing you
regret the most?"

David looked down, his hands twisting together. "I wasn't
always a good man," he admitted. "I hurt people. Not in big
ways, maybe. But I lied. I was selfish. I betrayed trust. I lost my
family because of it."

Ben exhaled, glancing at Peter, who simply raised an eyebrow as
if to say, this is your show now.

Ben folded his arms. "And what did you do to fix it?"

David hesitated. "I tried," he said. "Maybe not soon enough.
But I tried."

Ben watched him for a long moment, then gestured toward the
gates. "Then go on."

David's eyes widened. "That's it?"

Ben smirked. "Yeah. That's it."

A choked sound escaped David's throat; his disbelief written all
over his face. But as he stepped forward, crossing through the
threshold, a look of peace settled over him. For the first time, he
truly believed he was forgiven.

Peter let out a slow whistle. "You know, the old system
would've made him wait in some kind of cosmic purgatory for a
few centuries."

Ben rolled his eyes. "Yeah, well, the old system was bullshit."

Peter grinned. "Can't argue with that."

470

The next soul approached, then another, and another. Some were ready. Some weren't. Some carried guilt too heavy for them to lay down yet.

A woman named Claire wept as she approached. "I was angry," she admitted, her voice trembling. "I shut people out. I held onto grudges. And now it's too late."

Ben shook his head. "It's not too late. You're here. That means you still have a choice."

She blinked at him, fresh tears slipping down her face. "A choice?"

Ben nodded. "To let go."

Claire let out a shaky breath, and for the first time in a long time, she did. The tension melted from her shoulders as she stepped through the gates, leaving her burdens behind.

Peter sighed. "You're taking this whole 'understanding over judgment' thing seriously, huh?"

Ben smirked. "Damn right, I am."

Hours—or days, or maybe years, it was hard to tell—passed in a steady rhythm. The line of souls never ended, and Ben met each of them the same way: with patience, with curiosity, with the belief that people were more than the worst things they had done.

A young boy approached; his hands clenched into fists. "I don't deserve to be here," he muttered. "I barely even lived."

Ben knelt in front of him. "What's your name?"

471

The boy scowled. "Ethan."

"Well, Ethan, let me ask you something—do you think you're supposed to be somewhere else?"

The boy hesitated, glancing at the space behind him. "I don't know," he admitted. "I just... I didn't get to do anything. It's not fair."

Ben nodded. "It's not fair."

Ethan's eyes darted up to his. "Then why am I here?"

Ben placed a hand on his shoulder. "Because there's more for you, Ethan. Just because your life was short doesn't mean it didn't matter."

The boy's lip trembled. "You think so?"

Ben smiled. "I know so."

Ethan hesitated, then took a deep breath and stepped through the gates. The golden light embraced him, carrying him forward.

Peter nudged Ben. "You know, if you keep this up, you might make Heaven a better place."

Ben chuckled. "Yeah. That's the idea."

Peter grinned. "Well, damn. Guess I picked the right guy after all."

The line continued. The work continued. And for the first time in his life—and afterlife—Ben had something that mattered.

Purpose.

He turned back toward the never-ending line of souls, his hands in his pockets, his stance relaxed but resolute.

The doors opened wider, the golden light spilling forward.

Ben took a breath, straightened his shoulders, and smiled.

The story ended.

But the work had just begun.

ACKNOWLEDGEMENTS

Writing *The Unholy Gatekeeper* has been an intense and deeply personal journey, one that would not have been possible without the unwavering support, encouragement, and inspiration from so many people in my life.

First and foremost, thank you. Whether you've been following my artistic journey from the very beginning or are just now discovering my work, I'm deeply grateful for your support. Thank you for stepping into this world, for believing in these characters, and for letting their stories find a place in your heart.

To the ones who stood by me— thank you for your patience, for listening to my endless ramblings about plot twists and character arcs, and for reminding me to eat and sleep during those late nights of writing. Your presence, encouragement, and quiet belief in me have been my anchor.

A special thank you to those who read early drafts provided feedback and pushed me to refine this story into what it has become. Your insights, honesty, and constructive criticism have helped shape this book in ways I could never have done alone.

To the artists I have been fortunate enough to collaborate with—your creativity, passion, and dedication inspire me endlessly. The process of working with other creatives, sharing ideas, and seeing visions come to life has been one of the most rewarding parts of this journey. I am deeply grateful for the energy and artistry you have brought into my world.

To the medical professionals who helped me regain my focus— your patience, care, and expertise have been invaluable. Thank you for guiding me through the moments when I struggled to concentrate, for helping me find balance, and for reminding me that perseverance is just as important as creativity. Thank you for all the long appointments, for replacing lost documents, and for your unwavering support during the hardest time in my life. Your dedication made it possible for me to complete this work, and I am forever grateful.

To the musicians, artists, and creators who continue to inspire me— this story is, in many ways, a tribute to the struggle, passion, and resilience that comes with chasing a dream. The music industry, like so many creative fields, can be ruthless, but it is also filled with raw beauty. This book is for those who refuse to give up on their art, no matter the odds.

And finally, to the dreamers, the misfits, and the ones who feel like they don't quite belong—this book is for you. May you always find the courage to create, to express, and to fight for what you believe in.

With gratitude,

KJ C

ABOUT THE AUTHOR

K.J C is a multidisciplinary artist, writer, and creative strategist whose work moves fluidly between mediums—photography, painting, fiction, fashion, and direction. She's not interested in staying in one lane. Her career has been built on following instinct, chasing tension, and turning abstract ideas into tangible impact.

For over 20 years, she's worked both on and off the record—developing projects that span visual art, editorial work, immersive experiences, and story-driven initiatives. Some of her work hangs in private collections. Some was created under ghost contracts. And some she made just to see if she could.

In 2019, she founded a creative platform focused on supporting artists through mentorship, collaboration, and opportunity design. It operates quietly—without a need for headlines—but has helped a growing network of creatives build sustainable careers, take risks, and stay in the game. It's part business, part experiment, part open door for those who don't wait for permission.

K.J began photography professionally at 14 and started writing novels long before that—though she's the first to admit most of them should never see daylight. Still, storytelling has remained the constant across everything she does. Whether it's a portrait, a runway concept, or a novel, her work explores perception, power, and the moments where things begin to unravel.

She's drawn to what people hide. Her projects often center on overlooked systems, quiet patterns, and the fault lines between identity and performance. The question behind the work is always the same: What's really going on here?

Writing, for her, is where everything converges. It's the medium that requires the most honesty—and the one that leaves the most behind. Her fiction is rooted in emotional truth, social tension, and human contradiction. She writes the way she sees the world: layered, sharp, and never quite what it seems. From psychological thrillers to speculative fiction to surreal realism, her stories explore the cost of survival, the architecture of belief, and the thin space between the visible and the invisible.

She's not writing to entertain. She's writing to expose, to challenge, and to leave something behind that can't be unseen.

Published by Concept Jane Pty Ltd
In association with Blackthorn Press
In partnership with IARTA Creative Industries

www.blackthornpress.com.au
www.conceptjane.com.au
www.KJC.com
www.iarta.com.au

Blackthorn Press is an independent Australian publisher dedicated to nurturing unique voices, empowering creative expression, and reimagining storytelling across mediums. As the publishing arm of IARTA, we proudly support multidisciplinary artists and authors who blur the lines between art, healing, and innovation.

For publishing inquiries, submissions, or collaborations, visit:
www.blackthornpress.com.au/submissions
or contact: **info@blackthornpress.com.au**

Published by:

Concept Jane Pty Ltd
in association with
Blackthorn Press